Praise for *Relati*

"A fun and lively retelling of *Sense and* … s
it all—a gorgeous setting, delightful characters, and juicy drama… Prepare
to be swept away by the Bae-Woods."

—Lauren Edmondson, author of
Ladies of the House **and** ***Wedding of the Season***

"A zippy homage to Austen's *Sense and Sensibility*…full of so much heart."

—Natalie Jenner, Internationally Bestselling Author,
The Jane Austen Society

"I had a blast reading this literary power remix."

—Christina Clancy, Author of ***The Second Home*** **and** ***Shoulder Season***

"You don't have to be a Jane Austen fan to enjoy this sparklingly witty retelling of *Sense and Sensibility*… *Relative Strangers* will appeal to any reader who loves stories about sisters—and yes, surprise pairings. I absolutely loved it."

—Camille Pagán, bestselling author of
Life and Other Near-Death Experiences

"Prepare to stay up half the night, like I did, to finish this twisty romantic page-turner!"

—Julia Claiborne Johnson, author of
Be Frank with Me **and** ***Better Luck Next Time***

"Think *Sense and Sensibilit*y mixed with *Modern Family. Relative Strangers* is layered with the good, bad, love, heartbreak and true meaning of family."

—Viola Shipman, ***USA TODAY*** **bestselling author of**
Famous in a Small Town

"Welcome to a world of family secrets, inheritance disputes, and rescues in the rain, as sisters Amelia and Eleanor Bae-Wood meet an array of eligible bachelors. But expect some surprises too."

—Finola Austin, author of ***Bronte's Mistress***

"Austen enthusiasts will be charmed by this fresh retelling of Austen's *Sense and Sensibility*… Twists and turns at the end will leave the reader delighted."

—Suzanne Park, author of ***So We Meet Again*** **and** ***The Do-Over***

Also by A.H. Kim

A Good Family

Relative Strangers

A.H. KIM

Recycling programs for this product may not exist in your area.

ISBN-13: 978-1-525-81955-1

Relative Strangers

Graydon House
22 Adelaide St. West, 41st Floor
Toronto, Ontario M5H 4E3, Canada
www.GraydonHouseBooks.com
www.BookClubbish.com

Printed in U.S.A.

For Mom, Dad and Alice

Thank you for being part of this very special day. Looking around at all your faces, I see old friends, new friends, even a few people I don't know yet but am sure will become friends.

And, of course, I see the three women who are the most important people in my life: my mother Tabitha, my sister Eleanor, and my niece Maggie. Today's celebration is about you, about us, about the next chapter in our family's story.

Today's celebration is also about this place—this wild, windblown miracle of a place. When I first arrived here fifteen months ago I was lost, in every sense of the word. I had no idea Arcadia even existed. Today, there's no place on earth I'd rather be.

A cancer retreat center seems like an unlikely venue for a wedding, but I can't think of a more perfect spot. If there's one thing I've learned this past year, it's this: sometimes you find beauty in the most unexpected places.

And sometimes you find love with the most unexpected people.

Summer

1

They're throwing Mom out of the house. It would be nice if you could come home to support her.

Typical Eleanor. Her email is so straightforward and simple. But I'm her younger sister and only sibling. Over the years, I've practically earned a Ph.D. in Eleanor Bae-Wood passive-aggressive psychology. There's nothing straightforward or simple about her.

Let me translate.

They (the heartless judge and money-grubbing lawyers) *are throwing Mom* (our poor widowed mother, whom you've pretty much ignored for the past twenty years) *out of the house. It would be nice* (I know you're a "free spirit" and all, but grown-ups sometimes do things they don't want to do) *if you could come home to support her* (and think about someone besides yourself for once).

I'd like to think I would have complied with Eleanor's request even if I hadn't hit rock bottom in my own life, but I can't be sure. My recent brush with the law had depleted my already anemic bank account, and the Buddhist monastery I'd been hiding out in was ready to kick me to the curb. Whatever the reason—my daughterly duty or my debt-riddled desperation—there was something about Eleanor's email that convinced me to return home.

I'll be there in a couple days, I emailed back.

That was a week ago.

Now, I'm hunkered down in a Starbucks on El Camino Real having spent my last five dollars on a white chocolate mocha. I know Eleanor would say that's too much to spend on a medium-sized nonalcoholic beverage, but I needed the free electricity and Wi-Fi.

Also, they're so yummy.

My cell phone's been out of juice ever since I crossed the Oregon border into California over four days ago. As soon I plug my phone into the Starbucks outlet and the Apple icon glows back to life, I see a torrent of texts from my sister.

Amelia, have you left yet? I thought you said you'd be here in a couple days.

Ames, the sheriff is telling us we need to get out—where are you???

If you need money, I can wire it to you. Just tell me where.

Honey, I'm getting worried. Are you OK? Pls text ASAP.

OK, I'm guessing your phone's not working. Mom and I are heading out now. I'm leaving a note on the gate and hope you'll get here soon.

The five stages of grief, all in one text string.

It took me six sweltering days of hitchhiking to get myself from the outskirts of Portland, Oregon, to my parents' majestic estate in Atherton, California. When I finally arrived, there was a lockbox and legal notice on the wrought-iron security gate along with a note from Eleanor:

Ames,

I'm sorry we had to leave without you, but the sheriff ran out of patience. My friend Leo offered to let us stay at the Master's Cottage in Arcadia. Just keep taking 1 North until you see the signs for the center. If you reach Bodega Bay, you've gone too far. Cell reception is bad up there, so call the main line if you need help. It would be nice if you could join us.

Assuming you're still alive. ~E

No translation needed.

So, what exactly is Arcadia? I check Wikipedia. "Arcadia: an administrative unit of Greece. In literature, refers to a Utopian view of pastoralism and harmony with nature. May also refer to Arcadia (video game), Arcadia (sexual dysfunction medication), or Arcadia (cancer retreat center in Northern California)."

According to Google Maps, the Arcadia Cancer Retreat Center is over ninety miles away from my current location. The red locator dot appears along the Pacific coastline in rural Marin County, north of Point Reyes Station. I click the public transportation icon. No route available. By foot? About twenty-eight hours, including walking across the Golden Gate Bridge. I glance down at my fawn-brown suede gladiator sandals. These boots weren't made for walking.

I try a few online searches—"free shuttles to Marin," "South Bay to North Bay public transit," "desperately seeking ride to

Arcadia"—but the results are worthless. I wonder if I might be able to convince one of the well-heeled Starbucks patrons to give me a lift, but everyone seems heavily invested in their screens.

My only option seems to be to hitchhike…again. A hard knot forms in my stomach just thinking about it. Most of the drivers who picked me up on the road were creeps at best. How much longer until my luck runs out and I get a ride from a true psycho?

I nibble on my ragged cuticle. I can't remember the last time I had a manicure. There's a red dot next to my Instagram icon indicating that I have unread messages, so in classic procrastinator mode I open the app to catch up on my thousand-plus so-called friends. It's not lost on me that, if they were real friends, I'd be able to text one of them and mooch a ride.

Instagram Stories unspool on my cracked screen. There are photos of mouthwatering food, white sand beaches, happy selfies from weddings and honeymoons and parties, interrupted by the occasional ad for nonstick cooking pans, Korean face serums, and vegan shoes. I tap my index finger at warp speed on the screen like an old-timey telegraph operator sending out an urgent SOS.

I'm about ready to close out the app when the words *No Car? No Money? No Problem!* flash by. I've already tap-tap-tapped several stories ahead, so it takes me a few seconds of back-arrowing to return to the ad.

No Car? No Money? No Problem! the ad promises. *Barter-Ride… For a Better Ride. Tap here for your first free trip.*

I've never been more grateful for Big Brother and his eerie algorithms.

The Barter-Ride app is like Uber or Lyft but based on the barter system instead of cash. Examples of high-value barter items include personal services (massage, acupuncture, yoga, career coaching) and CBD gummies. I nearly laugh out loud. I wouldn't be in this mess if I had any valuable life skills, and I've long since consumed all my gummies.

I unzip my beat-up canvas duffel in search of something I can trade for the ninety-mile car ride from the heart of Silicon Valley to the remotest reaches of Marin County. Dirty socks and underwear, a clear zippered case of half-used cosmetics, a couple pairs of stretched-out yoga pants, some badly pit-stained T-shirts. I regretfully think about all the beautiful designer clothes that I donated to the Goodwill of Greater Multnomah County. Somewhere on the sidewalks of Portland, there's a waif wearing Stella McCartney and begging for change.

I have just two options: my phone or my lucky charm bracelet. Given how the past year has gone, it's a no-brainer. I take a photo of my bracelet—a small jade turtle on a bright red silk string—and upload it to Barter-Ride. I input my starting and end destinations. And then I wait.

I suck down the last bit of foam from my cup. I'm alive, I text to Eleanor.

She doesn't respond.

2

Shayna has a perfect five-star rating on Barter-Ride. Unlike the trucker who gave me a ride from Portland to Redding, Shayna appears to have all her teeth and doesn't remind me of Charles Manson.

"Amelia?" she asks, pulling up to the curb.

"Shayna?"

She flashes me a smile, and I crawl into the back seat of her Mini Cooper.

"Do you have the bracelet?" she asks.

I take the bracelet off my wrist and pass it to her.

"Oh, this is really nice," she says, slipping it on. "So, where to?"

"Arcadia Cancer Retreat Center in Marin County," I say, trying not to sound annoyed. I'm tempted to point out that I'd typed my destination into the Barter-Ride app, so she should already know where to. The whole exchange reminds me of those 1-800 numbers where, "in order to expedite service," you have to answer a dozen questions before you can speak to a live representative, and then the rep asks you for the same information all over again. But Eleanor is always telling me to check my New York attitude at the California border, so I shut my piehole.

I see Shayna inputting the location into her phone, and we're on our way.

"So, what kind of cancer do you have?" she asks as we hit traffic on 101.

"What?"

"What kind of cancer do you have…if you don't mind me asking."

I see her looking back at me through the rearview mirror. I'm confused for a moment, and then I remember: I'm bald.

"I don't have cancer," I respond. "I just shaved my head."

"That's cool," she says, although she seems a little disappointed.

The conversation now stalled, Shayna focuses on her driving, which is fine by me. I've had a long day. A long week. It feels like forever since I left the Buddhist temple up in Oregon to come home to California. I lean back in the car seat, close my eyes, and let the gentle rocking lull me to sleep. Soon, I'm dreaming. I dream about Nils, our cozy hideaway cabin in the Mendocino redwoods, the crackle of fire in our wood-burning stove, the gentle drip-drip-drip of raindrops on the cabin's metal roof.

The Mini Cooper screeches to a stop, and I wake with a start.

"What happened?" I ask.

"Stupid rabbit," Shayna mutters. "That's the third one I almost ran over."

"Where are we?"

She doesn't answer.

I look out the window. We appear to be driving on a country

road running parallel to the Pacific coastline. The windshield wipers are going fast—whoosh, whoosh, whoosh—and the rain falls in percussive rhythm. There's not a house or car in sight.

"Where are we?" I ask. "Are we almost there?"

Shayna doesn't say anything.

I pull my phone out of my hoodie pocket. No service. AT&T sucks.

"I'm almost out of gas," Shayna says. "I need to turn around."

"But we're not there yet."

"It's getting dark, and it's impossible to see anything on these roads. There was a gas station in the last town we passed. I'm going to fill up and head back to San Francisco."

"But we made a deal! I gave you my bracelet."

"Take it back then." She slides the bracelet off and practically throws it at me.

"It doesn't work that way," I say. "A deal's a deal."

But it's clear Shayna's made up her mind. She executes a three-point turn in the middle of the road and speeds back toward the city.

Up ahead, sitting on the bluff overlooking the ocean, a miracle appears. It's a stand-alone public phone booth with red metal panels on the side and a diamond-shaped sign on top. I haven't seen one in years. Eleanor's note had said to contact the center's main line if I needed help. I just hope they accept collect calls.

"Let me out here," I say.

Shayna doesn't hesitate. She slams on the brakes, and I crawl out of the car.

"Thanks for nothing," I mutter, my New York attitude back in force.

"Get a life!" Shayna yells.

"I'm trying!" I yell back.

By the time I've jogged over to the phone booth, my clothes are soaked through. I drop my duffel on the shiny metal floor, close the accordion-style door, and pull out my phone. I still don't have any cell reception, but the number for Arcadia Cancer Retreat Center is saved from my last Google search.

I pick up the public phone's heavy black receiver, but there's no dial tone. I hang up, pick up, and listen. Nothing. I repeat the cycle. Still nothing.

I bash the receiver onto the hook, shove the phone booth door open, and walk out. I scan the landscape for a car, a building, any sign of life. All I see is the ocean, the road, and vast stretches of empty beach.

"Damn," I say.

At that moment, something in the air changes. The previously steady rain starts coming down in buckets. The sky turns dark. I rush back into the phone booth for shelter.

"Come on, come on," I plead, pressing my thumb on my cell's home button. What I would give to see even one bar. No service.

"Damn it!" I scream.

"Pull yourself together," I mutter. "You've got a bag full of clothes and a vintage phone booth to protect you from the elements. You drank a 600-calorie beverage not so long ago. And it's the middle of summer, which means you've got a short night ahead."

I contemplate the idea of spending the night in an abandoned phone booth on a remote ocean bluff. Honestly? I've lived through worse.

There's a brilliant flash of lightning followed by an ominous clap of thunder. It's almost comical, this series of unfortunate events, except it's not so funny when it's happening to you.

I venture outside the phone booth again, just in case I missed something the first time. There's absolutely nothing as far as the eye can see, just the bluff and the sea and this completely random phone booth with a big metal sign on top. It might as well say, Strike Here. Weighing the risk of lightning against the certainty of getting drenched, I head back inside the booth.

When I was a little girl, there was a thunderstorm that was so loud, it woke me from my sleep. I got out of bed and saw my father at the living room picture window watching the storm. As I stood next to him and clutched his warm hand, Dad told me to count the seconds between the lightning and thunder to know how far away the storm is, whether it's coming closer or heading away. Dad always knew how to calm me down.

With the next flash of lightning, I peer out of the vintage phone booth and start counting. *One-one-thousand, two-one-thousand, three-one-thousand.* I get up to eight-one-thousand before the thunder crashes. I don't know if eight seconds is good or bad, near or far. It feels pretty bad.

What I wouldn't give to have Dad standing by my side again. Or my sister, Eleanor. She would know what to do in this situation. She always knows what to do. Since I don't have them to guide me, I turn to the next best option: God. I've never been religious before, but now seems as good a time as any to start.

"Dear God," I begin to pray. "I never thought I'd be talking to you."

Wait, that sounds wrong. Like one of those old letters from *Penthouse.* You know, before everyone got their porn online. Okay, stop thinking about porn. Start thinking about God.

"God, I could really use your help right now," I continue. "As you probably know—well, of course you know, being all-knowing and everything—things were going very well for me for a while. Thank you for that, by the way." I've never been good about thank-you notes. Eleanor, of course, always gets hers out right away.

There's another flash. One-one-thousand, two-one-thousand, three-one-thousand, four-one-thousand, five-one—CRASH.

"Anyway," I say, returning to my prayer, "I've run into a rough patch lately. I realize maybe I'm not at the top of your list of people to help. Probably nowhere even close. Still, I was hoping maybe—you know, being the all-powerful and merciful God that you are (shit, that sounds like the Wizard of Oz) (shit, I just said shit during my prayer)—maybe you'd give me a sign."

Another flash. I don't even bother to count this time.

"So, in summary," I say, getting to the point as quickly as possible—CRASH—"if you could tell me what I should do at this very moment, I'd really appreciate it."

Yet another flash.

"Are you there, God? It's me, Amelia." When in doubt, try humor.

Suddenly, I realize the last flash of light didn't come from the sky. It's coming from one of those super-bright LED flashlights, and it's headed straight at me. I open the phone booth's door. There's a tall, dark stranger standing two feet away.

"Hey, I was driving by," he says, "and it looked like you could use some help."

"Sorry, let me get that out of your way," the man says as he grabs a chainsaw off the truck's passenger side floor and moves it to the back seat.

I climb into the white pickup truck, half-relieved to be out of the thunderstorm and half-petrified by this mysterious chainsaw-wielding man in whose car I'm about to trap myself.

"Headed to Arcadia?" he asks.

"Yeah, how'd you know?"

"There's nothing else out here."

I stifle a gulp.

In space, no one can hear you scream.

"So, how'd you get into this mess?" he asks, "trapped in the Portal to the Dead?"

"Excuse me?" I croak.

"The phone booth you were standing in. It's an art piece, modeled on a phone booth from Japan. People come from all over to talk to their dead loved ones. I call it the Portal to the Dead."

"Oh, so that's why it didn't work," I say.

"How do you know it didn't work? Maybe you weren't listening close enough."

The man starts laughing, which does not seem like a normal reaction at all. I notice an ugly red scar on his left hand. His sinister hand. He notices me noticing and stops laughing.

"Old butchering accident," he explains.

Butchering accident?

"You didn't answer my question," he continues. "How'd you get stuck out here?"

I somehow find my voice and tell him about my first and last-ever experience with Barter-Ride.

"Next time you come to Arcadia," he says, "just call the main number and someone will pick you up."

"Seriously? Someone will just pick me up?"

"Well, you have to get yourself halfway close—like SFO or the ferry terminal—but yeah, someone will pick you up. That's the Arcadia way. We're like one big family out here. Some people think we're a cult."

Oh great, I just got into a truck in the middle of nowhere with a cult member who travels with his own chainsaw and is prone to butchering accidents. I'm tempted to throw my lucky charm bracelet out the window.

It's completely dark outside. Nothing to guide us along this twisty country road. By the dim lights of the dashboard, I can barely make out the man's features. He's got on a knit cap—I think they call it a watch cap—like you see cops or ex-military wear. The cap's pulled down low, almost covering his eyes, which are darting rapidly back and forth. I'm starting to think this dude's on drugs.

"You can't be too careful out here," he says. "I've killed one too many innocent creatures in my day. I feel terrible about it every single time."

I discreetly pull out my phone and check again. No service.

"People don't usually arrive midweek," he says. "Are they expecting you tonight?"

"Yes, they're expecting me," I lie. "They're probably worried sick. I hope they haven't called the police."

"Well, we're close now," he says.

As the road curves to the right, I see a small cottage on a hill. The lights are on in the windows. It looks like something out of those maudlin Thomas Kinkade paintings they sell in tourist traps everywhere.

"What's that?" I ask.

"The Master's Cottage."

I pull Eleanor's crumpled note out of my hoodie pocket. "My friend Leo offered to let us stay at the Master's Cottage in Arcadia," it reads.

"Stop right here!" I yell.

I reach over to the driver's side and start beeping the horn. The man brakes hard, and I leap out of the truck. I run up the hill to the cottage.

And I don't look back.

3

Eleanor opens the door before I even knock. Poor Eleanor. She hasn't changed one bit.

She's wearing one of her dowdy Lanz of Salzburg flannel nightgowns, navy wool scuffs, and a puffy down jacket she's probably had since her eighth-grade outdoor ed trip to Yosemite. On her head is a lopsided beanie, one of dozens she made while pregnant with Maggie and going through her third trimester nesting-and-knitting phase. Oh Lord, is that a ladybug pattern on her nightgown? Given how she dresses, it's a wonder my older sister ever got pregnant in the first place.

Meanwhile, my mother is looking as stylish as ever in her all-white velour tracksuit and hot-pink Uggs. Despite the tough times, she's maintained her appearance. She looks like a cross between Goldie Hawn and Helen Mirren. Mom puts the WOW into widow.

"Amelia," Mom says, hugging me quickly and pulling me through the door. "Your sister was worried sick about you."

"Don't exaggerate, Mom," Eleanor replies irritably. But

when she hugs me, it lasts longer than is customary. Longer than I'd expect.

The first thing I notice about the cottage is the fire in the fireplace, which you wouldn't normally see in the summer. Then again, this is Northern California. Everything about the place is wacky, even the weather.

The second thing I notice is the buckets and bowls scattered around the living room, collecting rain as it drips through the ceiling. One of the smaller bowls is starting to overflow. The Master's Cottage is sort of a ruin.

By the time Mom settles me in front of the fireplace, Eleanor's already grabbed a fluffy white towel for me to dry myself. Then she brings out a tray with three tumblers of Scotch on the rocks. Mom and I each grab one.

"Whatever took you so long to get here?" Mom asks. I'm about to answer when Eleanor gasps and drops her tumbler to the ground. Crash. Ice. Broken glass. Good thing she's wearing those scuffs.

There's a tall, dark stranger standing in the doorway.

"I'm sorry," he says. "I didn't mean to startle you. I just wanted to drop off your luggage. Where would you like it?"

"Oh my God, I'm so sorry," I apologize. I jump to my feet and walk to the door.

"Mom, Eleanor, this is…" I realize I don't know his name.

"Jett," he says. "My name is Jett."

Jett sets down my duffel, takes off his watch cap, and runs his fingers through his damp hair. He holds his cap bashfully in his hands, like a well-mannered boy meeting his sweetheart's parents for the first time. It's straight out of Norman Rockwell.

In the golden light of the cottage, I see Jett clearly for the first time tonight: soft brown hair, hazel eyes, sexy smile.

Thank you, God.

"Mom, Eleanor, this is Jett," I say, "the Good Samaritan who rescued me from the rain." My mother and sister greet Jett with something just short of idolatry.

"I'm afraid I didn't catch your name," he says to me.

"Mmmm-me?" I ask. OMG, did I actually stammer? Mom and Eleanor are positively grinning at me.

"My name is Amelia."

"It's a pleasure to meet you, Amelia," Jett says.

Eleanor is the first of the Bae-Wood women to regain her composure.

"Jett, please come in and dry off," she says. "I'm going to grab something to clean this mess up. May I get you a drink?"

"No, but thanks for the offer," he says. "I really should be running."

I try to imagine the scene from Jett's perspective. The ramshackle cottage spurting leaks like the fricking *Titanic*. Eleanor in her Old Mother Hubbard best, down on her hands and knees to clean up the broken glass and spilled booze. Mom with JUICY written in pink rhinestones across her Pilates-toned ass and self-medicating with Glenfiddich.

And then there's me.

I see my reflection in the mirror by the front door. My threadbare hoodie is plastered against my body. My well-worn jeans are ripped at the knees, and not on purpose as a design element. My gladiator sandals have fought their last battle. The past few years have taken their toll. I'm scrawny, pale, and bald.

"Are you sure you can't stay?" I ask Jett, whose smile is so brilliant it could sustain several planets.

"I've got some stuff in the truck that I need to unload right away," he says. "But if it's okay with you, I'll stop by tomorrow morning and check out those leaks. We need to fix them before the next storm."

"How can we ever thank you, Jett?" Mom asks.

"No thanks necessary," Jett replies. He pulls his watch cap back on, walks toward the door, and turns around.

"Welcome to Arcadia, ladies."

"What in the world did you do with your hair?" Mom asks, a worry-line furrowing her brow. "Your gorgeous hair."

"Your one beauty," Eleanor jokes. It's our favorite line from *Little Women*.

The three of us are sitting in front of the fireplace, our tumblers of Scotch in hand. The fire is slowly dying, but it's too late to put on another log.

Where to begin? I already told Mom and Eleanor about the Buddhist monastery I'd been staying at for the past few months. "An extended meditation retreat," was how I described it to them, although a more accurate description would be "completing my community service hours as far away from the public eye as possible."

"When I saw the photos of the monks on the temple website," I say, "I felt inspired by their serenity. They looked so enlightened, like they had a real purpose in life."

"Did they make you shave your hair?" Mom asks.

"No, that was my own idea," I admit. "I wanted to fit in."

"Even bald, I can't imagine you fitting in at a monastery," Eleanor says.

If she only knew the half of it. A few days into my stay, I overheard two of the female monks bad-mouthing me for wearing mink eyelash extensions. And then the head monk started getting on my case for not paying my monthly fees.

"But I'm working eight hours a day," I complained. "Cleaning bathrooms, picking weeds, harvesting crops."

"Yes, that's to fulfill your community service," Master Lee said. "You still need to pay your room and board."

I was shocked when Master Lee handed me the flyer with

the monastery fees, which seemed excessive given that my room consisted of little more than a single futon on the floor, and board was mostly porridge and boiled root vegetables. Clutching the piece of paper in my grubby hands, I tried to appear as pathetic as possible, hoping the head monk would take pity on me.

"Why don't you try selling some of your stuff on eBay," he suggested, "and use the proceeds to pay your past due fees."

Seriously, eBay? For someone who supposedly shunned materialism, Master Lee didn't cut me much slack. Besides, I'd already tossed everything worth anything into the Goodwill collection box outside the Carl's Jr. where I'd had my last pre-monastery meal. Yum, I can still taste that Western Bacon Cheeseburger.

"I still don't know why you'd want to vacation at a monastery," Mom says, snapping me back from my cheeseburger memories.

"I was feeling stressed," I explain. "I thought it would be nice to disappear from the face of the earth, just like my namesake Amelia Earhart."

"Eponym," Eleanor corrects me, not for the first time.

"No one knows what eponym means, Ellie."

"That's no excuse."

"Okay, you two," Mom says, just like she used to when we were bickering little girls, "I'm going to bed." She places her empty tumbler on the fireplace mantel, gives us both a quick hug, and heads down the hallway.

"Night, Mom," Eleanor and I say in unison.

Eleanor picks up Mom's tumbler and a full bowl of water, empties the bowl in the sink, and returns it back in place. She continues this sequence, walking around the living room and picking up another couple bowls. After all the bowls and buckets have been emptied and the fire completely put out,

Eleanor turns off the lights. I grab my duffel, and we walk down the hall.

"That's the main bedroom," Eleanor says. "Mom's got dibs on that."

"This is the bathroom," she says, flipping on the light.

"And this is our room," she says when we reach the end of the hall. "There's just one bed, so we'll have to share." Eleanor switches on the nightstand lamp. The walls are painted an apricot-peach color, and the queen-size bed is covered with a faded patchwork quilt.

"Here," Eleanor says, handing me a soft bundle: a bath towel, washcloth, and Lanz of Salzburg nightgown. "You should take a nice, long shower and change into something warm before bed." The flannel nightgown in my hands has a Tyrolean heart-and-flower print and eyelet lace trim. It feels wonderful.

I expect Eleanor to be asleep by the time I finish my shower, but when I open the door, my sister's still awake, sitting up in bed and reading a book. It's one of those pocket editions of some classic novel like *Anna Karenina* or *Madame Bovary*. Just seeing the cover makes me cringe, reminding me of my high school required reading lists full of boring old tomes by dead white men, but Eleanor has always had a soft spot for them.

"You look better," she says. She slips in a bookmark and sets the paperback on the nightstand. She slides over to make room for me on the bed, and when I get in, the spot is still warm.

"So, tell me about Jett," Eleanor says. Her voice is girlish, almost singsong. I haven't heard her sound girlish in years. Not since her husband, Edward, died.

"What about him?" I say.

"Come on, now, don't hold back on me. Tell me the whole meet-cute setup."

"You've been reading too many romance novels, Ellie."

"Seriously, Ames," Eleanor says. "Throw me a bone."

I regale Eleanor with the details of my near-disastrous day—from my 600-calorie white chocolate mocha at Starbucks, to the Barter-Ride debacle with Shayna, to Jett as Freddy Krueger appearing out of nowhere to rescue me from the Portal to the Dead.

"Oh, Ames," Eleanor sighs. She slides under the sheets and closes her eyes. "You always tell the best stories." I turn off the nightstand light and curl up next to my sister, who places her hands on my cheeks.

"I missed you, Ames," she says into the darkness.

"Your hands are cold," I reply.

"Sorry, it's from emptying those bowls of rainwater."

"Why does she say that?" I ask. "'Your hands are cold'?"

"Oh, don't get started on this now, Ames. It's too late, and I'm too tired."

Too tired? Eleanor is never too tired to talk about *Pride and Prejudice*. It's one of our favorite topics of conversation.

"I just don't get it," I persist. "Why doesn't Keira Knightley say, 'I love you too'?"

"It's implied."

"I know that. But when someone says something so heartfelt and beautiful as what Mr. Darcy says to her, the least you could do is say it back."

"I don't know why she says it, Ames. The line's not even in the book. Or the BBC version, which is so much better," Eleanor says.

"Let's agree to disagree on that," I reply.

"Anyway," Eleanor yawns, "Darcy's declaration of love is so obviously the work of an overzealous screenwriter. No one ever uses such flowery words in real life."

"Edward did," I say before I can stop myself.

Eleanor is quiet for a long time, and I worry that I've upset her. It's been over twelve years since Edward died. Is it still too soon to talk about him?

"Yes, he did," Eleanor finally admits.

"I love you, Mr. Darcy," I whisper.

"I love you too, Mr. Darcy."

4

The next morning, sunshine is streaming through the window. There's a shallow indent in the sheets where Eleanor slept, but she's already up and moving. The distinctive aroma of coffee wafts into the bedroom, and my stomach growls. I rub the sleep out of my eyes and pad down the hall to the kitchen.

"Good morning, starshine," Eleanor half sings to me.

"The earth says hello," I mumble back.

"Oh, I loved that movie," Mom says. "*Hair*, right?"

"Bingo, Mom," I reply and give her a peck on the cheek. Ever since we were young, Eleanor and I loved quoting movie lines at one another. Hitchcock thrillers, MGM musicals, John Hughes comedies, cult classics—Eleanor and I gobbled them all up. Mom almost never gets our movie references, so she's tickled pink on the rare occasion that she does.

"That Treat Williams was so handsome," Mom says. "Wasn't he just dreamy?"

Eleanor shrugs and passes me a mug of coffee.

"We've got toast or yogurt on offer," Eleanor says.

I wrinkle my nose like I smell something bad. After three months of plain porridge for breakfast, I was kind of hoping for Eleanor's famous blueberry streusel coffee cake or cinnamon-raisin rolls.

"Sorry, but this kitchen's impossibly tiny," Eleanor says. "Apparently, the Master never cooked." I take a sip of my coffee. Eleanor added lots of cream and sugar, just the way I like it. My sister knows me so well.

"Why's it called the Master's Cottage anyway?" I ask.

"The whole compound used to be a military school for wayward boys," Eleanor explains. "In the midseventies the school shuttered, and the property sat empty. Then a wealthy doctor bought it and created the cancer retreat center. When the doctor died, the center was at risk of closing until my friend Leo decided to take it over."

Eleanor goes on to describe the Arcadia campus. A large building that once served as the dormitory and cafeteria now houses the cancer center guest rooms and dining hall. Another large building that used to be classrooms and a library has been converted into the owner's personal residence. And a couple cottages formerly occupied by teaching staff have been turned into a yoga studio and meeting rooms.

"The Master's Cottage was where the school's headmaster lived," Eleanor says. "It was disused until Mom and I moved in, which explains the poor condition of the roof."

The front door to the cottage is wide open. A gentle breeze wafts in carrying the bracing scent of eucalyptus after a rainstorm. Two pale yellow butterflies fly in circles outside the door, chasing each other like young lovers. I pick up a piece of buttered toast, take a bite, and put it back down on the plate. It's fine, but it's not Eleanor's famous coffee cake.

"Hello?" says a voice at the front door. The three of us turn to look.

"I hope I'm not too early," Jett says.

Just like last night, I imagine the scene from Jett's perspective. Eleanor is still wearing her flannel nightgown and wool scuffs; she took off her knit beanie and down jacket, thank God. Mom remains in her Juicy Couture tracksuit. And dear Lord, here I am, all decked out in my Tyrolean-patterned, eyelet-trimmed flannel finery. I'm a bald Holly Hobbie.

"Oh, Jett, come in and join us!" Mom beckons, oblivious to the fact that neither Eleanor nor I are exactly dressed for guests. Jett holds out a willow basket and approaches the kitchen. The basket is lined with a red-checkered cloth and smells of butter and happiness.

"I thought you ladies might appreciate something sweet this morning," he says.

"What could be sweeter than a breakfast of eye candy?" Mom stage-whispers to me and Eleanor, who gives Mom the "hush up" look. Jett places the basket on the kitchen counter, and when I see its contents, I let out a high-pitched squeal like a stuck pig.

"Oops, did that come out of me?" I ask. Jett smiles, but my mother and sister don't even notice. After nearly forty years with me, they're immune to my quirky outbursts. Inside the basket is an array of butter croissants, chocolate croissants, and my favorite, morning buns.

"Where in the world did you get these?" Eleanor asks. My sister's an even bigger foodie than I am; she knows every top-notch bakery on the West Coast. If there were a place within twenty miles of Arcadia that could produce such impressive pastries, she'd already know about it.

"I made them," Jett says.

"You made them?" we cry out. Although, given that I've already stuffed half a morning bun into my mouth, my words come out like, "Mur meh meh?"

"In my rush to get the groceries into the fridge last night, I realized that I forgot to properly introduce myself," Jett says. "I'm the new chef at Arcadia."

Ah, the old butchering accident.

As Eleanor cross-examines Jett about his culinary training, I take a more ladylike bite of my morning bun and savor the craftsmanship. The flaky outer layer of sugar-dusted pastry gives way to the achingly tender inner layers of dough mingling with just the right amounts of brown sugar and cinnamon. But I sense something else. A secret ingredient.

"Orange zest?" I ask, interrupting Eleanor and Jett's conversation.

"What?" Eleanor asks.

"Yes," Jett replies. "Those are some sensitive taste buds you've got there."

"Amelia has always been a sensitive soul, my wild child," Mom says. "She's like a little butterfly flitting from flower to flower—flit, flit, flit—while Eleanor here is my wise, practical child. She was an old lady from the moment she popped out of my womb."

Eleanor turns as red as the ladybugs on her nightgown. Jett doesn't say a thing, seemingly thrown off by Mom's oversharing. I'm just relieved she said "womb" and not "vajayjay." Mom tries so hard to stay current on the lingo, although she's usually at least a decade behind.

"I should get going," Jett says. "The guests will be walking back from morning yoga, and I want to be in the dining room to greet them. I wouldn't want to disappoint them my first week on the job."

The three of us gaze at the dashing figure walking out the front door, and I know we're all thinking the same thing: *I can't imagine you ever disappointing anyone.*

About an hour later, Jett is back at our front door.

"Hello, Jett!" Mom exclaims. She's sitting on the couch and skimming through the latest issue of *Us Weekly* magazine. She still hasn't changed out of her tracksuit.

"Hey, Jett," I say, trying to sound casual and hoping he doesn't notice that I'm still at the kitchen counter, scavenging the remaining pastry crumbs from the basket. Thankfully, I ditched Eleanor's pj's and am wearing my own yoga pants and T-shirt. "What're you doing back?"

"I told you I'd stop by to check out your leaks."

"But it's not raining anymore," I say, pointing at the bright sunshine streaming through the windows.

"Yes, but the weather could change at any moment," Eleanor warns as she emerges from the bathroom. She's wearing her *Peanuts*-themed nursing scrubs and white plastic clogs.

"In fact, the forecast called for light showers last night," Eleanor continues, "and you saw what a thunderstorm we got. You can never predict what you're going to get these days with all the local microclimates. Not to mention global warming."

"Are you a nurse?" Jett asks, eyeing Eleanor's outfit.

"She's an OB-GYN nurse at Marin General," Mom says proudly. "I call her St. Eleanor. She spends all day pulling babies out of strangers' vajayjays, and then comes home to take care of me, her poor widowed mother."

"So anyway," Eleanor says, all businesslike, "here are the places where the roof leaked last night." At some point, Eleanor seems to have removed the buckets and bowls and marked the drippy spots with blue painter's tape on the floor. Jett follows Eleanor around like an obedient service animal—looking down at the X's, up at the stucco ceiling, back at Eleanor—and occasionally shoots me a smile.

"Eleanor," I interrupt, "Jett's a trained chef, not a home repair specialist. I think this Hobbit house needs professional help."

"What do you say, Jett?" she asks, ignoring me. "I've got the day off work tomorrow. We could at least get up on the roof and check if there's any obvious damage. Are you in?"

Jett glances over at me and runs his fingers through his hair. "Absolutely," he says. "I'm all in."

That evening, Eleanor gets back from work and makes a quick dinner of penne with curly kale and Italian sausage. I pop open a bottle of cheap red wine and pour three generous glasses. I don't say a word the entire meal. After months of near fasting, this food feels miraculous.

"I'm thinking of walking to the bluff to check out the sunset," Eleanor says. "Want to stretch your legs and join me?"

"No, thanks," Mom says, pouring herself a second glass of wine.

"Sure," I say. "I haven't left the house since I got here."

"What did you do all day?" Eleanor asks.

I shrug. Honestly, I don't know where the time goes.

We open the front door, and the air is unseasonably chilly. Eleanor dashes back to our bedroom and returns with her trusty down jacket and a knit beanie. She hands me an oversized cardigan and extra beanie before closing the front door and leading me up to a path behind the cottage.

"When is Maggie joining us?" I ask, adjusting the beanie to what I hope is a jaunty angle.

"I pick her up from camp on Saturday," Eleanor responds.

"What kind of camp is it?" I ask, envisioning friendship bracelets and s'mores.

"SAT camp. It's a one-week intensive study program at Berkeley."

Nix the friendship bracelets.

"How's Maggie doing these days?" I ask.

"Junior year was challenging," Eleanor says. "Not academically—she's still a straight-A student—but socially and emotionally. Maggie's just so hard on herself, and I'm worried senior year will be even more challenging."

"Is she still having panic attacks?" I ask.

"How did you know she was having panic attacks?" Eleanor asks. "I don't remember telling you."

"Maggie and I manage to stay in touch," I say, trying to keep it vague and hoping Eleanor doesn't press the issue. "Snapchat, DMs, you know, that kind of thing." I throw these words out with the full expectation that Eleanor doesn't have any clue what they mean.

"Maggie's been so negative lately," Eleanor says. "She says she doesn't want to go back to St. Isadore in the fall, that her classmates are all spoiled brats with overbearing parents who went to Harvard and Yale and Stanford, and that she has no way to compete with them because of the legacy preference system."

"I've heard the social pressure at SI can be pretty intense," I say. "Lots of entitled kids and their entitled helicopter parents. It's not the most supportive setting for a sweet and sensitive girl like Maggie."

"What's the alternative?" Eleanor asks. "Public school? Poor Maggie would be eaten alive there."

"Have you thought about homeschooling?"

"Yeah, right," Eleanor scoffs, "in my copious spare time when I'm not doing twelve-hour shifts at the hospital and commuting an hour each way."

"I hear there are a lot of online homeschool programs," I offer.

"Ames, Maggie is going to be a high school senior. She needs to retake the SATs and keep up her GPA and get teacher recommendations for college. The last thing she needs is to sit alone in a room all day glued to a computer screen."

We stop at a fork in the path, and I see a large white stucco house with a heavy oak door and red-tiled roof.

"What's that?" I ask.

"The old school building. That's where Leo lives."

"Who's Leo?"

"Surely, you remember me talking about my friend Leo?"

"If I remembered Leo, I wouldn't have asked. And don't call me Shirley."

Eleanor always laughs at that line. *Airplane!* An oldie but a goodie.

"Leo Lowenstein is my friend who owns Arcadia," Eleanor says. "He's one of the most generous people I know. You should remember his name. It's thanks to him we have a roof over our heads."

"Why are we living out here anyway?" I ask, following Eleanor along the left fork of the path, the one leading away from Leo's house. "Why can't we live in your place in the city?"

Eleanor stops for a moment and tucks her hair behind her ear. It's a tic she's had since we were girls. It means she's giving something serious thought.

"Mom's had a tough time since Dad died," Eleanor says. The gravel crunches under our feet as we make our way along the path. "She puts on a good face to the world, but she's in way over her head with all these legal issues. That's why I had to step in. The court froze Dad's assets when we lost the initial estate battle, so she has nothing to live on. And we had no idea how hard the court appeal would be. Or how expensive."

"How much money are we talking about?" I ask.

"The appeals lawyer wanted a $10,000 retainer to take our case," Eleanor says. "And that's on top of the legal fees for the case that we lost. I don't have that kind of money just sitting around, and I refuse to touch Maggie's college fund. So, when a visiting surgeon from Germany complained about how hard it was to find a short-term rental in San Francisco, I offered him our flat. I figured the three of us could spend the summer subletting a cheaper place in Oakland or Daly City and apply the savings toward the retainer. When Leo heard we were between homes, he offered us the Master's Cottage for free."

"Free is good," I say.

"Yeah," Eleanor agrees, "especially since it turns out nothing in the Bay Area is cheap anymore, not even in Daly City."

"So, you'll move back to the city at the end of summer?" I ask. The ocean breeze is even colder than when we left the cottage. I'm grateful for the cardigan and beanie.

"Yeah, that's the plan," Eleanor says. "Maggie and I will spend the next three months here with Mom and then move back to the city before Maggie's senior year begins. What about you, Ames? What are your plans?"

We're standing at the edge of a steep cliff, the azure-blue Pacific Ocean stretching out before us. The setting sun glints on the water's surface like an honest-to-God Monet. I gaze into the far distance, using the breathtaking scenery as an excuse to avoid my sister's question. A question that I can't answer.

What *are* my plans? What kind of future can I have? My lawyer had told me that people with criminal records—which, shockingly, is a category I now belong to—often have trouble finding work.

"California is one of the few states with a ban-the-box law," my lawyer had said, "which means employers can't technically ask potential hires about their criminal records. But in real life, most employers put candidates through at least a cursory background check, and criminal records are in the public domain."

My lawyer had been able to plead my case down from a felony to a misdemeanor, but I'm still technically considered a criminal in the eyes of the legal system. Who's going to hire a convicted criminal with no marketable skills? I can't remember the last time I've had to look for a job. I don't even have a résumé. But I can't admit any of this to Eleanor.

"Hey, I think we should have a signal," I say, trying to change the topic.

"A signal?" Eleanor asks.

"Yeah," I say, "in case one of us needs the bedroom for… privacy."

Eleanor laughs. "I don't think that'll be necessary."

"It's always good to be prepared," I say, remembering Jett and his warm hazel eyes. A girl could get lost in eyes like those.

"We could use our bedroom doorknob as a signal," I suggest, "like in college."

"I never had a signal in college," Eleanor says. "Edward had his own place off-campus, remember?"

"La-dee-dah," I say. "Not all of us dated fancy business school guys."

"Okay, then," Eleanor says, "how does this signal thing work?"

"I thought you'd never ask," I say, rubbing my hands together in mock–evil genius mode. "Let's say I hooked up with a preppie from Amherst. I'd hang his purple-and-white-striped rep tie on the doorknob. A French major from Hampshire? His beret. A hockey goalie from UMass? His jockstrap. A lax player from Smith? Her jog bra."

Eleanor chuckles. Then she stops.

"You're joking, right?" Eleanor asks.

"Of course," I assure her, "I would never sleep with a French major."

5

I wake to the sound of chainsaws. Eleanor's woolen scuffs are by the bed. I slip them on and head outside. It's another beautiful day in Arcadia.

"Sorry, Amelia, did we wake you?" Jett says.

I see Jett standing on the roof of the Master's Cottage sporting a pair of plastic safety goggles and holding his trusty chainsaw. Eleanor is by his side wearing paint-spattered overalls and purple work gloves. A metal ladder is leaning against the cottage, safely secured to the roof. Jett hands over a gnarly branch to Eleanor, who tosses it down to the ground where I see there's already a small pile of dead wood.

"Jett brought some banana-walnut muffins this morning," Eleanor shouts. "They're in the kitchen next to the coffee." I scurry back inside to the kitchen. The muffins are still warm. I take a bite from one and reflexively moan. The French press is half-full, so I pour myself a large mug and load it up with sugar and cream. I gobble down the rest of the first muffin, grab a second one from the basket, and head outside again.

"What're you guys doing?" I ask, sitting down on a flat slate stone.

"Jett crawled into the attic space and found a bunch of holes. We think some animals may have climbed this tree and gnawed their way into the house," Eleanor says. "We're cutting off all the dead and dying limbs and then we'll get to work patching the attic and roof."

I watch Eleanor and Jett working in silent partnership. At one point, Jett reaches into his pants pocket and offers my sister a handkerchief. It seems she's got some schmutz on her cheek. Even from my vantage point over twenty feet away, I can sense Eleanor blushing. She takes Jett's handkerchief and rubs the side of her face way harder than she needs to. When she tries to give the handkerchief back, Jett motions for her to keep it. Eleanor stares down at the handkerchief and then further down at me. We make eye contact for a microsecond.

I get up from my slate stone and pretend I didn't see anything. I head back into the cottage and find Mom sitting at the kitchen counter, picking walnuts off the top of a muffin.

"Terrible racket, don't you think?" Mom says.

"Yeah, it woke me up."

"Me too," she says.

I reach over and pour the dregs of the coffee into my mug and start on my third muffin of the morning.

"Mom, you haven't changed out of that tracksuit the whole time I've been here," I say.

"It's comfortable."

"Yeah, but you're starting to give off that creepy Miss Havisham quality."

"Who's that again?"

"The old lady in *Great Expectations* who sits around her decaying mansion wearing her wedding gown from when her fiancé left her at the altar."

"I don't think I've seen that one."

"Oh, Mom," I say, "I'm sure you have. There've been at least a dozen versions. The black-and-white one with Jean Simmons is my favorite. Once we get back to civilization, I'll add it to your Netflix queue." Then it occurs to me: Do people even watch Netflix anymore? I've been out of the loop for so long.

"Anyway, I *am* an old lady," Mom says, smoothing out her white velour sleeves. "No one cares how I look. But you don't have that excuse. You're still young enough to snag yourself an eligible man. What are you doing walking around the house looking like that? Completely bald and wearing Eleanor's frumpy flannel nightgown? What must Jett think?"

"What must I think of what?" Jett asks. He wipes his heavy work boots on the doormat before entering the cottage.

"Nothing," Mom and I say at the same time.

"I think I'll go lie down for a bit," Mom announces. She gives me a stage wink—is that even a thing?—before heading back to her bedroom.

I am tempted to have a fourth muffin, but I force myself away from the pastry basket. I make myself comfortable on the couch and start leafing through Mom's magazines. There's a photo of Beyoncé and Jay Z strolling casually down Rodeo Drive. Beyoncé looks as gorgeous and glam as when she took that selfie of the two of us together. That feels like a lifetime ago.

"Eleanor tells me you used to work with Nils Nilsson," Jett says, sitting down next to me.

I look around for Eleanor, who seems to have made herself scarce.

Nils Nilsson. I haven't heard his name in months. That's one of the benefits of living off the grid. In fact, it was the whole point of retreating to the Buddhist monastery. I'm pretty sure no one at the temple had even heard of Nils Nilsson. People who wear saffron robes and subsist on a primarily spelt-based diet don't normally follow the avant-garde culinary world.

"Yeah, I was the hostess at Amuse," I admit. I'm not ready to admit to anything else.

"I should have recognized you, but you look so different..."

"Without my hair," I say, finishing his sentence. My signature hair.

At the height of Amuse's popularity, Nils and I were such fixtures on the Manhattan social scene that people actually dressed up as us for Halloween: Nils with his shock of white-blond hair and sharply trimmed goatee; me with my cascade of jet-black curls and ironic nerd-girl glasses. We were the "It Couple" for a hot second before we turned our backs on it all and made a fresh start in Mendocino County.

I first met Nils when I was an undergrad at Hampshire College and he was a perpetual graduate student—a "gradual student" he used to joke—tending bar at a local dive. It was one of those meet-cute moments that would be perfect in a rom-com, except that rom-coms usually end in happily-ever-after. Spoiler alert: no HEA for us.

"Hell, no," Nils said, shaking his head as my friends and I walked into the dimly lit bar. "No one under twenty-one." He pointed at the sign next to the cash register.

"Asian women age well," I responded. I've always considered myself Asian even though my Asian American friends annoyingly point out I'm "only" half-Korean.

"I need to see some ID," Nils said brusquely. He had a thick Nordic accent.

I reached into my purse, pulled out my California driver's license, slipped it along with a crisp hundred-dollar bill into my cleavage, and leaned forward over the polished oak bar. My dad had given me the money when he and Mom dropped me off at college—“keep the bill hidden in your wallet in case of emergency,” he’d advised—and this seemed about as big an emergency as I was going to get.

Nils stopped and stared at me for a beat. Honestly, I’ve never had much of a rack, but something about the combination of sex, money, and laugh-out-loud ballsiness did the trick.

“What’ll ya have?” Nils asked as he plucked the Benjamin from my boobs.

What I ended up having that night was Nils. I’ve always been attracted to bad boys: James Dean, Marlon Brando, Christian Slater. And foreign accents? Don’t get me started. With his Billy Idol hair, Japanese sleeve tattoos, and “live fast, die young” attitude, Nils was all I ever wanted in a man.

What can I say? I was just a dumb nineteen-year-old girl.

He had me at “Hell, no.”

Things between me and Nils escalated rapidly after that initial hookup. Soon, I was spending more time hanging out at his studio apartment or the bar than I spent in the lecture halls, and my grades reflected it. Rather than risk getting kicked out of college, I decided to quit after my junior year and moved with Nils and a bunch of his filmmaker friends to New York City to start our lives. It was shortly after 9/11, and my parents and Eleanor were freaking out, begging me to reconsider. They urged me to finish school or at the very least come home to California, but I said no.

There was something about the devastation of post-9/11 New York City that Nils and his friends found inspirational. There were stories to be told, flowers to grow out of the ashes. And me? I just wanted to join Nils for the ride, to follow his passion, even if it meant upsetting my family and losing my monthly allowance from Mom and Dad.

Fortunately, the city was so desperate to revitalize downtown that the group of us were able to get a huge live-work loft space for practically nothing. Our friends worked a range of crappy jobs, everything from data entry clerk to phone sex operator. Nils found work chopping vegetables at a corporate hotel restaurant in Times Square, and I killed time as a salesgirl at Urban Outfitters.

Ah, the value of a liberal arts education.

While soul-crushing, the jobs paid decent hourly wages and had their fringe benefits. Nils would bring home aluminum trays of leftover banquet food, and I'd supply my loft-mates with clothes that would otherwise be trashed or donated to the Salvation Army. We all thought we were living the edgy, bohemian life, but come on, who were we kidding? Most of us were upper-middle-class kids from the coastal suburbs. We could always go back to Mommy and Daddy if things ever fell through. In retrospect, we were a lot closer to *Friends* than we were to *Rent*.

After working and saving for nearly a year, Nils and I spent a life-changing few months backpacking through Europe. We hitched from town to town, sleeping in spartan youth hostels or, in a pinch, on deserted beaches or in noisy train stations. We saved our hard-earned money for what really mattered: eating our way through the famed *Michelin Guide*. When our cash ran out, we returned to New York and got new jobs, building up our savings until we were ready to hit the road again.

Nils and I lived this vagabond life for almost ten years. As our destinations got more exotic, so did our epicurean tastes. In Asia, we went from curry-dusted noodles from hawker-stalls in Singapore, to still-wriggling octopus dipped in gochujang from pier-side vendors in Seoul, to sticks of salt-and-pepper-coated locusts from makeshift carts in Bangkok. In Africa, we covered everything from tagines to bunny chow to salt-cured kudu. South America introduced us to llama stew, fried guinea pig, and bull cock soup—I had to take a pass on that last one.

Each time Nils and I returned from our travels, we somehow managed to land even better jobs. Employers seemed to find our life experience interesting if not necessarily relevant. Over the years, I slowly worked my way up from lowly salesgirl to personal assistant to one of the head honchos at Bergdorf's, and Nils was hired as the sous-chef at Le Cocodrile.

Life was good, but by the time I approached thirty, I was more than happy to settle in for longer stretches at our now-prime-real-estate loft. I was getting tired of living like a nomad. But not Nils.

"I can't do this much longer," Nils complained to me after working another late night at Le Cocodrile. "I feel like I'm suffocating."

"Do you mean the job, or us?" I asked. Nils didn't respond.

"What would make you happy?" I asked, taking a different tack.

"I don't want to be happy," Nils muttered. "Happy is so American. Happy is boring. What I want is the opposite of boring. I want to be surprised, challenged, entertained. I want to be amused."

I spent so many years trying to figure out how to keep Nils amused. Only later, when everything came crashing down, did I realize that I'd spent so much time focusing on Nils' passions, I never thought about my own wants and needs.

A swift wind blows in off the Pacific and slams the front door of the Master's Cottage shut—bam!—and I realize Jett is still talking to me.

"When I read about the restaurant in the *Times*, I nearly kicked myself," Jett says. "The concept was so simple. Simple but brilliant. I couldn't believe no one had thought of it before."

That's what everyone says. Such a simple idea. A simple idea that took me and Nils three full years of crowdfunding, real estate negotiating, city permit wrangling, and local organic farm sourcing to bring to fruition.

"When Nils was working as sous-chef at Le Cocodrile," I explain, "he felt shackled by the classic French repertoire. The only time he could flex his creative muscles and experiment was for the amuse-bouches. Food critics who had long ago written off the restaurant as a relic of the past, a shadow of its former glory, started coming back just for Nils' inventive palate teasers. One day, I asked him, 'What's holding you back? Why not open your own place that only serves amuse-bouches?'"

"Are you telling me it was all your idea?" Jett asks. His face is a mixture of surprise and delight. I don't say anything, but yeah, it's true.

I was the muse of Amuse.

6

That afternoon, Eleanor, Jett, and I go into town to pick up some roof-fixing supplies and groceries. When we get back from shopping, Mom seems to be in her bedroom still, the only sign of her a tumbler on the kitchen counter with a telltale splash of Scotch at the bottom.

"What's up with Mom?" I whisper to Eleanor. "It's barely past noon."

Eleanor unpacks the groceries and starts putting things away in the tiny fridge. I hear Jett climbing back onto the roof and banging away at something. Man, don't these people know how to relax?

"I think she's depressed," I say.

"You'd be depressed too if your husband of forty-four years suddenly died of an undiagnosed heart condition," Eleanor responds. She pulls a chef's knife from the block and slices into a gorgeous green-and-white-striped watermelon. I can tell by the distinctive sound how ripe it is.

"It's been over six months, Ellie."

"There's not an expiration date on grief, Ames."

There's an unkind edge to Eleanor's normally kind voice, and I feel the sharp sting of judgment. Look who I'm talking to. I don't think Eleanor's gone on a single date in the twelve years since Edward died. Not that she would tell me if she did. All she ever does is work and worry, worry and work, rinse and repeat. I'm tempted to tell my sister to lighten up and enjoy life, but things are going so well between us right now, and I don't want to disrupt the peace.

"What're you making?" I ask.

"Watermelon and feta salad."

"Oh, I love that. It's so refreshing," I say.

"Yeah, I thought it would be nice in this warm weather." Eleanor rinses some mint leaves under the faucet and gives them a rough chop. The tingly scent fills the air.

"Could you squeeze some lime and grind some pepper into that small bowl over there?" Eleanor asks. After years of following Nils' detailed directions, I've become a pretty good sous-chef. I stifle a sneeze from the spicy aroma of the fresh-ground Tellicherry peppercorns.

I hand the bowl to Eleanor, who adds a generous glug of olive oil, gives the mixture a good whisk, and pours the dressing over the watermelon and feta. She picks a chunk of watermelon and pops it into my mouth.

"What do you think?" Eleanor asks.

The salad is sweet from the watermelon and salty from the feta, fresh from the mint and spicy from the black pepper, crisp and creamy, unexpected and comforting. It's a concoction of contrasts. Things that shouldn't go together but do.

"It's perfect," I say. "Just like everything you do, Ellie."

Eleanor beams at me. Acts of service and words of affirmation are her love languages. Ever since we were little, Eleanor's worked hard to earn everyone's praise. She was a straight-A student, Honor Society member, yearbook editor, French Club president. She kept her bedroom neat as a pin, practiced piano an hour every day without being prompted, and visited the old lady next door every Sunday to read to her from the Bible—and we weren't even religious.

It wasn't easy growing up in my sister's shadow. No matter how hard I tried—and to be fair, I didn't really try that hard—I could never be as perfect as Eleanor. I struggled to sit still in school and constantly got in trouble for passing notes in class. I hung out with my stoner friends after school instead of joining any clubs. My parents bought me almost every instrument in the music store—clarinet, violin, guitar, flute, even accordion—before they finally realized I had no interest in music. The only thing I had any interest in was watching movies and making up stories. That's how I ended up going to Hampshire College. It was the only school my guidance counselor could find that didn't require grades or SATs but still passed muster with my parents.

It wasn't until I was in my thirties that one of my friends, a licensed therapist, asked if I'd ever been diagnosed with ADHD. I hadn't. Come to think of it, I still haven't. I've never had the follow-through to get tested.

Eleanor sets the watermelon salad aside and opens some packages of assorted salami and arranges them on a platter. She then slices a sourdough baguette into ovals and adds them to the arrangement. I watch as she fiddles with the mound of bread to make it more symmetric. Ever the perfectionist, my sister.

"In New York," I say, "they'd call this an artisanal charcuterie platter and charge a small fortune." It always amazed me how much people would be willing to pay for simple, good food presented beautifully.

"I'm still disappointed in myself for never visiting when you had Amuse," Eleanor says. "I mean, how often do you have a chance to try a Michelin-starred restaurant run by your baby sister?"

"I was hardly running the place," I protest. "I was a glorified hostess."

"That's not how the press described you," Eleanor says, wiping her hands on a dishcloth. "Amuse's Comely Co-Owner. Gastronomic Go-Getter. Foodie Fashionista."

"Since when did you start reading gossip magazines?" I ask. "And why in the world have you memorized them?"

"Mom would clip the articles and send them to me," Eleanor says. "She was so proud of you. And so was I."

I can't help but notice Eleanor's use of the past tense. I wonder how my mother and sister feel about me now that I'm no longer successful. I wonder how they would feel about me if they knew what really happened to me and Nils.

I pray they never do.

It's evening, and we're getting ready for bed. It's been a productive day of chainsaws and hammering and generally making a ruckus. Eleanor takes out her contact lenses while I scrub my face with a washcloth. Our bodies engage in a subtle swaying rhythm as we jockey for space at the sink, just like we did when we were growing up and our bedrooms were attached by a shared bathroom. It's funny how quickly my sister and I fall back into old patterns even though it's been years, decades really, since we've spent quality time together.

"I think you got some color today," I say.

"You think so?" Eleanor asks. She leans closer to the mirror.

"Yeah, your cheeks have a spot of pink on them. It looks good on you."

"Thanks, Ames. It felt good to work outside. In the fresh air."

Eleanor turns on the faucet to wash her face. She's almost four years older than me, but when we were in our teens and twenties, people sometimes used to mistake her for the younger sister. I think it was because I was taller, and she had soft, rounded features in contrast to my sharp, more angular ones. Now I can't help but notice how much my sister has aged. There are delicate lines around her eyes and mouth, silver strands peeking out at her temples.

"So, how much more work is there to do on the roof?" I ask.

"We made good progress today," Eleanor says. "We replaced the plastic barrier and attic insulation, and Jett's coming back tomorrow to patch up some holes in the roof and lay down a new membrane."

"When did you become such an expert in home repair?" I ask. I regret the question the moment it comes out of my mouth.

"Never mind," I say.

It always comes back to Edward. Ever since Edward died, Eleanor's had to be everything for their daughter: the mom and the dad, the breadwinner and the meal maker, the disciplinarian and the cheerleader. Now, she has to be everything for me and Mom too.

"You through?" I ask.

Eleanor nods. I turn off the bathroom light, and we head to our room. As she climbs into bed, Eleanor winces slightly and rotates her shoulders.

"Feeling sore?" I ask.

"A little. I must not be used to working those muscles."

"Here, let me give you a massage," I say. For once, Eleanor gives in.

"Wow, you're super tight, Ellie. You've got a knot the size of a golf ball. When was the last time you got a massage?"

"The cobbler's children go barefoot," she responds. In addition to being a full-time nurse and single parent, Eleanor makes time to volunteer as a massage therapist for cancer patients at Arcadia. Mom isn't too far off when she calls her St. Eleanor.

"How many years have you been volunteering here?" I ask.

"Oh gosh, I don't know. Edward and I first came out here when we learned his cancer had returned. That was…what, maybe twelve, thirteen years ago? Based on that, I've probably been volunteering about ten years."

"How about Jett?" I ask. "Do you know how he ended up here?"

"He says he heard about the place through an old friend, came up a few times to visit," Eleanor says. "When the longtime chef announced his retirement, Jett decided to quit his day job to take on the role."

"What was his day job?" I ask.

"I can't believe I forgot to tell you," Eleanor says. "Jett used to be the head pastry chef at La Reverie." La Reverie is a legendary San Francisco restaurant perched at the tippy-top of Nob Hill with million-dollar views of the city. Consistently included among the Top 50 Restaurants in the World, La Reverie has a six-month waiting list and its employees have gone on to open their own successful restaurants in Napa, Portland, and New York.

"No way!" I say in an exaggerated Valley-girl accent.

"Yes way!" Eleanor responds in kind.

"Well, that explains the orgasmic pastries."

"Amelia!" Eleanor says in mock-astonishment. She always uses my formal name when she's being prim and proper.

"Eleanor!" I reply. Two can play at this game. I stop massaging her shoulders and whisper huskily into her ear, "Don't try to deny your feelings, Eleanor. I saw you checking out his hot, sticky morning buns."

Eleanor's face turns pink, and then we fall apart in a fit of laughter.

7

"Where's Ellie?" I ask, shuffling into the living room with my eyes half-closed. Mom's sitting on the floor with one of those adult coloring books that's all the rage among the senior serenity-seeking set.

"And good morning to you, Amelia," she says. She lifts her dewy face to allow me to give her a peck on the cheek.

"Eleanor went down to the center to volunteer with the guests," she says.

"Oh yeah, I forgot," I say. I wander over to the kitchen and poke my nose around.

"No Jett this morning either," Mom says, sussing me out. "You'll have to make do with toast." Toast doesn't sound in the least bit appealing. Only Jett's pastries will do. I've become spoiled in just two days.

"I think I might walk down the hill and try to find Jett," I say. "Wanna join me?"

"And leave my decaying mansion?" Mom asks, spreading her white velour arms.

"Good one, Miss Havisham," I say, smiling.

I go back to the bedroom to change out of my nightgown. I think about whether to take a shower. I take a quick sniff of my pits. Fresh as a daisy. Eleanor and I always say how lucky we are to have gotten the "no BO" gene from our Korean dad, but I like to check from time to time anyway, just to be sure. I stroke my head and feel the prickly stubble of my hair growing back in. That's at least one benefit of being bald: you save a lot of money on shampoo.

I toss on a T-shirt and yoga pants and borrow a pair of Toms from Mom's closet and start walking down the road. It's the same road that Jett and I were driving on that first night before I spotted the Master's Cottage, but it looks a lot less ominous in the broad daylight.

As I walk along the country lane, I spy a couple of floppy-eared rabbits darting into the brush up ahead. I'm reminded of Shayna the Barter-Ride driver and then again of Jett. "I've killed one too many innocent creatures in my day," he'd said. I laugh out loud thinking about how Jett's words had terrified me.

I round the bend, and I'm gobsmacked by the scene before me. Now I see why they call this place Arcadia. There's a white stucco building in the Spanish colonial revival style nestled among a grove of ancient redwoods and fragrant bay trees. Serving as backdrop: the cerulean Pacific, glittering with the diamond dust of morning light. Above the doorway of the building is a wooden sign with the words *Welcome to Arcadia* artfully carved into its surface. Behind the half-open door, I hear the tinkling of classical piano music, and I smell the intoxicating perfume of Jett's just-baked pastries.

Like a *Looney Tunes* character being lifted off the ground and floating toward the source of some delicious aroma, I find myself following my nose through the empty foyer and toward the bustling dining room. I am met by a dozen sets of curious eyes dispersed among three round tables. Half of the people in the room are bald. A few are wearing knit beanies.

I shouldn't be here.

I stand stock-still, trying to think of a way to make a hasty retreat, when a trim, silver-haired man wearing a powder blue tracksuit glides over to greet me. He has a certain lightness to him, Fred Astaire's delicacy and grace. The man nods placidly to the room, which goes back to its previous state of friendly chatter and careful chewing.

"Hello, my dear," he says. "Welcome. Won't you join us for breakfast?" He cradles my back with his hand and ushers me gently to his table.

"I don't have cancer," I blurt, remembering how Shayna the Barter-Ride driver assumed that I had cancer because of my bald head. I don't want to be accused of getting a free breakfast under false pretenses. Even I wouldn't sink that low.

The silver-haired man blinks his bright blue eyes in surprise and then smiles.

"Well, that's good to hear," he replies. "Neither do I."

On the sideboard is a plate of muffins, a clear glass trifle bowl filled with something creamy-looking layered with berries, and a shiny chrome-plated urn. The silver-haired man goes to the sideboard, loads up a plate and fills a mug, and brings the bounty to me.

"Please," he says, motioning to the food, "enjoy yourself."

I don't need to be asked twice. I go straight for the muffin. OMG. The toasty warm pear muffin has bits of candied ginger and the distinctive taste of maple syrup. Inside, there's a soft center of lightly sweetened mascarpone. My eyes go sideways in ecstasy. The silver-haired man grins and leans over to the petite, middle-aged woman on the other side of him.

"I'll have what she's having," he says.

They both start laughing. I stop chewing for an instant and stare at the man. Handsome, kind, and able to quote *When Harry Met Sally*? I'm instantly smitten.

"I love you," I blurt.

Wait, did that really come out of my mouth? Or did I just think it super-hard?

"Well!" he responds. "This is a surprising turn of events. But before we go any further with this relationship, I should probably introduce myself. I'm Leo Lowenstein."

"You're Leo Lowenstein?" I ask with amazement.

"The one and only. And you are?"

"Amelia?" Jett calls from the kitchen.

"Amelia!" Eleanor cries as she enters the dining room.

"Amelia," I say, brushing the crumbs off my fingers before reaching out to shake Leo's hand.

The dining room is empty except for me, Leo, and Jett. The Arcadia guests have retreated to the meeting rooms for their therapy sessions, and Eleanor has left for the first of six massage appointments she has scheduled for the day.

"Eleanor never told me she had such a beautiful sister," Leo says.

He takes a sip from his cardamom and cinnamon-spiced almond milk chai. Normally, when older men say stuff like that, it gives me the creeps, but there's something about Leo that manages to avoid the creep factor.

"Then again, Eleanor is so beautiful," Leo continues. "Why should it surprise me that her sister is as well?" Jett looks across the table at me and nods.

"You should see their mother, Leo," Jett replies. "The three Bae-Wood beauties."

"Actually, there's a fourth," I say. "Maggie, Eleanor's daughter."

"Eleanor has a daughter?" Jett asks.

"Eleanor never mentioned a daughter to me," Leo says. "Although, come to think of it, Eleanor never seems to talk about herself. She's always too busy taking care of other people."

Good old St. Eleanor.

"Maggie was at summer camp this week," I say, "but Eleanor's picking her up from the Larkspur Ferry Terminal this afternoon."

"I have a brilliant idea," Leo exclaims, snapping his fingers. "Why don't the four Bae-Wood beauties come to my home tomorrow night for an impromptu dinner party? Amelia, would you be so good as to extend the invitation to your family?"

"Of course," I say. "And, on behalf of my family, I accept."

"Marvelous! And, Jett, can I count on you?"

"To cook or to dine?" Jett asks.

"Both, of course," Leo replies.

Jett stands up to clear the dishes, which Leo takes as his cue to leave. I follow Jett into the kitchen, perch myself on the metal kitchen counter, and grab another pear-ginger muffin.

"So, tell me about your name," I say.

"My name?" Jett asks. He turns on the spigot to let the dishes soak.

"Yeah. Jett—it's unusual. Is it short for something?"

"You could say so. Jettison."

"Seriously?" I ask.

"No, not seriously, but I did jettison my parents' first two efforts."

"Okay, you got me," I say. "There's a story here. Spill."

"Well," he begins, washing each of the breakfast dishes in soapy circular strokes, "it all started when my dad decided to take a post-college year in Oxford, supposedly to get a master's degree but really to delay going into the family business. Dad was invited to this mixer at the president's house, where he meets this very proper English girl. Tweed skirt, string of pearls, you get the picture."

"Your mom," I say.

"Exactly," Jett says. "To hear my parents tell it, Dad was in love with Mom the moment he set eyes on her face, but it took some time for Mom to let down her British reserve and warm up to Dad's arrogant American style."

"Classic opposites attract love story," I say. "Katharine Hepburn and Spencer Tracy. Vivien Leigh and Clark Gable. Molly Ringwald and Judd Nelson. I'm imagining a young Emily Blunt or maybe Felicity Jones in the role of your mother."

"You've got a fertile imagination," Jett says. "Anyway, Mom and Dad ended up getting married before the year was through, and eight months later—yes, eight—I was born— Willow Bartholomew Jett."

"Willow?" I ask.

"Yeah, apparently I was conceived in the shade of a willow tree," Jett says, wincing.

"Gross," I say.

"Yeah, tell me about it."

"But that still doesn't explain why you go by Jett," I say.

"I'm getting to it," Jett says. "Growing up, I was small, scrawny, constantly getting teased. Every year on the first day of classes, we'd have an all-school assembly at which the headmaster would insist on introducing each student by their full name. The entire school would laugh whenever he called out my name. I should have sued my parents for intentional infliction of emotional distress."

"Bartholomew's not so bad," I say.

"Yeah, I went by Bart until middle school," Jett says, "and then *The Simpsons* came out and ruined everything all over again."

"Don't have a cow, man."

"Exactly," Jett says. "And thanks for that, by the way. Middle school traumas all rushing back to me now."

"Well, Jett's a very cool name," I say. "Like, you could pretend you're part of the Jett family."

Jett suddenly seems unable to maintain eye contact.

Damn, I think this guy's part of the Jett family.

The Jetts are San Francisco royalty. The Jett patriarch made a fortune in the oil business in the early 1900s, and the extended family's been living off the spoils ever since. The society pages are always full of splashy photos of the Jett family members attending the SF Symphony Gala, Opera Ball, and other money-soaked charitable events. I thought it was strange that the former pastry chef at La Reverie would quit to work at a remote retreat center, but now I'm doubly intrigued. Why would a member of the super-rich Jett family be working at all?

I hardly have time to consider the mystery, though, as Jett indicates for me to get off the kitchen counter so he can bleach it down. Then Jett gathers up the food scraps and invites me to join him as he heads outside to throw the scraps into the compost bin. He shows me around the carefully tended garden where we pick baby lettuces, pole beans, and heirloom tomatoes. We gather some speckled eggs from the resident heritage-breed chickens. Jett plans to make a salade Nicoise for today's lunch. I half expect him to head out to the beach to hand-spear some tuna.

Just before lunchtime, I run over to the Master's Cottage to drag Mom away from her bedroom and down to the center. I introduce her to Leo, who couldn't be any more charming. Mom and Leo hit it off right away. I notice their velour tracksuits practically match. For the first time in forever, Mom lets her sunny personality shine through.

That evening, my heart skips a beat when I spot Eleanor's

car in front of the cottage. Maggie should be finished with summer camp. I can't wait to see my niece again.

"Hey, Ellie," I say, entering the dark living room. "Where's Maggie?"

"She went to bed already. Mom did too."

"But it's barely eight o'clock."

"She was tired from the long drive," Eleanor says, making excuses.

I don't press the issue. Maggie's told me how hard it's been for her to fit in at her ritzy private high school. She's not cool enough for the beautiful crowd but not nerdy enough for the brainy crowd. I keep telling her that things will get better soon, that she'll find her own tribe in college, but that's not much comfort in the moment. Back when I was Maggie's age, everything felt overwhelming for me too. Sleep was the one respite from depression.

"What did you do all day?" Eleanor asks.

"This and that," I say. "I helped Jett in the garden and prepping lunch. I can't believe how hard he works, and it's just him in the kitchen."

"Well, this is his first week working at Arcadia," Eleanor says. "He probably wants to do a good job."

"You won't guess what I found out today," I say. "Did you know Jett's part of the Jett family?"

"No!" Eleanor gasps. "*The* Jett family?"

"None other," I say.

"I wonder what he's doing out here at Arcadia," Eleanor says.

"We're having dinner with him at Leo's house tomorrow night," I say. "You can ask him then."

8

"Psssst, Aunt Amelia," I hear someone whisper.

I wake from my peaceful slumber and open one eye to see Maggie curled up in bed next to me. I open both eyes to take a good, long look at my beloved niece, whom I haven't seen in person for nearly six months. Not since Dad's funeral.

The morning light filters through the bedroom curtains and accentuates the sprinkling of pale brown freckles on her small nose and high-boned cheeks. I recognize the round brown eyes with speckles of gold and green, still the same as when she was a little girl.

Looking at Maggie is a little like staring at myself in a mirror. Eleanor likes to joke that she somehow gave birth to my baby. The only physical trait Maggie shares with Eleanor is her heart-shaped lips. They got those lips from Mom. Meanwhile, I'm stuck with Dad's rubbery Julia Roberts-meets-Joker mouth.

"Maggie!" I murmur. I wrap my arms and legs around her body and close my eyes again. I have a sense memory of Maggie as a newborn. The first night we met, I fell asleep on the couch with Maggie nestled peacefully on my chest. Her tiny, precious body felt weighty and weightless at the same time. How did that baby grow up into this lovely young woman?

"Is there Wi-Fi here?" she asks.

"No, and no cell reception either."

"You're kidding, right?"

"I wish I were," I respond—although now that I think about it, I kind of like being disconnected from the rest of the world.

"Is this some evil plot Mom came up with? Like a punishment or something?"

"Why would your mom punish you?" I ask.

"I don't know!" Maggie cries. "Why does Mom do anything?"

I could deliver a three-hour lecture on my theories of Eleanor Bae-Wood's psychology, but it's too early in the morning and I haven't had any caffeine yet.

"What is there to do around here anyway?" Maggie asks plaintively. I rack my brain for something that might interest my teenage niece, but I come up empty. No TV. No stereo. No movie theaters or stores or restaurants.

"We're going to a party tonight," I say with false cheer.

"A party?"

"Well, not a party-party. A dinner party."

"With adults?"

"Yes," I say apologetically. Maggie groans and pulls the covers up over her head.

"Wake me up when summer's over."

Four women, one bathroom. It's a formula for disaster.

"Maggie, other people need to use the bathroom too," Eleanor shouts into the crack between the bathroom door and jamb. "And it's almost time for us to leave."

"I'm coming!" Maggie yells.

"She's been in there nearly an hour," Eleanor grumbles.

"It's okay," I say. "If I really need to go, I can go outside."

"You are not peeing outside," Eleanor orders.

"Wouldn't be the first time," I reply.

Maggie emerges from the bathroom wearing a navy-and-white-striped French sailor's shirt and neatly pressed, flat-front khakis. Her long, wavy hair is freshly washed, blow-dried, and pulled into a low ponytail. She's even wearing a touch of mascara and smear of lip color. I'm glad to see she's learned a little something about glamour from her aunt Amelia.

"Oh, you look lovely, sweetie," Eleanor sighs. All is forgiven. Eleanor has never been one to hold a grudge.

"Très chic," I concur. I rush past my niece to get to the toilet.

"What's that you're wearing, Ames?" Eleanor asks when I come out of the bathroom. She casts an uncertain eye on the shimmery teal tube dress I found in Mom's closet. It's a far cry from the shapeless smock dress she's wearing.

"This old thing? Why, I only wear it when I don't care how I look," I say with an exaggerated drawl. I usually flip my hair too, but being bald, I can't.

"What's that line from?" Maggie asks.

"It's a Wonderful Life," Eleanor and I respond at the same time.

"My God, it's exhausting being around you two," Mom groans as she enters the living room from her bedroom. "Everything's an inside joke."

It's the first time all week I've seen Mom in something other than that white velour tracksuit. She's wearing a bright fuchsia-

and-orange Moroccan print wrap dress that accentuates her cute figure.

"Oh, Mom, you look beautiful," I say.

"You do," Eleanor concurs.

"You're gorgeous, Grandma," Maggie adds.

"You girls," Mom says, glowing.

The four of us make our way uphill from the Master's Cottage to Leo's house. When Eleanor knocks on the front door, it's answered by a very tall man with a stiff, formal quality. With his dark suit and precisely combed hair, the man reminds me of Alfred the Butler from *Batman*.

"Good evening," he intones. "You must be the Bae-Woods."

"Good evening," I reply using my deepest *basso profundo*.

"Hello, I'm Eleanor," Eleanor says warmly. She reaches out to shake Alfred the Butler's hand. "This is my mother Tabitha, my daughter Maggie, and you've already met my lunatic sister, Amelia."

Eleanor has always had such good manners.

"Heavens, they're here!" Leo trills as he rushes to the entryway to greet us. "Ladies, ladies, please come in." Alfred the Butler steps back from the door to allow us to enter Leo's house.

"Leo, thank you so much for inviting us to your home," Eleanor says. "I believe you've already met my mother and sister, but I'd like to introduce you to my daughter, Maggie."

"Oh my," Leo gasps, "another Bae-Wood beauty!"

"It's nice to meet you," Maggie replies politely.

"And you've all met Master Allyn here," Leo says.

"Please, call me Brandon," he says. I detect a slight British accent. Brandon smiles in a way that looks almost pained and makes eye contact with each of us in turn. It feels forced, like something he might have learned in an etiquette book, or maybe they teach it in butler school.

"Nice to meet you, Brandon," Eleanor replies, shaking his hand.

"You already shook his hand, Mom," Maggie mumbles.

"Oh, did I?" Eleanor says. I could swear she's blushing. The rest of us nod hello.

"Please come into the dining room and let me get you a drink," Leo says. He leads the way to a richly paneled room with an enormous oak table and chairs.

"Leo, this room is just splendid," Mom says. "Tell us all about it." Leo describes each detail of his tastefully appointed house, and Mom acts like every word is a revelation. I haven't seen her this animated since Dad died.

"Wine?" Brandon asks. He presents me with a glass of deep ruby liquid.

"What kind is it?" I ask.

"Ridge Monte Bello 2005," Jett says, entering the dining room from the kitchen. "Mostly Cabernet and Merlot, with Petit Verdot and Cabernet Franc for added interest. Parker gives it a 97, and it's drinking perfectly now." Jett holds the bottle in his hand and is wearing a Kiss the Cook apron. His hazel eyes are extra sparkly tonight.

"Yummy," I murmur, even though I haven't taken a sip.

Soon, Leo calls us to sit down for dinner. We sit boy-girl-boy-girl around the oak table: Leo, Mom, Brandon, Eleanor, Jett, me, and Maggie. If only we had one more boy to make the pattern perfect.

"Jett, this salad is really delicious," Eleanor says.

"Everything from tonight's dinner is sourced on-site or made locally," Leo brags. "Jett, tell the ladies about the ingredients."

Jett looks slightly embarrassed, like a teenage boy forced to talk about his science fair project to his parents' boring friends, but he gamely proceeds to describe the salad ingredients: arugula, figs, and herbs all grown at Arcadia; honey for the vinaigrette from the on-site beehives; olive oil and goat cheese from small local producers.

While Jett talks, I have a flashback to the restaurant up in Mendocino County that Nils and I opened after we shuttered Amuse. So many hopes wrapped up into that one place, so many dreams shattered in an instant. I get agita just thinking about it.

"May I help you clear the dishes?" Eleanor asks Jett when everyone has finished their salads. She pushes back her chair to stand.

"No, please, let me," Brandon says. He gets up and motions for Eleanor to sit.

"Thank you," I say as Brandon takes my plate.

He looks at me a half second too long, like he might disapprove of my shimmery tube dress. Okay, so maybe it's a little inappropriate for a casual dinner party with friends, but how was I to know the dress code? What if the glittery Jett family had shown up in their top hats and tails?

Jett and Brandon walk out with the next course: hand-cut pappardelle with a meat ragout. I can scarcely wait for everyone to be served before I dig in. Brandon stands up to get the wine bottle from the sideboard and tops off my glass.

"Yum!" I blurt as soon as I taste the ragout, "is this rabbit?"

Jett grins at me. "You *do* have sensitive taste buds, Amelia."

"Don't tell me these are the bunnies I see hopping all over Arcadia," I say without thinking. From the corner of my eye, I see Maggie turning a slightly greenish color.

"No," Jett says, "the meat comes from a small family farm near Marshall."

"The local rabbits aren't meant for eating," Leo adds. "Right, Brandon?" With that cue, Brandon proceeds to drone on about the different breeds of rabbit that are native and non-native to Northern California and the various kinds of parasites and diseases they carry. It's not exactly appetizing dinner table conversation, although it does nothing to affect my enjoyment of the meal.

"How do you know so much about the local fauna, Brandon?" Eleanor asks. I don't know if it's the free-flowing wine, but my sister seems extra-animated, almost flirty. I'm not the only one who notices either. Mom sneaks me a sly sidelong smile.

"Why, Brandon here is a noted expert in ornithology and other local wildlife!" Leo says, clapping his hands together. "Brandon has degrees from King's College in London and Cornell University and taught at Davis for many years before serving as the founding headmaster at the Muir Academy. Fortunately for me, Brandon's taking a well-deserved year-long sabbatical, and he's agreed to stay on as my houseguest and personal bird-watching guide."

Mom and Eleanor look over at Brandon in admiration, but all I can think about is getting seconds of the pasta.

After dinner, Eleanor insists on helping Jett with the dishes, and Mom, Leo, and Brandon linger at the dining table nibbling on the remnants of dessert and sipping tiny glasses of *eiswein*. Maggie and I sit outside on the back porch, listening to the sound of the ocean and observing the scene through the large picture window.

"Leo's nice," Maggie comments.

"Yes, he is. Very nice."

"And Jett's cute."

"Uh-huh."

"Do you like him?" Maggie asks.

"You know me, I like everyone."

"But do you like him?" she asks. "Like, you know, like?"

"It's a little early for that," I say. "We just met."

Maggie eyes me suspiciously.

"What do you think of Mr. Allyn?" Maggie asks.

"You mean, the Master?" I say, putting an ironic emphasis on the final word.

"Yeah."

"He seems very smart," I say. "Maybe a bit on the stiff side." A lot like Eleanor, I think but don't say.

"I think he's kind of handsome," Maggie says.

"Really?" I reply, surprised.

"For an old guy," Maggie backpedals. "He reminds me of Professor Snape."

"The head of Slytherin House?"

"You know your *Harry Potter*, Aunt Amelia!"

I take a moment to bask in her praise. Never mind that I couldn't make it past the first few movies. I didn't like the new Dumbledore.

"Isn't Snape a bad guy?" I ask.

"You think so until Book Seven, and then you realize he's just misunderstood."

"Ah, that old trope."

Maggie and I watch as Leo pours more *eiswein* into Mom's glass. Mom makes a girly show of protesting but finishes the glass off in one sip. Brandon stares grimly at his fork.

"Mom says you have a thing for bad boys," Maggie giggles.

I don't know how to respond. How much of my past has Eleanor told her daughter about? I'm tempted to tell Maggie the story of my first encounter with Nils but think better of it. Eleanor would kill me if she thought I was putting inappropriate ideas in her daughter's head.

"Close your mouth please, Aunt Amelia," Maggie quips. "We are not a codfish."

I'm caught off guard for a moment before I break out laughing.

"Ten points to Gryffindor," I say, wrapping Maggie in a tight hug, "for pulling a *Mary Poppins* line out of thin air."

9

I love to sleep. I got in trouble all the time at the Buddhist temple for missing morning prayers and barely getting to breakfast on time. You could practically hear the monks singing, "How do you solve a problem like Amelia?"

It's different here at Arcadia. I feel different. It's Monday morning, and I'm up before eight o'clock. I don't know what's gotten into me. Maybe it's going to bed early because there's no TV or internet. Maybe it's sleeping like a baby for the first time since—well, since I was an actual baby. Or maybe it's being greeted every morning by the brisk, salty ocean air. Whatever the reason, for the first time in forever, I feel like I have a reason to wake up.

Oh, who am I kidding? My reason for waking up is Jett's pastries.

I jump out of bed and change out of my nightgown into my day clothes. The cottage is quiet. Eleanor is nowhere to be seen, and I can tell from the quiet snuffling sounds behind the closed bedroom door that Mom and Maggie are still sleeping.

"Good morning, rabbits," I shout as I walk down the road,

a little bounce in my step. "Good morning, birds," I yell toward the twittering trees. I feel like one of those bizarrely happy women you see in commercials for laxatives or tampons. Soon enough, I'm at the cancer center.

"Hello?" I say, entering the empty dining room. "Hello?"

"Amelia?" Jett calls out from the kitchen.

"Hey, Jett, where is everyone?" I ask.

"What do you mean?"

"Like, you know, the center guests."

"They left yesterday morning."

"Oh," I reply, disappointed. I liked the center guests. I can't believe they left without saying goodbye.

"When will the new guests arrive?" I ask.

"Next month."

"Not today?"

"We don't have retreats every week. We only hold seven retreats a year. One a month from April to October."

"So, what do we do between retreats?" I ask.

"If you mean what do the Arcadia employees do between retreats, most of us go back to our regular lives. Michaela and Frank have their psychotherapy practice in Mill Valley. Gisela and her partner, Sage, have a yoga and Pilates studio in Sausalito. And I promised to help a buddy with his new pop-up bakery in SoMa."

"Are you going away?"

"I'll be back," Jett says.

"Ah'll be baack," I repeat reflexively in *Terminator* mode.

"Excuse me?"

"Nothing," I mumble. Mom's right: everything's an inside joke with me and Eleanor. Not everyone gets our silly sense of humor.

"So, when are you leaving?" I ask.

"After breakfast," he says, gesturing to a bowl on the counter.

"So soon?"

"There's nothing for me to do here."

"There's our roof," I offer.

"Eleanor and I finished most of the work yesterday," he says. "We just need to replace some of the tiles, which are on order. The tarp we laid down should protect you in the unlikely event of another storm. I'll finish the job when I come back next month."

I must appear pathetic because Jett asks, "Hey, is everything okay?"

I suddenly feel foolish. Why am I making such a big deal about a guy I met only five days ago? A guy I thought was going to dismember me with a chainsaw.

"I'm just hungry. What's on the breakfast menu, Chef?" I ask, trying to sound cheerful. I point at his bowl.

"Steel-cut oatmeal. Do you want some?" Jett picks up the bowl and shows it to me. The pale beige contents bear an uncanny resemblance to spelt porridge.

"No, thanks," I reply. Jett returns to eating his breakfast. I have a queasy feeling in my stomach. Maybe I shouldn't have gotten up so early.

When I arrive back at the cottage, Mom and Maggie are sitting on a plaid woolen blanket just outside the front door. They have a plate of buttered toast, two steaming mugs of coffee, and a vintage Hills Bros. tin full of fine-point markers and colored pencils in between them.

"Where's Eleanor?" I ask. "I thought she had today off from work."

"She went into the city to meet with the lawyers," Mom says.

Eleanor didn't tell me she was meeting with the lawyers today. I wonder why she didn't ask me to come along. Not that I would have been much help with the legal stuff, but I could at least have kept her company during the drive.

"What's that you're working on?" I ask. I point at the sketchbook on Maggie's lap. She shows me a detailed color drawing of a hummingbird.

"Wow, did you draw that yourself, Maggie?" I ask. "You've really got talent."

"It must run in the family," Mom says, showing me a page from her coloring book.

"Ho, ho!" a voice shouts in the distance. We turn our attention up behind the cottage, where Leo and Brandon are fast approaching. They're wearing matching khaki shirts and zip-up cargo pants and floppy sun hats. They look like retired librarians on safari. Brandon's carrying a black backpack the size of a mini-fridge.

"Ho, ho," Mom shouts back. "What are you doing out this morning?"

"Brandon and I are embarking on our first bird-watching expedition of the season," Leo says. "Would you lovely ladies care to join us?"

"No, thanks," the three of us say in unison.

"Bodega Bay is one of the finest bird-watching destinations in the country," Leo says, "and Brandon here is one of the region's foremost experts." Mom nods absently, I reach down to grab a slice of toast, and Maggie returns to her drawing.

"My dear girl," Leo exclaims, focusing on Maggie, "is that your work?"

Maggie blushes. I know my niece well enough to recognize a hint of pride mixed in with her typical teenage embarrassment.

"Brandon, come take a look at this. It's really quite remarkable." Brandon walks over and extends his left hand to Maggie.

"May I?" he intones. Maggie obediently passes her sketchbook to him.

"The Anna's hummingbird," he says. "Formerly limited to

the southernmost parts of California, it's now the most common hummingbird on the West Coast." He pauses to make a closer inspection of Maggie's drawing.

"Common, but uncommonly beautiful," he says. "Based on the gorget, I'd say you've drawn a female."

"Gorget?" Maggie asks.

Brandon returns the sketchbook to Maggie and reaches into his backpack to pull out a well-thumbed guidebook. He flips through and finds the page he's looking for.

"You see here," he says, plopping himself down next to Maggie, "the iridescent red patch is called the gorget. Male Anna's have gorgets that cover their entire head and throat—the females have just a tiny spot of color."

"May I see?" Maggie asks. Brandon hands the guidebook over to Maggie.

"Does the word *gorget* come from the French word for *throat*?" she asks.

"Very good!" Brandon answers.

"Amazing," Maggie says. She starts skimming through the rest of the book.

"Are the checkmarks for all the birds you've seen?" she asks.

"Correct," Brandon says.

"Not exactly," Leo chimes in. "Those are just the North American birds he's seen since the book was published. You should see the volumes of books of all the birds he's seen before then, not to mention the ones from around the world."

"And what are these scribbles?" Maggie asks.

"Annotations," Brandon says.

Leo chuckles, glancing affectionately in Brandon's direction. "Dearest Brandon is constantly in search of perfection."

"Wow, that's really amazing," Maggie says. She hands the book back to Brandon.

"Leo is correct. Your drawing is excellent," Brandon says. "You have a special gift, young lady."

Maggie's face is radiant.

"Now, are you sure you don't want to go bird-watching with us?" Leo asks.

"Thanks, but I'm fine right here," Mom says. She smiles and returns to her coloring book. I pretend like I'm inspecting my piece of toast but can't help spying Maggie's eager face. It's like when she was a little girl and would ask me to take her to the boring science museum instead of playing like a normal kid in Golden Gate Park. "Please, please, pretty please, Aunt Amelia?" she'd plead. After so many years, Maggie doesn't need to say a word; I can see the pleading in her eyes.

Damn, the things I do for my niece.

"This is far enough," Brandon announces. We've been hiking for over an hour. I'm so relieved I could almost kiss him. My feet are killing me. Mom's old Toms aren't great for long distances.

Brandon takes the enormous backpack off his broad shoulders, lays it on the ground, and unzips the largest compartment. He pulls out a tripod and telescope and begins setting them up. Maggie watches his actions in quiet fascination, while I drop down on the bare dirt and take off my shoes to inspect my blisters.

"Brandon, I'll finish that up," Leo says, "it looks like our fair Amelia needs some of your ministrations."

"Oh, no, please don't worry about me," I say.

Without a word, Brandon pulls a red zippered pouch from the monster backpack. Inside, there's an impressive collection of first-aid items. It's like a portable Walgreens.

"A damsel in distress," Leo chuckles, "is there anything more disarming?"

"Expelliarmus!" Maggie and I shout.

"Pardon me?" Leo asks.

"Nothing," Maggie and I say at the same time, giggling like schoolgirls.

"It's from *Harry Potter*," Brandon explains to Leo. "The disarming charm."

Brandon crouches down, picks up my feet, and inspects them. I notice that his hands are large and capable looking, his nails neatly trimmed. I like that in a man.

WTF? Why am I noticing Brandon's hands?

"Mr. Allyn, how do you know about *Harry Potter*?" Maggie asks.

"I've been teaching high school for over a decade," he says without looking up. Brandon rifles through his bag of magical medical tricks, rips open some packets of wipes, and cleans my feet.

"Maggie, based on your earlier question about the word *gorget*," he says, lightly pressing my blisters, "you might be interested to know that *expelliarmus* is derived from Latin, combining *expellere* meaning to force out, and *arma* meaning weapon."

"Do you speak Latin, Mr. Allyn?" Maggie asks.

"It's one of the classes I teach," he says. Brandon pulls a sheet of moleskin from the first-aid kit, cuts off several small strips, and places the velvet-soft pieces on my blisters.

"Is Latin hard to learn?" Maggie asks.

"Not for someone as bright as you," he says. "Latin can be very helpful for the vocabulary portion of the SAT. In fact, there's a book in Leo's library that you might like. Remind me to get it for you."

Brandon remains crouched on the ground. He seems to be done attending to my blisters, but he's still got my feet in his hands. I wonder whether I should clear my throat.

"Mr. Allyn, what's that bird up there? Is it a hawk?" Maggie asks. She points to a silhouette in the sky. Brandon stands up and turns his eyes toward the sky.

"Turkey vulture," he declares. "Commonly mistaken for a hawk but much larger in size. Notice the V-shape to his wings and the fingerlike feather tips."

"The scope is ready," Leo says. "Miss Maggie, come over here and tell us what you see."

Maggie steps toward the tripod and puts an eye to the scope.

"Wow, I've never seen so many birds," she says. Her voice is hushed. "Amazing," she whispers under her breath.

"Did you know that Alfred Hitchcock filmed *The Birds* here?" Brandon asks me.

"Did he really?" I respond. "That movie scared the heck out of me. I still freak out whenever a pigeon flies too close." Brandon's jawline starts to twitch.

"Brandon and I like to play this game," Leo says to Maggie. "Pick a bird. He'll ask you three questions, and then he can tell you what it is."

"It's Leo who likes to play the game," Brandon says, "and I have no choice but to accede."

Accede? What kind of person uses the word *accede* in regular conversation? Brandon probably uses the word *eponym* too. Brandon and Eleanor would be perfect together. Mr. and Mrs. Vocabulary.

"Okay," Maggie says, looking through the scope, "I've got one."

"Size," Brandon begins. "Is it large like an egret, medium like a dove, or small like a chickadee?"

"Large," Maggie answers.

"Color," Brandon continues. "How would you describe the bird's coloration?"

"It has a soft white breast, and the body is mottled in browns and buff. The head is striped, alternating in brown and buff, and its legs are slate gray."

"Excellent description!" Leo declares. He looks at me with a smile.

"She's an artist," I say proudly.

"And its bill," Brandon says, "is it fairly long but not too long, dark, and downward curving?"

"Yes!" Maggie cries out. "How did you know?"

"It's a whimbrel," Brandon says. He pulls the guidebook out of his backpack and hands it to Maggie, who quickly locates the appropriate page.

"You're right!" Maggie says.

"Whimbrels are very common to this area," Brandon explains. "And Leo is correct, you did an exceptional job describing its coloration."

"Can we play again?" Maggie asks.

Brandon humors my niece in several rounds of "Name that Bird"—surf scoter, least sandpiper, marbled godwit, willet—while Leo and I sit together soaking up the midday sun and enjoying the scenery.

"I don't know about the three of you," Leo says, "but all this hiking has made me hungry."

"Indeed," Brandon says, scanning the horizon, "it's well past noon."

"Already?" Maggie asks.

Brandon reaches into his backpack and extracts a brightly patterned bedsheet, three large Tupperware containers, and a string bag of apples. With the ocean breeze picking up, I help Brandon spread the bedsheet on the dusty ground. The colorful dahlia pattern is so un-Brandon-like. It makes me wonder if there's a feminine influence in Brandon's life.

As we sit down on the bedsheet, Leo removes the lids from the Tupperware: one holds BLT sandwiches cut on the diagonal;

another reveals deviled eggs garnished with paprika and fine herbs; and another contains homemade chocolate-chip cookies.

"Did Jett make this?" I ask.

"Ho, ho, Brandon," Leo laughs, "Amelia just paid you the highest compliment."

"You made this?" I ask Brandon, who nods almost imperceptibly.

While everyone else digs into the sandwiches, I grab a chocolate-chip cookie. I've got a terrible sweet tooth. Life's short; always start with dessert. I take a bite of the cookie, and it's exactly the kind I like. Crisp but chewy, not in the least bit cakey. The chocolate chips are soft and almost melted. I can taste that he used good, fresh butter.

"What kind of apples are these?" Maggie asks. She practically inhaled her BLT and has grabbed an apple and two cookies. It's a relief to see her with an appetite again, a flush of color returning to her cheeks.

"Gravensteins," Leo answers. "Brandon picked them this morning from the tree behind the house. They're just coming into season."

"They're yummy," she says. She takes another crisp bite.

Gravensteins are my favorite apple. The dull outside belies the complex flavor inside, the perfect balance of sweet and tart. They're good for pies and tarts, applesauce, and eating out of hand. Versatile.

"How are your blisters, Aunt Amelia?" Maggie asks.

I stare down at my neatly bandaged feet and then up at the delicious picnic foods spread out before me. I see Maggie leaning back with her eyes closed to enjoy the warmth of the sun on her freckled cheeks. I glance over at Brandon, who's absentmindedly tracing the dahlia pattern on the sheet with his fingertips. He's taken off his floppy hat, and the wind is wafting through his gray-streaked hair. Maggie was right about Brandon: he really is kind of handsome. He's not my type, but he might be Eleanor's. It's worth a try anyway.

"I'm feeling just fine," I say, reaching for an apple.

10

The afternoon fog starts rolling in, obscuring the ocean view, so Brandon packs up the bird-watching paraphernalia and we head back to Arcadia. Not a moment too soon, if you ask me.

"Mr. Allyn, I think I see something in that field," Maggie says, pointing.

"Maggie, let's just call it a day on the bird-watching," I say. I'm tired and a little sunburnt. Lunch was the highlight of the trip.

"Size," Brandon says, ignoring me.

"Medium," Maggie replies.

"Color."

"Jet-black with patches of bright red on each wing. Oh, and a small bar of white."

"A small bar of white?" Brandon asks.

"Yes," Maggie says.

"Are you sure?" Leo asks, suddenly joining in the game. He grabs the binoculars around his neck and lifts them to his eyes.

"Yes," Maggie says. She turns around to take in Leo's piqued interest.

"Brandon, isn't it rare to see one here?" Leo asks.

"It is," Brandon replies, looking through his own set of binoculars. "Especially at this time of year."

"What?" Maggie asks. "What is it?"

"A tricolored blackbird," I say, not missing a beat. The three of them stare at me, openmouthed.

"Beginner's luck," I lie.

Three years ago, I couldn't have told you the difference between a tricolored blackbird and the Triborough Bridge. Three years ago, I was your typical Manhattan urban canyon dweller whose only encounters with wildlife ended in a call to the building superintendent or a citation from the City Health Department. Three years ago, I was sitting in my downtown loft, looking at the piles of moving boxes that contained all my worldly possessions and having a severe panic attack. I picked up my cell and dialed the steadiest person I knew: Eleanor..

"Good news, Ellie," I said. I hadn't seen my sister in over a year, not since Maggie's fourteenth birthday. "Nils and I are moving out to California."

"Moving out here?" she asked.

"Yeah, we decided to close Amuse and start a new place up in Mendocino County."

"But why? You only just opened the place last year, and already you've been named *Bon Appétit*'s number one new restaurant," Eleanor said. "Mick Jagger tweeted that your oyster puff is the best thing he's ever put into his mouth."

"Excluding a certain celebrity's private parts," I added for accuracy. I love to say things that make my sister squirm.

"I know what you're thinking, Ellie," I said. "That Nils and I have been working our entire lives to get to this point.

That we've put our heart and soul, our blood, sweat, and tears into Amuse. That we're stupid to give it all up."

"Yes," Eleanor said.

"And I agree with you. I'm not an idiot. I know how special Amuse is. This is the first time we've owned our own place. The first time we've made real money. The first time we've had freakin' health insurance."

"This is the first time you've had health insurance?" Eleanor gasped.

"But Nils is a genius, and genius can't be tamed."

"That's a line from *Chef's Table*," Eleanor said.

I could never BS my sister.

"Stop being such a wet blanket and look on the bright side," I said. "I'm finally moving back to California, just like you've been begging me to do for years. Now we'll be within a few hours' drive from one another, and we can spend loads of time together." There was a long silence on the line.

"Tell me about your new restaurant," she finally replied.

Nils and I started with the name: Loca. As in locavore. And crazy. Everyone told us we were crazy to leave New York, to abdicate our throne as rulers of the gastronomic universe to open a twenty-four-seat, $500 per person fine-dining bistro on the fringes of Northern California cannabis country. Even crazier was the concept: we would personally source everything on the menu. If we didn't forage, grow, or kill the food with our own hands, we wouldn't serve it.

"You've never foraged, grown, or killed anything in your life," Eleanor said. "How do you expect to begin now?"

"Oh, Ellie," I replied, hoping to deflect the question. There was another long silence on the line. It was so quiet that I thought we might have lost the connection.

"I'll pick you up at baggage claim," Eleanor said. "Just email me your flight info."

Eleanor had greeted me and Nils so warmly at the airport, and she went out of her way to help us get settled in Mendocino. And then I got completely sucked into our new restaurant—the permits, the plans, the build-out, the promotions—that I lost touch with her and everyone else in my life. It wasn't until Dad died that I made time to be with my sister, mother, and niece again.

I don't know if it's the sight of the tricolored blackbird or the memory of Dad's sudden death or the guilt of neglecting my family for so long, but my legs start to wobble.

"Are you okay, Aunt Amelia?" Maggie asks, rushing to my side.

"I just need a moment," I say. "Not used to so much exercise, I guess."

I sit down on the nearest rock for a few minutes. Brandon offers me his walking stick, which I wave off as unnecessary. During the long hike home, I try to block out Leo's animated chattering about our marvelous bird-watching luck. I'd be happy never to see another tricolored blackbird again.

When we get back to the comfort of Leo's house, Maggie can't wait to search through his library and read everything she can about the birds of Bodega Bay. Brandon walks her through the library's collection, while Leo and I doze like lazy cats on the overstuffed couches.

Hours later, I come home to find Eleanor sitting cross-legged on the Master's Cottage living room floor surrounded by piles of mail. I plop down next to her.

"That's a lot of crap," I say.

"I stopped by the PO box to pick up our forwarded mail," Eleanor says. She adds a glossy *Vanity Fair* to the thick pile of magazines. *People, Us Weekly, In Touch.* Mom never met a gossip magazine she didn't love.

"Wow, all that mail in just one week?"

"Most of it's junk," Eleanor says.

I walk to the kitchen and pour myself a glass of wine. Eleanor is squinting at a letter, the corners of her mouth turned downward. I pour an extra-large glass for her. I set Eleanor's wine down on the steamer trunk that we use as a coffee table and join her on the floor.

"How'd it go with the lawyers today?" I ask.

"Extremely frustrating," Eleanor responds. "They say we can't do anything at this point except wait. We're waiting for the court to rule on our appeal, which could take weeks or even months, and we're waiting for Chong Bae to respond to our request for temporary funds while the appeal is pending."

Chong Bae. It's bad enough that imposter kicked Mom out of her house and made her go through this expensive estate battle. It makes my blood boil to think he's using Dad's name—our family name. Although, according to the judge who ruled in his favor, the man is Dad's family. His secret family.

Oh, Daddy, could it be true? Did you really have a family before us?

Mom, Eleanor, and I were still reeling from Dad's unexpected death last winter when Mom got an email from someone in Seoul claiming he was Dad's long-lost son. We didn't believe it, of course, and assumed it was a cruel hoax. Dad's death had been reported in a number of media outlets given his prominent role as founder, president, and CEO of a successful Silicon Valley tech company, and the publicity brought out the worst sorts of people—everyone from con artists trying to get us to invest in their Ponzi schemes, to suspiciously handsome "widowers" extending their sincerest condolences to Mom and hoping to meet her beautiful self in person. Eleanor told Mom to ignore the emails and phone calls, and Mom was happy to comply.

After Dad's funeral, I went back up to Mendocino County

to work through my own troubles. I didn't give the long-lost son a second thought until I got a call from Eleanor a few weeks later.

"Did Dad write you a big check last winter?" Eleanor asked.

It felt like a bomb exploded in my chest. I had hoped no one—least of all my perfect big sister Eleanor—would find out that Dad had given me money shortly before he died. I wondered how I could answer Eleanor's question without giving away too much, without prompting more questions.

"Yeah, I needed some money for Loca," I said, which was sort of true.

"The lawyer is asking whether the money was a loan or gift," Eleanor said.

"Lawyer?" I asked. "What lawyer?"

"Our probate lawyer," Eleanor said.

"Why do we need a probate lawyer?" I asked. "I thought you said Dad's estate was pretty straightforward and you could handle it on your own."

"Well…" Eleanor began. "Remember that guy who claimed to be Dad's long-lost son? Mom ignored him like I told her to do, but he wouldn't give up. He kept emailing her, claiming he had proof that he was Dad's son. Mom was getting pretty upset, so I hired a lawyer to scare him away, and the imposter responded by filing an official legal claim with the probate court."

"You're kidding," I said, wondering why she hadn't told me any of this before.

"Worst of all," Eleanor continued, "the probate court is taking his claim seriously. We're going through all of Dad's documents now to get an accounting of his full financial situation and to disprove this imposter's bogus claim. I can't believe we have to go through all this bother, but I'll make sure this whole thing gets resolved as fast as possible."

That was almost six months ago. Since then, what should have been a slam-dunk case turned into a financial fiasco. We lost the case despite incurring thousands of dollars in legal fees, and Mom got kicked out of her Atherton estate. Time certainly flies when your life has been flushed down the toilet.

"I can't believe it," Eleanor exclaims, looking at the letter in her hand.

"Everything okay?" I ask.

"Yup, everything's fine," Eleanor responds too quickly. She places the letter on a small stack of papers. I recognize the St. Isadore seal on the letterhead.

"Fundraising appeal?" I ask.

"Tuition bill. They're increasing tuition by another $1,200 this year. Without any notice or warning, as if we have piles of extra money just lying around."

"I thought Maggie didn't want to go back to SI in the fall."

"We don't have a choice," Eleanor sighs.

We do have choices, I want to say. Maggie should have choices, but Eleanor never lets her. Instead, Eleanor makes the decisions—for Maggie, for Mom, for all of us. But now is not the time to criticize my sister's control issues.

"Brandon gave Maggie her very own copy of a guidebook that he wrote," I say. "Maggie was so impressed, she asked Brandon for his autograph."

"That's wonderful," Eleanor says. "Maybe Brandon can encourage her to take AP Bio next year. Maggie could use another AP class or two to get her GPA up."

"Doesn't she already have like a 4.2?"

"The average GPA to get into Berkeley is 4.4."

"That's stupid," I say.

"That's reality, Ames."

Eleanor says this as if I have never had to live a day in the real world. I know she thinks my life is oh-so-glamorous, globe-trotting with Nils, hobnobbing with celebrities, rubbing elbows with famous chefs. What she doesn't see—what no one sees—is all the hard work and self-doubt and moments of sheer panic that lurk behind that enviable façade.

"What if Maggie doesn't want to go to Berkeley?" I ask.

"Has Maggie said something to you?" Eleanor gasps.

My big fat mouth.

"No," I lie, "it's just that Berkeley's so darn competitive these days. Maybe Maggie should think about other colleges too."

"Of course," Eleanor says, her tone returning to normal. "Davis, Santa Cruz, and Santa Barbara are also on her list. And a couple nearby private colleges if we can get financial aid."

"You'd let her go as far away as Santa Barbara?" I joke.

"It's on the border of the approved zone," Eleanor says, completely missing the humor. "A five-hour drive. I Google-mapped it."

Eleanor opens a large manila envelope and pulls out a thick, binder-clipped document. She scans the contents, tucks her hair behind her ear, and places it on top of the SI tuition bill.

I glance over. Park and Associates, it says on the expensive letterhead. They're Chong Bae's lawyers. I'm tempted to take the document from the pile and read what it says, but I hold myself back. I don't want to upset Eleanor. I need to stay on task. I promised Maggie.

"Maggie spent the whole afternoon reading in Leo's study," I say. "She's reading a book about the Miwoks who used to inhabit this area. And she's borrowing a book of poems by a local woman that Leo recommended. She's even planning to teach herself some Latin to improve her verbal SATs."

"Maggie's always been a good reader," Eleanor says absently. She glances at a dozen or more college brochures and puts them into the discard pile. The collection of unopened mail has dwindled down to a few business-sized envelopes and mail order catalogs. I feel my window of opportunity closing.

"Hey, Ellie, remember how I suggested homeschooling for Maggie?"

"And I told you that was a nonstarter," Eleanor responds. "I mean, who's going to teach her? You?" My sister says this like she can't imagine I could teach Maggie anything—anything worth knowing, at least.

"No, I was thinking of Brandon," I say. That gets Eleanor's attention.

"You know Brandon's on sabbatical this year," I explain. "He mentioned at dinner tonight that he's looking for something meaningful to do to fill up his days. Something besides cooking for Leo and taking him out on bird-watching hikes."

"You had dinner with Brandon?" Eleanor asks.

"Yeah, we all did. Mom and Maggie are still there, finishing up a game of Scrabble."

"That makes two nights in a row," Eleanor says. "I don't want you imposing on Leo's generosity. We're already beholden to him as it is."

Leave it to Eleanor to use good manners as an excuse to avoid the subject. I can tell her defenses are up. I need to be strategic in how I break down those defenses.

"I think Leo and Brandon are happy for the company," I say.

Eleanor nods. "That's probably true," she admits. Her voice trails off, as if she wants to say something more. "Yes, I'm sure they appreciate your company."

"Anyway, like I was saying," I continue, "Brandon mentioned over dinner that he needs something productive to do. I asked if he ever thought about tutoring. Like, you know, would he ever consider tutoring Maggie and helping with her college applications. You should've seen his reaction, Ellie. Their reaction. I've never seen Maggie look more excited."

To my relief, Eleanor doesn't shoot down the idea. Her eyes dart to the growing pile of important papers needing her attention, including the Park and Associates law firm letter on top of the St. Isadore private school tuition bill.

"Leo offered to let us stay here in the Master's Cottage indefinitely," I continue. "Leo says the cabin would otherwise be empty anyway, and he likes knowing that someone's taking good care of it."

Staying at Arcadia until the estate battle is finished could help with Eleanor's financial woes. And if I'm being honest, it wouldn't be so bad for me either. It would buy me more time to figure out what the heck I'm going to do with the rest of my life.

"Maggie could spend her senior year focusing on her studies instead of stupid high school social cliques," I say. "Brandon would have a purpose during his sabbatical. And Mom would be a lot less lonely if we all stayed out here together. Plus, she and Leo seem to really get along."

Eleanor tucks her hair behind her other ear.

And that's when I know I've got her.

Fall

11

The delicate Japanese maple outside the Master's Cottage is flaunting its autumn colors. The once-bare walls are covered with Maggie's sketches of birds, plants, rocks, the sea, and the sky. The soft-worn wooden floors are littered with books—novels, textbooks, chapbooks, nature guides—and crumpled sheets of blue-lined notebook paper. There's a gnawed apple core nestled with some empty pistachio shells in a buttercup-yellow bowl.

"It's chaos in here," Eleanor says, glancing around. Normally, chaos and Eleanor don't play well together, but my sister looks content.

"Yes, happy chaos," I say.

Eleanor bends down to pick up the bowl and empties it in the compost bin in the kitchen, but she leaves the rest of the clutter alone. Not that Maggie would care or even notice if anyone tidied up after her. But there's something about the mess that feels organic, genuine, alive. You just don't want to tame it.

I don't know if it's the financial freedom that comes from renting her flat in the city and saving on private school tuition, or if it's the relief of seeing Maggie emerge from her bottomless pit of teenage angst, but Eleanor's been a lot more relaxed in the weeks and months since we decided to stay in Arcadia. We all have.

"You headed to the center later?" Eleanor asks. She's dressed in her pastel-pink scrubs and magenta Crocs. She must be expecting a bunch of baby girls today.

"Yup," I say.

"Say hi to Jett for me," she says, smirking.

"I think he'd rather hear it from you," I say, smirking back.

It's become our new family joke: Which of the Bae-Wood women will end up with Jett? Eleanor insists he's only got eyes for me, and he's too young for her anyway. I say Jett and she have more in common, and four years isn't much of an age difference. Mom says if one of us doesn't do something soon, she might just nab Jett for herself.

Eleanor grabs her purse and heads for the door. As she checks her face in the entryway mirror, I could swear I see my sister's smirk turn into a genuine smile.

It's Monday morning, and I'm looking forward to welcoming the arriving cancer center guests. It's part of my new routine. Every month, a fresh batch of guests appears at Arcadia, and I help Jett with meal prep, setup, and cleanup. I don't do a whole lot, but Jett seems to appreciate the company and I appreciate having something to do. The weeks in between retreats are harder for me, with Jett and the other Arcadia staff returning to their normal lives, leaving me to search for ways to fill my days. Usually, I go up to Leo's house and annoy Brandon by trying to distract Maggie from her studies.

As I enter the Arcadia kitchen, I'm greeted by the familiar scent of cardamom, cinnamon, and cloves. Jett's making the almond milk chai that's as much a part of the Arcadia experience as the guided meditation, yoga, and massages.

"Hey, you," Jett says by way of hello.

"Hey, you," I say back.

"What's for breakfast?" I ask, opening the oven door.

"Careful," he warns. He says it nicely, but I know there's seriousness behind the warning. Baking is a science. Chemistry mixed with physics and maybe a touch of black magic. Opening the door lowers the temperature of the oven and throws everything off. Maybe it even releases the magic. I heard it from Nils a thousand times.

"Do I smell apple?" I ask, closing the door gently.

"You must be part bloodhound," Jett says. "I made apple-walnut bread from the last of the Gravensteins."

My mouth starts to water thinking back to those homely apples Brandon brought on our first hike when I had just arrived at Arcadia: the paper-thin peel giving way to crisp flesh and nectar-sweet juice. Gravensteins are notorious for their short season. They're all but unavailable now. The autumn brings a whole new array of apples: Golden Delicious, Pippin, Jonagold, Gala, Rome. All more beautiful on the outside, more durable for traveling to market, but rather one-note in flavor—in my humble opinion.

"The last retreat of the year," I say. I try to keep my tone even, but my mood is more than a little melancholy. I've grown to love the weeklong cancer retreats: the influx of new guests, the daily rhythm of nourishing meals and intimate discussions, the emotional arc of starting the week as strangers and ending as lifelong friends.

"Spring will be here before you know it," Jett says. He ladles some chai into a ceramic mug and passes it over to me.

I sip the comforting beverage while Jett pulls the two loaves from the oven and places them on the cooling rack. Their puffed exterior deflates a little, as if letting out a sigh. Little bits of apple and walnuts add texture to the otherwise satiny smooth surface. After a few minutes, Jett runs a spatula around the interior of the pans and releases the loaves from their confinement. He cuts a slice, places it on a plate, and pushes it over to me, still warm.

Jett's given me the end slice. We call it the "butt piece" in our family, and it's the best slice of the whole loaf. Dad and I used to fight over the butt piece whenever Eleanor made her yummy Maui banana bread. I gobble up the slice and push my plate over for more.

After polishing off my second slice, I help Jett set up the dining room before the center guests arrive. I stack the mugs next to the urn filled with the almond milk chai. I carefully wipe the silverware and place them in the antique wooden milk-bottle holder. The large Mason jars are already filled with lightly roasted almonds, Turkish apricots, and candied ginger. Healthy snacks to quell queasy stomachs.

Jett brings out the platter of apple-walnut bread and places it next to the Spanish tortilla and colorful arrangement of sliced fruit. As always, the buffet spread looks like it's been styled for a *Bon Appétit* photo shoot.

"Ready?" he asks.

"Always," I say. I hear the rumbling of tires on the gravel driveway. I fight the impulse to rush to the entryway. Leo doesn't like us to overwhelm the guests all at once.

"They're here, they're here!" Leo exclaims. He breezes through the building, his hands fluttering like small doves.

"Leo's welcomed hundreds of guests to Arcadia," Jett chuckles, "but he's still like a mother hen every time."

Jett and I wait at our spots in the dining room as Leo greets the first guests on Arcadia's front porch. I peek out the window and see them: a young couple, probably in their early to midthirties. Slightly younger than me and Jett. The woman is tiny, barely five feet tall, with wide-set eyes, pixie-cut auburn hair, and sunny smile. The man reminds me of a young Ben Stiller: small and lean, hollow eyes and dark hair.

"You have matching hairdos," Jett observes.

I reach up to stroke my growing-in hair. Eleanor calls it my *Rosemary's Baby* look, and I'm kind of loving the 1960s Mia Farrow vibe.

"I wonder which one of them is sick," I say.

"The girl," Jett replies. "It's usually the happy-looking one who has cancer. It's the spouses who look terrible. Like they'd rather die than be left behind."

Jett's words hit me hard, reminding me of the losses in my own family. Is that what Mom feels like since Dad died? How Eleanor feels even after all these years? Eleanor never talks about Edward. I wonder whether she still thinks about him every day or whether the painful memory of his premature death has receded to the corners of her mind. I wonder if the pain ever truly goes away.

"And here, what I'm sure you're looking forward to the most," Leo says, leading the couple into the dining room. "Our celebrated Arcadia kitchen."

The couple visibly perks up as they see and smell the glorious breakfast offerings. They exchange appreciative looks. The pallor recedes from the man's face. It's always been my experience that good food—even the promise of good food—is miraculous in its restorative powers.

"Chloe and Andrew, this is our in-house chef, Jett, who I brazenly stole away from La Reverie in San Francisco," Leo says. His chest is puffed up with pride. Chloe and Andrew nod hello.

"And this," Leo says, gesturing to me, "is the lovely and charming Amelia."

Everyone smiles, but the words echo in my head: the lovely and charming Amelia. Yup, that's me. That's what I've always been. The sassy sidekick. The amusing accessory. But is that all I am? All I will ever be?

"It's nice to meet you, Amelia," Chloe says, extending her hand.

Chloe's voice is small, almost childlike, and utterly charming. Andrew looks over at his wife with absolute devotion. Nils never looked at me like that. I don't think anyone ever has.

"Amelia?" Jett says, clearing his throat.

I pull myself away from my midlife crisis moment and come back to the present. I reach for Chloe's hand.

"Welcome to Arcadia," I say and give her my most charming smile.

12

It's just the second day of the retreat, and I've already fallen in love with the cancer center guests. I'm willing the days to go slower and dreading Sunday morning when they have to leave.

I sit in the back of the yoga studio watching the other participants. A soft snoring sound comes from the older man next to me. His name is Erik, and he's a retired English Lit professor from Morro Bay with Stage IV lung cancer. Never smoked a day in his life. On the other side of him is Lynnly, a kick-ass photographer from San Francisco recently diagnosed with ovarian cancer. Both her mother and maternal aunt died of the disease in their early fifties. Over in the corner, Chloe and Andrew are resting in child's pose and wearing coordinating yoga outfits. Jett was right: Chloe's the sick one. BRCA-positive breast cancer with metastases to the liver and lungs. She's on a clinical trial now, having exhausted the standard treatments.

The morning's quietude is broken by the gentle tinkling of meditation bells. Slowly, my yoga mates emerge from their contented cocoons and stretch like waking kittens. No one bothers to pick up their mats. Gisela, our classically beautiful and impossibly lithe instructor, does that for us. It's Arcadia custom to remain silent as we leave the yoga studio and walk together along the gravel path back to the main center building.

I'm usually the one leading the morning yoga pack to breakfast, but I notice Gisela is rubbing her belly absentmindedly. Gisela doesn't do anything absentmindedly. She's perhaps the most mindful person I've ever met—and I once met the Dalai Lama. I linger behind until all the guests have left, and then I approach Gisela.

"When are you due?" I ask, picking up a couple yoga mats.

Gisela takes a moment before responding.

"April," she says.

"So, how far along does that make you?"

"I just passed twelve weeks," she says. "Please don't tell anyone."

I'm dying to know who the father is, but I don't know Gisela well enough to ask. Of all the cancer center staff, Gisela is the most reserved, the one least likely to join the others for a glass of wine at Leo's place after the week's guests have departed.

Gisela winces slightly as she touches her belly again.

"Are you okay?" I ask.

"I've had these weird pains the past few days. Probably just gas."

It's hard for me to imagine Gisela having gas. Goddesses don't fart.

"My sister Eleanor is a baby nurse at Marin General," I offer. "I could ask her to check you out when she comes back from work."

"That's so nice of you, but I've got a doctor's appointment tomorrow. I'll be fine."

Gisela winces again.

"Are you sure?" I ask.

"I think I just need to lie down."

I drop the yoga mats into a neat pile and follow Gisela out of the studio, down a short hallway, and through a heavy oak door. Most of the Arcadia staff have dorm-style bedrooms in the main center building, but Gisela has her own private room in the same building as the yoga studio.

The room is just what I'd expect of Gisela: eclectic and artistic while still warm and welcoming. The studio apartment is dominated by a full-size bed, which is covered in quilts and pillows in a riot of colors and patterns. The bold, bright fabrics remind me of the bustling bazaars and open-air markets Nils and I used to explore in Marrakesh, Delhi, and Bali.

"Do you want some tea?" Gisela asks.

"You lie down," I say, "and I'll make us both a cup."

Gisela's room has a small kitchenette similar to the one at the Master's Cottage, complete with double-burner hot plate and mini-fridge. There's an electric kettle on the counter that I fill halfway with water from the tap.

"The teas are in the right-hand cabinet," Gisela says from her bed.

"What kind do you want?" I ask.

"Ginger-peach would be good."

I open the tin of tea, drop the tea bags into two hand-painted ceramic mugs, and pour in the boiling water. The round tea bags float to the surface like deliciously scented jellyfish.

Gisela sits up and uses both hands to accept the mug from me. We hold our tea to our faces and breathe in the aromatic steam, allowing it to permeate our nostrils, our pores, our eyes. Above Gisela's bed is a sepia-toned photograph of a woman's bald head, perfectly egg-shaped and ornamented with intricate henna designs.

"Is that you?" I ask.

"Yes."

"It's beautiful. How long ago was it taken?"

"Almost ten years," she says. "I had it taken when I finished chemo. It was my way to commemorate that milestone."

"Ten years ago? Wow, you must have been really young."

"Twenty-eight."

Twenty-eight years old. So young. I think back to what I was doing at that age.

I was twenty-eight when Nils and I traveled to Southeast Asia for the first time. We covered Vietnam, Cambodia, Thailand, and Laos. Everything was so cheap—the food, the hostels, even occasional luxuries like massages and tour guides—that we were able to make our savings last almost nine months before we had to return to New York. My memories from that year are a blur of tuk-tuks and temples, neon-green rice paddies and crystalline sand beaches, savory street food and ice-cold lagers. It was a blissful time. A far cry from what Gisela had to go through.

"Do you have a family history?" I ask.

"Why do you ask?" Gisela says.

"I'm sorry?"

"Why does it matter if I have a family history?"

"I'm sorry," I say. "It's just that twenty-eight is awfully young to get cancer, and I was trying to make sense of it."

"Cancer doesn't make sense, particularly if you're the one who has it."

"I'm sorry," I repeat. This time I really mean it.

"It's okay," Gisela says. She gives me a compassionate smile. "But if you're going to live in a cancer community, you should know there are certain questions you shouldn't ask."

"What are the others?"

Gisela closes her eyes as if reciting a poem from memory.

"Do you smoke? Do you drink? Do you eat red meat? Do you exercise?"

Shoot, I've probably asked those questions a hundred times since I got here, and no one told me not to. I wonder how many people I've inadvertently hurt or offended.

"I get it," Gisela says, "people want there to be a reason why someone gets cancer. It's a normal human impulse. It creates a false sense of security, like, if I don't smoke or drink or eat red meat or whatever, I'm safe. The people I love are safe." Gisela takes a long sip of tea. "But what the questions really do is make the person who has cancer feel like they somehow deserve it. And no one deserves it."

Gazing at Gisela with her lovely, placid face shrouded in swirls of steam, the shimmering sunlight catching her loose-flowing hair, I realize that if a vegan yoga instructor can get cancer at the age of twenty-eight, no one is safe. Life's a crapshoot.

"Is there anything else I shouldn't ask? Anything I shouldn't do?" I ask.

"There are no hard and fast rules," Gisela says. "I'd recommend that you try to spend more time listening than talking. Most people will tell you what they want you to know if you open your heart and just listen."

"How long have you been teaching at Arcadia?" I ask.

"Four or five years. I tried yoga for the first time when I was a guest here, and it changed my life. I went to school to become a certified instructor, and I found my calling. Once I opened my own studio and got my life together, I decided it was time for me to start giving back."

Gisela's story reminds me a bit of Eleanor's. She, too, started volunteering at Arcadia in order to give back after she and Edward had been guests. I wonder what Jett's motivation is to work here.

"I had a few tough years in my late teens and early twenties," Gisela continues. "I was just starting to get my feet back under me when I found a lump and got diagnosed with cancer. After more than a year of horrific treatments, I couldn't figure out what to do next, what I wanted from life, whether I'd even have much life to live. I was a lost soul. And then I came here, and Arcadia helped me find my way."

Gisela takes a sip of her tea. She dreamily rubs her stomach.

"And it's thanks to Arcadia that I have this tiny miracle," she says.

It takes all my self-control not to ask Gisela what she means by that. What does Arcadia have to do with her baby? My mind races through the possibilities.

Gisela sets her mug on her nightstand, leans back on her pillows, and closes her eyes. A moment later, the Goddess is snoring. I quietly let myself out of the yoga studio and head back to the center. As I walk along the gravel path, birds twitter exuberantly in the nearby brush, and far in the distance is the ever-present whisper of the ocean surf.

Jett is wiping down the tables when I enter the dining room. The guests appear to have finished breakfast and started their morning sessions.

"Sorry to be late," I say.

"I was wondering what happened to you," he responds.

I follow Jett into the kitchen, where I'm happy to see plenty of leftovers. I'm about to tell him about Gisela's stomach pains when I remember that she asked me to keep her pregnancy a secret. I've always been terrible at keeping secrets. My mouth seems to blather before my brain has a chance to filter.

"I went to Gisela's room to have a cup of tea," I say. I grab a clean plate and help myself to some spinach frittata and mixed berries. Jett raises one eyebrow inquisitively.

"What?" I ask.

"Nothing." Jett pours a mug of chai for himself and sits down at the counter with me.

"What?" I repeat.

"Gisela's very private. I've never heard her invite any guests to her room."

"What, are you jealous?" I joke. A look flashes across Jett's face, a look that says I've struck a nerve.

"Did I say something wrong?" I ask. I seem to be messing up a lot today.

"No, it's nothing," Jett mutters.

"It's clearly not nothing," I say. "Is there something between you and Gisela?"

"No. Well, yes. Not really."

"Oh, that's definitive," I tease.

"Gisela and I went out when we were in high school," Jett admits. "Eons ago."

"You and Gisela were high school sweethearts?"

"Yeah, like I said, it was eons ago. A lifetime ago."

"Wow, isn't it weird working in the same place as your ex?" I ask.

"No, not at all," Jett answers. I can usually tell when someone's lying to me, but Jett's face doesn't reveal anything. He reaches over and eats a blackberry off my plate.

"What an amazing coincidence," I say. "The two of you dating in high school, and now, decades later, working side by side in the same place."

"Oh, it's not a coincidence," Jett says. "Gisela's the whole reason I'm here." And with that, Jett turns to start doing the dishes, the conversation apparently over.

All day, I can't help but think about Gisela and Jett. Could Jett be the father of her baby? Is that the "whole reason" why Jett's here? My natural inclination is to pry and find out more, but Gisela's words of advice keep reverberating in my head. Patience is not one of my strengths.

After helping Jett clean up from the dinner service, I stop by the yoga studio to check on Gisela. I've been worried about her all day. I find her sitting in lotus position, her eyes closed, on the kilim-covered floor of the studio's foyer.

"Hi, Gisela," I whisper, and she opens her eyes.

"I just wanted to stop by to make sure you were okay," I say. "Are you feeling better?"

"A little better," she replies. She beckons for me to sit by her side. "I've still got some cramping, but it's manageable. I'll just ask about it at my appointment tomorrow."

"Is someone driving you?" I ask.

Like the baby's father, for example?

"Yeah, I've got a ride," she says, glancing toward the door.

"Are you sure?" I ask. "Because I'm happy to drive you." I conveniently leave out the fact that I don't have a car, but I figure I could probably borrow Leo's or Jett's. I'm not sure what to do about my expired license, though.

"You're sweet to worry, but I'll be fine," she says. Gisela stands up and stretches her slim arms overhead.

"Thanks for checking in on me," she says. "I think I'll head to bed now." She leans forward and gives me a soft kiss on the cheek. She smells deliciously of almond oil.

"Be careful walking home," she says. "It's dark out there."

As I push open the front door to leave the building, I walk smack-dab into a man. He's about my height and age, slim, with smooth dark brown skin. His wavy black hair falls well below the chin, and he's wearing loose cotton pants and a tight tank top that accentuates his muscular shoulders.

"Oh, sorry," I say, flustered.

"My bad," he says. There's something about his voice, his

intonation, that makes it sound more like a promise than an apology. Gisela silently glides in behind me.

"You're late," she says, pulling the Mystery Man inside.

"You're stunning," he replies, standing back in admiration.

She gives him a mock-exasperated look, grabs his arm, and leads him back toward her bedroom.

"You're forgiven," I say, completing the *Pretty Woman* dialogue before letting the door click shut behind me.

13

It's still dark outside when I wake with a start. The light from the harvest moon spills through the window and fills the bedroom with its magical glow. I reach over to the other side of the bed and feel around, only to find it empty. Eleanor has apparently left for work.

I check the nightstand clock. It's barely 5:00 a.m., and St. Eleanor is already on her way to Marin General so she can spend twelve-hour shifts helping women bring precious life into the world. Then she'll drive back another hour-plus to make dinner for her widowed mother, fatherless daughter, and no-good freeloader of a sister. Eleanor lives every day with purpose and clarity and commitment. She's the opposite of me.

"Today's the day," I say. "Today's the day I start to get my act together."

I throw the quilt off my body, hoping the autumn air will energize me, but it just makes me feel cold. I start to have second thoughts. Maybe I should wait until this week is over and the center guests have left before I start on my resolution. I pull the quilt back over my body, happy for the warmth. As I drift back into blissful slumber, my thoughts turn to Gisela and our talk from the morning before. "I was a lost soul," she'd said. "Arcadia helped me find my way."

"Ugh," I grunt as I throw the quilt off my body again. Maybe Arcadia will help me find my way too, but only if I get my sorry butt out of bed.

I open the closet door and see Eleanor's decades-old down jacket and collection of lopsided beanies. I used to laugh about my sister's grandma-style clothes, and now I'm borrowing them on an almost daily basis. Oh, how the mighty have fallen. I don't want to change out of my nice, warm nightgown, so I layer the down jacket on top. I doubt I'm going to run into fashion police at five in the morning.

I slip on Mom's old Toms—which, by now, have become mine—and quietly make my way outside. I take the moonlit gravel path to the rock labyrinth in the clearing behind the cancer center. I've never walked the rock labyrinth at Arcadia before, but there was one at the Buddhist temple that the monks would walk for meditation every morning. If walking the labyrinth helped the Buddhist monks to feel enlightened, I might as well give it a shot myself.

When I arrive at the circle of river stones, I'm surprised to see another person. A slim shadow of a person.

"Gisela?"

"Amelia?"

"What are you doing up so early?" I ask.

"I can never sleep during the full moon."

"Yeah, me too," I lie.

I follow Gisela as she steps gracefully on the hard-packed sand that forms the foundation of the labyrinth. The labyrinth is surprisingly difficult. I thought it was just a spiral going around and around, but it's really a complex series of curves, backtracks, and tight turns. Gisela seems to have no trouble navigating it, but I falter more than once. Even on the parts of the labyrinth that look easy—actually, especially on the parts that look easy—I lose my balance and stumble. I'm better with the tight turns. Gisela and I make three rounds of the labyrinth before the first soft shimmers of daylight appear on the horizon.

"Let's go watch the sunrise," Gisela says. "I know the perfect place."

We walk up the sloping hill, Gisela leading the way. I shiver from the autumn chill and wonder how much farther we're going when, there in the distance, I see the miraculous vision from my first night at Arcadia. It's a little like running into an old friend.

"The Portal to the Dead," I say. The diamond-shaped sign on top of the phone booth creaks softly in the wind as if to say hello.

"You've been talking to Jett," Gisela replies.

I try to imagine Gisela and Jett together in high school. They must have been a beautiful couple. I wonder what happened to break them up, why they're back together here in Arcadia. Soon, we're standing at the desolate bluff overlooking the ocean, the same bluff I searched so desperately for signs of life my first night in Arcadia.

"This is my favorite spot," Gisela says, settling herself down on the brittle dry grass.

"I can see why," I reply.

At first, the ocean seems to be a vast expanse of nothingness, but as my eyes adjust and focus, details emerge. I spot tiny figures in the distance—seabirds patrolling for their morning meal. Too bad I don't have Brandon's or Maggie's talent for bird-spotting. To me, they're just dark specks against a blue-black background. I couldn't tell the difference between a whimbrel and a whip-poor-will if you held a spotting scope to my head.

"Jett tells me you're old friends," I say.

"Yeah, we go way back," Gisela says.

A lifetime ago—that's how Jett had put it.

"Jett was my first boyfriend," Gisela says after a long pause. "He and my brother were friends from grade school, and I always thought he was cute. At first, I was too shy to even talk to him. But over time, the shyness sort of melted away, and he became my first love."

Jett didn't tell me they were once in love, but I should have guessed. I wait for Gisela to continue talking when something in the water catches her attention, breaking the moment of intimate reflection. My eyes follow hers into the distance, and a shape leaps from the water's surface.

"Is that a dolphin?" I gasp.

"Please don't let him know you said that," Gisela says. "He's already insufferable."

I watch the dolphin transform into the silhouette of a man, who rides the surf into shore. Dolphin Man tucks the surfboard under his arm and walks up the beach before disappearing in the shadows of the bluff. Gisela stands and walks to the edge, and I get up to join her.

"The great whites' spawning ground is just around the corner, you know," Gisela yells.

"That's what makes it so fun," Dolphin Man yells in return. There's a rope hooked into the side of the cliff that the man uses to climb from the beach to the spot where Gisela and I are standing.

"Nothing makes you feel more alive than to tempt death," Dolphin Man says, pulling the hood of the wetsuit off his head. It's the Mystery Man. He gives his head a shake, like a puppy after a bath, spraying me and Gisela with salt water.

"You're such a child," Gisela says. She gives him a playful push.

"My bad," Mystery Man says, looking straight at me.

"Oh goodness, where are my manners," Gisela says. "Hari, this is my new friend, Amelia. She's volunteering at the center and living at the Master's Cottage with her family."

Before Gisela can finish the introductions, Hari reaches for my hand.

"Nice to see you again, Amelia," he says. "I'm Hari."

"Ha-Ha-Hari?" I say. Damn, there I go, stammering again. There must be something in the Arcadia air that interferes with my brain function.

"I like the whole *Little House on the Prairie* look, by the way," he whispers. I'm momentarily baffled before I remember, mortified, that I'm wearing a full-length flannel nightgown. This one has a particularly embarrassing pattern of a spotted cow jumping over a smiling moon.

"Feel free to ignore my brother," Gisela says. "He's a notorious flirt."

Her brother. Of course. I should have seen the family resemblance. The three of us walk along the crest of the bluff, which takes us back to the cancer center. When we arrive at the yoga studio building, Gisela stops and points at Hari.

"You," Gisela says, "clean up before you step one foot inside."

"She's so bossy," Hari says, grinning at me as he unzips his wetsuit.

"Listen to your elders," Gisela says. She walks around to the side of the building and uncoils a green plastic hose.

"Older by fifteen minutes," Hari shouts in Gisela's direction.

"You're twins?" I ask.

"You wouldn't know it, right?" Hari says. "Me being so devastatingly handsome, and Gisela…well…" He pulls off his wetsuit and shakes his head in false pity. Gisela turns the hose on full strength and douses Hari with cold water. Hari lets out a yelp and runs to grab the hose from her.

"I've gotta get ready for morning yoga," Gisela says, handing off the hose and laughing. "You're welcome to join, but don't you dare get a grain of sand or a drop of water on the studio floors. This is a registered historic building, you know."

"Bring me a towel at least," Hari says. He adjusts the hot and cold spigots. He closes his eyes as he holds the hose over his head, letting the steamy water roll down his face, his torso, his legs. It's hard not to ogle his lean surfer's physique. Hari would give even Ryan Gosling major body image issues.

"You get ready for class," I tell Gisela. "I'll take care of your brother."

After getting Hari a towel, I rush home to change out of my nightgown and into my yoga clothes. I spend the whole morning yoga class waiting for Hari to show up, but he doesn't. When class ends, I skip the silent walk to breakfast for a second straight day and follow Gisela back to her room. We find Hari lying on the bed, a brightly colored bag of snack chips propped up on his stomach.

"Oh my God, you're killing me," Gisela says.

"No, actually, I'm killing myself," Hari says. "Very slowly."

"Want some?" he asks, offering me the bag from his reclining position. "I special order them by the case from India. They're extra spicy. Even hotter than Flamin' Hot Cheetos."

"We need to head out soon," Gisela says. "My appointment is at ten thirty."

"Okay, I'm ready," Hari says, licking the neon-orange dust off his fingers.

"Is that what you're wearing?" Gisela asks. She pulls a floral-print dress from her closet and heads into the bathroom.

"What's wrong with what I'm wearing?" Hari yells. He has on the same white tank top and loose pants that he wore last night, but his shoulder-length hair is pulled into a man-bun with a batik-print scrunchie.

"You look like a billboard for Grindr," Gisela yells back. I hear the shower turning on behind the closed door.

"My sister is *so* not-P.C.," Hari says to me.

"I can still hear you!" Gisela shouts.

Hari looks over at me with a grin and says, "C'mon, I know you're curious." He reaches into the crinkly bag, plucks a single chip, and holds it out with two fingers.

Something about Hari's gesture reminds me of the time Nils and I went to the art-house theater in Amherst and watched Roman Polanski's *Tess.* The strawberry scene with Nastassja Kinski was the most erotic thing I'd ever seen. I wanted to jump Nils' bones right then and there. Now here I am, decades later, a decidedly unvirginal Tess acting out the same scene, the Masala spice–dusted chip taking the place of the ripe strawberry. I lean closer to Hari, open my mouth, and accept the chip onto my tongue. My eyes open wide, and Hari laughs in delight.

"Damn, it's really flamin' hot," I say.

After bonding over our shared love of extra-spicy snack chips, Hari insists I come along for Gisela's doctor's appointment. I was expecting Gisela to see an earth mother–type doctor in Marin County, so I'm surprised when she directs Hari over the Golden Gate Bridge to a modern high-rise building in San Francisco's techy and trendy Mission Bay district. The quietly efficient elevator delivers us to the fifth floor, where we're greeted by an etched glass sign that reads Bay Area Fertility Clinic.

"So good to see you again," the receptionist says as Gisela checks in. The woman looks over at me and Hari. "Where are Jett and—"

"I brought my brother and friend this time," Gisela interrupts. My ear catches on the mention of Jett's name.

"Well, you know what to do," the receptionist says. "Ultrasound first, then Dr. Rose will see you after. You'll be in Room 5 today."

In the examination room, Hari and I sit on the padded vinyl chairs while Gisela closes the pastel-hued privacy curtain and gets changed into her hospital gown. The ultrasound tech comes into the room, sits on a rolling chair, and opens Gisela's hospital gown just enough to expose her still-taut tummy. Honestly, I've had food babies bigger than that.

"Come closer and watch," the tech says to me and Hari. We each pull our chairs on either side of Gisela as the tech squeezes some clear blue gel on Gisela's stomach.

"It looks like a lima bean," Hari says when the image of Gisela's twelve-week-old fetus appears on the ultrasound screen.

"The most precious lima bean ever," Gisela replies. After the ultrasound tech prints a couple copies of the black-and-white image for Gisela to take home, Hari and I exit the exam room so Dr. Rose and Gisela can have some privacy. Barely fifteen minutes go by before Dr. Rose and Gisela come out into the waiting room where Hari and I are sitting.

"The baby is developing perfectly," Dr. Rose says, writing something on Gisela's chart. "You don't need to schlep into the city to see me anymore. My work is done. Your regular OB can take it from here. Just be sure to take it easy and drink plenty of fluids if you feel any more cramping. And promise me you'll send a photo of your beautiful baby."

On the drive back to Arcadia, Gisela falls asleep in the back seat. All along the Pacific Coast Highway, there are ramshackle stands promising fresh oysters, farm-fresh produce, and other regional delights. I realize that, except for the couple of extra-hot chips I had with Hari in the morning, I haven't eaten anything all day.

"Are you hungry?" Hari asks.

"I'm always hungry," I say.

"How about we drop Gisela off at the studio and then grab a late lunch?"

Hari and I spend the rest of the afternoon exploring the epicurean delights that dot Route 1 from Point Reyes Station on up toward Jenner: briny oyster farms and pastoral family dairies, craftsman bakeries and artisanal cheesemongers, tasting rooms offering fresh-pressed olive oils, infused vinegars, and sparkling honey mead. Just when we think we can't eat another bite, Hari and I spot a road sign for a barbecue joint with mesquite-smoked ribs and Boont Amber on tap.

Hari and I seat ourselves at an empty booth by the front window. The clientele ranges from burly Harley riders to REI-togged day hikers. Patsy Cline is crooning "Crazy" on the jukebox in the corner. The waitress comes and takes our order, and then we wait.

"What's this?" Hari asks. He reaches over and fingers the bright red string around my wrist. Instinctively, I pull my hand away.

"What wrong?" he asks.

"Nothing," I say, twisting my hands together on my lap. "It's just…" I hesitate.

I lift my hands out of my lap and place them on the table. I play with the bracelet around my wrist and start to tell the story. The story of my lucky charm bracelet. The story of my dad.

"When I was little, I used to sit in my parents' bathroom and watch my dad get ready for work. Every morning, Dad would shave, brush his teeth, and then squeeze a dab of white cream in his palms and comb it through his jet-black hair." I can practically smell the mix of Barbasol, Colgate, and Brylcreem.

"Dad was an engineer at this old-school tech company doing work on transistors and stuff like that," I continue. "My dad would usually dress business casual—jacket and slacks—for his job. One day, he got dressed in a suit. A plain black suit. The one he wore to weddings and funerals. The only suit he owned. He told me that he was going to the bank for an important meeting—a meeting to get money to start his own company."

Hari strokes my forearms and takes my hands in his, but his eyes are riveted to my face.

"He opened his top dresser drawer and pulled out a small box," I say. "It was shiny black with intricate mother-of-pearl inlays. It had a strong smell—almost like nail polish remover but not exactly. He opened the box and pulled out a set of cuff links. He asked me to help him put them on." I keep expecting Hari to interrupt me and ask questions, but he just continues to stare into my eyes and hold my hands.

"I peered into the lacquer box," I say, "and saw that it was empty except for one thing—this bracelet. I remember thinking it was funny that my dad had a bracelet. Boys aren't supposed to wear jewelry, I thought. 'What's this?' I asked, and he said, 'Can you keep a secret? A special friend gave that to me a long time ago.' I took the bracelet out of the box and asked, 'It's pretty—can I have it?' I was just a little girl, maybe six or seven, so I didn't think twice about it, about taking something special from my dad. And my dad didn't think twice about it either. He tied the red string around my wrist—I was so small, I think the string went around two or three times—and he told me to keep it safe. He said it would bring me luck."

My voice catches on the last word. I haven't had much luck

lately. I've had the opposite of luck. Maybe that's why I was so willing to trade my lucky charm bracelet for a ride to Arcadia.

I'm wondering how to end the story—if there is an end to the story—when the waitress comes with our food and drinks. Hari releases my hands to make space on the table for our meal, but something about the way he looks at me makes me feel like we're still holding hands.

It's late evening by the time Hari drives me back to the Master's Cottage. He turns off the car ignition, and we sit there in silence. We stare at the golden glow coming from the living room window and the moonlit outline of the tiled roof against the dark sky.

"The cottage looks so pretty at night," I say.

"I can't see anything but you," Hari says. He leans in and kisses me—long and slow and soft. I'd forgotten how incredible it feels to kiss someone for the first time. It's been nearly twenty years since I first kissed Nils, and almost a full year since I last kissed him.

Why am I thinking about my stupid ex-boyfriend when I've got this hot guy right here?

Out of the corner of my eye, I see a shadowy figure appear and quickly disappear in the living room window. I reluctantly pull myself away from Hari.

"Thank you for an amazing day," I say. "I really enjoyed myself."

"Me too," he says.

I've barely shut the car door when Hari drives away, the tires kicking up a light spray of gravel. I make my way slowly up the hill and into the Master's Cottage, where I find Eleanor sitting on the couch in her nightgown.

"Sorry to be late," I whisper.

"You're an adult," Eleanor responds, not looking up from her book.

"Sorry anyway," I say, cuddling up next to her.

Eleanor lets out a small sigh as she sets in her bookmark and sets aside her annoyance. Like I said, my sister's not one to hold a grudge.

"Where were you?" Eleanor asks.

I'm about to tell Eleanor about Gisela's doctor's appointment when I remember: Gisela's pregnancy is a secret. Ugh, I hate secrets.

"I met Gisela's brother this morning, and we kinda hung out all day."

"You hung out with Hari?" Eleanor asks.

"You know Hari?"

"Everyone at Arcadia knows Hari," Eleanor says.

"What does that mean?"

"It doesn't *mean* anything," Eleanor says. She gets up from the couch and checks to make sure the front door is locked. "Just that Hari is a known quantity around here."

"How so?" I ask. I follow my sister from the living room to the bathroom.

"Let's just say Hari has a reputation with the ladies," she says.

"That doesn't surprise me," I say. "I mean, he's pretty gorgeous."

Eleanor takes out her contacts, the first step in her nightly routine. The same routine she's followed since we were teenagers.

"Please be careful around him," Eleanor says.

"I just met him, for Pete's sake," I protest. "I'm not about to elope with him."

"Okay, if you say so. I don't want you to get hurt, that's all," Eleanor says. "Rumor has it that Hari's parents want him to marry a nice girl from a respectable family and eventually take over the family business. If he doesn't find a wife soon, Hari's parents will do it for him."

I wonder how soon is soon. We're both in our late thirties, and the big 4-0 is just around the corner. That seems like an appropriate deadline.

I squeeze a pale blue blob of Crest on my toothbrush and start brushing. I feel the minty foam cleaning away all traces of the day's delights. The flaming hot chips. The freshly shucked oysters from the roadside stands—Kumamoto, French Hog, Golden Nugget, Sweetwater. The flutes of sparkling mead we sipped in the field of sunflowers and thistles, the golden elixir so crisp and clean, I could've sworn it was Champagne but for the lingering hint of honey. The samples of cheese and bread and olive oil, all created by humble hands. The smoke-suffused barbecue meat, so achingly tender it was falling off the bone.

And, of course, that kiss.

I glance down at my bracelet and remember what it felt like to hold Hari's hands in that barbecue joint. How he looked at me like I was the only person in the world. How it seemed like we'd known each other far longer than just one day.

Perhaps my luck is finally starting to turn around.

14

"Aunt Amelia," Maggie whispers.

I open my eyes to find my niece curled up next to me on the bed.

"What?" I whisper back.

"Mr. Allyn offered to drive me to his school today so I can use the computer and research some college stuff," Maggie says, "but only if you come along as my chaperone."

"What time is it?" I mumble.

"Almost ten?"

"Oh my God," I say. I sit straight up and check the clock on the nightstand. Sure enough, it's 9:55. After getting up super-early to walk the labyrinth with Gisela and staying out late with Hari, I must've been really exhausted. I can't believe I slept through morning yoga and breakfast.

Especially breakfast.

"Mr. Allyn brought some lemon poppy seed muffins," Maggie says, as if reading my mind.

"Brandon brought muffins?" I perk up.

"Yeah, he's in the living room talking to Grandma."

Knowing Brandon, I'm pretty sure he's not actually talking to my mother. I imagine him brooding darkly while Mom dithers on about the latest royal wedding or trendiest diet for colon health.

"Is Leo here too?" I ask.

"No, Leo went into the city for some business thing. It's just Mr. Allyn today."

"Isn't it too early to be applying to college?" I say. "It's only October."

"UC applications open November first."

Maggie's eager face practically begs: *Please, please, pretty please, Aunt Amelia?* Maggie's puppy dog eyes could melt even the toughest cynic's heart.

"Go bring me two muffins and a cup of coffee, plenty of milk and sugar, and you have a deal," I say, giving Maggie a kiss on her pert nose.

I gobble up breakfast in my bedroom and slip into some clean clothes before heading out to the living room. Mom is standing by the front door and admiring Brandon's car. I'm surprised to see him next to a vintage creamy white Land Rover. I don't know what I expected Brandon to drive—a hearse maybe?—but I certainly didn't expect something so retro-cool. The thing even has a front winch and knobby tires.

Brandon walks to the passenger side door and pulls it open for me. Maggie is already sitting in the back seat. He makes sure I'm safely inside before carefully closing the door.

As we pull away from Arcadia and toward the Muir Academy, Maggie leans her head out of the back window taking in the passing scenery. The pale blue ocean sparkles in the distance. I've never seen Maggie so contented.

"Brandon, this is magical," I say when we pull into the school driveway. The Muir Academy is tucked into a grove of old-growth redwoods just off the highway but seemingly a world away from the rest of civilization.

"That's the main schoolhouse," Brandon says, pointing to a classic Arts and Crafts–style building. "Rumored to have been designed by Julia Morgan as her personal weekend home but never completed in her lifetime." His voice is deep and mellifluous, like the narrator of a BBC nature program.

"And here we are," he says, parking in front of a wisteria-covered bungalow. "My humble abode." Brandon opens the door of the cottage to reveal an entryway with Mexican floor tiles and weathered brass wall hooks. We walk into a cozy sitting room. The hardwood floors are covered in richly colored carpets, and the sun streaming through the side window illuminates the delicate dust motes in the air.

Next to the sitting room, where a dining room might normally be, is a library with rough-hewn shelves filled with books. The endless rows of leather-bound spines with gold-leaf writing bring to mind an older, more refined era—an era when people read books instead of memes.

"Would you like something to eat or drink?" Brandon asks.

"Now that you mention it, I am feeling a bit peckish," I reply.

I follow Brandon to the back of the bungalow to a modest kitchen. It's larger than the kitchenette at the Master's Cottage but still barely able to accommodate two full-grown adults.

"The cupboard is rather bare, I fear," Brandon says.

Brandon fills the kettle with water from the sink and places it on the white enamel stove. He pulls a fine bone china tea set from the nearest cabinet and carefully arranges three cups and matching saucers on a silver tray. The delicate pattern on the china—pale pink roses against an ecru background—seems out of place in this masculine, academic environment. I'm reminded of the dahlia-printed sheet that Brandon brings to our picnics. Who provided these feminine touches in his life? I know so little about Brandon, who is even more secretive than Gisela.

Brandon opens a tin of Fortnum & Mason English Breakfast tea and spoons a couple generous scoops into a teapot.

"When was the last time you were here?" I ask.

"Not since I started my sabbatical," he says. "The day I first met you, actually."

He looks me directly in the eyes with an unusual intensity. The small kitchen suddenly feels much smaller and warmer. The kettle lets out a faint whistle, breaking the spell. We both reach over to turn it off, and our fingers barely brush.

"Why don't you take this out to the sitting room," he says, handing me the teapot. "I'll try to scrounge up something to eat."

Back in the sitting room, I place the teapot on the doily-covered table. Maggie stands by the window admiring the artwork on the walls. She waves me over to examine an arrangement of framed Audubon-style bird prints. "Everything's so precise and meticulous," she marvels. She's talking about the drawings, but she could just as well be describing Brandon. Leo had said at our first bird-watching trip that Brandon is constantly in search of perfection. Reminds me of Eleanor.

"Sorry for keeping you," Brandon says, entering the room. He sets the silver tray on the table. Having been away from his home since summer, I can't imagine what Brandon could have scrounged up to eat. I don't have great expectations.

"Are those crumpets?" I ask, eyeing the pale griddle cakes speckled with air bubbles.

"From my freezer," Brandon says. "They're better fresh but toast adequately."

"And what is that?" Maggie asks.

"Clotted cream and lemon curd," Brandon says.

Maggie watches curiously as I reach for the butter knife and slather a thick layer of clotted cream on my warm crumpet, topped with a healthy dollop of the lemon curd.

"The British have a knack for preserving foodstuffs so they last," Brandon says. He holds a sterling silver strainer and pours the tea into the three cups. It's strong and dark and hot.

I'm about to take a bite of my crumpet when Brandon offers me a delicately filigreed teaspoon. I look into the cup that Brandon has placed in front of me and notice the black tea has started to turn cloudy.

"I know you take your coffee with sugar and cream," Brandon says, "so I hazarded to guess that you might like your tea the same way as well." I swirl the spoon in my cup, take a bite of crumpet, and then a sip of tea. The combination is perfect.

After tea, Brandon leads us to his library and logs on to the shiny iMac computer perched on his desk. "I'll give you some privacy," Brandon says once he opens the browser. "But let me know if you need any help." He leaves Maggie and me alone in the library.

Maggie types "UC admissions" into the Google search box. I expect to see bright and happy photos of multicultural kids walking along sun-soaked campuses. Instead, I'm assaulted by an impenetrable wall of words.

The phrases "minimum of 15 college-preparatory courses," "minimum weighted GPA," and "must rank in the top 9 percent" pop out at me. I feel my own blood pressure spiking, and I'm not even the one applying to school.

Maggie clicks to see the admission stats for each UC campus. Eleanor was wrong about Berkeley. The average admitted student's GPA isn't 4.4. It's 4.45. I see Maggie's leg jittering up and down, her hands clutched together with her right thumbnail pressed hard into her left palm.

"Hey, move over and let me drive for a while," I say. Maggie scoots her chair to the side to allow me to take control of the computer.

"I wonder what my old college is up to these days," I say, typing "Hampshire College" into the Google search box. "They didn't even require an SAT score when I applied."

"Everyone looks so serious," Maggie says as the images appear on the screen. It's true. When did my alma mater become so earnest?

"These photos really don't do the school justice," I say. "Hampshire was a ton of fun. And Western Mass is breathtaking in the autumn. It's the quintessential college setting." I run a search of "Western Mass in the fall" to prove my point. I click the Images icon on the Google search results page.

"That looks nice," Maggie says, pointing. Now that's more like it. Happy, friendly faces. Flourishing forests in hues of carnelian red and flaming gold. Chunky hand-knit sweaters and cozy collegiate hoodies.

Wait, the hoodies are the wrong color.

"Oh, this isn't Hampshire," I say.

"Where's Mount Holyoke?" Maggie asks, leaning closer to the computer screen.

"Holyoke? It's just down the road from Hampshire."

"It looks nice," Maggie says. She takes back control of the mouse and starts clicking through the college website. She pauses on the photo of a dark-haired young woman standing in what appears to be a dreamy woodland setting. Her ethereal beauty and the bucolic backdrop are reminiscent of Liv Tyler in *The Lord of the Rings.* Only on closer inspection do I realize that the young woman is standing in front of a large mural artfully illuminated to create the illusion of dappled sunlight through leafy branches.

"Wow, can you believe she's only nineteen?" Maggie says. "She won a contest, and her design is being used by the Williamstown Theatre Festival for *A Midsummer Night's Dream*. She even has a summer internship to work at a Hollywood studio designing movie sets."

"You could do that," I say.

"No, I couldn't."

"Yes, Maggie," I say, looking directly at her, "you absolutely could."

"I don't know..." Maggie says.

I reach over and click the print button for the Holyoke admissions application and scholarship rules. The printer next to Brandon's desk comes alive and whirrs softly.

"Anyway, Mom would never let me go all the way across the country," Maggie says. She clicks the X in the upper right of the computer screen and closes the Mount Holyoke window. She returns to the UC site and prints out the essay prompts.

"You could always apply and see if you get in first," I say. "No need to tell your mom."

Maggie tucks a loose strand behind her ear.

After printing out everything she needs, Maggie closes the browser and makes herself comfortable on the couch. I pretend to be perusing the bookshelves but secretly spy on my niece as she pulls out her iPhone for the first time in months. She immediately opens her social media apps.

Even though more than twenty years have passed since I was Maggie's age, seeing her Instagram feed brings up feelings from my own high school days. The popular girls and cocky jocks and petty social hierarchies. The crippling insecurities and pressure to perform. The awful, overwhelming feeling like your entire life depends on those four stupid years of school.

I started to have terrible panic attacks junior year when I got my SAT scores and realized I could never live up to my parents' expectations or my older sister's legacy. Those panic attacks sent me to the school psychologist and nearly caused me to drop out of high school without even graduating. It wasn't until my senior year, when I applied early decision to Hampshire, that those panic attacks stopped. After I got in, I packed my bags for Western Mass and never looked back.

"How did the research go?" Brandon asks.

Maggie clicks off her phone and looks up.

"I've got a lot of work to do," Maggie says. "I wrote a couple essays last year with my advisor at SI, but I don't know if they're good enough."

"Would you like me to review them?" Brandon asks.

Maggie bites her lip, unsure.

"Or how about me?" I say.

Maggie brightens, and when I see the trust in her eyes, so do I. Maggie once confided that she felt like she could tell me anything without the kind of judgment or worry that she'd get from her mother. It felt good to hear her say that, and it feels even better to see it remains true today.

"Excellent idea," Brandon says. "Your aunt Amelia will be the perfect advisor. She was a film studies major. She knows all about creating a compelling narrative. A good college essay is very much like a good film—original, engaging, and tightly edited."

"How did you know…?" I begin. I stop talking when I notice Brandon staring at a framed photo on the shelf. His normally steely eyes are softened around the edges.

"Your mother told me about your college years this morning," Brandon says, coming back to the present. "Your mother is very proud of you, Amelia. And given how much you have already achieved in life, that pride seems to be fully justified."

Brandon discreetly turns the frame ninety degrees so that it's facing the wall. I'm both dying of curiosity about the photograph and stunned by Brandon's effusive praise. Here is a guy with multiple advanced degrees and decades of achievement, whereas I'm just a college dropout with little more to my name than a famous ex-boyfriend and shady criminal record. Still, it feels nice to be seen in a positive light.

"If you're done here, Maggie, perhaps we should head back," Brandon says. "Leo will start worrying if we're away too long."

"Mr. Allyn," Maggie says, "could I use your restroom before we go?"

"Of course," he says. "This place is a bit of a maze. Let me show you the way."

As soon as Brandon and Maggie leave the room, I dash to the shelf to examine the framed photo. It's a faded Kodachrome image. Based on the fluffed and feathered hairstyles, I'd say it was taken in the late '80s or early '90s. The backdrop appears to be a lush English garden, and the gathered guests are in their formal best. It could practically be a movie still from *Four Weddings and a Funeral.*

In the center of the photograph is Brandon dressed in a traditional morning coat and matching slacks. On one side of him is a slim, attractive woman wearing a tea-length pale pink chiffon dress. On the other side of him is another woman, also attractive and maybe a decade older, wearing a silvery silk pantsuit. Both women have brilliant, sparkling blue eyes. I squint at the second woman in the photograph, the one wearing the silvery pantsuit, and hold back a gasp. I'd recognize that impish grin anywhere.

It's Leo.

And etched in the sterling silver frame are two words: *Our Wedding.*

15

On the meandering drive from the Muir Academy back to Arcadia, Maggie is lulled to sleep, but I'm wide-awake with curiosity. I keep looking at Brandon's profile and wondering: whose wedding was that in the photo? Brandon and the pale pink lady, or Brandon and Leo? When did Leo decide to transition? And what happened to that other woman?

If Brandon were a different sort of person, I wouldn't hesitate to ask him about the photo, about Leo, about their relationship. But Brandon is exactly the wrong sort of person to ask such questions to. There's something about his upright posture, formal bearing, even his British accent—they're like the royal guards at Buckingham Palace, rigid and humorless, protecting what hides within from tacky American onlookers like me.

We pull up in front of the Master's Cottage, and Brandon jumps out of the Land Rover to open my door. I'm impressed by his gentlemanliness. Despite my feminist convictions, I have to admit I like a man with good manners.

"Mom?" Maggie says sleepily. She uses her hand to shade her eyes and looks skyward.

Eleanor and Jett are back on the roof again.

"What are you doing up there?" I yell. Eleanor and Jett finished fixing the leaky roof last month. What else is there to do?

"Cleaning the gutters before the rainy season," Eleanor yells back. "There's a bunch of debris that needs to be cleaned out before winter's rains."

"I want to keep you ladies warm and dry this winter," Jett says. The afternoon sun glints off his safety glasses as he passes a bundle of leaves and twigs to Eleanor. There's a large brown leaf stuck in his hair that he's apparently unaware of and Eleanor is too shy to point out. For such a handsome man, Jett really is kind of a dork sometimes.

"Doesn't Jett look cute today?" Maggie says, elbowing me in a not-so-subtle manner. It's like she's playing the role of the nosy next-door neighbor in a sitcom. She really needs to stop hanging around with her giddy grandmother so much. Brandon gives Maggie a bemused look.

"Brandon, can you stay for lunch?" Eleanor calls down.

"Thank you, but I should head back," Brandon says, clearing his throat. "Leo fusses when I'm away for too long."

"Thank you for letting me use your computer, Mr. Allyn," Maggie says. "Could I go back when I'm done with my essays to turn in my applications?"

"You're welcome," Brandon says. "And yes, absolutely, you both have a standing invitation to come back anytime." He turns to me and tips his head in greeting, and I instinctively tip my head in return.

"There's matzo ball soup in the kitchen," Eleanor says.

"I'll race you," I say to Maggie before making a mad dash to the cottage. Matzo ball soup has always been a family favorite, and Eleanor makes the best chicken broth: rich in flavor, with just the right balance of salt and schmaltz.

I sit at the kitchen counter with my steaming bowl of soup and watch as Maggie sits cross-legged on the cottage floor, absentmindedly spooning soup into her mouth and perusing the pile of admissions materials she printed out at Brandon's. Maggie seems lost in her thoughts—thoughts of what college will be like, dreams of what the rest of her life could be. As soon as Eleanor walks in, Maggie reshuffles the papers so the UC materials are on top.

"I think I'll head up to Leo's to do some studying," Maggie says. "I'll be back in time for dinner." Maggie drops her empty soup bowl in the sink, stuffs the papers into her backpack, and slings the pack over her shoulder as she trots out the door.

"How'd it go today?" Eleanor asks as soon as Maggie is gone. I know she's asking how Maggie is handling the college application process, but I pretend otherwise. I want so much to keep Maggie's trust.

"We had a beautiful drive along the coast. The weather was perfect. And have you ever been to the Muir Academy? It's spectacular. Brandon has this very charming cottage with the most amazing library," I say, as if I cared about libraries.

"Maggie seems eager to get as far away from me as she can," Eleanor says. She picks up Maggie's bowl from the sink and starts washing.

"Why do you say that?" I ask. I try to sound cool while silently panicking that Eleanor spotted the Holyoke admissions materials before Maggie tucked them away.

"Well, she certainly made a beeline for Leo's as soon as I walked in."

"I'm sure it was just a coincidence," I say, relieved. I pass my empty bowl and spoon over for Eleanor to wash.

"You'd tell me if there's anything I needed to know about

Maggie, wouldn't you, Ames?" Eleanor asks. "Like you said, Maggie does seem happier since we moved out here and pulled her out of SI, but I'm still worried sick about her. Everyone says the college process is so stressful. I'm afraid she could backtrack into her old habits."

My heart melts when I see Eleanor's weary face. I see now why she's using eye cream. She must be exhausted from all those twelve-hour shifts—not to mention Dad's death, the estate battle, and Maggie's ongoing struggles with anxiety. When did life become so hard?

"Of course, I'd tell you," I say. I walk over to the sink and grab a clean cloth to dry the dishes and put them away. Eleanor ladles the remainder of the matzo ball soup from the pot into a bowl and sets it aside for later. She takes the empty pot from the stove and fills it with warm, sudsy water. As she scrubs the pot's interior, an iridescent soap bubble drifts up and floats above the sink and pops just short of the ceiling.

"Hey, where did Jett go?" I ask, registering his absence.

"He had to run back to the center to start dinner," Eleanor says. "We were so busy cleaning the gutters that we completely lost track of time."

"Cleaning the gutters, huh?" I growl, trying to make it sound dirty. "You know, I can't remember the last time I had a good gutter-cleaning." I set down the bowl in my hands and start tickling my sister's ribs. Eleanor splashes water at me, and we laugh like we used to as girls.

"What's all the commotion?" Mom says. She rubs the sleep from her eyes as she emerges from her bedroom. Her wispy blond hair is puffed and messy from sleep, giving her a vague resemblance to a Dr. Seuss character.

"Sorry to wake you, Mom," Eleanor says. "How was your nap?"

"It was a very good nap," Mom says. "I saw your father again."

"Oh, Mom," Eleanor says, "how is he?" Eleanor asks this without batting an eye, like my mother just said she ran into the mailman on the street.

"As handsome as ever," Mom says. "In my dream, I was wandering this great big field—a field of California wildflowers—looking for something I lost. I was searching and searching when I suddenly felt like turning around. And when I did, I saw him, your father. He was backlit by the sun so I couldn't make out his features, but I could tell it was him. He was standing on a hill, wearing his favorite blue seersucker suit."

"The one he wore to Ellie's wedding," I say.

"Yes," my mother says.

"Was he wearing the same lilac bow tie?" I ask.

"Of course," Mom answers.

"And then what happened?" Eleanor asks.

"Well, I was so shocked to see him standing there," Mom says, her voice high and thin. "I stood there with my mouth hanging open, just staring at him. I didn't dare make a noise or take a breath. It was like standing in front of a wild animal. I didn't want to scare him away. I just wanted the moment to last forever.

"After a while, I moved the least little bit, just so he wasn't backlit anymore. I wanted to see his face. Oh, girls, he was smiling so wide. Your dad was positively glowing with happiness."

I glance over at Eleanor, and she's giving Mom her full attention.

"I said, 'You're here,'" my mother continues. "And your dad said, 'Of course I'm here. I've been here all along. Where did you think I'd gone?'"

My mother stops talking.

"And then what?" I ask.

My mother looks at me, stunned and confused.

"And then what?" I ask again.

"And then she woke up," Eleanor says. She wraps her arms around our mother's narrow shoulders and leads her to the couch.

"I want to go back to sleep," Mom says, resisting Eleanor's pull.

"You've slept enough today," Eleanor says firmly. "It's time to spend some time with the living."

"Okay," Mom says, her voice small and obedient.

"There's still some matzo ball soup left, Mom," Eleanor says. "I want you to finish the entire bowl, and then the three of us can go out for an afternoon walk."

Mom does as she's told. She seems to perk up after her soup. She even changes out of her tracksuit and into some warm clothes.

"How far are we going?" Mom asks moments after we leave the cottage.

"To the bluff," Eleanor says. "It's a good long walk, and the view is breathtaking."

"It's so cold up here," Mom complains. "Not like Atherton. It was always nice and warm in Atherton." She zips her creamy white shearling vest and pulls the fuzzy collar close to her neck. Mom is dressed in her après-ski finest. She doesn't ski, but she loved to hang out at the lodge reading magazines and napping in front of a roaring fire while Dad, Eleanor, and I would schuss the black-diamond slopes of Tahoe.

With her honey-colored hair peeking out of her furry hat and grazing her wide-set eyes, Mom reminds me of Julie Christie in *Doctor Zhivago*. Even without a drop of makeup, my mother is stunning. She looks at least a decade younger than her sixty-five-plus years. You can still see hints of the groovy hippie chick she was nearly five decades ago when my dad first laid eyes on her at Berkeley. She was the quintessential all-American beauty, the kind of long-haired, slim-waisted girl you used to see in Coppertone ads, the kind who inspires young men to write bad poetry and sappy love songs.

"How are things going with Jett?" Mom asks me. A light wind sends ripples through her shearling vest and furry hat. "You seem to be spending a lot of time together in the kitchen."

"What do you mean?" I say, glancing over to catch Eleanor's reaction. "There's nothing going on between me and Jett. We're just friends, that's all." I sidestep a pile of rabbit droppings in the gravel path.

"If you say so," she responds.

"And what about you, Ellie dear?" Mom says. "You seemed quite taken with Brandon when we first met him. You might consider him as a mate. You're both so brainy and serious. And he's already acting like a second father to our dear Maggie."

"I think Brandon is more interested in Amelia, Mom," Eleanor says.

"Yes, you're probably right. But Amelia can't have them all," Mom says. "So many men, just one Amelia."

"That's true," Eleanor says.

"See, Amelia?" Mom says, returning her attention to me. "Even your sister agrees that it's time you finally got over that Nils and found a good man to settle down with."

"That's not what Eleanor said, Mom," I say.

"But that's what she meant. You know your sister. Ellie's too nice to say things directly. You're not getting any younger. And anyway, how are we all supposed to keep living like this? Crammed together in this tiny cottage, mooching off poor Eleanor with just her nurse's income. This isn't any way to live."

While Mom goes on about how I should be trying to find myself a husband before I get too old, I sift through my mental calendar and realize that it's been exactly one year since Nils and I kissed our tearful goodbye at the Chevron gas station outside of Portland. I haven't heard anything from or about him—which is what you'd expect when your ex-boyfriend has fled the country and gone incognito somewhere in the world. But still. How is it that someone I spent every day with for nearly twenty years is now gone from my life? How is it that the person who once mattered most to me is now relegated to a footnote in my book of life? How does that happen?

"And here we are," Eleanor announces.

Mom and I look up from the dusty path and see the Pacific Ocean spread out before us.

"Oh my gosh," Mom gasps.

"I thought you'd like it," Eleanor responds, pulling me and Mom closer.

The three of us sit down on the bluff, two generations of Bae-Wood women taking in the incomparable view. I breathe deeply from my diaphragm like Gisela taught us to do in yoga class.

"It's so clear today you can even see the Farallons," Eleanor says.

"What's that?" Mom asks.

"See that tiny outcropping of rocks?" Eleanor says, pointing. "Those are the Farallon Islands. They're famous for their abundant wildlife. Seabirds, seals, sea lions, even gigantic elephant seals. And those waters are teeming with sharks and whales."

Eleanor sounds so authoritative. I didn't realize she was such a nature expert. Further proof that she and Brandon would make a good couple. Just as I start to imagine Eleanor and Brandon living happily ever after in their fairy-tale cottage at the Muir Academy, a dark shadow emerges from the waves.

"Mom, did you know you loved Dad the moment you saw him?" I ask.

"Are you kidding?" she says. "When I first met your father, I thought he was the biggest nerd. He had horn-rimmed glasses and—honest to God—even wore a pocket protector. But I was failing freshman math, and the TA recommended your dad as a tutor, and the rest—as they say—is history."

"Did you just see that leaping dolphin?" Eleanor gasps.

"Please don't tell him you said that. He's already insufferable," I mumble, smiling at the memory of Gisela saying those very words to me.

"Tell who what?" Eleanor asks. "Is that a line from a movie?"

"No," I say, "just a private joke."

I stand up and watch Hari as he rides the cresting wave. Once he reaches shore, he pulls off the hood of his wetsuit and waves at me. In that moment, with his crooked, sexy smile and long, soaking hair, Hari reminds me of a cross between Brad Pitt in *Thelma & Louise* and Keanu Reeves in *Point Break*. Is it a bad omen that both characters turn out to be scoundrels who steal money and break hearts?

"Who's that?" Mom asks, squinting.

"Hari," Eleanor and I say at the same time.

"Another of Amelia's admirers?" Mom asks.

"Yes," Eleanor says at the same time I say, "No."

We all watch as Hari pulls his hood back on, turns his board around, and paddles back out to the horizon.

"Uh-huh, very interesting," Mom says.

After catching another wave and gliding to the beach, Hari tucks his surfboard under one arm and trots to the spot where the rope is hooked into the cliff. He gesticulates for me to meet him at the top of the bluff. I walk over as Hari climbs up the rocky slope.

"Hello, beautiful," Hari says. In a reprise of last night, his kiss is long and slow and soft. Even though he's dripping cold seawater, I feel a current of warmth flowing down from my lips throughout my body. As he pulls his lips away, Hari glances sideways and smiles.

"Hello there," Hari says to Eleanor and Mom sitting several feet away. Eleanor seems reluctant to stand up, while Mom practically leaps to her feet and dashes over to meet Hari.

"Mom, Eleanor, this is my friend, Hari..." My voice sputters to an awkward stop as I realize I don't know Hari's last name. I shudder to imagine what Mom and Eleanor think of me. They both married their college sweethearts, guys they met freshman year at Berkeley, the first men they ever slept with—probably the only men they ever slept with. Meanwhile, I'm traipsing around making out with guys whose last names I don't even know.

"Pleased to meet you," Hari says. He bends his sleek figure forward and does a little hand flourish, like a courtier greeting the queen. "Hari Mistry, at your service."

Mistry, what a cool last name. I laugh to myself, thinking about that first night I ran into him at Gisela's cottage. I thought of him as the Mystery Man. Turns out I was right.

The four of us head back to the cancer center. Hari and Mom walk together, practically joined at the hip and engrossed in conversation. Eleanor and I follow a few paces behind.

We reach the spot where the gravel path diverges into three directions: one way to Leo's house, another way to the Master's Cottage, and yet another way to the cancer center and yoga studio.

"Well, ladies, this is where I must leave you," Hari says. "I very much hope to see you all again soon." He kisses me lightly on the cheek and does another hand flourish in my mother and sister's general direction.

"Amelia, now I understand why you've lost interest in poor Jett," Mom says before Hari is even out of earshot. "Jett's rich and handsome, but Hari is something else altogether. What a charmer! How many other secrets have you been keeping from us?"

I think about Gisela's pregnant belly, Maggie's printout of the Mount Holyoke college admissions materials, the framed wedding photo in Brandon's library. And those are just the secrets I've collected in the past day or so.

"Don't be silly, Mom," I say, brushing off the question.

Soon, we're back at the Master's Cottage, full of energy and hungry for dinner. Eleanor heads to the kitchen while Mom and I settle down on the couch.

"What were you and Hari talking about, Mom?" I ask. "It looked really juicy."

"I'm going to start dinner now," Eleanor says, "but talk loudly so I can hear you."

"I was just making small talk with him at first," Mom yells. "You know, where is your family from? What do they do? When he told me his parents originally came from India, I told him that your father and I once went there on vacation, and he asked where we stayed, and I told him, 'The Raj,' and he said, 'You have good taste—my family owns that hotel.'"

There's a clatter of pots crashing in the kitchen.

"Hari's family owns the Raj hotels?" Eleanor and I shout at the same time.

Over the course of two decades, Nils and I traveled the world several times. We started out in youth hostels and fleabag motels, worked our way up to pensiones and quaint B and Bs, and were only able to stay at luxury hotels in the few halcyon years between the rise of Amuse and the fall of Loca.

In all that time, we'd only experienced a Raj hotel once—the Raj Stockholm in Sweden—booked and paid for by some global food conglomerate that wanted Nils to endorse its frozen fish products. In many ways, the hotel wasn't much different from the other ultra-luxe hotels we had visited, with its deliciously soft linens and designer toiletries. What set the Raj apart, though, were the personal touches. The masses of lilacs (my favorite flowers) in crystal vases tucked in every corner. The princess cakes decorated with Nils' and my initials in calligraphy royal icing. Sinfully soft sheepskin slippers embroidered with the Raj logo and custom-selected in Nils' and my exact shoe sizes.

"Yes," Mom says. "I couldn't believe it myself."

Eleanor walks over with two glasses of rosé and hands one to me and the other to Mom before returning to the kitchen.

"Congratulations, Amelia," Mom says. "Looks like you've snagged yourself a keeper. A rich and handsome bachelor who's clearly entranced by you. Hari could be the solution to all our problems."

Mom picks up a random magazine and flips through the pages, humming "Here Comes the Bride" to herself. Her words nag at me. Is Hari really the solution to all our problems? What does that even mean? That our family's problems would be solved by money, or that my own problems would be solved by a man?

Neither seems right, but neither seems exactly wrong.

16

On Friday morning, I get out of bed the instant the alarm clock goes off to make sure I get to yoga on time. I only have two more days with the cancer center guests before they leave, before the last retreat of the year comes to an end. I don't want to miss a single moment. As I walk into the studio and pick up my mat from the neatly stacked pile, I see Chloe in the far corner. Alone.

"Where's Andrew?" I whisper, setting up my mat next to hers.

"He's taking the day off," Chloe whispers back. "My poor husband. He's not used to so much rest and relaxation. He misses his daily dose of podcasts and streaming news. I told him I'd be fine without his company for just one day. He drove off this morning in search of espresso and 5G service."

Gisela rings the meditation bells to signal that it's time to start. She gives Chloe and me a placid but pointed stare that says, "No judgment, girls, but it's time to stop your gabbing." Chloe and I exchange not-so-guilty smiles.

After yoga, Chloe and I lead the group back to the center for breakfast. Over the past few days, the two of us have bonded over our shared love of food. Despite her tiny frame, Chloe has an impressive appetite, savoring every bit of Jett's cooking. Chloe is equally enthusiastic about my stories of working with Nils at Amuse and Loca—and I must admit it's been fun to reminisce about my glory days at the apex of the celebrity chef world.

When we walk into the dining room, the breakfast spread looks and smells divine. Chloe and I head straight to the sideboard, where Jett has set up his award-winning pastry selections.

"Morning buns," Jett says to Chloe. "Amelia's favorite."

"You remembered!" I swoon in mock devotion. Jett shakes his head, laughing, and walks back to the kitchen. Chloe and I fill our plates and sit down at a table near the front window. The ocean is just barely visible from our seats, a spectacular sliver of aquamarine wedged between sand-colored dunes and sage-green brush.

"Oh my God," Chloe exclaims as soon as she takes a bite of the pastry.

"I know, right?" I say, biting into my own treat.

I notice that Chloe's eyes seem to change color depending on where she is and how she's feeling—from flat gray to soft brown to pale green—like a mood ring. Right now, they're almost the exact same color as the jade turtle on my lucky charm bracelet.

The tables in the dining room are filled with guests and staff, all enjoying the delicious food and good company. Leo's holding court as usual, drawing peals of laughter from the ladies at his table. Michaela and Frank, Arcadia's resident therapists, sit at one of the smaller tables, nodding and cooing as Jane, a kindly kindergarten teacher in treatment for a third cancer (thyroid, breast, and now ovarian), passes around photos of her beloved nieces and nephews. Jane showed me the same photos over dinner the first night of the retreat. The youngest one, a baby girl, has Jane's fair complexion and saucer-wide eyes.

"You and Jett seem very friendly," Chloe says. "Anything going on between you?"

Before I have a chance to deny everything, Hari appears out of nowhere and leans over our table. "Yes, is there anything going on with you and Jett?" he whispers.

Chloe looks up at Hari, who's dressed in a faded Stanford hoodie and his baggy cotton pants. His hair is damp and pulled into a loose man-bun with the same batik-print scrunchie that he wore the day of our outing to Gisela's doctor's appointment. Hari smiles and gives me a kiss on the cheek before sitting in the chair next to me. He sits so close that our bodies are practically overlapping.

"Hi, I don't think we've met yet," Hari says. "I'm Hari."

"He's Gisela's brother," I say by way of explanation, although I can tell by Chloe's curious expression that she suspects more.

"How was surfing this morning?" I ask. I scoot my chair away from Hari so I can talk to him without craning my neck sideways.

"Not nearly as much fun without an audience," he says, scooting his chair back closer to mine. "I kept hoping you and your mother would show up."

"Hey, keep your hands off my mother," I say. "She's not a cougar."

"You never know," Hari says. "Maybe she just hasn't met the right prey." He makes a low purring sound and paws at me playfully, like a kitten batting at a ball of yarn, and I swat his hands away.

"Did you say you went surfing this morning?" Chloe asks.

Hari turns his attention to Chloe. The way he looks at her, as if she's the only person in the room, reminds me of Eleanor warning me that Hari is a known quantity around Arcadia. Of Gisela saying that he's a notorious flirt. Just as I start to feel a pang of jealousy, he reaches under the table to take my hand in his. Something about the surreptitiousness of it feels illicit. Holding hands hasn't felt this hot since middle school.

"Yeah, I try to get out every morning. Do you surf?" he asks.

"No, but my dad used to take me to Mavericks every year," Chloe says. "I loved seeing all the top surfers braving those incredible waves. I haven't gone in almost ten years, but I'm hoping to go back this winter with Andrew, knock on wood."

Chloe's phrasing reminds me that, despite her outwardly healthy appearance, she is very sick. Her cancer is metastatic, meaning it's incurable and ultimately fatal. How much time do the doctors give Chloe? Will she be alive long enough to experience Mavericks with Andrew? Over a decade ago, when Eleanor phoned me to say Edward's cancer had come back, she said the doctors gave him up to a year to live. He was gone in less than six months.

"If the weather holds up, I'll probably go out again this afternoon," Hari says. "If you're interested in watching, why don't you stop by Gisela's studio around four and we can head out to the beach together?"

That afternoon, Chloe and I walk over to Gisela's studio to find Hari already in his sleek black wetsuit. By the time the three of us reach the bluff overlooking the ocean, clouds of fog are beginning to roll in.

"If you want to come down to the beach to watch, I can help you down," Hari says to me and Chloe. He points to the twisted cable bolted into the bluff. "But the view is probably just as good from up here."

"We'll stay up here," I say. Hari nods and gives me a quick kiss.

"Wish me luck!" he says, climbing down the rope.

Chloe and I sit down on the ground. It's the same spot I sat with Gisela earlier this week after walking the labyrinth. The same spot I came with Mom and Eleanor just yesterday. My new favorite place on earth.

"It's normally so beautiful here," I say. "I'm sorry for the fog."

"Don't worry about it," Chloe says. "I've gotten used to the fog." I intuit from Chloe's absent gaze that she's not talking about the weather. Remembering Gisela's advice, I don't say a word. If Chloe wants to share more details with me, she'll do so without my prompting.

"The drugs are messing up my brain," Chloe says. "It's a known side effect of one of the medications. Last night, I told Andrew I was thinking about quitting the clinical trial, that I don't want to spend whatever time I have left in a mental fog. He didn't say anything, but I knew he was mad. And this morning, when I brought it up again, he told me he needed to get some air. That's when he drove off."

"I'm sorry," I say. The first time I met Chloe and Andrew, he'd looked at her with such absolute devotion. I envied them both in that moment, which is admittedly strange considering their circumstances.

"Andrew didn't want us to come to the retreat this week," Chloe says. "He thinks it's a complete waste of time and money. He'd rather that I stay at home and focus on getting better. He actually believes that if I just focus harder, I can beat this thing." Chloe says the final two sentences with teary-eyed exasperation.

Back in Gisela's studio, she had talked about how the words we use with cancer patients can make them feel like they're being judged for being sick, as if it's their fault for not doing the right things. Those words must be so much more painful coming from a loved one.

"When I was first diagnosed, I did everything I was supposed to do," Chloe says. "I can't tell you how many surgeries and rounds of chemo, radiation, and hormone treatment I've gone through. I kept a positive attitude, just like everyone told me to. I exercised and went to support groups and even tried to go vegan. In the end, I couldn't give up butter and cheese."

"I could never give up butter and cheese," I agree.

"When the cancer came back in my liver and bones," Chloe says, "I was devastated to think all my efforts to be good had been for nothing. Then I picked myself back up and focused on getting better, living as long as possible. Andrew and I researched clinical trials. Between the two of us, we know more about cutting-edge cancer treatments than most doctors. Every time a drug would seem like it's working, we'd be elated. And then after a while, I'd go in for another scan, and there'd be new tumors. Andrew and I have spent so many years that way, living from scan to scan. Standing on the precipice of life and death."

I can't imagine the stress of living with such uncertainty, never knowing when a lab test will come back with bad news. My heart breaks for Chloe and Andrew and all they've had to go through in their young lives. I put my arm around Chloe's shoulder and pull her close.

"I'm done with treatments," Chloe says. "At our group session yesterday, we talked a lot about regret. What would we regret at the end of our lives? It occurred to me that I would regret spending my final days glued to a computer screen trying to find another clinical trial to qualify for, another way to torture myself in search of a miracle cure. I would regret not appreciating the wonderful things this earth has to offer. I don't care anymore about living as long as possible. I just want to live as well as possible for however many weeks or months that I have left."

As if on cue, an ebullient whoop pierces the air. Chloe and I see Hari getting ready to mount a wave. It's a spectacular, nearly vertical wall of water rising like a mythological sea creature and threatening to swallow him whole. Chloe and I stand and watch breathlessly as Hari maneuvers his body to tame the monster and glides gracefully in toward shore. Hari reaches the beach, takes off his wetsuit hood, grins up at Chloe and me, and waves with wild abandon. Chloe waves back at him, her face aglow, and I am overcome with something resembling love for Hari. Despite his first impression as a bad boy and reputation as a Lothario, Hari has a heart as wild and open as the ocean. You can't help but be drawn to him.

"Hari seems awfully fond of you," Chloe says as Hari paddles out again and we settle back down on the ground.

"We just met this week," I say.

"I wouldn't have guessed. You both act as if you've known each other much longer."

She's right. Something about Hari feels so familiar to me. There's a lightness to him, an optimism and playfulness, that reminds me of myself when I was a child, back before my panic attacks and bad decisions and chasing after other people's dreams. Having spent so many years in Nils' chilly shadow, I'd forgotten what it felt like to live fully as myself, to show my colors in the sun. Maybe it's time I changed all that.

"Oh look," Chloe says, pointing.

There, out on the horizon, a golden light breaks through the fog and illuminates everything.

17

Gisela is standing on the porch of the yoga studio when Hari and I return from dropping Chloe off at the cancer center's main building.

"Where have you been?" Gisela asks.

"Where do you think?" Hari says, gesturing to his surfboard.

"Rigo called," Gisela says. "The lady from the museum is at the house. You were supposed to be there thirty minutes ago."

"Shoot," Hari says. "Is it Friday already? I completely lost track of time."

"Mom and Dad will be royally pissed if they find out you blew off the meeting," Gisela says. "You know how important this is to them."

"Stop it with the lecturing," Hari says, hosing himself clean. "Tell Rigo to tell her I'll be there as soon as I can—an hour, hour and a half tops. We're the ones making the huge donation. She can cool her jets for another hour." Gisela flashes him a frustrated scowl before walking off toward the center's main building.

"Hey, wanna go into the city with me?" Hari asks. He wraps a large towel around his bottom half, which only accentuates his ridiculous abs. "I've got this thing I need to do for my parents, and we can grab something to eat afterwards."

"I'm not exactly dressed for dinner," I say, pointing at my tattered and sandy clothes.

"That's fine," Hari says. "We won't go anywhere fancy. Maybe pick up a burrito in the Mission or some Chinese from Henry's."

I'm thinking I should tell Eleanor not to expect me for dinner—she hates not knowing where I am at all times—when I remember she told me that she's doing a double shift at work. She won't be home until tomorrow morning.

"Sure, I'd love to," I say.

Hari goes into Gisela's bedroom to shower and change, and I wait for him in the yoga studio. Just as I'm about to nod off to sleep, Hari comes in looking like a heartthrob movie star. He's changed into a form-fitting button-down shirt and ink-blue jeans. I feel even more self-conscious about my stretched-out hoodie and ripped Levis, but I know Hari's in a hurry, so I don't want to go back to the Master's Cottage to change.

"Who's Rigo?" I ask as Hari whips his car along the curves of Route 1.

"He's my parents' personal assistant," Hari says. "He's basically the person who answers the phone when my parents are unreachable."

"What's this thing you're doing for your parents?" I ask.

"It's kind of embarrassing," Hari says, not looking the least bit embarrassed. "My parents have a bunch of Indian art they want to donate to the Asian Art Museum, but only if the museum agrees to keep the collection together and display all the pieces. That means the museum would have to dedicate an entire room, maybe an entire wing, to the collection. The curator of Indian art wants to inspect the pieces in person to determine whether to seal the deal. My parents are out of the country right now, and they don't trust anyone besides me or Gisela to show anyone around our house. They also don't want to give anyone a chance to discover Gisela's pregnancy until they're ready to make a formal announcement, so I agreed to help them out. The curator made the appointment weeks ago, and I got so caught up showing off for you and Chloe today that I forgot about it."

"I'm ashamed to admit I don't know much about Indian art," I say.

Hari proceeds to describe his parents' collection of ink and watercolor paintings from Northern India, mostly from the sixteenth to nineteenth centuries: bold and vibrant images of Hindu gods and goddesses, rajahs and ladies, lovers and warriors. Hari stops talking as we pass under the rainbow hues of the Robin Williams Tunnel, the honking from other cars echoing all around us. When we emerge from the darkness, the Golden Gate Bridge is directly before us with millions of city lights twinkling in the distance.

"This view never gets old, does it?" Hari asks.

Traffic slows to a crawl as we approach the bridge. Hari pushes a button, and the roof of his convertible goes down. An expensive sports car passes us on the right. The driver looks like he's barely out of high school, another tech billionaire headed into the city for a night of overpriced cocktails. How is it that some people get their lives together in their twenties, and here I am, on the verge of forty and still completely rudderless?

I close my eyes to blot out my self-critical thoughts.

"Hey, beautiful," Hari whispers in my ear. "We're here."

I open my eyes to find that we're stopped in the driveway of a gleaming mansion. The canyon-like walls are made of a light-colored stone with huge windows of reflective glass. It's as if Frank Gehry had been commissioned to construct a contemporary version of the Taj Mahal. I'm so awestruck by the architecture that I don't notice the dark gray Audi sedan parked farther up the driveway. A slender, elegant woman wearing a black sheath dress emerges from the car and walks toward us.

I pull down the passenger side visor to check myself in the mirror. The wind has whipped up my short-cropped hair so I look like that guy in *Eraserhead*. The mascara around my eyes is badly smudged, lending me a distinctly punk raccoon look. I glance down at my ripped jeans and stretched-out hoodie and beat-up Toms slip-ons. What was I thinking coming into the city looking like this?

"I'm in no state to be meeting anyone," I say, "least of all fancy museum curators."

"Don't be silly, darling," Hari says, kissing me lightly on the lips, "you look fine."

Hari gets out of the car and introduces himself to the curator. I'm so flabbergasted by my own appearance that I can't make eye contact with her. Hari punches a code into the security module and opens the front door. The interior of the mansion, like the exterior, is clean lines and white surfaces. Soft lighting automatically illuminates as we enter the open space foyer.

"May I get you something to drink?" Hari asks the curator. "Champagne, Chablis?"

"Nothing for me, thank you," the curator says. I could really use a glass of Champagne right now, but I keep quiet.

"Shall we start the tour then?" Hari asks, and the curator nods.

Hari leads us to the second floor, where the long, white-painted hallway is lined with colorful watercolor prints in simple ash frames. The curator dons a pair of very expensive-looking glasses and peers closely at each picture.

"I believe I saw similar images at the Met several years back," the curator says.

"Yes, that collection had almost a hundred paintings," Hari says. "Ours has over two hundred."

Over two hundred paintings? We're going to be here forever. I feel a stomach growl coming on, and I clench my abs tight in a feeble effort to contain it.

"And here," Hari says, turning the corner, "are my parents' most prized pieces. The ones they know will be controversial, but they insist must be displayed as part of the collection."

The curator adjusts her glasses, and I see her fig-colored lips curl into a smile.

"Lakshmi," she murmurs.

The brightly painted image is of a blue-colored man and his bare-breasted lover clearly doing the humpity-hump in a lush grove of flowers. The next image shows what appears to be a man with four women in various states of undress and ecstasy. I feel a warm flutter in my nether regions. Am I really getting hot and bothered over three-hundred-year-old Indian watercolors?

"I've seen enough," the curator says.

How can she be done? We've barely looked at a dozen or so images. I can't tell if the curator is outraged or impressed.

"Mr. Mistry," she says, extending her hand to Hari, "the Asian Art Museum would be honored and grateful to receive a gift of your parents' unique and exquisite collection. I can offer you my personal assurance that we will display every single work with the care and reverence they so richly deserve.

I will have our legal department start drawing up the papers tomorrow for review by your parents' lawyers."

"Great," Hari says. "My parents will be delighted to hear the news."

As Hari shows the curator out of the house and back to her car, I poke around the house and examine the framed photos on the white-lacquered grand piano. I'm pleasantly surprised by the contrast between the extravagant mansion and the modest photos in the sterling silver frames. The images of Hari and Gisela as children echo those of Eleanor and me when we were young. The same awkward school portraits with bad haircuts and metal-mouth braces. Snapshots taken at the Santa Cruz beach boardwalk and Disneyland. Portraits from proms and graduations.

My focus turns to the pictures of Gisela and Hari at high school prom. Hari and his date mug it up for the camera, laughing as if sharing a private joke. Meanwhile, Gisela looks achingly innocent in her canary yellow dress and gardenia wrist corsage. Neither Gisela nor her handsome escort is looking at the camera. Jett and Gisela only have eyes for each other.

"Well, that was a resounding success," Hari says, finding me by the piano. "You must be my lucky charm."

"I love your family photos," I say. "It gives me some insight into the younger Hari."

Hari picks up a photo of himself in a soccer jersey. He looks to be about six or seven, and his wavy black hair is pulled off his face by a sweatband—the kid equivalent of a man-bun. He's standing next to a plump and pretty woman who I assume is his mother. She has her hand on his shoulder like a proud parent.

"I didn't grow up rich, you know," Hari says. "This house, all the artwork, my parents worked hard to get them. They didn't have their wealth handed to them on a silver platter."

Not like Jett, I think to myself, and then I wonder if the unstated comparison was intentional on Hari's part.

"My mom was the fifth of nine kids," Hari says. "Her parents came from nobility but didn't have much money. They made sure each of their children married into the right kind of family. My dad's own background wasn't notable, but he was super-smart and ambitious. His first job out of university was as an accountant at the Raj Hotels' head office in Mumbai, and he quickly gained the attention of the higher-ups. My mom's parents still thought he wasn't up to their standards. When the Raj Hotels decided to open their first hotel in the US, they sent my dad to oversee the construction finances, and that's when he and my mom decided to marry. It was only when Dad became president of US operations that my grandparents finally accepted him as worthy of our family. Now that he's head of the investor group that owns the Raj Hotels, my dad can do no wrong."

Hari focuses on the pretty woman in the photo.

"Growing up," he says, "Gisela and I hardly ever saw my dad. He was always flying from continent to continent, working on the next big project, leaving my mom to raise two kids pretty much by herself. She never once complained."

Hari sets down the photo of himself in the soccer uniform.

"I'm not sure why I told you all that," he says. "I guess I just didn't want you thinking I'm some spoiled brat or something."

"I would never think that," I lie.

"I usually don't care what people think of me," Hari says, "but you're different, Amelia. In all the best ways."

Hari pulls me close and kisses me in a way that I haven't been kissed in a long time. As a prelude to something else. He slides his hands down my spine, grabs me tightly, and presses his body into mine. I feel Hari getting hard and myself getting soft.

Something vibrates near my pelvis. Wow, am I really so sex-starved that I can be turned on so easily?

"Sorry," Hari says to me, pulling away. "What do you want?" Hari says into his phone. "I'm in the middle of something."

"Uh-huh," he says, motioning to me that it'll only be a minute.

"Yeah, it went great," he says, "they agreed to everything."

"Tonight?" he asks. "I just drove all the way to the city."

"Okay, I'll be there soon," he sighs, clicking off his phone.

"Who was that?" I ask.

"Gisela," he says. "She wanted to make sure I kept the meeting with the curator. And she can't find her inhaler anywhere and needs me to pick one up for her at the drugstore. Her asthma isn't too bad lately, but she gets panicky if she doesn't have an inhaler close to her at all times."

"I'd get panicky too," I say.

"I'm so sorry, babe," Hari says, giving me another kiss. "I know I promised you dinner. Let me grab some snacks and a bottle of Champagne to make up for it."

"You don't need to apologize," I reply, once again admiring the photographs on the grand piano. "Family always comes first."

The Master's Cottage is quiet by the time Hari and I leave the city, run Gisela's errand, and walk back from the yoga studio, a bottle of Dom Pérignon in hand. The porch light is on, but the rest of the house is pitch-dark. Mom and Maggie must have gone to sleep already. Eleanor's car isn't anywhere to be seen. She should still be at the hospital working her double shift.

"Do you want to come in so we can have that drink?" I ask.

"What do you think?" he says. He pulls me close, shuts his

eyes, and kisses me—first on my lips, and then working his way down to the hollow of my neck.

"Well, we're in luck," I say. "My sister won't be home until seven or eight in the morning. I've got the whole bedroom to myself tonight. You just need to leave before she gets back."

Hari's eyes open wide. We stare at one another for a moment and then laugh.

"Shhh," I say, before opening the front door. "I don't want to wake Mom and Maggie."

Hari nods and kisses me softly in response. I take his hand in mine and lead him through the dark living room, down the narrow hallway, and into Eleanor's and my bedroom. I close the door quietly and turn on the bedside lamp. Hari sets the bottle of Champagne on the nightstand, pushes me down on the mattress, and gets on top of me. His taut surfer body is lighter than Nils' brawny build. Sometimes when Nils used to put his body on mine, I almost couldn't breathe for the weight.

"Now, where was I?" Hari whispers as he kisses the hollow of my neck again. Hari has a whole catalog of kisses—from casual pecks to erotic erogenous explorations—and his fun and flirty neck nibbling is one of my favorites. I feel another vibration near my pelvis, and it's not Hari's phone this time.

I sit up and pull both my hoodie and T-shirt over my head. Hari unbuttons his shirt to reveal those incredible abs, and then he wriggles out of his dark denim jeans. I can't believe I'm in bed with this perfect specimen of manhood. Things continue to heat up as pieces of clothing come off one by one.

"Are you sure your sister won't be coming home tonight?" Hari whispers in my ear.

I pause for a moment, double-checking my memory. I'm fairly confident Eleanor said she wouldn't be coming home until tomorrow morning, but I shudder to think of the scene if I'm mistaken.

"Just one sec," I say.

I jog over to the bedroom door and hang his batik-print scrunchie on the knob.

18

When I wake up the next morning, I'm alone. I check the clock, and it's not yet eight. Hari must have left in the night, but I don't know where Eleanor is. Perhaps her double shift at the hospital ran long, or maybe she's asleep on the couch, not wanting to disturb me. I walk out of the bedroom and notice the scrunchie isn't on the knob. The door to Mom and Maggie's bedroom is still closed. I head out to the living room, and it's empty.

I hop into the shower. The hot water pelts my body, and I rub the sliver of soft white soap over my neck and shoulders, down my breasts and belly, and in the tender space between my legs. I think about Hari and last night. I dry myself off with a towel and clear the steam from the bathroom mirror. I stare at my reflection and smile.

"Stop looking so damn happy," I say to myself. I change into a fresh set of clothes and walk down to the yoga studio to start my day.

There's always a bittersweet quality to Saturdays at Arcadia.

After a week of intense group sessions full of self-reflection and revelation, the center guests have bonded in ways that would normally take years or even decades to develop. It feels rare, almost sacred, to share space and time with one another.

With only one more day together, the guests do everything more slowly—they walk more mindfully from morning yoga, chew more carefully at meals, even breathe more deeply in their quiet moments—as if by slowing down their actions, they could somehow slow down time and delay leaving this place.

Neither Chloe nor Andrew shows up for yoga this morning, and I don't see them in the dining room for breakfast either. I'm worried for them, given what Chloe said yesterday about Andrew driving off in a huff. I hope he returned safely from his excursion, and I hope the two of them made up their differences.

"Amelia!" I hear someone whisper.

Through the open window, I see Chloe sitting outside on the porch. Her heart-shaped face is radiant, almost lit from within. There are glints of golden sparkles in her wide eyes and a blush on her apple cheeks. She motions for me to join her.

Up close, I see that Chloe's cheeks aren't just blushed; they're cherry red. I detect something in the air and sniff in Chloe's general direction.

"Chloe, have you been drinking?" I ask.

Chloe holds her finger up to her lips as if shushing me.

"Just a little," she whispers. "But Andrew is out cold. Poor baby. He never did have much of a tolerance." Chloe starts giggling.

"What happened?" I ask. The cancer center doesn't serve any alcohol to guests in case of possible adverse drug interactions.

"Andrew and I were sitting on the porch this morning," she says, "waiting for the sun to rise, when we saw Hari going by."

I imagine Hari walking from the Master's Cottage to the

yoga studio after our incredible night together. In college, we used to call it the "walk of shame."

"Hari came over to chat with me and Andrew," Chloe says, "and then one thing led to another, and soon the three of us were drinking Dom Pérignon straight from the bottle. At six in the morning!"

"What were you and Andrew doing up so early?" I ask.

Chloe waggles her eyebrows and laughs. Then her face turns serious.

"It's been almost a year since Andrew and I last had sex," Chloe says. "He always said he was too tired, too stressed from work, but I didn't believe him. I figured all the scars on my body turned him off, or the idea of screwing a dying girl made him lose his mojo. After a few months, I stopped even trying. Honestly, I thought I would die never having sex again."

Chloe closes her eyes and leans her small body against mine.

"So last night," she continues, "I was taking a bubble bath after dinner when Andrew finally came back from town. We hadn't seen one another all day, not since he drove off in the morning, and I wasn't sure what kind of mood he'd be in."

Chloe stops talking, her eyes still closed.

"And then?" I ask.

"I thought about our talk on the beach," she says, "about my grand proclamation that I wanted to live as well as possible in however many weeks or months I have left. And I thought: what the hell, and I pulled Andrew into the tub with me."

"Chloe!" I say. "You little minx!"

"Let's just say, Hari wasn't the only one riding some killer waves yesterday," Chloe says, opening her eyes and grinning. "Sorry, TMI," she adds.

"That's great, Chloe," I say. "I'm so happy for you. And for Andrew."

"Speaking of Andrew," Chloe says, sitting up straight, "I was about to drive into town and get him some coffee. I think he's gonna need it this morning. Want to come along?"

"We've got coffee at our place," I say, "and I'm not sure you should be driving."

Chloe sways a little as she stands from the bench.

"Good point," she says, aiming her finger at me and jabbing me in the chest.

It's unusually warm for late October. The sun beats down on Chloe and me as we walk from the cancer center building to the Master's Cottage. All the dense fog from yesterday seems to have burned off, and the gentle ocean breeze provides welcome relief from the sun's rays.

"Oh my God, this is adorable," Chloe exclaims when I open the door to the Master's Cottage. It really is adorable: the soft-worn floors; the homely but comfy couch; the steamer trunk with its dark leather straps and tarnished brass fixtures; Maggie's hand-colored drawings hanging on the walls. I walk to the kitchenette and put some water on to boil. Chloe sits on a stool and watches me.

"How long have you and Eleanor lived here?" Chloe asks.

"We moved in this past summer," I answer, pouring the ground beans into the French press. "Along with my mother and Eleanor's daughter, Maggie."

"Wow, the four of you here?" Chloe says. She looks around the small space again.

"Yeah, it's just a temporary thing," I say. "Until we work some family stuff out."

"Where do you live normally?" Chloe asks.

How do I answer this seemingly simple question? The truth is: I'm homeless, Eleanor can't afford to stay in her San Francisco flat, and the judge evicted Mom from her Atherton home to turn over to my supposed half brother that my father never told us about. Ugh, when did the truth become so complicated?

"I told you she'd be here," Maggie says from the doorway.

Chloe and I turn toward the door. Maggie is wearing her new favorite uniform: loose-fitting khaki pants and safari shirt and a big floppy hat, just like Brandon and Leo always wear. Behind her, Brandon is carrying the same mini-fridge-sized backpack that he straps on whenever they go bird-watching. Meanwhile, Mom looks ready to play mixed doubles at the tennis club in her white Nike visor and neon-pink top and skort set.

"Are you just getting up?" Mom asks. She settles down on the stool next to Chloe. Leo comes inside and makes himself at home on our couch.

"Hi, I'm Tabitha. Amelia's mom," she says to Chloe. "That's my granddaughter, Maggie, in the doorway, Brandon's outside, and I'm sure you know Leo."

"I'm Chloe," Chloe says, smiling.

"Grandma, we need to get going," Maggie says. She's still standing in the doorway, and I can practically hear Brandon huffing in impatience behind her. "The birds are waiting.

"Aunt Amelia, are you going to join us?" Maggie asks. "You haven't been out birding in weeks."

"I need to deliver this pot of coffee to Chloe's husband over at the center," I say, happy for an excuse to avoid another boring bird-watching hike, "so I'll have to take another rain check."

"Are you going bird-watching?" Chloe asks. "If you don't mind waiting for me to drop this off with Andrew, I'd love to join you. I've never been before."

"We're in no rush at all," Leo says, jumping to his feet. "Are we, Brandon? Especially if it means the lovely Amelia and Chloe will be joining us."

Oh, Chloe, how could you betray me so? I thought we were friends.

"I'll have to change my shoes," I say, feebly trying to make an excuse.

"My sneakers are still in my closet," Mom says. "We can wait."

When I walk back into the living room wearing Mom's Gucci sneakers, I see a Scotch-plaid thermos on the counter. It looks like the one Dad used to fill with coffee for our drives to Tahoe. Mom would sit in the passenger seat of our beat-up station wagon and pass the red plastic cup to Dad, the two of them taking turns sipping while Eleanor and I snoozed or played "I Spy" in the back seat.

"Is this…?" I begin, but the words somehow get stuck in my throat.

"Yes, it's Daddy's thermos," Mom says. "Eleanor found it in our basement and brought it here. That girl is so sentimental. Of all the things in our house to pack, your sister picked this old thing, can you imagine? Well, at least we're putting it to good use today."

The group of us troop down to the main center building and wait on the porch while Chloe runs upstairs with the thermos. I sit on one of the rustic chairs and wonder which one Hari sat in just hours ago. I picture him drinking Dom straight from the bottle, getting Chloe and Andrew drunk while the sun comes up. It's such a Hari thing to do.

"How far are we going today?" I ask, putting my feet up on the porch railing.

"We're thinking of heading back to Thrashers Point," Maggie says. She sits in the chair next to me and unlaces then relaces her hiking boots. She uses double knots, just like Eleanor. "You remember that place, don't you, Aunt Amelia? The place where we spotted the tricolored blackbird."

"Amelia identified the bird before Brandon or I could even say a word. She claimed it was beginner's luck," Leo stage-whispers to Mom. "But I don't believe her. I suspect she's got a secret she's hiding from us.

"Don't you agree, Brandon?" Leo says, his voice booming.

"It's not polite to ask about people's secrets, Leo," Brandon says humorlessly.

"You're so right, my dearest Brandon," Leo says humorously. "You always are."

"Sorry to keep you waiting," Chloe says. She's changed into a T-shirt and hiking pants and pulled her hair into a ponytail slipped through the back of a Giants baseball cap. With her deep dimples and freckled face, Chloe looks barely older than a teenager.

"Shall we, ladies?" Leo asks, hooking arms with Mom and Chloe.

Maggie jumps up to lead the way, with me and Brandon pulling up the rear.

I'm famished by the time we reach the appointed spot. Brandon sets his backpack on the ground and unzips the main compartment. Maggie is quick to grab the spotting scope and set it up on the tripod, and I'm equally quick to offer to help lay out the picnic lunch.

"What are those?" Chloe asks. Her eyes are fixed on the flaky pastries that Brandon removes from a Tupperware container and places in neat rows on a rustic wooden board.

"Chicken hand pies," Leo says. "One of Brandon's specialties."

Leo reaches over to grab one of the hand pies directly from the Tupperware and receives a light wrist slap from Brandon. I can't tell if Brandon is being playful or is actually annoyed.

"To give credit where it's due," Brandon intones, "I adapted the chicken pot pie recipe from the Amuse cookbook."

I've just bit into the hand pie when Brandon says this, and my jaw drops.

"Your cookbook, Amelia," Brandon adds.

I'm about to protest that it's not really my cookbook but decide it's not worth talking about. Nils and I argued about this same thing when the book was going through the lengthy publication process. In fact, it was Nils' idea to list me as a co-author.

"But you're the chef— I'm just the hostess," I argued.

"And the muse," he said.

"They're your recipes, not mine."

"Who came up with the idea of adding fresh mint and pine nuts to the burrata salad?" he asked. "Who thought to put a Korean twist on French ratatouille with the addition of gochujang and sesame oil?"

"Yeah, so I gave you some ideas for tweaking your recipes," I said, "but that doesn't mean I'm a co-author."

Ultimately, it was the publishing company who decided.

"Sorry, Amelia, but you have no choice," the publisher's marketing director said. "This guy here might be the best chef in the freaking universe, but he's a big fat zero when it comes to promotion. People can't understand a word he says."

"I love his accent," I said. "It's so charming."

"Well, not everyone agrees," the marketing guy said. "The accent is a big problem. The folks at *CBS Sunday Morning* had to subtitle his last interview—even though he was speaking English—because no one could understand what the hell he was saying.

"You're the face of Amuse," the marketing guy said, turning to flattery, "the hostess with the thousand-watt smile, the reason people set their alarm clocks ninety days ahead to try to score a reservation. Hard-core foodies will buy the book for Nils' recipes, but regular folks will pick it up just because you're on the cover."

That's how I was made co-author.

"I have that cookbook too," Chloe says, gobbling down one hand pie before reaching for another. "Andrew got it for me as a birthday gift last year, but I've never made anything from it. I just like to stare at the pictures and drool."

I take my barely eaten hand pie and wrap it up in a napkin, as if I'm saving it for later. I'll throw it away the first chance I get. I scan the rest of the picnic spread and grab a blondie. Brandon makes the best blondies, the moist-chewy bars studded with chunks of dark-chocolate peanut butter cups.

"Andrew and I even talked about taking a vacation to New York City to eat at Amuse, but it closed before we could get a reservation," Chloe says.

"Yes, I never could understand why you decided to close Amuse, darling," Mom says to me. "You were at the peak of your success. All the newspapers said so."

"When did you start reading newspapers, Mom?" I say irritably. "I thought you got all your news from *People* magazine."

Mom turns bright pink, and I notice that Leo, Brandon, and Chloe are stunned by my sudden outburst of unkindness.

"Miss Maggie," Leo shouts to break the tension, "you've been very quiet over there! Have you seen anything notable today?" Leo stands to join Maggie at the spotting scope, and Brandon and Chloe quickly follow, giving me and Mom a wide berth.

"Sorry, Mom," I say, reaching over to squeeze her lightly freckled arm. "It's just a sensitive topic for me."

"I know you must miss Nils," Mom says, "just like I miss your dad." She gives me a sad half smile. My parents would have celebrated their forty-fourth anniversary this year. They were college sweethearts and lifelong friends. As much as I miss Dad, I know it's nothing compared to how much my mother misses him.

"To be honest, Mom, I don't miss Nils all that much," I

say. "In a way, it's a relief to be free from him." As the words come out of my mouth, I realize I'm admitting this more to myself than I am to her.

Mom turns her eyes to me but doesn't say a word.

"The first thing that drew me to Nils was his raw charisma, his sense of adventure," I say. "Going to New York after 9/11, traveling all over the world with only our passports and change of clothes, working just enough to fund our next six months of travel. He was the mad genius with a million crazy ideas, and I was the game girlfriend happy to follow along."

Brandon is standing next to Chloe and pointing toward the beach below. He looks his usual serious and steady self. I imagine him teaching her about using size, shape, color, and field markings to identify birds, the same way he taught Maggie and tried without success to teach me.

"To Nils, Amuse was just another adventure, another mountain to climb. It's like he said one day: Hey, let's see if we can open a fine dining restaurant in the toughest culinary market in the world. And I said: Sure, why the hell not? I went along with his ideas for Amuse, just like I went along with every other harebrained scheme he came up with."

"That's the sign of a good girlfriend," Mom says. "A good partner."

"Maybe," I say, not convinced.

"Anyway, Nils had the shortest attention span ever. When we were traveling, as soon as we learned how to navigate one city or country, he was ready to move on to the next, even if we were having a great time. Sure enough, as soon as Amuse got its second Michelin star and racked up a bunch of best-of awards, Nils wanted to move on. He was ready for his next challenge."

Just telling this story aloud sets my heart racing. I'm instantly pulled back to all the long talks Nils and I had over the decades. It didn't matter where the conversations occurred—

on a postcard-perfect beach in Tahiti, in a seedy apartment in Rio, or at the lavish 50 Best Restaurants in the World awards ceremony in Milan—the topic was always the same: what Nils wanted to do next.

"Anyway," I continue, "when he told me he wanted to close Amuse and open a brand-new restaurant, something changed inside of me. I was just done. I told him I wanted to break up. That I was ready to grow up, get married, maybe even start a family. He begged me for one more chance, one final adventure. He told me his vision of moving to California, opening a restaurant far away from the grind of New York City, and finally settling down. He seemed genuine in his promises—or maybe it's just that I wanted so desperately to believe those promises."

"When you told us you'd be moving back to California," Mom says, "Dad and I were over the moon. So was Eleanor."

"I'm sorry I didn't spend more time with you," I say. "But Nils and I were working 24/7 getting the new restaurant set up, and it was an eight-hour round-trip drive to Atherton."

"Don't worry about it," Mom says. She blinks away tears. "Dad and I had been planning to come up to Loca on your birthday, but it closed so quickly."

Mom stops talking, and her unasked question—why did Loca close?—hangs in the air like a gossamer filament. I reach over for Maggie's water bottle and take a big gulp, wishing it contained something stronger.

It's finally time to tell Mom the truth.

19

“The concept for Loca was extreme locavore,” I explain.

“Locavore?” Mom asks.

“Yeah, if we didn’t forage, grow, or kill the food with our own hands, we wouldn’t serve it,” I say, repeating the same line Nils and I shared with countless investors, reporters, and food bloggers. “While we were waiting for the permits to be approved and the carpenters to build out the restaurant, Nils and I focused on finding the best places to forage for mushrooms and herbs and berries, created an enormous vegetable garden, and uncovered hidden coves of mussels and oysters and crabs. We learned how to dive for abalone, make hard apple cider and blackberry wine, even grind our own acorn flour.

“Finally, after nearly a year of hard work, Loca had its grand opening,” I say. “All of the seats were filled by critics and celebrities, and everyone agreed the food was amazing. Within weeks, we were getting rave reviews in newspapers and magazines all over the world, and we were once again marching toward success.”

I pause to take a breath and notice that Brandon, Leo, Maggie, and Chloe seem to have disappeared. I scan the landscape as far as I can see, but they're nowhere to be found.

"They went down to the beach, darling," Mom says.

"That's weird they didn't invite us."

"You were in the middle of your story."

"What was I saying?" I ask.

"You were marching toward success."

"That's right. And then winter came," I say. "We started to run out of things we could forage or grow, so Nils focused on the last part—things we could kill."

"Oh my, I don't like the sound of that," Mom says.

"Yeah, neither did I. But Nils got obsessed with the idea of killing and butchering his own meat. He hired a local guide to help him stalk wild boar, but all he got for his hard-earned money was a sprained ankle and a bad case of poison oak. Once, he somehow managed to trap and kill a gray squirrel, but the meat was so stringy and gamey that we couldn't imagine serving it at the restaurant.

"And then one day, we were both in the garden when we saw a flock of blackbirds in the field nearby. Nils talked about how he used to shoot blackbirds with a BB gun when he was a kid in rural Norway. His farmer grandfather used to pay him a kroner for each bird killed. The next day, Nils went to the closest Walmart and bought an air rifle. The next thing you know, we're up to our ears in blackbirds."

I shudder thinking about the bags full of glossy black feathers Nils would give me to add to the compost pile after he was done de-feathering his victims. To his credit, Nils never made me participate in the killing or cleaning of the birds.

"That winter, the Loca menu was more delicious than ever. Our lucky guests feasted on Merle à la Mûre, or blackbirds in blackberry sauce, which was Nils' Nordic-Californian riff on duck à l'orange. Food critics couldn't find enough superlatives for our Merlo Cacciatore with hedgehog mushrooms and dry-farmed heirloom tomatoes. But everyone's hands-down favorite was Nils' locavore version of his most popular dish from Amuse: mini chicken pot pies. Which, at Loca, we called Petit Merle en Croûte."

"Did your customers know they were eating blackbird?" Mom asks. She casts a sideways glance at Brandon's chicken hand pies on the wooden board.

"I don't think so. Nils always used a foreign word for blackbird—most people were too afraid to appear unsophisticated to ask what the words meant—and for the few who did ask, we simply described it as 'a local game bird similar in flavor to squab.'"

"Tastes like chicken," Mom quips, and I'm momentarily surprised by her wit.

"Anyway, while business was booming, other aspects of Loca became more challenging. Our country neighbors didn't like all the city folks coming out to their remote neck of the woods. They complained about the traffic, the noise, the foodie entrepreneurs offering foraging tours of Mendocino County's backwoods. And then it turned out one of our neighbors was also good friends with the state fish and wildlife commissioner."

Mom shakes her head, figuring out how the story will end.

"It's completely legal to kill blackbirds," I say, "which—like Nils remembered from his childhood—are widely seen as pests. But what Nils didn't know is that some of the birds weren't ordinary blackbirds. They were tricolored blackbirds, which are classified as an endangered species."

Brandon, Leo, Maggie, and Chloe suddenly appear in the distance, their cheeks rosy with exertion from climbing the steep hill.

"It can be a felony to kill tricolored blackbirds," I say, waving in welcome to the returning birders. "Punishable by penalties of $20,000 per bird or imprisonment of up to three years in county jail."

For the rest of the bird-watching hike, Mom looks over at me like I'm a wounded animal. She keeps stroking my hair and removing invisible pieces of lint from my hoodie. This is exactly the reason I never told Mom or Eleanor or anyone about why Nils and I closed Loca and split up: I didn't want to be the pathetic object of their sympathy. I already felt bad enough about myself without everyone piling on to the Amelia pity party. Given my mother's teary reaction, I refrain from telling her the details of the pivotal final scenes of the Nils-Amelia disaster movie.

Nils and I had put in another fourteen-hour day preparing and serving an inspired twelve-course meal to our discriminating Loca patrons when we finally collapsed into bed. I was barely asleep when I heard pounding on our cabin door.

"Sheriff's department, open up," a voice shouted.

I stood behind Nils in my silky pajamas as he opened the cabin door to a barrel-chested sheriff with a couple of rifle-toting deputies providing backup.

"What's the matter, Sheriff?" Nils asked through the screen door.

"We've got reason to believe you've been engaging in unlawful activities at this establishment in violation of Section 597 of the state penal code," the sheriff shouted in a rat-a-tat voice. He sounded like Tommy Lee Jones in *The Fugitive*.

"I'm sorry, I don't understand," Nils said. From the confusion on the sheriff's face, it was clear the feelings were mutual. Nils' Norwegian accent was always more pronounced when he was tired, and in that moment, Nils was exhausted.

"Do either of you speak English?" the sheriff asked, elongating the words and looking from Nils to me and back again. As the two deputies exchanged goofy grins, I glanced down and realized my cheongsam-style pajamas made me appear as if I had just stepped out of *The World of Suzie Wong*.

"Yes, we speak English," Nils said, speaking more loudly, "I just don't understand the charge." He stepped forward to open the screen door, causing the deputies to raise their rifles.

"Hey, guys, I don't think that's necessary," I shouted, emerging from behind Nils. "We run a restaurant here. What do you think we're going to do, julienne you to death?"

Apparently, the Mendocino County sheriff's department didn't have a sense of humor or working knowledge of French cooking terms. They took my little joke as a personal threat. The sheriff and deputies handcuffed me and Nils on the spot, pushing us into separate cruisers. When we got to the sheriff's department, we used our one phone call to leave an urgent voice mail for our business lawyer in Manhattan. We spent the rest of the night in his and hers concrete-block cells, with two obnoxious drunks as Nils' cellmates and a very twitchy meth-head as mine.

Our New York lawyer referred us to a local criminal defense specialist who advised us to make a plea. He said the evidence against us was overwhelming. The sheriff's office found Nils' air rifle, boxes of BB pellets, and dozens of printed menus featuring "merle" or "merlo" (damn you, Google Translate!). But the most incriminating evidence of all was discovered outside the restaurant walls: the compost pile filled with bird feathers. It was then that I learned tricolored blackbirds have a white bar on the shoulder, distinguishing them from the more common (and not at all endangered) red-winged blackbirds.

"They're offering forty hours of community service for each of you and $200,000 total in restitution," the lawyer said. We were sitting at a four-top in Loca's dining room. "And you'd have to give up your business license."

"We'd be losing everything," Nils argued.

"You'd be keeping your freedom," the lawyer said, looking to me for support.

I surveyed the restaurant's simple interior: a half-dozen cherrywood dining tables and twenty-four matching chairs that we commissioned from the local fine woodworker, long strings of Edison bulbs that we crisscrossed along the ceiling to give the room a golden glow, an antique walnut sideboard filled with crisply ironed vintage linens and random pieces of English bone china and sterling silver flatware that we bargained for at flea markets and estate sales up and down the coast. These things were priceless to me and Nils but practically worthless to the general public. Even if you threw in the high-end kitchen appliances, I didn't see how we could raise anywhere near $200,000 in the limited time the prosecutor was willing to offer the plea deal.

"I think we should take it," I whispered to Nils.

"Well, I don't," Nils replied. He got up from the table and walked over to the open-style kitchen. He started banging around some pots and pans, searching for something to make. "What would prevent us from just leaving this country, going to live in Europe, without paying any fees or doing any community service?"

"I will pretend I didn't hear that," the lawyer said. "And I would advise you not to say that ever again. You do not want to live as fugitives on the run from the law."

I closed my eyes so the lawyer couldn't see the fury I felt in that moment. How many times had Nils and I argued about what we should do with our careers, our relationship, our money, and how many times had I given in to Nils' wishes? I'd abandoned my family, my friends, my SoHo apartment, even my hopes of getting married and having kids, all because they didn't fit with Nils' half-baked plans. But this time, it was different. This time, my very freedom was on the line.

"Tell the DA I'll accept the deal," I said, my eyes open at last. "I'll do the forty hours of community service and pay my half of the restitution—$100,000."

"And where do you think you'll get that kind of money?" Nils shouted from across the room.

There was only one person who could give me that amount of money on such short notice: Daddy. Even though I hadn't spoken to him in months, I knew my father would do anything for me, his baby girl. I also knew Dad could keep a secret.

I just didn't know back then how many secrets he kept.

By the time Eleanor and I arrive in the cancer center's dining room that evening, most of the tables are filled. Leo sits at the largest table surrounded by his adoring guests, and Chloe and Andrew sit at a smaller table with Hari and Gisela.

"Amelia, Eleanor, come join us!" Leo beckons welcomingly.

My sister and I walk over to pay our regards. Everyone at Leo's table scoots closer together, trying to make room for an extra chair.

"Don't worry about it," I say to Leo's tablemates, "I can sit over there." I gesture over to Chloe's table.

"I can't compete with the youngsters for Amelia's attentions," Leo says, "but, Eleanor, won't you please honor us with your presence?"

"Of course," Eleanor says, smiling.

Eleanor and I make our way to the lavish buffet spread. Jett's outdone himself again. From the house-cured salmon appetizer to the grilled portobello mushrooms with avocado chimichurri sauce, the curried couscous salad to the olive oil and sea-salt roasted cauliflower, everything on the buffet is healthful and delicious.

"Where are Mom and Maggie?" I ask Eleanor, piling my dish as high as it'll go.

"They went up to Leo's place to have dinner with Brandon," Eleanor says.

"Why isn't Brandon here?"

"If you haven't noticed before, Brandon doesn't eat at the center."

"Why not?" I ask.

"Because Brandon's neither a cancer center guest nor a staff member."

"Well, neither am I. Or Hari."

"I believe Brandon is a little more…" Eleanor pauses to find the right word, "reserved than the two of you."

Something about Eleanor's tone makes me wonder: Did she get home early and see the batik-print scrunchie on the doorknob this morning? Well, if she did, I'm not going to apologize for it. I'm an adult, after all, and unlike my sister, I'm not ashamed of my adult urges.

"Hey, everyone," I say as I approach Chloe's table. My tone is casual like I'm talking to the entire table, but of course I'm thinking only of Hari whom I haven't seen since last night.

"Amelia, sit next to me," Chloe says. "Andrew won't mind moving." She motions for Andrew to move to the empty chair across from her, and he picks up his plate to comply.

"Chloe was just telling us about your bird-watching hike," Hari says. He emphasizes the last two words, grinning, like he can't believe I'd do anything as dorky as that.

"Yeah, it was kind of an impromptu thing," I say.

As Chloe talks excitedly about the day's bird sightings, Hari sneaks me a sweetly sly smile. I suppress my own smile and stare down at my cauliflower.

"I'm gonna miss everything about Arcadia," Chloe says, "but mostly this food!" She holds up a forkful of the curried couscous as if to emphasize the point.

"Yeah, where is Jett anyway?" I say. "We should thank the chef."

"He ran off," Gisela says. "Right after setting up dinner."

"Ran off?" I ask.

"Yeah, he got an urgent message from the switchboard and had to leave," Gisela says.

"But he's coming back, right?" I ask.

"I don't know," Gisela says. "Probably not. It's the last retreat of the year. Most of us go back to our day jobs for the winter."

I reach for my water glass. My throat has gone unexpectedly dry. As hard as it is for me to say goodbye to the cancer center guests every month, I can't imagine saying goodbye to Jett and Gisela and the rest of the staff for the entire winter. They've become like family to me.

Over at Leo's table, Eleanor nods and smiles as Leo and their tablemates engage in playful banter. As usual, she's listening more than talking. I wonder if she knows that Jett has left, that he might not come back until spring.

"I wish I had known," Chloe says. "I'd have liked to say goodbye and thank you."

"Goodbye and good riddance is more like it," Hari mumbles.

"Hari!" Gisela says.

"What?" Hari protests. "C'mon, you may have forgiven him, but I'm not as spiritually evolved as you."

Gisela stands up, crosses the room, and refills her mug of almond milk chai. Then she sits down at another table to chat with other cancer center guests.

"Ooh," Chloe coos, leaning into Hari, "what was that all about?"

I expect Hari to hesitate, but he jumps right in with his story.

"Gisela hates when I talk about this," Hari begins, "but Jett's not the good guy everyone thinks he is. In fact, he's kind of an arrogant jerk."

Chloe and I are all ears.

"Jett and I—we go way back," Hari says. "From kindergarten through middle school, Jett and I were best buds. We were both scrawny, bad at sports, and had funny names. No one else at our fancy-pants boys' school wanted to be friends with us two dweebs, so we became friends with each other."

Jett had told me how he used to dread the first day of school when the headmaster would say his full name aloud to the entire assembly: Willow Bartholomew Jett. I'd never imagined that Hari had been witness to Jett's childhood humiliations, let alone Jett's best friend.

"By the time we reached high school, things changed," Hari says. "Jett changed. He grew practically a foot in just one summer, while I grew at a more leisurely pace." Hari pauses to flash a smile. It's true that Hari isn't very tall—five-seven or five-eight, tops—but no one would ever think twice about it. With his toned torso and sculpted limbs, Hari's a far cry from the scrawny kid he apparently once was.

"Every October, our school would hold a mixer and invite the girls from our sister school next door. We never dared to go to the dance before, but Jett decided one year that it would be cool to check it out. As soon as we arrived, I could see the girls all ogling Jett. Including one girl in particular—Gisela."

I've known for some time that Jett and Gisela had been high school sweethearts. I've even seen the photo from their prom at Hari's parents' house. But this is news to Chloe, who lets out a delighted squeal.

"Oh my God, I love this," Chloe says. "It's like a YA novel or something!"

"It gets better," Hari says.

"From that moment on, Jett and Gisela were inseparable," Hari continues. "Which, as you can imagine, was very awkward for me. Not only was my best friend dating my twin sister, but I had to help them keep it a secret from our parents."

"Why?" Chloe asks. "Why was it a secret?"

"You have to understand, Jett comes from San Francisco old money," Hari says. "His mother sits on the board of every cultural institution in the city. The Jett family donated an entire new wing to the city's main library. Our high school's dining hall even has this bronze bust of Jett's grandfather in the entryway. The blue-blood heir to the Jett family fortune isn't about to be seen with a no-name brown-skinned girl."

"Are you saying Jett's family wouldn't have approved of him dating Gisela because she's Indian?" Chloe asks. She sounds appalled.

"You got it," Hari replies.

"And would your parents have approved of Gisela dating a white boy?" I blurt.

Hari waits a beat before asking, "Why're you taking Jett's side?"

"I'm not taking anyone's side," I answer. "I'm just saying, the prejudices probably went both ways."

I know from personal experience about family prejudices. When I was in kindergarten, I asked my mom why I didn't have a grandma and grandpa to come to Grandparents' Day like all my friends did. "Your dad's parents in Korea didn't want him to marry an American girl," Mom explained, "and my parents in Ohio didn't want me to marry a Korean boy.

We were sad about it at first, but then your dad and I decided it didn't matter. 'Fine, we'll just start our own beautiful family,' we said to one another. And we did."

Mom and Dad filled our home with so much love, I never questioned the absence of grandparents ever again.

"The final straw happened our senior year," Hari says, resuming his story. "Gisela and I had gotten our Stanford admissions letters, fulfilling my immigrant parents' wildest dreams. Ever the smart cookie, Gisela seized on the moment and told my parents she wanted to go to the prom with Jett—'just as friends,' she lied—and my parents said okay. At that point, my parents were so over-the-moon happy, they would've agreed to almost anything."

It's striking how much Hari's parents have in common with my parents. When Eleanor got her admissions letter from Berkeley, Mom and Dad were so proud of her, they practically glowed. I was just excited that she would be going to college close enough so we could see each other on the weekends. That was back in the day when Eleanor and I were still thick as thieves. Little did I know that she'd fall in love with a business school student named Edward her freshman year and barely make it home for the holidays.

"While my parents knew about Gisela and Jett going to the prom together," Hari says, "Jett was too chicken-shit to tell his own parents. Instead, Jett got this blonde girl he knew from another school to pretend to be his prom date, but she was actually going to be mine. Jett's mom insisted on inviting all the guys from the varsity basketball team and their dates to come over to their Pac Heights mansion for a pre-prom party—a party that, of course, neither Gisela nor I was invited to."

"Oh, poor Gisela!" Chloe cries.

"Poor Gisela?" Hari says. "What about poor me? Anyway, Jett and the blonde girl show up late at our house because the pre-prom party ran long. Gisela was so upset, knowing that Jett had been taking photos with this other girl at his house and pretending to be going with her. We all somehow muddled through the prom, but the Monday after, Jett and Gisela broke up. Jett told Gisela he decided to turn down Stanford in favor of Yale, and he didn't think the long-distance thing would work out. Gisela was so heartbroken that she had a mini nervous breakdown and had to take a gap year in India.

"So, now you know," Hari concludes, "why Gisela and I don't see eye to eye on Jett. Gisela did some major soul-searching after her cancer experience and managed to find it in her heart to forgive Jett. But like I said before—I'm not as spiritually evolved as my sister."

Chloe, Andrew, and I silently absorb Hari's story. In a few short months, Jett has gone from being a chainsaw-wielding criminal to a rain-soaked romantic hero to an adorably dorky handyman/chef and friend. Now, it seems he was once a cowardly and callous heartbreaker. Which is the real Jett?

After an especially long and emotional dinner, all the cancer center guests head upstairs to their rooms to sleep. Hari accompanies Gisela—who still hasn't told anyone other than me and Hari about her pregnancy—back to the yoga studio, while Leo mutters something about getting home to Brandon in time for their nightly snifter of cognac.

Normally, Jett and I would clean up after dinner, but there's no Jett tonight. There's only me and Eleanor, who picks up the plates and silverware scattered around the dining room and collects them in a plastic tub. I pick up my own plate and utensils and follow her into the kitchen.

I'm feeling confused about Jett. Even though I'm upset with him for breaking Gisela's heart, that was over two decades ago. He's been so kind to me and Eleanor ever since we arrived at Arcadia. But has he really changed? When the rubber meets the road, would he ever consider bringing someone like Gisela, Eleanor, or me to meet his high-society parents?

"Did you hear Jett got called away unexpectedly?" I ask Eleanor. I grab a dirty plate from the plastic tub and scrape the bits of food into the compost bin.

"Leo told me," Eleanor responds. "I mean, he told all of us at the table." She turns on the tap to fill the basin with hot soapy water. I stand side by side with my sister at the sink, scraping dishes and lowering them into the steaming suds.

"It's the last retreat of the year," Eleanor says. "It's not like he had any reason to stick around here much longer." She sounds like she's trying to convince herself. She pulls a plate from the soapy water, gives it a swipe with a dishcloth, and passes it to me to rinse and stack in the drainer.

"Still, I would've liked to say goodbye," I reply, saying out loud what I suspect Eleanor feels but is too proud to admit.

"Isn't it enough that both Hari and Brandon are head over heels in love with you?" Eleanor says sharply. "Do you really need to add Jett to your doorknob collection?" Eleanor passes me a soapy dish, which I am too stunned to receive. The dish crashes to the ground.

"What in the world are you talking about?" I yell. "I'm not the least bit interested in your precious Jett. You might consider putting yourself out there and making your feelings known to him rather than criticizing me for caring about a friend."

The kitchen is suddenly very quiet. Eleanor looks down at her soapy hands. They are wrinkled and red from the hot water.

"I'm sorry, Ames," Eleanor whispers, not looking me in the eye. "I don't know what's gotten into me. I think I'm just exhausted from lack of sleep." Eleanor bends over to pick up the broken pieces.

"I'll take care of all this," I say, crouching down to take the jagged shards from her hand. "You go home and get some rest." And for the first time in our collective lives, Eleanor leaves the mess for me to clean up.

It takes me nearly another hour to finish washing, drying, and putting away the dishes, pots, and pans. I sweep up the floor and empty the dustpan in the garbage, where I see a pink While You Were Out phone message slip lying on top of the empty almond milk cartons. I pluck the slip out of the bin and read the handwritten note:

To: Jett
Message: A man called at 5:25pm but wouldn't leave his name. Said to tell you, "It's been arranged. There's a ticket waiting for you at the Air India counter. Flight leaves SFO at 10:30 tonight. She'll be waiting to meet you outside customs. Good luck!"

I reread the note several times trying to make sense of it. Who in the world could Jett be flying halfway around the world to meet? Why did he have to leave in such a hurry? How long will he be gone? Will he come back to Arcadia?

But the biggest question of all is: Should I tell Eleanor?

20

It's a glorious Sunday morning, and the Arcadia staff assemble on the porch of the main building to bid farewell to the guests. There are lots of hugs and more than a few tears. Eleanor, Maggie, Mom, and I stand off to the side of the building—not quite staff but not quite guests either—watching the scene. After receiving warm embraces from all the staff, Chloe walks over and pulls me aside to have a private conversation.

"Thanks for everything," Chloe says. "Keep in touch, please?" She hands me a slip of paper with her contact information.

"I will," I promise. "Just remember there's no cell service out here, so we'll probably have to communicate by snail mail or carrier pigeon."

"That's okay. Brandon explained to me that, while the passenger pigeon is extinct, several other forms of carrier pigeon are not. He even gave me this book to take home and study for the next time I come out to Arcadia." Chloe shows me a pristine copy of *The Allyn Guide to Birds of Northern California: Second Edition*.

"That Brandon—such a charming conversationalist," I say.

"He's no Hari," Chloe says, "but he's not so bad."

"No, he's not," I admit.

"You've got quite a group of eligible bachelors here at Arcadia," she says, turning her head to watch Leo and Hari laughing with the guests while Brandon sits respectfully off to the side. "Great guys one and all. I'm dying to know who you'll end up with."

"If I end up with anyone," I say, "I'll be sure to send you a carrier pigeon."

I hug Chloe's body tight to mine, knowing it might be the last time we see each other. When we pull apart, we both wipe the corners of our eyes and then start laughing.

Chloe says goodbye to Eleanor, Mom, and Maggie. The four of us watch as Chloe hurries to catch up with Andrew, who's rolling their luggage down the road to the parking lot.

After the last of the guests leaves, the staff disperses. Only Leo and Brandon remain on the porch, sitting in the deck chairs and taking in the quiet beauty of the late autumn day. There is something a little sad and lonely about the two of them together, although I can't quite put my finger on it. Reluctantly, Mom, Eleanor, Maggie, and I start walking up the hill to the Master's Cottage.

"When do the center guests come back again?" Maggie asks. There's a plaintive tone to her voice that reflects our collective mood.

"Not until next spring," Eleanor says. She reaches over to stroke her daughter's tousled hair. There's so much to look forward to in the spring: milder weather, longer days, wildflowers. Next spring, Maggie will be learning which colleges she got into.

We are almost at the crest of the hill when a dark blue Mercedes speeds past us toward the cancer center building, trailing a billowing cloud of dust.

"Who could that be?" Eleanor asks.

The Mercedes stops in front of the cancer center, and the dust starts to settle. From a distance, I see a tall African American man getting out of the driver's side. With his tailored pinstripe suit and colorful pocket square, he looks out of place here at Arcadia. He certainly doesn't look like a cancer patient.

"Oh…my… God," Eleanor says.

My sister looks like she's seen a ghost.

"What is it?" I ask.

I turn around and notice another person emerging from the passenger side of the car. He's an Asian man, dressed in bright, casual clothing like he's ready to play a round of golf at Pebble Beach. My heart stops.

"Daddy?" I say.

Mom, Eleanor, Maggie, and I watch dumbstruck as the two strangers walk up the steps of the cancer center building and talk to Leo. After a minute, Leo points toward the hill, spots the four of us standing there stock-still, and proceeds to accompany the two men toward us. Brandon stays behind on the porch.

"I'm very sorry to barge in unannounced on you like this, Mrs. Bae-Wood," the older, African American man says by way of greeting. His body language is respectful. "But my client was very eager to meet you face-to-face."

"I'm not a client," the younger, Asian man says exuberantly. "I'm their Opa—their older brother!"

"You're my brother?" I blurt.

"Amelia! The Muse of Amuse!" he says, outstretching his nicely tanned arms. "You are just as beautiful as your photo in The 100 Most Beautiful People of 2017! But what's happened to your signature hair?"

"Keep your hands off my sister," Eleanor snarls, pulling me back from the man.

"I know this is unsettling," the older man says in a soft, soothing tone. "My client flew in from Seoul to meet you in person. Neither your home nor cell numbers appears to be working. I tried to convince my client to wait until we could provide you with advance notice, but he was quite insistent."

"I don't believe we've properly met," my mother interrupts. She extends her right hand in greeting to the older man. "I'm Tabitha Bae-Wood, and these are my daughters Eleanor and Amelia, and my granddaughter, Maggie."

"I'm Douglas Park of Park and Associates," the man responds, "and I represent this man, Chong Bae."

Mom, Eleanor, and I gasp as if stung by a bee.

"Chong Bae, the younger," Mr. Park clarifies, apparently remembering that my father's name was also Chong Bae. "Your husband's son and namesake."

I instinctively shoot a glance at Eleanor, wondering whether this is the correct use of the word *namesake* and then realizing what a stupid thing that is to be wondering at a moment like this.

"Now that I've introduced you," Mr. Park says, "I need to excuse myself. Legal ethics prevents me from speaking with you without your counsel present." Mr. Park leans over to the younger man—my supposed half brother—and whispers, "I'll wait for you in the car."

"I should excuse myself too," Leo says halfheartedly.

"Oh, don't be silly," my mother says, grabbing Mr. Park and my supposed half brother by the arm. "It's a long drive from San Francisco—you must both be tired. Let's sit down inside the cottage, and Eleanor can make us some refreshments. And, Leo, don't even pretend you're not dying to join us!"

"Actually, we came even farther—from Atherton," my supposed half brother says. "What a beautiful home! And so comfortable! I haven't slept so well in years."

Eleanor visibly blanches. Mr. Park gives my supposed half brother a pointed stare indicating that it's not cool to talk about sleeping in the beautiful home that he stole from us.

"Thank you for vacating your home so promptly," Mr. Park says to my mother. "I'm sorry for any inconvenience it may have caused you."

My mother opens the front door of the Master's Cottage, and it's clear from Mr. Park's and my supposed half brother's faces that they now realize the extent of the inconvenience they have caused us. Compared to our mansion in Atherton, the cottage is little more than a tool shed.

Mom ushers Leo and my supposed half brother to the couch. Maggie bids a hasty retreat to her bedroom, realizing it would be a good idea to get out of the line of fire. Eleanor, Mr. Park, and I linger by the front door, ready to bolt at a moment's notice.

"Now, Eleanor, don't just stand there," Mom says. "Why don't you run and make our guests a nice pot of tea?" Eleanor glares at Mom for a moment before stomping to the kitchenette like a petulant child.

"And, Mr. Park, I'm sure we could squeeze together and make room for you," Mom says. She motions for Leo to scoot over to make some space for the pin-striped lawyer.

"Really, Mrs. Bae-Wood," Mr. Park says, "I must leave."

Mom stands up, grabs Mr. Park by the hand, and forces the uptight lawyer to sit next to her. Somehow the four of them—Leo, Mom, Mr. Park, and my supposed half brother—manage to sit together on the creaky old couch that usually accommodates just two.

Most people would find this situation awkward, sitting shoulder-to-shoulder between the man who claims to be your dead husband's firstborn secret son and the man who filed the civil lawsuit that got you evicted from your home, but Mom looks tickled pink. She seems genuinely fascinated by these two strangers, peppering them with questions about their drive to Arcadia, their marital status, their hobbies and activities. It's like watching an extremely bizarre version of *The Bachelorette.*

With no place to sit and nothing to add to the conversation, I walk over to the kitchenette, where Eleanor is staring at the electric kettle waiting for the water to boil. I'm tempted to crack a joke but see from her face that my sister's in no mood for hilarity.

"Need any help?" I ask.

"Do you know any good exterminators?" Eleanor says through gritted teeth. "Because I need to get rid of a couple rats."

My mind is going all over the place at a thousand miles per hour. I've trusted Eleanor to handle every detail of Dad's estate, but now I'm questioning myself—and her.

"Ellie, did you know," I begin, my voice tentative.

The kettle clicks off, indicating that the water is boiled. Eleanor pours the hot water into the ceramic teapot.

"Did you know…" I say again. I pause to think how to phrase the question.

"Did I know what?" Eleanor asks. She arranges some store-bought shortbread cookies on a pretty plate, tucking a few fresh raspberries in between for color. Despite her fury, my sister can't help but be the perfect hostess.

"Did you know he looks just like Dad?" I muster the courage to blurt.

I hold my breath, fearing Eleanor's reaction, but she doesn't say anything. Even she can't deny the resemblance.

"That doesn't prove anything," Eleanor finally answers. "I mean, he could have had his face fixed to resemble Dad's. Everyone knows South Korea is the plastic surgery capital of the world." Eleanor picks up the tray with the teapot and cups and saucers, and motions for me to bring the plate of cookies.

Mom is still chattering away when Eleanor and I emerge from the kitchenette and set the tea and cookies on the steamer trunk. There is a buzzing of "oh, how lovely" and "you shouldn't have gone to all this trouble" murmurs of appreciation.

Everyone watches Eleanor as she pours the tea into the cups, which lets me sneak a closer peek at my supposed half brother. It really is uncanny how much he looks like Dad. He has the same broad forehead, the same bushy eyebrows, the same Julia Roberts-meets-Joker mouth—the same mouth that I have. These aren't the kind of features that plastic surgery could fake, are they? Eleanor passes the cups to each of the guests on the couch. When she passes the cup to my supposed half brother, I hear a gentle ping. It sounds musical, like a bell.

It's only then that I notice a flash of color on my supposed half brother's wrist. It's a small jade turtle on a bright red string. "A special friend gave that to me a long time ago," my father told me when I first saw the bracelet in his lacquered wooden box.

"Opa," I say, reaching for Chong Bae's hand. We raise our joined hands together like Olympic medalists on the podium so that everyone can see our matching bracelets. Chong Bae's eyes crinkle as he smiles, and in that moment, it feels like I have my dad back.

"Don't call him Opa!" Eleanor shouts, practically ripping our hands apart. Both Chong Bae and I are stunned by the physical intrusion.

"What's an Opa?" Leo whispers.

"Older brother," Mom whispers back.

"I think you should both leave," Eleanor says, staring bullets into Chong Bae and Mr. Park. She's got her arms crossed, legs wide. The Wonder Woman power pose. The two men get up from the couch, but Mom pulls them back down. I'm surprised by how strong Mom is. Must be all those Pilates classes.

"Now, now, Eleanor," Mom says, "you're being ridiculous."

"I'm being ridiculous?" Eleanor shouts. "Me? You're sitting here making small talk with the two men who threw you out of your own home, and I'm the one being ridiculous?"

"Well, technically..." Chong Bae begins.

"Do. Not. Talk!" Eleanor shouts at him. "Do not say a single word!"

"We should go now," Mr. Park whispers to Chong Bae.

"Once again, I'm so sorry to have intruded on you, Mrs. Bae-Wood," Mr. Park says to Mom, bowing in respect. "I'm so very deeply sorry—for everything."

Leo, Mom, Eleanor, and I are silent as the two men leave the Master's Cottage. Eleanor's normally kind and generous face has turned to stone. I hesitate before asking, "Eleanor, what in the world is going on?"

"Dad is dead," Eleanor says. "Don't destroy his memory by believing their lies."

Winter

21

"Merry Christmas, Aunt Amelia!"

Maggie jumps on the bed and snuggles next to me. She's wearing her candy-cane-striped flannel pajamas, and her hair is a tangle of dark curls. I roll over to give her a sleepy hug. It feels comforting to have this warm body so close. After more than six months of sharing a bed—first with Eleanor at Arcadia and then with Hari at his Nob Hill penthouse—it feels strange to me to be sleeping alone in Eleanor and Maggie's San Francisco flat.

Technically, I'm not sleeping alone. Maggie and I have been bunkmates, with my niece occupying the upper bunk and me the lower one. The visiting doctor and his family who were renting Eleanor's place went home to Germany for the month of December, so the Bae-Wood women decided to decamp from Arcadia—which felt especially cold and lonely with the cancer center guests, staff, and volunteers gone for the season—and spend Christmas and New Year's in the city.

Eleanor's place is your classic San Francisco flat: three bedrooms and one bathroom with a living room and kitchen on the upper floor of a two-story Edwardian house. The downstairs unit is occupied by an older Chinese couple who seem to keep to themselves most of the time, although I once met the wife in the basement laundry area shared by the two households.

Things have been strained between Eleanor and me ever since Chong Bae showed up uninvited at Arcadia and we had that lucky charm bracelet bonding moment. I spent most of the late fall at Hari's place to avoid Eleanor and her cold shoulder treatment, but Maggie said all she really wanted for Christmas was to spend the holidays together as a family, which is how we ended up as bunkmates. I can never deny my niece anything, plus I don't have the money to get her a real gift.

Despite the simmering tension, it's been fun being part of Eleanor and Maggie's holiday traditions. We spent nearly a full hour at the Christmas tree lot debating the relative merits of spruce versus fir before finally settling on a ten-foot Noble Fir. Eleanor and Maggie filled every inch of the kitchen counters with baking sheets and cooling racks of hand-decorated Christmas cookies, while Mom and I taste-tested each batch. We sipped mugs of mulled wine (or spiced cider for Maggie) as Eleanor plucked delicate blown-glass ornaments from their storage boxes and hung them on the tree.

Last night, instead of having a traditional Christmas Eve meal, the four of us went to a little Vietnamese place on Clement Street to feast on crispy roast pork banh-mi and steaming bowls of chicken pho. Apparently, it's something Edward and Eleanor started doing when my sister was pregnant with Maggie and suffering from bad morning sickness. The elderly owners greeted Eleanor and Maggie like lifelong friends. Just before going to bed, Eleanor and Maggie set out a plate of sprinkle cookies on the fireplace hearth beneath the monogrammed stockings and evergreen garland. Life with Eleanor sometimes feels like living in a Hallmark commercial.

"Girls, it's time to open gifts," Mom says, peeking her head through Maggie's bedroom door. "Ellie's been bustling about for hours, waiting for you to wake up."

Maggie and I make our way to the living room, and I'm stunned by the pile of wrapped packages under the tree. I have no idea when Eleanor found the time to go shopping, let alone to wrap the gifts so festively. On top of her normal schedule, Eleanor's been working extra shifts at the hospital. She claims it's to cover for the nurses who need to travel to visit their families, but I suspect my sister wanted an excuse to keep away from me.

A video of a crackling fire plays on the television while Maggie acts as Santa, picking out the gifts from under the tree and passing them to their designated recipient.

"This one's for you, Grandma," Maggie says, "from me."

Mom tears off the wrapping paper to reveal a framed watercolor painting of wildflowers.

"California poppies," Mom says. "Grandpa's and my favorites. Thank you, sweetheart. You're so thoughtful...and talented."

"And this one's for you, Aunt Amelia," Maggie says. "From Grandma."

"Mom, you didn't have to get me a present," I say, and Mom waves vaguely as if to indicate, "it's nothing." Inside the wrapping are two new pairs of yoga pants and a zip-up hoodie.

"The tags are still on," Eleanor says, "in case you want a different size or style."

"These are perfect," I say, making a show of admiring the fabric. We exchange smiles. Mine is genuine; I hope Eleanor's is as well. The two of us have barely spoken a direct word to one another all week. I'm hoping things will thaw as the days pass.

In the evening, Mom and I are sitting at the kitchen table pinching off the ends of the French green beans while Elvis Presley croons "Blue Christmas" on the stereo speakers. The landline rings.

"I bet it's Hari," Maggie says. She's standing at the kitchen sink and dumping a pot of boiled russet potatoes into a colander. Maggie loves mashed potatoes. She makes them with two whole sticks of Irish butter and tons of heavy cream. They're a heart attack waiting to happen, but what a lovely way to go. Eleanor peeks into the oven and checks on the prime rib. The heat gives her face a rosy glow.

"It's Hari," Mom agrees.

I rush to the landline and check the digital screen.

"Hey, Hari," I say into the handset. I glance over at my mother, who exchanges a smirk with Maggie.

"Hey, beautiful," Hari murmurs. "How's Christmas?"

"Couldn't be better," I say, aware that every ear in the room is attuned to my every word. I shrug a halfhearted apology to Mom for leaving her with all the green beans and make a quick escape to Maggie's bedroom. Like a lovesick teenager, I lie down on the bottom bunk with the cordless receiver glued to my ear.

For the past two months, Hari and I have been nearly inseparable. After the final retreat of the season, my daily routine went up in smoke: no morning yoga class, no helping Jett in the kitchen, no new cancer center guests to greet, no torturously long hikes with Brandon or wine-soaked evening meals at Leo's. Instead, I found myself spending hour upon hour with Hari, exploring the hidden parts of the Northern California coast, venturing out to the latest hot spots in the city, or lounging in bed in Hari's condo apartment atop the luxurious Fairmont Hotel.

Being with Hari has been revelatory. For nearly twenty years, Nils had been my only partner, sexual and otherwise. While things were passionate early on, Nils became so preoccupied with himself and his own agenda that he seemed to lose interest in me or my needs. Hari meanwhile seems to delight in my every pleasure.

"Was Santa good to you?" Hari asks on the phone.

"Yes, very," I say. "But I felt awful not being able to give anything in return."

"Your presence is your present," Hari says. "I read that on an e-vite once."

"How about you?" I ask.

"I'm miserable without you. The maid just did the laundry, so I don't even have your scent to keep me company. And there was nothing in the fridge but a bottle of Dom and your leftovers from Henry's."

"You better not have eaten my Kung Pao Shrimp," I say.

"It went really well with the Champagne. Best breakfast I've had all day."

"You rotten scoundrel!"

"I love it when you talk dirty to me," Hari growls.

"And I love…" I whisper.

"Yes?" he whispers back.

"The tantalizing aroma of prime rib wafting over from the kitchen," I say.

"Ooph! You sure know how to hurt a guy," Hari says. "I told you I'll be having a vegan dinner tonight. Probably nothing but a pile of acorns and twigs."

"Hey, I invited you over here for dinner. You're the one who said no to me."

"I didn't say no to you," Hari says. "I just said yes to Gisela.

I didn't have the heart to turn her down. I think the pregnancy hormones are making her extra-clingy."

Earlier in the week, Hari had told me that, with their parents out of the country, Gisela insisted he come over to Sausalito for a family Christmas dinner with her and her partner, Sage.

"Trust me," Hari continues, "I'd give anything to come over right now and partake of your juicy prime rib."

"Now who's talking dirty?" I purr.

"Aunt Amelia?" Maggie says, walking into the room.

"What, sweetie?" I say, worried that she heard my last comment.

"You've never called me sweetie before," Hari says.

"I'm not talking to you," I answer, laughing.

"Aunt Amelia?" Maggie says again.

I cover the phone receiver so Hari can't hear.

"What, sweetie?" I say.

"Mom wanted me to tell you dinner's almost ready."

"Okay, I'll be right there," I say.

When Maggie leaves the room, I put the receiver back to my ear.

"Dinner's ready," I say. "I gotta go now."

"Could I swing by on the way back from Sausalito?"

"Sure," I say, "but we'll have to keep it short. We've got a full lineup of holiday movie classics tonight."

"Like I said, you sure know how to hurt a guy," Hari says. "But I'm hoping you'll help me get over it when I stop by later."

"Call me when you're leaving Gisela's."

"Will do," he says.

"Aunt Amelia, it's time," Maggie says, coming back into the bedroom. I try not to be annoyed; I know she's just doing Eleanor's bidding. I crawl out of bed and follow Maggie into the kitchen. My family is waiting for me.

★★★

The gentle beep of a car horn wakes me from my upright nap. Michael Caine is shouting, "The spirits have done it all in one night!" Like me, Mom and Eleanor seem to have nodded off, but Maggie's eyes are glued to the closing scene of *The Muppet Christmas Carol.*

"It's Hari," Mom mumbles, her eyes still closed.

"Of course, it is," Eleanor mumbles back, her eyes also still closed.

"Sorry to wake you guys," I say.

I walk into the hallway to grab a jacket. Maggie follows me.

"You're not leaving, are you?" she whispers.

"I'm just going down to say hello and Merry Christmas," I assure her. "I'll come back up in a jiffy. I promised you I'd stay here through New Year's, and I'm a woman of my word. No need to pause the movie. I've seen it a million times." I give Maggie a quick kiss on the cheek before heading outside. Hari's car is parked in our driveway.

"You didn't call," I say as I get into the car.

"Sorry, I forgot," he says. "I was in such a rush to see you." He holds my face in his hands and kisses me. His tongue is soft and warm as it explores my mouth.

"That's a good apology," I say, pulling back to catch my breath. I check to see if Eleanor or Mom are watching from the second-floor windows, but the curtains are drawn shut.

"Merry Christmas," Hari says, handing me a gift bag.

The trademark robin's-egg blue makes my heart skip a beat. I reach into the bag and pull out a medium-sized box tied with a glossy white ribbon. The box is too big to hold a ring—not that I expected a ring.

I tug on the ribbon, which unravels like a sigh, and inside the box is a sleek silver iPhone in a robin's-egg blue pebbled leather casing.

"I got tired of not being able to text you," Hari says.

"It's beautiful," I say.

"It's limited edition," Hari says. "Check out the back."

I take the phone out of the box and turn it over. There, on the backside, is one of those loopy things you use to hold the phone on your finger like a ring. Except this ring looks just like the iconic platinum-set, six-prong engagement ring.

"Try it on," Hari urges.

The simulated diamond is laughably large, like something only a rap star or professional athlete would be ballsy enough to give his fiancée. I slip the loop on my ring finger and flash it playfully like a real engagement ring.

As much as I want to make a joke about it, there's something unsettling about seeing this ridiculous ring on my hand. There were countless times when Nils and I would be walking past jewelry stores in New York, Paris, London, Seoul, and I'd secretly harbor this pathetic hope that Nils would say, "Hey, let's go inside and check out some rings—just for fun." But he never did.

Now, I feel relieved that Nils and I never got married. If anything, I'm frustrated with myself for having squandered so many years in his self-absorbed orbit. What I wouldn't give to have those years back.

"I love it," I say, leaning over to show Hari how much. We kiss and kiss some more until Eleanor's front porch light comes on and the living room light turns off.

"I better go," I say, reluctantly pulling myself away.

"Yes, I suppose so," Hari sighs a bit more heavily than usual.

"Everything okay?" I ask.

"Everything's great," he says, kissing me lightly on the forehead. "It's just my parents are coming back into the country this week, and there's something very important I need to discuss with them. Something I've delayed talking about for far too long."

In that moment, I sense something different in Hari. Maybe it's the softness in his liquid brown eyes or the tenderness in his raspy voice. He seems vulnerable, almost boyish.

"Wish me luck?" he asks, kissing each of my fingertips.

The word *luck* gives me an idea.

"Wait," I say, "I have something for you."

Hari looks at me with bemused curiosity as I wiggle my lucky charm bracelet off my right wrist and untie the red silk knot.

"I want this back at some point," I say, "but consider this a long-term loan. I hope it will bring you all the luck you deserve." I reach for Hari's right hand and tie the red string around his wrist. Hari strokes the small jade turtle and then kisses the spot on my wrist where the turtle once lived. As I open the car door to leave, he says to me:

"The only luck I need is you."

22

"Are you sure the library is open?" I ask, not for the first time.

"Yes, Aunt Amelia," Maggie says with the patience of a saint. "I checked the library website. Twice."

Sure enough, when Maggie and I arrive at the local public library, the sign in the front is flipped to OPEN. The Richmond branch is one of those classic Andrew Carnegie libraries with an impressive sandstone façade, heavy oak door, and leaded windows. This being San Francisco, the library is flanked by two tall palm trees, and there's a pair of elderly Chinese women sitting on a bench out front, feeding a flock of pigeons.

Maggie leads me through the high-ceilinged reading room where patrons of all ages and colors sit at long wooden tables perusing books and magazines. We pass by the neatly organized shelves of books in Russian, Chinese, Spanish, Korean, and yes, even English. We settle inside a small private room outfitted with a table, two chairs, and most important of all, an electric outlet and Wi-Fi password.

"Wow, is that one of yours?" I ask as the screen saver on Maggie's laptop appears. It's a delicate watercolor of the bluff at Arcadia where Hari and I first met. My talented niece has captured the beauty and tranquility of the place without any trace of artifice or sentimentality.

"Yeah," Maggie says bashfully. "Mr. Allyn scanned a bunch of my art so I could use them for my portfolio." She quickly opens the settings icon on her laptop and hooks up to the library's Wi-Fi.

"I recycled a couple of my essays from the UC applications," Maggie explains, clicking through the Mount Holyoke online application form. "You don't want to go over them again, do you?"

"Nope," I say. The University of California application deadline was almost a month ago, and I already read and reviewed Maggie's essays.

"The only thing I really need you to review is my essay about 'Why Holyoke?'" Maggie says. She clicks SAVE on the application and opens a Word file.

"I've always been taught to color inside the lines," the essay begins. "Until senior year, that's what I did. But I'm tired of playing it safe, doing exactly what everyone expects, trying to please everyone around me. In this college admission process, I want to focus on the one person who should matter most: me."

Reading these words takes my breath away. The other college essays Maggie asked me to review were well-written but, honestly, rather dry. One essay described her interests in drawing and reading and her plan to major in fine art with a minor in English literature. Another essay was about her volunteering experience with the local food bank. This essay feels different from the others. This essay provides insight into Maggie's thoughts, hopes, and dreams. This essay is personal.

"I'm going to get a boba tea while you review this," Maggie says. "Text me when you're ready for me to come back. No hurry."

I nod and pull my chair closer to the table. As I read through Maggie's essay, I'm struck by how familiar her sentiments are to mine at the same age. The same undercurrent of frustration—or it is resentment?—at the pettiness of high school. The same crippling anxiety about leaving the security of home accompanied by the ardent desire to leave everything behind and branch out on one's own.

I think about the two decades since I left home and set out for college in Western Mass. Did things turn out the way I had hoped? Sure, I was able to chart my own course, make my own mistakes, defy my parents' expectations, but where did it get me? Single and childless at the age of thirty-nine, unemployed and broke, wholly dependent on the charity of my older sister to keep me housed and fed and clothed. Is that what I want for my sweet Maggie? Maybe Eleanor is right. Maybe Maggie should stay closer to home and focus on a practical major like accounting or nursing. Why am I encouraging her to move all the way across the country and try to make it as an artist?

A man of indeterminate age with a weary face and mismatched shoes peers into the glass window of my room. His windbreaker is torn and flimsy, reminding me of the paper-thin hoodie I wore for so many months before Eleanor convinced me to put it in her ragbag. I can't imagine how cold this homeless man must feel on foggy San Francisco nights.

My cell buzzes. I pick up my Bling Phone and see a text from Maggie: Do U want a boba? Or egg puff? In line now.

Sure, boba would be great, I text back. Thai iced tea pls. Come back anytime. I'm almost done.

By the time Maggie returns to the library, I've marked up her essay with some suggested edits. Less passive voice. Don't repeat the word *amazing* so often. Truth be told, the essay was fine as written, but I want to demonstrate my value. I remember how Brandon had told Maggie back at his cottage that I'd be a good person to review her essays, that I knew how to tell a good story, and for some reason, it's important to me to prove him right.

I sip on my Thai iced tea and watch Maggie as she makes and saves the edits to her essay. Then she double-checks every page of the online application, clicking OK and NEXT several times before finally getting to the payment screen.

Payment screen?

I nearly choke on a ball of tapioca as it lodges in my throat. How are we going to pay the sixty-dollar application fee for Holyoke? If I were a good aunt, a real grown-up, I'd have a credit card that I could whip out to pay for my only niece's admissions application to her dream college. If Maggie uses her mother's credit card or even her own Teen Saver banking account, Eleanor will surely notice it on the monthly statement, ruining everything. Eleanor would blow her top if she knew I was encouraging Maggie to apply to a school far beyond the mother-approved five-hour driving radius of San Francisco. She'd most likely kick me out of the house and force Maggie to withdraw the application before it could even be considered.

While these thoughts are racing in my brain, Maggie fishes her hamburger wallet from her backpack—I got the wallet for her a few Christmases ago because it reminded me of the hamburger phone in *Juno*—and pulls out a small strip of paper.

"What's that?" I ask.

"Mr. Allyn gave me his credit card number to use for Holyoke," Maggie says.

"That's awfully trusting of him," I say.

"He said I seemed trustworthy," Maggie answers. She stifles a giggle.

"What's so funny?" I ask.

"It's funny that he finds me trustworthy even though he knows I'm doing all of this behind Mom's back."

Hearing the words from my niece's mouth puts the situation in stark relief: Maggie is sneaking around behind Eleanor's back, and Brandon and I are helping her. I feel simultaneously guilty at our deception and grateful to have someone like Brandon as a partner in crime.

"Congratulations, your application has been successfully submitted," it says on the screen. The hint of a smile on Maggie's face erupts into a huge grin.

"I'm officially finished with my college apps," she says. She closes her laptop and slips it into her backpack. She looks jubilant, and I give her a high five.

"Now, all we need to do is wait," I say.

"Did you go to the library today?" Eleanor asks Maggie.

Eleanor just got back from work, and the four of us are sitting at the kitchen table eating leftovers from Christmas dinner. Maggie's fork stops midway to her mouth, and she gives me a panicked look. When I was young, I used to think Eleanor had ESP because she seemed to know when I was about to do something even before I did it. I still sometimes wonder about Eleanor's superpowers.

"Uh, yeah," Maggie says, gulping down her forkful of mashed potatoes. "Why?"

"I just saw the stack of Blu-rays," Eleanor says. "*The World According to Garp, Dead Poets Society, Good Will Hunting.* They're some of Amelia's and my favorites. Are you doing a Robin Williams marathon?"

"Yeah," Maggie lies convincingly. "He's amazing."

The real reason I chose the movies was to give my California born-and-bred niece an education in all things New England: woolen sweaters and L.L.Bean duck boots and summers on the Cape. The fact that Robin Williams, one of my favorite actors ever, happens to star in all of them was just icing on the cake.

"If everyone's done eating," Eleanor says, "I'll do the dishes while you start the movies. We need to return them to the library before we head back to Arcadia this weekend."

"Speaking of this weekend," Mom begins. She pushes aside her half-eaten plate of food and takes a long sip from her glass of red wine. "Leo called to make sure we're coming to the party on Saturday night."

"A New Year's Eve gala at the Jett mansion?" I ask. "Wouldn't miss it for the world."

"How about you, Eleanor?" Mom yells toward the sink.

Eleanor shuts off the water and stares down at her soapy hands.

"I don't know," she says, "I'm thinking I'll just stay home with Maggie and rock in the new year with Dick Clark." She pulls a clean dishcloth from the drawer and starts drying the few dishes in the drainer before putting them away in the cabinets.

"Didn't Dick Clark die, like, ten years ago?" I ask. I pull out my Bling Phone to google it. How quickly I have fallen back into my technology-addicted ways.

"Eleanor, don't be ridiculous," Mom says. "All four of us have to go to the party. It's a fundraiser for Arcadia! And don't pretend you're not dying to see Jett again. Now that Amelia's practically engaged to Hari, you don't have any reason to hold yourself back."

My heart thumps as Eleanor marches across the kitchen.

"I think you've had enough," Eleanor says. She reaches for Mom's wineglass.

"Pish-posh, Eleanor," Mom says. Instead of handing over

her glass, Mom hands Eleanor her dirty plate. "You haven't had nearly enough."

"I've never been to a gala before," Maggie says in a transparent effort to distract. "What should I wear?" Eleanor glances over at her daughter's wide-eyed innocence.

"I probably have a little black dress that'll fit you," Eleanor says. "And I'm sure your grandmother has a shiny necklace or something to fancy it up."

"Don't listen to your mother, dear," Mom says to Maggie. "This is an occasion for a new ball gown, not a boring old dress from Talbots' evening collection circa 1999. The four of us will have to go to Union Square tomorrow to get something suitable to wear."

"You may have forgotten, Mother, but our bank accounts aren't exactly flush these days," Eleanor says. "So, unless a fairy godmother shows up soon, I don't think we're in any position to be acting the part of Cinderella this New Year's."

"My point exactly," Mom says. She strides over to the sideboard, squints as she holds up the bottle of red wine to the overhead light, and empties the contents into her glass. "How are you expected to snag Prince Charming wearing nothing but rags?"

I gather the remaining dishes off the table and set them on the counter next to the sink for Eleanor to wash, while Maggie takes a damp dishcloth and wipes the table clean. Then we both perch at the kitchen counter, watching the conversation volley back and forth between Mom and Eleanor like a Grand Slam tennis match.

"We're hardly going to be wearing rags," Eleanor says. "And besides, Amelia's the only one doing any snagging these days, and I don't think Prince Hari cares what she wears."

"Don't underestimate your old mother," Mom says, "I used

to turn quite a few heads in my younger days. Perhaps I'll be the one snagging an eligible bachelor at the ball."

Eleanor and I exchange surprised looks while Mom smiles in a self-satisfied way.

"Now that you mention it," I say, "you are looking pretty foxy these days, Mom. Which Prince Charming are you hoping to sweep off his feet?" Color blooms on my mother's freckled chest and rises to her high cheekbones.

"Grandma," Maggie says, "are you blushing?"

"I bet it's Leo!" I shout. "Or maybe Mom's got her heart set on Brandon."

"I'm not against considering a younger man," Mom admits coyly.

"OMG!" Maggie says, drawing out each syllable. "Grandma and Mr. Allyn?"

"Now, now, don't go jumping to conclusions..." Mom protests.

"I know Mr. Allyn's been really lonely ever since his wife died," Maggie says.

"What do you know about Brandon's wife?" I ask. I never did figure out a discreet way to ask Leo or Brandon about that wedding photograph in Brandon's study.

"Only that she died of some rare kind of cancer," Maggie says. "And that she's Leo's younger sister. That's how Mr. Allyn found out about Arcadia, and the reason why Leo decided to buy it."

Now, all the pieces are starting to come together. I must admit that I'd wondered if Leo and Brandon were the married couple in the photograph, but this makes more sense. Somehow the relationship between Leo and Brandon never struck me as romantic.

"I think it would be really nice if you and Mr. Allyn got

together, Grandma," Maggie effuses. "That way, the two of you could keep each other company."

Mom leans over to kiss Maggie on the cheek.

"Thank you, sweet Maggie," Mom says, "but I don't think that's in the cards. Anyone with eyes can see poor Brandon's smitten by your aunt Amelia, but she's too preoccupied with Prince Hari to notice."

"I wouldn't be so quick to dismiss Maggie's matchmaking skills, Mom," I say. "I could totally see you and Brandon as a couple. There's a certain *Something's Gotta Give* appeal to the idea."

Seriously, if Diane Keaton can get Keanu Reeves—playing a doctor, no less!—to fall hopelessly in love with her, then my glam mom should definitely be able to snag a middle-aged fuddy-duddy like Brandon.

"Enough of this silly talk," Eleanor says, shooing us out of the kitchen. "Go and start the movie. I'll bring out the popcorn."

Robin Williams is dressed in drag, attending his sainted mother's memorial service. Mom and Maggie are cuddled together under the fleece throw, while Eleanor sits in the plaid armchair and wipes away tears with her shirtsleeve. I've always thought of *Garp* as a comedy, but I forgot how much sadness there was in it. Maybe you become more attuned to sadness as you get older.

My Bling Phone quietly buzzes.

"It's Hari," my mother, sister, and niece all say at once.

I check the screen.

"Hi, Hari," I say, leaving the room. "What's up?"

"Just checking in before I head to bed," he says.

"How was vegan Christmas dinner at Gisela's?"

"Let's just say my jaw muscles got an excellent workout,"

he says. "And my bowel movements should be very regular for a good long time."

"Ewww," I say. "TMI."

"There's no such thing as TMI between soul mates," Hari says.

Did Hari just call us soul mates?

"So, when are your parents coming back?" I ask. "I'd love to meet them."

"Rigo just texted me that they're flying into SFO tomorrow," Hari says. "And they're going to the Arcadia thing on Saturday. You can meet them then."

"Your parents are going to the fundraiser?" I ask.

"Gisela insisted they come," Hari says. "Or, more accurately, Gisela insisted they write a big fat donation check, gala attendance optional. My parents said if they're going to make out a check with that many zeroes, they might as well get a decent dinner out of it. Besides, my mom can never pass up the chance to pull out her finest jewels and flaunt them for all the so-called high-society dames to drool over."

"Now I'm getting nervous," I say. I hadn't thought about the other attendees at the gala.

"Nothing to be nervous about," Hari says, sounding uncharacteristically nervous.

"I don't have anything appropriate to wear," I say.

"I've loaded my Amex on your phone," Hari says. "Buy whatever your heart desires. Just make sure it's sexy and sophisticated. I want to show you off."

"Besides you, Gisela, and Leo," I ask, "will there be anyone else I know at the party?"

"Anyone in particular you're wondering about?"

"Brandon?" I ask, remembering Maggie's matchmaking idea. I imagine that Brandon would look handsome in a tux. He's certainly got the height and posture for it. A mental image of Brandon and Mom standing together pops into my head. They remind me of the bride and groom figurines on top of the wedding cake only with graying hair and wrinkles.

"Brandon? No idea," Hari says. "I thought you might be asking about Jett."

"I assumed Jett would be there Saturday," I say. "After all, it's at his parents' house."

None of us have seen Jett since he abruptly left Arcadia on the last night of the last retreat over two months ago. I never told anyone—not Hari, not Mom, and certainly not Eleanor—about the pink message slip I found in the garbage that night. Why was he in such a rush to leave? And who was the "she" he was so eager to meet?

"It's hard to predict what Jett will do," Hari says. "Particularly if it involves his parents. They've got this weird power play relationship. As much as I hate Jett for how he treated my sister, I suspect it was his parents and not him who put the kibosh on their relationship. They probably threatened to cut off his trust fund if he continued to date Gisela. Why else would he have turned down Stanford and run off to Yale? I mean, Yale sucks."

It's weird to think of Jett going to Yale. He doesn't seem the stuffy Ivy League type. It's weirder still to think of him as a trust fund baby. You wouldn't know it by his casual clothes and down-to-earth demeanor. Then again, maybe being filthy rich is what gives Jett the freedom to not care about material things.

"I hear his parents practically disowned him when he refused to get his MBA and went to cooking school instead," Hari continues. "But now that the senior Mr. Jett is getting on in years, I'm sure Jett will buckle down and play the role of obedient son. He can't afford to be cut out of the will now."

"Speaking of wills," I say, "don't breathe a word of this to anyone, but I've arranged to meet Chong Bae on Wednesday."

"You mean your supposed half brother?" Hari asks. "What for?"

"To discuss my dad's will—or, rather, his lack of will. Eleanor assured me and Mom that settling Dad's estate should be straightforward despite the absence of a will because my parents were married for so long. Even if Chong Bae were able to prove he was Dad's child, California law would entitle Mom to all their community property and a share of any other property Dad might have had. It doesn't make sense why the judge gave Chong Bae everything."

"How do you suddenly know so much about California law?" Hari asks.

"There's this amazing function on the phone you gave me," I say. "It's called Google. Have you heard of it?"

"Soon you'll be arguing cases before the Supreme Court," Hari teases.

"I just don't understand how we could have lost everything," I say.

"Maybe your sister's not being fully honest with you."

Or maybe she's not being fully honest with herself, I think.

23

"What do you think about this one?" I ask. I emerge from the dressing room, twirl around in a circle, and inspect my reflection in the floor-length mirror. I'm not quite sure how I feel about this Saint Laurent gown, a wispy slip dress in silver silk chiffon trimmed with black lace.

"You are simply stunning, darling," Mom says. "Hari will have to fight off every man at the ball for your attention." She motions to the nearest saleswoman to top off her still half-full flute of Champagne.

"You don't think it's too…" I struggle for the word.

"Sexy?" Maggie offers cautiously.

"Skimpy?" the nearest saleswoman suggests.

"Inappropriate," an older saleswoman says.

"Yes, that's the word," I say, pointing to the older woman.

"Don't be silly," Mom says. "You said Hari's mother wanted to flaunt her jewels at the party. This dress is the equivalent of you flaunting your own jewels."

"You do look beautiful in it," the first saleswoman says.

"I can't believe Hari loaded his credit card on your phone," Maggie sighs. She picks up my Bling Phone from the accent table next to the love seat. Maggie slips her finger in the faux-diamond ring, trying it on for size. "He must really love you."

"Of course, he loves her," Mom says. "He's rich, and she's beautiful. It's a classic combination."

"Hari's not so hard on the eyes either, Mom," I point out.

"Perhaps this would keep you a bit warmer," the older saleswoman suggests. She walks over with a black velvet shrug jacket that matches the black lace on the slip dress. "What with all the rain forecast for the weekend."

"Or how about this?" the other saleswoman says. She plucks a salmon pink fake-fur stole from a mannequin and brings it over. "The bright color provides a nice contrast to the gown."

"Ooooh, it's so soft!" I say, tossing the stole over my bare shoulders. "Maggie, come here and feel this."

Maggie hobbles over to me, one foot in a sparkly Jimmy Choo pump, the other foot in her red Converse slip-ons.

"Oh my God, it feels amazing!" Maggie says. We both stroke our faces with the luscious stole.

"It feels like burying your face in a kitten's fur," I say.

"A kitten's belly fur," Maggie adds.

"A Persian kitten's belly fur!"

"A really fat Persian kitten's belly fur," Maggie laughs.

"Darling, you won't believe this," Mom says, interrupting our girlish goofing. "You've made the gossip rags."

"What are you talking about?" I ask.

"Here, read for yourself," Mom says. She holds out her iPad to me.

Maggie and I walk over to my mother and squeeze together on the love seat. Under the bold-faced headline, "Who's That Girl?" I see an article that practically shouts at me in all caps.

WHO'S THAT GIRL?

Readers of *THE NOB* are well-acquainted with the amorous antics of a certain HARI MISTRY—billionaire playboy, heir to THE RAJ family of luxury hotels, and notorious occupant of the FAIRMONT penthouse suite—but lately, the yummy Mr. Mistry has been spotted all over town with another mystery: an exotic beauty with a pixie cut reminiscent of JEAN SEBERG and who is rumored to leave men similarly BREATHLESS.

So, the question on everyone's lips is: WHO'S THAT GIRL? In an exclusive scoop, *THE NOB* has identified the lithesome looker as AMELIA BAE-WOOD. Name sound familiar? You might remember her as the slinky sidekick of NILS NILSSON, the FOOD NETWORK celeb and MICHELIN two-star chef who crashed and burned after trying to re-create his New York City glory in the rough-and-tumble redwoods of Mendocino County.

THE NOB's sources say Amelia may be more than just another notch in Mr. Mistry's proverbial black belt. What proof do we have? Check out the slideshow below and see if you can spot THE ROCK on Amelia's left ring finger. With a TIFFANY trinket like that, how soon before the stunning duo start calling one another BAE?

I click on the slideshow, which reveals about a dozen photos of me and Hari, apparently snapped by random strangers on their cell phones while we were walking around town, eating dinner out, or taking the elevator up to Hari's suite. In the last photo, you see me wearing what appears to be a glittery twenty-carat diamond ring on my left hand.

"This is hilarious," I say, laughing. "I can't wait to show Hari." I take my Bling Phone from Maggie and start texting.

"Or maybe it's not so funny," Mom says. "I've noticed the way Hari looks at you. It's clear that you two have chemistry.

I have a sneaking suspicion that the fake ring he gave you was just warming you up for the real thing."

I stop texting and think about the moment Hari gave me the Christmas gift. He seemed so different that night: softer, more tender. He's been that way for a while. His sexy swagger and braggadocio from our initial meetings are gone, replaced by a sweet sincerity. Even our sex life has been different, less like a performance and more like true intimacy.

"Hari did tell me on Christmas night that he had something important to talk to his parents about," I admit.

"And what could be more important than telling his parents he wants to get engaged?" Mom asks. She looks around the dress boutique for confirmation. The saleswomen all nod in assent, even though they have no idea what Mom is talking about. Maggie dreamily strokes the fake-fur stole like a beloved pet.

I decide not to text Hari after all.

"Oh, Aunt Amelia, could that be true?" Maggie coos. "Do you think Hari's going to ask you to marry him?"

Maggie, Mom, and I reread the article on Mom's iPad and re-scroll through the photos. Meanwhile, the first saleswoman refills Mom's flute and offers me my own, which I gladly accept. Maggie smiles shyly and says "no thank you" to the offer of bubbly.

I flip my Bling Phone over and slip my finger into the six-prong setting. I stretch my arm out to view my hand from a distance. From this angle, it could be mistaken for a real engagement ring.

"I have some shoes that would be perfect with that dress," the first saleswoman says. "You've got great legs, and these will really show them off." She holds up two different pairs of sandals: a strappy one with four-inch stiletto heels, and a closed-toe mule with a demure kitten heel.

"Look, Aunt Amelia," Maggie says, her eyes scanning the ceiling.

The faux diamond on my finger catches the light streaming through the boutique window and sends twinkles all over the room. It's like being in the center of a glitter-filled snowball.

I get up from the love seat and smooth out the silk chiffon fabric of my gown.

"Let's try on those stilettos," I say.

After our dress-shopping excursion, I treat Mom, Maggie, and myself to a late lunch at the Neiman Marcus Rotunda. Their popovers with strawberry butter are to die for, and the bottle of sommelier-selected Chablis isn't too bad either. Then we take a black car home and settle in for a well-deserved nap. It's my favorite way to spend an afternoon.

When I wake an hour later, I can hear Maggie still snoozing above me. The rest of the house is quiet. I reach under my pillow and pull out my Bling Phone. I haven't heard from Hari all day.

Got my dress for New Year's, I text him. I put it on your Amex. Along with lunch. Don't hate me.

Can't talk now, Hari texts back. Family stuff.

Everything OK? I text.

No answer.

Dinner tonight? I text.

No answer.

Let me know when you're free, I text. Then I stick my Bling Phone under my pillow and resolve not to check it for a while. At least another thirty minutes.

Maybe twenty.

I immediately pull my Bling Phone back out and search for that article in *The Nob* that Mom showed me. Each of the all-caps words has a hyperlink. I click onto HARI MISTRY and land on a special page of *The Nob* with an index of all the articles about all the women he's been spotted with over the years. There are actresses, singers, socialites, athletes, two pairs of twins, and even a senator's daughter. I have to hand it to Hari: he doesn't have a type. Blonde, brunette, redhead, platinum-and-magenta-striped, even a bald woman (a striking Ethiopian runway model). Hari seems to take an equal opportunity approach to dating.

I click THE RAJ and FAIRMONT and get directed to their corporate websites. When I click AMELIA BAE-WOOD, there's the photo of me standing next to Nils, my long black curls and ironic nerd-girl glasses in stark contrast to his shock of white-blond hair and goatee. It's the standard shot that the media used whenever there was an article about Amuse or Loca—the two of us looking like some hipster-foodie version of *American Gothic*.

I search my name in Google Images and scroll through the pictures that appear. Hipster *American Gothic* is the first and most common image, followed by posed photographs of me and Nils with random celebrities standing in front of Amuse. Further down the search results are the surreptitious snaps of me and Hari gallivanting around San Francisco's hot spots. As image after image passes before my eyes, I realize I'm almost always alongside Nils or Hari, my handsome paramours. It's like I don't exist as my own person, just as one half of a bold-faced-type couple. I feel a nagging sense of disappointment. How have I allowed myself to be defined by the men in my life?

Finally, down in the bowels of the search results, there's an image of me alone. I laugh out loud at the absurdity. It's my mug shot from the Mendocino County jail.

I inspect my face in the photograph. My hair is a complete

mess. My eyes are shadowed with exhaustion. My normally full lips are pressed tightly into a ragged line. Most people would assume the woman in that mug shot was an addict or an extra on *Orange Is the New Black*. Had it not been for Dad and his generous check to pay off my plea deal, I'd have become a real-life inmate. I suddenly miss my dad so much that my whole chest aches.

Still sleepy from the Champagne at the dress boutique and Chablis at lunch, I decide to go back to napping and have the strangest dream. In it, Leo, Brandon, Jett, and Hari are standing in a police lineup, an image straight out of *The Usual Suspects*. I'm looking at them through a one-way mirror, and Nils is by my side interrogating me.

"Which one is it, Amelia?" Nils asks. His voice is rough, his accent strong.

"What do you mean?" I ask.

"You need to choose one," Nils says. "Which one will take care of you?"

"I don't need anyone to take care of me," I say. The four men in the lineup are different shapes, sizes, ages, and colors, but they've got one thing in common: they're all staring straight ahead with an intensity that makes me uneasy, like they can see through the one-way mirror into my very soul.

"Not even me?" Nils asks gently. Except that it's not Nils. It's Dad.

"Daddy," I say, reaching out. The emptiness in my chest is filled with warmth as I touch his face, his soft smooth skin, the tiniest bit of stubble on his cheek. My father is so alive, so real.

Then just as quickly as he appeared, he's gone. I turn around, and the men in the lineup are gone too. I'm all alone. I lift my hand to look at my fingers, which moments ago had been touching my father's face, and see the small jade turtle dangling on my wrist.

The lucky charm bracelet that Dad entrusted to me and I so casually gave away.

24

It's Wednesday morning, the day I've arranged to meet with Chong Bae and get to the root of what's going on with our family's estate battle. I hop out of bed and peer into the upper bunk. It's empty.

"Good morning, Mom," I say, walking into the kitchen.

Mom is seated at the counter, playing Solitaire on her iPad and sipping coffee from a mug. I check the kitchen clock; it's almost noon. Ever since we left Arcadia, I've fallen back into my old habit of waking up late and squandering the day doing nothing.

"Where is Maggie?" I ask.

"Maggie left a little while ago to check out the vintage shops on Haight."

"When did Maggie start buying vintage?" I ask.

"When she saw what you were wearing for the gala, Maggie realized that the little black dress Eleanor picked out for her won't quite do. She knows how worried Eleanor is about money these days, so she's hoping to find a nice vintage dress with the cash that Santa gave her."

"What a good kid," I say, and Mom nods.

"I'm thinking about doing a little shopping myself," Mom says. "When we were having lunch yesterday, I saw that Neiman's is having a post-Christmas sale. Want to join me?"

"I can go as far as Union Square with you," I say, "but I'll have to take a pass on Neiman's. I'm meeting someone for lunch."

"Someone?" Mom asks, arching her brow.

"You have to promise not to tell Eleanor," I say.

"Cross my heart."

"I told Chong Bae that I'd meet him to talk about Dad's estate. I'm thinking maybe I can help break through the legal logjam."

"That sounds wonderful," Mom says. "As much as I love living with you girls, it's not exactly sustainable in the long term. It would be nice to have my own bathroom again."

"Well, don't count your chickens yet," I say. "I'm not promising a resolution. I just have this nagging feeling that something's getting in the way of ending this estate battle, and I need to know what it is."

"I've always loved that about you, Amelia," Mom says. "Once you set your mind to do something, you don't let anything stand in your way."

I give Mom a double take. Is that really how she perceives me, as a go-getter? I'm pretty sure most people would think of me as a screw-up, a stunted adolescent, Matthew McConaughey in *Failure to Launch*. Only someone who loves me as much as Mom would see me so charitably.

"Seriously, Mom," I say, "you cannot breathe a word of this to Eleanor. She would be apoplectic."

Mom makes the "my lips are sealed" gesture.

I text Maggie on my Bling Phone to let her know we'll be gone for a few hours. It's drizzling outside, so Mom and I call a Lyft to Union Square. Traffic is already slow because of the rain, but it comes to a standstill as we approach San Francisco's commercial center.

"What's going on?" I ask the driver.

"They've blocked off the area for the holidays," the driver says. "All the cars are being diverted to the other side of Market. This is the closest I can get you."

I check the time on my Bling Phone. I'm five minutes late already.

"Where are you meeting him?" Mom asks.

"At the café on the opposite corner," I say, pointing. There's a small patch of clear sky overhead. "We'll have to make a dash for it."

Mom and I are panting by the time we finish speed-walking the two city blocks to the far corner of Union Square.

"Beautiful sister!" Chong Bae says, his arms outstretched. "How wonderful, you brought your mother!"

I haven't seen Chong Bae since the time we met that October day in Arcadia, but once again, I'm taken aback by his uncanny resemblance to my dad, right down to his fleshy earlobes and unruly cowlick.

"You remember my lawyer, Douglas Park?" he says.

Mr. Park emerges from the café, impeccably dressed in a gray flannel suit and holding a classic black umbrella, the kind with the cane handle that Gene Kelly dances with in *Singin' in the Rain*. With his short-cropped black hair and handsome features, Mr. Park reminds me of Nat King Cole on the cover of his greatest hits album. When Eleanor and I were kids, Mom and Dad used to play that album every Friday night and dance cheek to cheek in our living room, which I used to think was weird but now realize was incredibly sweet.

Chong Bae, Mr. Park, Mom, and I engage in some light

pleasantries under the café awning until Chong suggests we go inside where it's dry.

"I'll wait outside for your counsel to arrive," Mr. Park says to me.

"Counsel?" I ask.

"Your lawyer," he says. "I thought you'd be coming with your lawyer."

"I don't have a lawyer," I say. Which isn't entirely true, but I don't think Mr. Park was expecting to meet with the criminal defense guy who sprang me from Mendocino County jail.

Mr. Park appears unhappy as he says something in Korean to Chong Bae.

"Do you speak Korean, Douglas?" Mom asks pleasantly.

Mr. Park looks surprised to be spoken to by my mother.

"Yes," he says. "I was born and raised in Korea but went to university and law school in the States. My father's Korean, and my mother is African American. They met when my mother was in the army and stationed near Seoul."

"How fascinating!" Mom says. "I'd love to hear more."

"I'm very sorry to you both," Mr. Park says, "but I had the erroneous understanding that your lawyer would be here today." He gives Chong Bae an exasperated look. "I see that we had a miscommunication."

"But Chong and I can talk without you, right?" I ask. "There's nothing to prevent us from talking—no legal or ethical prohibitions?"

Mr. Park pauses a moment before saying, "No, I suppose not."

"Douglas," Mom says brightly, "these two have their hearts set on catching up, and I have my heart set on doing a little post-Christmas window-shopping. But foolish me, I left the house without an umbrella. Would you be a perfect gentleman and escort me down to Neiman's? I promise we won't talk about anything legal. If it makes you feel better, we don't have to talk about anything at all."

Mr. Park looks flummoxed by my mother's request. So flummoxed, in fact, that he's powerless to resist as my mother drags him outside and down the rain-soaked street.

"Two for lunch?" the maître d' asks in a thick Gallic accent.

A black-vested waiter walks by with two steaming crocks of French onion soup, the Gruyère cheese melted and dripping down the side of the bowls. Chong Bae gestures for me to make the decision.

"Pourquoi pas?" I respond, exhausting my entire memory of high school French.

The maître d' leads us into the back of the café and seats us in a corner table right next to the floor-to-ceiling windows. I settle down on the cushy chintz-covered bench, and Chong Bae takes the bent-cane café chair.

"I'm so happy you agreed to meet me, little sister," Chong Bae says. "May I call you little sister? In Korea, we don't call our sisters or brothers by their name."

"Uh, sure," I say.

"And you can call me big brother," he says, "or Opa, if that's easier."

"Okay, Opa," I say.

Our waiter comes by and takes our order. As he turns to leave, I glance at the chic couple next to us, who are enjoying a bottle of Bordeaux.

"Oh, good idea, little sister!" Chong Bae says. He beckons back the waiter and orders a bottle of Pomerol. I don't even try to fake-protest.

"You seem very sensible to me," Chong Bae says. "I can tell that your sister is the more emotional one."

I suppress my impulse to burst out laughing. He's got such an earnest face.

"I think my requests have been very reasonable," Chong Bae continues, "and my lawyer agrees. Yet your family refuses to even consider them. I'd like to understand why."

The waiter comes back with the bottle of wine. I slather butter on a bit of baguette and eat the whole piece while waiting for the waiter to pour me a glass.

"You know, my sister wasn't very clear to me," I say, "about exactly what your requests are." I'm being disingenuous. In fact, Eleanor has never told me anything about the legal dispute other than that Chong Bae claims to be our father's first-born son and that the court granted him my dad's entire estate.

"As you know," Chong Bae says, "I'm not doing this for the money."

I practically choke on my wine.

"No," I say, "I didn't know that."

"Your sister didn't tell you? My family is very prominent in Korea. We own one of the largest construction companies in the country."

"I didn't know that either," I say.

"Even though she didn't need the money," Chong Bae says, "my mother appreciated the financial support your father gave us during the last years of her life. It meant so much to her to know that he had accepted me as his son."

I reach for my wineglass only to find it empty. I reach over for the bottle—manners be damned—and refill my glass. I glug it down all at once and pour myself another.

"Opa," I confess, "I have no idea what you are talking about. Eleanor hasn't told me a thing. Please start from the beginning."

"My mother met our father in high school," Chong Bae explains. "They were like Romeo and Juliet. You've read it, I'm sure."

I nod vaguely, but I've never actually read Shakespeare's play. I have seen the Leonardo DiCaprio movie, though, so I understand the whole star-crossed lovers concept.

It turns out Dad was a diamond in the rough from a working-class background who tested into the most prestigious high school in Korea. Meanwhile, Chong Bae's mother was the jewel in the crown of a hoity-toity family that not only owned a profitable construction company but also included uncles and grandfathers who were prominent members of government.

When my dad was admitted to UC Berkeley, which was pretty much unheard-of back in those days, he promised Chong Bae's mom that he'd come back to Korea after graduating. They agreed to be secretly engaged. My dad couldn't afford a ring, so they exchanged bracelets. In Asian tradition, the red silk thread symbolized their destiny as soul mates, a magical cord that would stretch or tangle over time but never break, and the jade turtle represented steadfastness.

And then my dad met a beautiful hippie chick in California.

Chong Bae's mom didn't know that our father had fallen in love with another woman. All she knew was that his letters arrived less and less frequently until they stopped altogether.

"I don't blame your father," Chong Bae says. "Our father, I mean. He was just eighteen years old, little more than a child, when he left Korea. According to my mother, they fell in love very easily, and it seems he fell out of love just as easily."

"You're being awfully generous," I say. "I mean, he left your poor mother alone and pregnant."

"He didn't know my mother was pregnant," Chong Bae says. "My mother didn't want to give him the news by letter or even long-distance telephone. She wanted to tell him in person when he came home for winter break—"

"But he didn't come home," I interrupt.

When Eleanor and I were young, Mom would often tell

us about her and Dad's very first Christmas together. They had started dating the fall of their freshman year. Dad hadn't realized living in the US would be so expensive, so he didn't have the funds to fly back to Korea for winter break. Mom hated the idea of leaving Dad for the holidays, so she decided not to go back home to Ohio either. Instead, she cashed in her plane ticket, and the two of them spent winter break huddled up in a cabin in Yosemite.

"By the time my mother received the letter from your father—our father—saying that he was breaking off their engagement," Chong Bae says, "my mother's parents had already decided he was garbage. They ordered my mother to forget about this garbage man in America and never to contact him again. After giving birth to me, my mother went back to her studies at university, and my grandparents raised me as their own son."

Chong Bae pauses his story while we eat our lunch. I notice he has a tiny dimple on his right cheek that appears and disappears when he's chewing, just like Dad.

"When did my father finally learn about you?" I ask while the waiter clears our plates.

"Maybe four or five years ago," Chong Bae says. "Like I said, my grandparents forbade my mother from contacting him. Honestly, I think they were worried that he would use me as a way to gain access to our family fortune. But when my mother got sick, she started thinking about her life, and she wondered whatever became of her first love. She found an article on the internet about this Korean American man named Chong Bae from UC Berkeley who became a very successful businessman in Silicon Valley, and she recognized his face. She gathered up her courage and reached out. It was only then, over forty years after they last spoke, that my mother told our father the truth. About the girl he left behind and the son he never knew he had."

My heart aches for Chong Bae's mother—for this innocent girl left behind—and for my father who must have been devastated when he heard the whole story.

"You said my father gave your mother financial support before she died," I say.

"Our father," Chong Bae corrects me.

"Right, our father," I correct myself.

"Yes," Chong Bae says, distracted for a moment by his buzzing cell phone. He holds up a finger, checks his screen, and smiles as he texts a quick message back.

"Once our father learned about my existence," Chong Bae continues, "he was full of remorse. He wrote my mother a letter saying that he acknowledged me as his son and would like to provide financial support. Even though my mother was well-off, and I was a full-grown man myself, she accepted the money as a token of our father's contrition and honor."

I lift the wine bottle and peer into the dark opening, hoping there's still a tiny bit left, but it's empty. Listening to Chong Bae's story, I sift through my memories of Dad in the past four or five years. Did he ever give us any reason to think he had a secret family back in Korea? Did he drop any clues, hints, casual mentions that he'd hoped we'd pick up on? Or did he just keep it all to himself, a source of guilt and shame that he couldn't share with us?

"Our father was a decent man, an honorable man," Chong Bae says. "That's what my mother told me before she died. Please know that my mother died at peace with her life, with her decisions, and with our father."

"Did you ever meet our father in person?" I ask.

"Once," Chong Bae says. "At my mother's funeral. After that, we chatted on Kakao but only a few times. I was so busy with my work and..." His voice trails off. He doesn't need to say anything more. The regret is written all over his face.

The place is nearly empty now, with just another couple in the far corner and a busboy sweeping under the tables and chairs. I've been so absorbed by Chong Bae's story that I didn't notice the lunchtime crowd dispersing from the café.

"You said you didn't file the lawsuit for the money," I say. "So, what are you doing it for? Why has my mother been evicted from her home, my sister forced to support us all, my niece worried about getting college financial aid, if it's not about the money?"

"Your sister really hasn't told you," Chong Bae says. I can't tell if he means it as a question or a statement.

"No," I say.

"When I heard our father had died, I wrote an email to your mother directly," Chong Bae says. "I didn't want to involve any lawyers. I didn't even think of this as a legal matter. I thought we could treat this as a family would, person to person. But when I didn't receive any response to my numerous emails, I grew concerned. I thought maybe my English was too blunt or unclear, so I engaged Mr. Park to write on my behalf, to help convince you and your family that I was a legitimate relation and not some fraudulent blackmailer."

Eleanor had told Mom to ignore the emails. I can only imagine how frustrating it must have been to be on the receiving end of such protracted silence.

"Instead of agreeing to our request for a face-to-face meeting," Chong Bae says, "your lawyers filed papers in the probate court seeking to bar me from making any claim to our father's estate. I hadn't asked for any part of the estate, but your lawyers forced me into the position of having to prove my claim of paternity or else admitting that my claim was false. Once lawyers got involved, things went out of everyone's control. In the end, the judge ruled that Korean law applied, and that I as his firstborn son was entitled to his entire business enterprise. Since almost all of our father's wealth derived from his business, that meant I inherited the bulk of our father's estate."

There's a light tapping on the window behind me. I turn around and see Chong Bae's lawyer Mr. Park standing on the sidewalk underneath his big umbrella. Behind him, my mother is waving at me from inside a black car, her face aglow, holding up a Neiman Marcus garment bag.

"I told Mr. Park to pay for your mother's ball gown," Chong Bae says.

I can barely comprehend what he's talking about. I'm still struggling to absorb the details of the legal case and the judge's ruling.

"Please believe me when I tell you," Chong Bae says, "I didn't want to take over your father's—our father's—estate. I still don't. I've been trying to see you and your family in person so you could hear from my own lips—the only thing I ever wanted is to be acknowledged as our father's son."

Chong Bae clasps his hands together as if in prayer.

"And as your brother," he says.

25

By the time the black car drops me and Mom back at Eleanor's flat, I'm seething inside. Thank God my sister is still at work. I don't think I have enough self-control not to tear into her about lying to the family for nearly a year. To think of all the hardship she's made us go through as a family just because she's too stubborn to admit that this man—this man who looks exactly like Dad, by the way—is our brother.

Oblivious to my inner turmoil, Mom and Maggie decide to throw an impromptu fashion show of the dresses they bought to wear at the Arcadia gala. Mom sashays out of her bedroom wearing a midnight blue floor-length gown in sparkly, stretchy wool. Its body-conscious style evokes classic Azzedine Alaïa but is still age-appropriate for a woman in her sixties.

"Oh, Grandma, that dress is beautiful on you!" Maggie says.

"And that dress looks fetching on you, Maggie," Mom says. She reaches to examine the slubby silk fabric. "I love the funnel neck and midi length, and that rose color goes so well with your complexion. You look like Audrey Hepburn in *Funny*

Face. I have the perfect drop pearl earrings to go along with it. I just need your mother to dig them out of storage."

"Why don't you model your gown for us, Amelia?" Mom says.

"I'm not in the mood for playing dress-up," I mumble.

Mom and Maggie exchange "what's with her?" eyes.

"Is something wrong, Amelia?" Mom asks, shimmying back to her room. "Didn't your talk with your brother go well?"

"Are those Spanx?" I ask. I am momentarily distracted watching my mother grunt and groan as she struggles to extricate herself from her shapewear like a butterfly trying to wriggle out of its cocoon.

"Don't judge, darling," Mom gasps. "You'll be needing a little foundational help too when you're my age."

"No judgment here," I say, holding my hands up as if in surrender. "I'm no stranger to the double-gusseted crotch."

"You have such a charming way with words," Mom says. She exhales in relief when she's finally released from her spandex straitjacket.

"Mom, what do you know about Chong Bae's claim to Dad's estate?" I ask. "What has Eleanor told you?"

"The only thing your sister told me," Mom says, "is that the clerk at the probate court said most cases can be handled without a lawyer, even if there's not a will. When we got the email from Chong Bae, Eleanor and I both assumed it was some terrible joke, so we ignored it, along with the half-dozen or more emails after that."

Mom changes into a pair of slim-fitting jeans and an open-necked blouse. It occurs to me that I haven't seen her wearing that white velour tracksuit in a while. At some point in the past few months, Mom seems to have emerged from her state of extended mourning and returned to something resembling her old effervescent self.

"I'd nearly forgotten about Chong Bae," Mom continues, "when your sister came to visit me in Atherton and showed me a letter she received from the law firm of Park and Associates. I remember being struck by the name: Park and Associates. Sounds so fancy, like Park Avenue in New York. I had no idea what a gentleman Douglas would be. Don't you think he's very refined?"

Mom looks through some cosmetics by her bedside, selects a lipstick, and applies it expertly to her lips. She leans over to apply some on me, but I decline.

"What did the letter say?" I ask, trying not to get hung up on Mom's commentary on Mr. Park's refinement. And when did she start calling him "Douglas"?

"I can't remember all the details," she says, furrowing her brow in concentration. It's been so long since her last Botox treatment that her brow actually crinkles. "I remember the letter was very long. The main point was that the firm represented a Mr. Chong Bae of Seoul, South Korea, who had proof that he was your dad's son."

"Did you see the proof?" I ask.

"The lawyers included a photocopy of a letter written in Korean, along with what they claimed was an English translation. In the letter, your dad supposedly admitted he was Chong's father and wanted to accept financial responsibility for him."

"Did the letter seem legit?" I ask.

"How was I to know? I don't read Korean. And besides, I was still so upset about your father's death, the horrible suddenness of it all, I couldn't even begin to process what the whole thing was about. Eleanor said she had a lawyer friend who could probably help, so I let her take care of things. You know, the way Eleanor always takes care of things."

"What else?" I ask. "Did Eleanor tell you anything else about the case?"

"Not really," Mom says. "Once Eleanor got the lawyer involved, I assumed everything would work out. And sure enough, months passed, and I was still living in our home, my credit cards were still working fine, there were no more letters from lawyers. I figured everything was settled, and the imposter son from Korea had given up.

"Then one day, Eleanor came over and asked me where your father kept all our important papers—marriage license, your birth certificates, that kind of stuff. She went through Dad's study with a fine-tooth comb. She asked me if I knew where Dad's citizenship papers were, saying that she needed them to resolve an important issue. When I told her the answer, she nearly bit off my head."

"Why?" I ask. "What was the answer?"

"Your father never became a US citizen," Mom says. She stares at the four-diamond anniversary ring on her left hand. When Dad gave it to Mom for their twenty-fifth anniversary, he said each diamond symbolized a member of the Bae-Wood family. He didn't know back then that there was a fifth family member.

"He could have gotten his citizenship after he married me," Mom says, "but he never bothered to fill out the paperwork. I kept reminding him, and he kept putting me off. After a while, I stopped asking."

Chong Bae had mentioned at the café that Korean law had been applied to our case. The fact that Dad was still a Korean citizen helps explain why.

"Why do you think he never became a US citizen?" I ask.

Mom doesn't say a word, but I see her eyes welling up.

"Mom, what is it?" I ask.

"You know your dad loved you girls," Mom whispers.

"Of course," I whisper back. "And he loved you, Mom."

"He really did," she says, nodding. "I have no doubt.

"But as much as he loved us," Mom continues, "I always sensed something was missing for him here in the US. Maybe it was the language or the culture or the food. Or maybe he just missed his parents who never spoke to him after we married. Whatever the reason, it seemed like your dad left a piece of himself back in Korea. I just didn't realize—and I don't think your father did either—that the missing piece was his son."

Eleanor comes home from work, and I give her a wide berth. Still processing everything that I learned today, I don't breathe a word about my lunch with Chong Bae or heart-to-heart talk with Mom. I feel like a prosecutor preparing for a big oral argument; I want to make sure I have all my ducks in a row before confronting Eleanor about her deception.

As soon as Eleanor goes to bed, I sneak down to her basement where she stored Mom and Dad's stuff. There must be evidence of Chong Bae's claim to Dad's paternity hidden among the boxes, and I want to find it to wave accusingly in Eleanor's face.

"I'm just looking for Mom's drop pearl earrings," I practice saying in case Eleanor catches me poking around. "They'd be perfect with Maggie's vintage dress."

Eleanor's basement is tidier than most people's living rooms. U-Haul boxes are stacked in neat piles, with the contents of each box written in Eleanor's careful print: Mom's Clothing, Mom's Shoes, Amelia's Memorabilia, and so forth. I keep searching until I find a box labeled Letters and Correspondence. I slit open the box and find several smaller boxes within. Each of the smaller boxes has a P-touch printed label affixed to it: Dad's Letters, Mom's Letters, Eleanor's Pen Pals, Amelia's Postcards. I feel nostalgic thinking about the many postcards I wrote my parents during my years of world travel and grateful that they cared enough to save them.

I see a box labeled Love Letters, which strikes me as promising. Maybe there are letters to Dad from his old fiancée in Korea. Inside, however, the letters are from Edward to Eleanor. The postmark on the top letter is dated June 1997 from New York, New York. I vaguely recall that Edward worked on Wall Street the summer after his first year of business school. Eleanor pretended to be okay about it, but I'd hear her crying in her room at night, so I knew she missed him dreadfully.

I'm tempted to open the envelope and read Edward's letter—he was a hopeless romantic and loved to quote poetry any chance he could—but hold myself back. As angry as I am with my sister, I know it would be wrong to read her old love letters. I'm almost done riffling through the stack of envelopes when I come upon a letter that isn't addressed to Eleanor. It's addressed to a Tina Gallagher in New York City and is written in Edward's neat script. The letter is stamped but not postmarked.

Curiosity overwhelms my sense of morality, and I pull the letter out of the unsealed envelope. In it, Edward thanks Tina for being "such a dear friend" over the years. He talks about how much he loves Eleanor and Maggie and wouldn't change his life for the world but admits that he has wondered from time to time what might have happened if he had stayed in New York after that summer. Would he and Tina have married? Would they have had children, and would they have had Tina's curly red hair? What would that alternative life have been like? The letter ends with Edward apologizing, saying he knows it's wrong to unburden himself like this to her, but he wanted Tina to know how special she was to him, how much he appreciated their long-distance friendship, and how he wished her a healthy and happy life.

I check the date at the top of the letter. It was written a few weeks before Edward's death. My heart is galloping, and my breathing is ragged. Did Edward cheat on Eleanor that summer he was in New York? Did Eleanor know? Is that why she was crying? Does it count as cheating if you're not married? Edward and Eleanor had only been dating for less than a year when he went to New York for that summer internship.

And then another question pops into my mind that I wish I could banish: Did Edward cheat on Eleanor during their marriage?

There's no way to know the answers without asking Eleanor directly, and that would be unthinkable. Given the date on the letter and the lack of postmark, Edward must have died before he could mail it. And Eleanor must have discovered it afterward.

I hear some bustling upstairs and worry that it's Eleanor. I shove the letters back into the Love Letters box and return the smaller boxes back into the larger Letters and Correspondence container. I hear a toilet flush, shuffling footsteps, and then nothing. As quietly as I can, I sneak back upstairs to my bunk bed and slide under the covers.

I try to fall asleep, but my mind is racing. I went to the basement looking for answers. But now I have more questions than ever.

26

"Wow, that's a lot to process, babe," Hari says. "I don't know what's more shocking, Chong Bae's story or the letter from Edward."

The two of us are sitting in his car and eating pastries from this fantastic French bakery on Arguello. We are the only people parked at Inspiration Point, which has a postcard-perfect view of iconic Alcatraz and the San Francisco Bay. In contrast to yesterday's gray clouds and intermittent rains, it's hydrangea-blue sky as far as the eye can see.

"You're telling me," I say. "My head is spinning."

"Do you believe this guy, Chong Bae?" Hari asks. "You don't think he's conning you, trying to get you on his side?"

"I don't know why he'd do that," I say. "He's already got everything—the house, the money, even Dad's name."

"Yeah, that's true," Hari says. "But you've only met this guy once before your lunch yesterday. You've known your sister your entire life. I think you need to withhold judgment on who you're going to believe until you've given your sister a chance to tell her side of the story."

In my heart of hearts, I know Hari's right, but I'm petrified about letting Eleanor know I went behind her back and met privately with Chong Bae. I can just hear her now, accusing me of being disloyal and poking my nose where it doesn't belong and where the hell was I when she and Mom really needed me. I wouldn't be so afraid of her accusations if I didn't believe they were in some part justified.

"And that letter you found in the basement," Hari says, "that's so effed up. Your poor sister. But it totally explains her extreme reaction to the lawsuit."

"What do you mean?"

"Put yourself in Eleanor's shoes," Hari says. "Edward has just died, and she's still reeling from the loss, when she finds a letter admitting that he cheated on her."

"The letter doesn't explicitly say he cheated," I interrupt.

"Okay, believe what you want," Hari says. "Regardless of whether he cheated or not, it's clear from the letter that Edward was still thinking about this woman on his deathbed, imagining an alternative life with her. How would you feel in that situation?"

"I don't know," I say, mulling over the scenario. "Angry, hurt, confused? Mostly angry, if I'm being honest."

"Exactly," Hari says. "But what do you do with that anger? You can't go to marriage counseling when your husband is dead. Based on what you've told me about your sister, I'm guessing she just stuffed that anger down in her chest and never dealt with it. And then years later, she's dealing with another big blow—your father's sudden death—and this random guy comes along and says your dad cheated on his first love, and he's the product of that love."

I let Hari's words sink in. I think about how angry I would have been in Eleanor's shoes, but I have never heard her say one negative word about Edward. To the contrary, she has done everything she can to remind Maggie of what a wonderful father he was, of all their good times together as a family. How does she do that without exploding? As hard as life has been for me, I now realize life has been even harder for Eleanor, but she hides it so well with that Hallmark commercial exterior.

"They say that women end up marrying men who remind them of their fathers," Hari says, "and the parallels between Edward and your dad are spot-on. The big difference of course is that your dad ended up marrying his second love—your mom—and living that alternative life that Edward could only dream about to his dying day."

I stare out in the far distance, trying to absorb Hari's hypothesis. It's as if he's put together the pieces of a complicated jigsaw puzzle, but I'm still struggling to see the whole picture.

"How did you figure that out so fast?" I ask.

"I was a psych major in college," Hari says. "Plus, I watch a lot of Korean dramas."

"You know," I say, "I think you may be right. Right after Eleanor threw Chong Bae and his lawyer out of the Master's Cottage, she said something like Dad is dead so we shouldn't ruin his memory by believing their lies."

"Just like Eleanor doesn't want to ruin Edward's memory," Hari says. "If you believe that Edward cheated on her, then what does it mean for Edward and Eleanor's marriage? And if you believe that your dad cheated on his Korean fiancée, then what does that mean for your parents' marriage? Does it somehow affect your memories of who Edward was, of who your father was?"

"I'm gonna need more time to think this all through," I say. I reach over to Hari's side of the car and check inside the bakery bag. There's an almond croissant still left. I tear the croissant in two, sliced almonds and powdered sugar raining down on my lap, and I offer Hari half.

"Sorry for hogging all the conversation," I say, licking the almond paste out of the middle of the croissant. "What's going on with you? How did your family thing go? You've been sort of MIA the past couple days. I was starting to get worried about you."

"Yeah, sorry about that," Hari says. "My parents got back from India on Tuesday and called an all-hands-on-deck family meeting, and it's been chaos ever since. I'm only able to see you right now because my parents are off with their PR team trying to come up with a ten-point communications plan."

"Communications plan for what?" I ask.

Hari hesitates. "I'll tell you as long as you don't tell another soul. Not even your sister," he says. "Especially not your sister. Not until we've told the people who need to know."

"C'mon, I just spilled a bunch of Bae-Wood family beans to you," I say. "I think it's only fair to even the playing field with some Mistry family mysteries."

"Seriously, Amelia," he says, "you have to swear yourself to secrecy."

"You're scaring me, Hari," I say. "Is everything okay? Is Gisela okay?"

Hari pulls his phone from his pants pocket and shows me a photo of a slender young Indian woman standing next to Jett. She appears to be around Maggie's age, in her late teens, and has a similar fresh-faced quality.

"Who's that?" I ask, immediately thinking of the pink message slip in the Arcadia trash. Did Jett fly off to India to hook up with this young woman? That seems highly inappropriate and not something Jett would do.

“Her name is Laila,” Hari says. “And she’s Gisela’s daughter. The one she had with Jett.”

“What?!?”

“Yeah, it was a shocker for me too.”

“But how? When?”

“Remember the story I told you last fall about our senior prom? About how Gisela was so upset when Jett showed up late? Well, it turns out he wasn’t the only one late that night.”

I shove the last bite of almond croissant in my mouth, grab the phone out of Hari’s hand, and pinch-to-zoom on the young woman’s face. Laila looks like the perfect mix of Gisela and Jett.

“Apparently Gisela had taken one of those EPT tests the morning of prom,” Hari says, “and she’d been trying to reach Jett all day about the positive result, but this was back before cell phones and texts, so there was no way to track him down. When Jett finally arrived at our house with his fake date, Gisela was barely able to hold herself together.”

“Did your parents know Gisela was pregnant when they took those prom photos?” I ask.

“No, not before prom,” Hari says. “You can imagine how much it tore Gisela apart to pretend everything was okay, to smile for the camera, all the while knowing that she had this huge secret that was going to rock everyone’s world.”

“What happened next?” I ask.

“When Gisela broke the news to Jett, he responded like you’d expect any eighteen-year-old guy to do. He said he knew a place where Gisela could ‘have it done’ and that he would ‘totally pay for everything.’ It didn’t cross his mind for a second to keep the baby.”

“Ouch,” I say. While I agree Jett’s reaction was typical of a guy his age, it doesn’t make it any less painful to hear.

“Later that night,” Hari continues, “while I was out getting hammered at the Takahashi twins' after-prom party, Gisela came home to tell my parents."

"They must've been devastated," I say.

"You don't know my parents," Hari says. "They're problem-solvers, and they're fiercely protective. When they heard how Jett reacted, they weren't surprised. 'He's a member of the Jett family,' they explained to Gisela. 'There's no way a member of the Jett family is going to marry a little brown girl and raise a little brown baby together. Do you really believe he would give up going to Stanford to be a teen dad? That's not going to happen.'"

"How did Gisela react?"

"She didn't have any say in the matter," Hari says. "My parents sent her to India to spend the rest of her pregnancy with my mom's youngest sister who, coincidentally, had been trying to have a baby herself but without success. After Gisela gave birth to Laila, she got on a plane and came back home, her 'gap year' at an end."

"When did Jett find out about Laila?" I ask.

"Laila's adoptive parents—my aunt and uncle—always intended to tell her the truth when she turned eighteen, to give her the choice of reaching out to her birth parents if she wanted. As soon as Laila learned who her birth parents were, she contacted Jett, and right away, he wanted to meet her. He flew out to India that last night of the last cancer retreat, and he's spent the past several months making arrangements for Laila to move to the US for college."

"Do Jett's parents know?" I ask.

"Not yet," Hari says. "Which is why I'm swearing you to secrecy. This isn't the kind of news you deliver by text or even phone. Jett and Gisela want to be very deliberate about how to tell the people they love. They broke the news to me Tuesday night, and they plan to tell Jett's family tomorrow. After that, we assume the news will leak out to the public, and so my parents are trying to have a communication plan in place now. Once people get wind of the Jett-Mistry love child, the gossip rags will be all over it. We want to protect Laila from the media hordes."

I'm very familiar with the media hordes. My thoughts return to the Buddhist monastery that I called my temporary home. I wonder how Laila would do with a shaved head and living on spelt porridge. Hopefully it won't come to that.

"That's so weird," I say, slowly absorbing Hari's revelation.

"What's so weird?" Hari asks.

"The fact that both my dad and Jett had secret children from when they were in their teens," I say. "I mean, what are the chances?"

"It's probably more common than you'd think," Hari says. "I've read that with these new home DNA tests, people are finding surprise relatives all the time. The world is filled with little secrets everywhere."

Little secrets like Edward's letter to Tina Gallagher? Or my mug shot buried deep in the bowels of a Google image search? Or Maggie's application to Mount Holyoke? How many other secrets are the Bae-Wood women hiding from one another?

"Hello? Earth to Amelia," Hari says, waving his hands in front of my eyes.

"Oh, sorry," I say. "I got lost thinking about Jett and Laila."

"I know you told me this was just a loan," Hari says, pointing to my lucky charm bracelet on his wrist. "I had hoped to return it to you by now, but Laila's surprise arrival kind of messed up my plans. Could I hold on to it for just another day or two? I'm hoping to have that talk with my parents tonight or tomorrow. Definitely before the Arcadia fundraiser on Saturday."

"Of course," I say. "There's no rush. Like I said, it's a long-term loan."

"Long-term sounds good to me," Hari says.

27

Despite the beautiful weather on Thursday, another storm front blows into the Bay Area on Friday, ruining my plans for a taco-tasting walking tour of the Mission District. I rummage around the bottom of Eleanor's fridge in search of some frozen tamales or burritos to satisfy my Mexican food cravings. I practically whoop with joy when I discover the Trader Joe's cheese and chile tamales hiding beneath the box of Pepperidge Farm puff pastry.

"Amelia, darling," Mom says, coming into the kitchen, "would you be an angel and use your Bling Phone to call me a car? I need to stop by the Fairmont today, preferably sooner rather than later."

"Sure, I'd love to come along if you can wait for me to have a midmorning snack," I say, "I'm kinda bored." I pop the tamales into the microwave and wait for them to heat up. As much as I'm enjoying being in a city again, I miss the days in Arcadia when Jett, Eleanor, and Brandon would make me home-cooked meals on a regular rotation.

"Why do you need to go to the Fairmont?" I ask between bites of cheesy masa.

"Eleanor found my drop pearl earrings down in storage," Mom says, "but the setting is coming loose on one of them. Maggie has her heart set on wearing the earrings to tomorrow's gala but doesn't want to risk losing a pearl, so I promised to get it fixed. Thankfully, my dear friend Mario the jeweler said he could squeeze me in today. He owns that adorable little shop in the lobby of the Fairmont."

It's not lost on me how ridiculous it is that my mother has a personal jeweler who works out of the five-star Fairmont Hotel. Mom has come a long way from her farm-girl upbringing in rural Ohio and her early Top Ramen–eating days with Dad.

When Eleanor and I were growing up, my parents weren't rich. Far from it. My dad was a midlevel engineer at a large tech equipment company, making a pretty decent salary but always getting passed over for promotion despite his superior education and innovative thinking. Mom blamed discrimination, but Dad refused to complain. "America has always been fair to me," he said. "I just need to work harder."

Then one day, Dad was standing by the dot matrix printer waiting for a document to rat-a-tat-tat out when he noticed a thick document in the printout hopper. He pulled it out and saw that it was a listing of salaries by employee name. Scanning the pages, he discovered he was making considerably less than all of his colleagues, even those who had less experience or went to less prestigious schools. The next week, Dad donned his black suit and went to the bank for funding to start his own company—a company that ended up being one of the biggest suppliers to Samsung, LG, and countless other international companies needing specialized electronic bits.

When the Lyft driver pulls into the Fairmont's circular

driveway with Mom and me in the back seat, I immediately recognize Benicio, the head valet.

"Good afternoon, Miss Amelia," Benicio says, rushing to open the door, a giant umbrella emblazoned with the hotel logo in hand. "Welcome back to the Fairmont." Benicio used to play semi-pro soccer back in his native country of Colombia, and it shows in his speed and agility, not to mention his charming South American accent.

"Hello, Benicio," I say. "I'd like to introduce you to my mother, Tabitha Bae-Wood."

Benicio and Mom exchange quick but cordial greetings.

"Are you both headed up to the penthouse, Miss Amelia?" Benicio asks.

"Not today," I say. "My mother and I are actually going to the lobby."

"Ah, very well then," Benicio says, escorting us under the umbrella and opening the front door to the hotel.

The lobby of the Fairmont is bustling. Even though Christmas has passed, there's a throng of people—tourists and locals alike—milling about and ogling the magnificently lit Christmas tree and two-story-tall gingerbread house. The hotel's welcoming interior smells intoxicatingly of spruce and cinnamon and cloves.

"Mario!" Mom gushes as soon as she enters La Petite Etoile, the elegant jewelry shop just off the main lobby of the Fairmont.

"Tabitha!" Mario gushes back as the two old friends exchange air kisses.

Mom introduces me to her jeweler friend and then takes the drop pearl earrings out of a velvet pouch. Mario cradles the earrings in his palm like a hallowed relic or baby chick.

"I remember when Mr. Bae picked these earrings out for you," Mario says, holding a loupe up to his eye and examining them. "He said they were a gift for your thirtieth wedding anniversary."

"Yes," Mom says, smiling at the memory. "When I opened the present, Chong said to me, 'Superstition says you shouldn't give a gift of pearls because they are an omen of sadness. Pearls represent tears. I hope these are the only tears I will ever give you, my dear wife.'" The corners of her smile quiver, her eyes glistening. An instant later, Mom blinks her tears away.

"Do you see, Amelia, why I won't go anywhere else for my jewels?" Mom says to me before giving Mario a warm squeeze of the hand.

"I'm glad you came here today, Tabitha," Mario says. "I have missed seeing your lovely face. This setting is quite loose but easily fixed. May I offer you some tea and biscuits while you wait? Or else you can walk around the lobby and take in the holiday decorations. It should only take me fifteen or thirty minutes."

I've never turned down an offer of free refreshments, and Mom knows it.

"Some tea and biscuits would be wonderful, thank you, Mario," Mom says.

Mario leads Mom and me to a private room in the back of the boutique with a marble-topped coffee table and royal blue velveteen settee. We make ourselves comfortable on the settee while an elegant young woman with dark brown hair pulled into a neat chignon serves us a pot of Mariage Frères tea and a bone china plate of sweets.

"My name is Inés," the young woman says. "Please let me know if there is anything else I can get for you."

When Mario said the word *biscuits*, I pictured some dry McVitie's digestives, not these delectable delights: pale pink macarons, tender madeleines, and buttery-light palmiers. I forgot that the French have a different definition of biscuits than the English. I'm hoping Mario takes a very long time with Mom's earring repair.

Mom nibbles a macaron while leafing through the glossy pages of *Paris Match*, which gives me an excuse to check my Bling Phone again for any word from Hari. What I wouldn't give to see those three blinking dots at the bottom of my screen. I always think of them as the beating heart of the person thinking about you on the other end.

I've been trying hard not to imagine the so-called "important conversation" Hari wants to have with his parents. The way he looked at me when he talked about it—it felt practically like a marriage proposal. We've only been together for a few months, though, which seems short for an engagement. Then again, neither of us is getting any younger.

"Monsieur Montand," someone calls out. Mom and I both look up. There is a handsome young man standing in the hallway. He's holding a small royal blue box in one hand, knocking on Mario's office door with the other. Mario comes out of his office, and the two men converse in French. They talk so fast I can't make out a single sentence, but I recognize certain words from freshman year French class: *important*, *fiancée*, *famille*. It helps when the words are basically the same in French as in English. The man pulls a slip of paper from his pocket, shows it to Mario, who nods in confirmation. Then the man walks away, leaving Mario to return to his office.

I'm debating whether to have another macaron or madeleine when Mario reenters our room. He's holding a royal blue velvet tray with the repaired pearl earring resting in its center.

"She is perfect," Mario says, presenting the tray to my mother.

Mom picks up the earring and gives it a jiggle to make sure the pearl is firmly fastened. "Merci, Mario!" Mom cries out.

"My granddaughter will be so excited to wear these at the ball tomorrow night. You have saved us!"

"C'est mon plaisir, chere amie," he says, kissing Mom's hand.

Mom tucks the earring into its velvet pouch, and Mario gestures for us to return to the boutique's main showroom. I bid a silent adieu to the unfinished plate of biscuits. I figure it would be gauche to ask for a doggy bag.

"Tabitha," Mario says, "I know you're not interested in anything new right now, but I want to show you an enchanting little piece that I just finished creating."

"It never hurts to look, right?" Mom says, glancing mischievously at me.

I let Mom have some bonding time with Mario and wander among the shiny showcases of twinkling treasures. I've never been much of a jewelry person, although I wouldn't turn down a gift of diamonds or rubies if offered. Even with my untrained eye, I can tell the pieces at La Petite Etoile are exquisitely designed and made of the finest gemstones. It's a place that caters to the rich and discerning.

Another customer walks into the boutique and places her umbrella in a blue-and-white porcelain stand near the entrance. I wonder if it's still raining. There may still be time for me to do a quick jaunt through the Mission for some tacos. Out the front window, I see Benicio in the circular driveway talking to the young man with the small blue box. Benicio says something that makes the man laugh and then helps him into a waiting taxi.

When Mom has finished up with Mario, we stroll arm in arm through the lobby and wait under the awning for a ride back home. Benicio apologizes that there's a shortage of cabs due to the weather, but Mom and I don't mind. It's fun to be out and about in the city.

"Did you enjoy the holiday decorations?" Benicio asks my mother.

"Oh, I only saw them in passing," Mom says. "Amelia and I had a meeting with Mario at La Petite Etoile."

"What a coincidence!" Benicio says. "I was just talking to Olivier."

"Olivier?" I ask. "Is that the man in the white shirt?"

"Yes," Benicio says. "Very nice guy. We play soccer on the weekends together."

"It looked like he had an important delivery to make," I say.

"Yes, he did," Benicio says, "which is why I thought it was so coincidental!"

"What do you mean?" I ask.

"The delivery was to the Mistry mansion," he says. "Hari's parents' home."

The ride back home from the Fairmont is almost unbearable. Mom will not stop gushing and speculating about my impending engagement to Hari.

"We don't know that it's an engagement ring, Mom," I say. "It could be anything. Hari said his mom couldn't wait to show off her jewels at the gala. Maybe she decided to buy a new piece especially for the event."

"First of all," Mom says, "it's not true that it could be anything. That box was small—I saw it with my own eyes! It was much too small for anything other than a ring. Second, if Mrs. Mistry wanted a new bauble to debut at the gala, it wouldn't be a ring—it would be a necklace or brooch or tiara, something big and flashy that you can see from across the room. She wouldn't choose a ring because even if it was Elizabeth Taylor huge, you'd have to hold it up right next to your face for anyone to notice." Mom holds up her hand right next to her face in demonstration, as if I couldn't grasp her meaning otherwise.

As the taxi signals to turn left on California Street onto Divisadero, I can't help but think that the Mistry mansion is just a few blocks uphill to the right. I imagine Hari and the rest of his family gathered in that immaculate white mansion and talking with their PR team through the ten-point communication plan for news of Jett and Gisela's love child. Or maybe they're done with that topic of discussion, and Hari is having his all-important talk with his parents alone.

"And finally," Mom says, "even though I don't speak any French, I clearly heard Mario say the word *fiancée*—you heard it yourself. Ring plus fiancée equals engagement, no doubt about it."

If there's no doubt about it, then why haven't I heard from Hari in over twenty-four hours? Why is there a knot in the center of my stomach as big and hard as a baseball? I don't think I ate that many macarons. And why would the ring be delivered to the Mistry mansion instead of right upstairs to Hari's penthouse apartment at the Fairmont?

Somehow, I have the nagging feeling that all is not right.

28

"I can't believe it's still raining," Mom says. She looks out the window of Eleanor's flat at the slick streets below and sighs with the exaggerated emotion of a telenovela actress.

"It's been raining off and on all week," Eleanor says curtly. She motions for Mom and me to lift our legs as she vacuums under the couch we're sitting on. "Why should today be any different?"

"Because Amelia needs to look her absolute best tonight," Mom answers. She reaches over to pat my cheek and smooth my hair, which has now grown out into a stylish shag, a cross between Jane Fonda in *Klute* and Meg Ryan in any number of 1990s rom-coms.

"Why?" Eleanor asks. She switches off the vacuum. "What's so special about tonight?"

Before Mom can say something wildly inappropriate like "tonight is the night Hari will finally propose to Amelia," I jump into the conversation.

"Doesn't everyone want to look their best on New Year's Eve?" I ask.

"Well, I'm usually wearing my pajamas and eating a bowl of ice cream before going to bed at 9:01, right after the ball drops in Times Square," Eleanor says, "so I don't think I'm the best person to ask." Eleanor bends over to unplug the vacuum from the wall socket and lugs the machine into the hallway.

"Exactly," Mom says. "If you don't seize the opportunity tonight, Amelia, you could end up like your sister."

"I can hear you, Mom," Eleanor shouts from down the hallway. Mom and I stay silent until we hear the roar of the vacuum in the far back of the apartment.

"Have you heard anything from Hari?" Mom asks. "Anything at all?"

"No, Mom," I say, trying not to sulk.

"Whatever could he be thinking?" Mom asks. She keeps looking out the window, as if Hari could show up at any minute.

"I don't know," I say. It's all I can do to resist checking my Bling Phone again. I've already set it to blast ABBA's "Does Your Mother Know" when Hari texts or calls. It's an inside joke, a nod to the time we drunk-watched *Johnny English* in his penthouse.

"Do you think he saw the article in *The Nob*?" Mom asks. "Maybe it's caused a ruckus in his family, and he's having second thoughts about proposing?"

"Really, Mom, I have no idea whether he's having first thoughts about proposing," I say, "so it would be quite a stretch to say he's having second thoughts about it." I glance down at my toenails, which I had done earlier in the week at the nail salon to match my faux-fur stole. The peachy salmon color looked so pretty in the bottle, but now I wonder if it's too summery for a New Year's Eve party.

"I don't understand young people these days," Mom says. "You act like you have all the time in the world. By the time I was your age, Eleanor was already graduated from high school and getting ready to leave for college, and you weren't too far behind. But you, Hari, even Jett—you all seem to be in no rush to get married and have children."

"There's more to life than getting married and having children," I say. I don't dare reveal to Mom that Jett already has a child—a fully grown child, the same age as Eleanor's daughter—and that Gisela is pregnant with her second child. All of a sudden, I feel like the odd man out, the only one without a child, the only one who has failed to launch.

The day trickles by as slowly as the raindrops on the windowpanes, but at long last, it's time to get bathed and dressed for the Arcadia fundraiser. We take turns using the one bathroom in Eleanor's flat. By the time the four Bae-Wood women are ready, the entire flat smells of scorched hair from the flat iron, Mom's flowery Chanel No. 5, and Maggie's cherry-almond Jergens lotion.

Traffic is, once again, terrible. When our Lyft car pulls up to the Jett mansion, there's a legion of valets dressed head-to-toe in black caps, black suits, and black raincoats, each of them holding a black umbrella large enough to accommodate a family of four.

One line of valets ushers the guests out of their Teslas and Mercedes and Porsches and under the striped canvas awning that appears to have been specially set up to protect the gala attendees as they make their way up the grand staircase to the mansion's front door. Another line of valets expertly whisks the cars from the circular driveway to parts unknown. Rumor has it the Jetts rented an entire floor of a nearby parking garage for tonight's gathering.

A valet opens the door of our Hyundai Sonata with the

bright pink logo glowing in the front window. I'd tried to convince Eleanor to splurge for a larger car, but she refused to spend a dime more than she had to and would not let me put it on Hari's Bling Phone account. The four Bae-Wood women breathe a collective sigh of relief as we wriggle out of the midsize sedan. I feel like a sexy clown emerging from a decidedly unsexy clown car.

"Oh my God," Maggie says, her head tilted upward, "is this where Jett lives?"

The splendid building is lit up like the White House or Eiffel Tower. Eleanor's face grows increasingly paler with each step that we climb.

"Welcome to Le Petit Trianon, ladies," another valet announces as we reach the top of the stairway. He tips his cap while another valet opens the door to the mansion.

Decades ago, Nils and I took a self-guided tour of Versailles on our first trip to Europe together. The glossy visitor's pamphlet said that Le Petit Trianon was the little château that the then-twenty-year-old King Louis XVI of France gave to his nineteen-year-old queen—a spoiled vixen named Marie Antoinette. Despite its pseudo-royal moniker, the Jett mansion on top of Pacific Heights is no little château.

It's a fricking huge château.

The moment the valet opens the front door, we breathe another collective sigh, but this time it's in wonderment. The grand entryway is festooned with twinkling Christmas lights and fresh pine garlands. The air smells of wood fire, silver polish, and roasted meats—in essence, of old money. A slender young woman with a blond bob and starched white apron walks by with a platter of foie gras torchons on toasted brioche. And everywhere, the men are tastefully decked out in classic black tuxedoes and the women are respectably dressed in St. John knits and Chanel suit sets.

Wait, what? Respectably dressed?

As Eleanor hands her beleaguered L.L. Bean raincoat to the coat attendant, I survey the sea of silver-haired matrons in their nubby tweeds and modest necklines. I'm frozen in place. What should I do? Is it better to walk around in my clearly inappropriate Blanche DuBois-goes-Victoria's Secret slip dress or to keep on my salmon-pink stole as a faux-fur fig leaf? The attendant holds his gloved hand out to me along with a ticket, and I feel like I have no choice but to surrender my fig leaf.

"The Bae-Wood beauties!" Leo shouts, spotting the four of us in the foyer. It's a relief to see a friendly face in the crowd. And behind him, as usual, is Brandon looking dashing in his tux. Brandon might be a dour fussbudget, but even I can't deny that he's a class act.

"You both look so handsome, gentlemen," Mom says. She hugs Leo and Brandon in turn, kissing them each on both cheeks, much to Leo's delight and Brandon's apparent discomfort.

Eleanor, Maggie, and I just wave hello.

"Can you believe this place?" Mom says, helping herself to a passing crystal coupe of Champagne. "I've driven by it a million times. Everyone has, of course. The Palace of Pacific Heights, isn't that what everyone calls it? I've always wanted to see the inside, and now here we are." She giggles like a giddy teenager.

"I've been dying to see it too," Leo says. "Even though Jett and I have been friends for years, he's very private about his family. I don't think he's ever even mentioned his parents more than once or twice in all our years together. But when I casually suggested that I was looking for a venue for our annual fundraiser, Jett offered to host it here. Can you imagine? I think it's your influence—the Bae-Wood beauties are my good luck charm.

"Ladies, you must try the escargot lollipops," Leo says, stopping another young blonde woman carrying another tray of appetizers. "They are simply to die for."

Mom and Eleanor make small talk with Leo and Brandon, and I check my Bling Phone for the millionth time today. Still no message from Hari.

I'm at the party, I text. Where are you?

"Oh, hello there!" Leo shouts, waving toward the foyer.

We all turn around to see who Leo is shouting at. Mom and Eleanor have expectant looks on their faces, and I probably do as well. Only Mom looks pleased with what she sees.

Chong Bae enters the living room with his lawyer Mr. Park. As usual, both men are the picture of good taste from the top of their neatly trimmed hairstyles to the bottoms of their patent leather tuxedo shoes. Eleanor gives me a suspicious sideways look.

"Did you invite them?" she asks.

"No, honest," I say. "I had nothing to do with them being here."

"Oh, Eleanor," Mom says. "Turn that frown upside down and say Happy New Year to Chong Bae and Mr. Park."

"Please call me Douglas," Mr. Park says.

"And please call me Opa!" Chong Bae says.

"How did you get an invitation?" Eleanor asks coldly. "I can't imagine you know the Jett family."

"We don't! Would you be so kind as to introduce us?" Chong Bae responds with the most genuine of expressions. Eleanor practically rolls her eyes in derision.

"Your mother was so kind as to invite us to this event," Mr. Park says in a suave baritone. "We were told it was a fundraiser for Arcadia, and we very much wanted to support this worthy cause." Mr. Park bends his head deferentially in Leo's direction.

"Yes, I brought my checkbook and am ready to write a big check," Chong Bae says.

"A big check?" Eleanor sneers. "Your checkbook?" She glares at Chong Bae in a way that suggests she is not going to be embracing him as our brother anytime soon.

"Come along, Maggie," Eleanor says. "Let's see if we can find something nonalcoholic to drink. I'm feeling suddenly warm." Eleanor drags Maggie by her sleeve, and the two of them disappear into the crowd.

"Did I say something wrong?" Chong Bae asks.

Before I can even begin to apologize for Eleanor's behavior, someone behind me calls my name. I turn around, and I see Gisela standing by herself near the grand staircase. I walk over to hug her hello.

"You're here," Gisela says.

"Of course," I reply. "Why wouldn't I be here?"

Like everyone else at the party, Gisela seems to have gotten the memo on appropriate gala attire that nobody bothered sharing with me. She's wearing a burgundy velvet Empire-waisted dress—perfect for camouflaging baby bumps—with garnet and seed pearl chandelier earrings.

"Have you heard from Hari?" Gisela asks in a hushed tone.

"I haven't spoken with Hari since Thursday morning."

"So, you don't know about the announcement?" Gisela asks.

"No, what announcement?"

"Did I hear someone mention something about an announcement?" Leo asks, his trilling voice breaking through the din of party guests. Leo, Mom, Chong Bae, and Mr. Park make their way over to us, with Brandon keeping a respectful remove.

"Oh, hello, Leo," Gisela says. She smiles at the gathered group, her eyes resting on Chong Bae and Mr. Park, whom she's never met before. "Hello, everyone."

"You look especially lovely tonight, dear," Mom says, leaning in to give her a kiss on the cheek. "You're practically glowing."

Gisela's hand instinctively reaches for her belly.

"Isn't this a wonderful party?" Gisela says. Her tone is light and breezy, but her face is shadowed by concern. "It's so generous of the Jetts to be hosting it."

"Speaking of the Jetts," Mom says, "look who's coming our way."

Jett walks toward us, flanked on one side by his very elegant parents and on the other by a pretty young woman I instantly recognize from Hari's cell phone photos as Laila.

"Mother, Father," Jett says, "I'd like to introduce you to Leo Lowenstein, the head of Arcadia Cancer Retreat Center and my very good friend."

Leo and the Jett parents shake hands warmly, exchanging greetings of mutual admiration and appreciation. Jett then proceeds to introduce his parents to Brandon, Mom, and me, followed again by handshakes and polite mumbling.

Jett smiles at Chong Bae and Mr. Park and surreptitiously raises his eyebrows at me as if to ask, "Do you know those guys?" Meanwhile, Gisela and Laila have also been conspicuously omitted from the formal introductions.

"Gisela here was just telling us there's going to be an announcement today," Leo says. I admire Leo for finding a not-too-awkward way of including Gisela in the group.

"An announcement?" the elder Jett asks. His bushy, dark eyebrows look almost exactly like Jett's. He's got that sexy older man look, Sam Waterston crossed with Ciarán Hinds, *Law & Order* meets *Persuasion*. Meanwhile, Jett's mom looks just as I'd imagined from Jett's stories: creamy complexion, her smooth ebony hair pulled back in a tartan headband, a three-strand pearl necklace accenting the modest neckline of her long-sleeved black velvet and tartan taffeta gown. She looks like Snow White crossed with an American Girl doll.

"Well, we weren't intending to make a formal announcement about it," the elder Jett demurs, "but given that you are such good friends of our son, it only seems fitting to share the news now. We're happy to introduce you to the newest member of the Jett family. Please meet Laila, our granddaughter. Jett and Gisela's daughter."

Leo and Mom audibly gasp as Laila steps forward.

"It's nice to meet you," Laila says, dipping in a sweet curtsey.

People have barely had a chance to absorb the news when Mom interjects, "Speaking of new family members, I'd like to introduce you all to Mr. Chong Bae—Eleanor and Amelia's half brother—and his lawyer, Mr. Douglas Park. We just discovered Chong's existence as well."

Mom makes this announcement delightedly, seemingly unaware of how awkward the entire situation is, as if having a hitherto-secret family member is a point of shared pride instead of a rock-your-world revelation.

"Eleanor, Maggie, over here!" Mom beckons, spotting them in the distance. Eleanor looks perplexed as she makes her way through the crowd. She pats her hair nervously when she sees that Jett and his parents have joined our gathered group.

"Mother, Father," Jett says, "I'd like you to meet Eleanor Bae-Wood. She's Amelia's older sister and a longtime volunteer at Arcadia. And this is her daughter, Maggie."

We endure another round of handshakes and murmured greetings. Everyone is on their best behavior, but the whole situation couldn't be more awkward.

"Eleanor, Maggie," Jett says, "I'd like to introduce you to my daughter, Laila."

Even Eleanor, with her practiced talent for putting on a

fake smile at will, can't hide her confusion. She stares at the delicate young woman who somehow manages to look exactly like both Jett and Gisela and then slowly pans around the circle of people until her gaze rests on me.

"Well, well, well," Leo says, chuckling. "To be completely honest, I was expecting a different kind of announcement, but this one is just as delightful." His eyes twinkle and then focus on Gisela's belly. "A double delight!"

"Oh, Leo," Gisela sighs. "You are such a gossip."

"Not true!" Leo protests. "Not true at all."

"Well, most people here know anyway," Gisela says, "so I may as well let everyone else in on the not-so-secret secret." Gisela gently draws Jett and Laila closer to her and kisses them both lightly on the cheek. For the second time in one night, Mom lets out an audible gasp.

"I'm excited to announce that in four months," Gisela says, "Laila will have a little sister."

29

While everyone fusses over Gisela and her baby announcement, Eleanor quietly backs out of the circle and retreats to a corner to sit down in an upholstered wing chair. I follow and crouch down at her feet.

"Are you okay?" I ask. "You're so pale."

"I'm fine," Eleanor says. She stands up and walks into the foyer.

"You're not fine," I say, shadowing her every move. The two of us bump and bustle our way through the throngs of partygoers. Heads turn, people whisper.

"Stop following me," Eleanor says.

"Where are you going?" I ask.

"To the ladies' room," Eleanor says.

"I need to go too," I lie.

While neither of us has ever been to the Jett mansion before, the ladies' room is easily recognizable by the queue of women waiting their turn. Eleanor takes her place at the end of the line, and I stand right behind her.

"Eleanor," I begin.

"Not here," she cuts me off.

We stand there in silence, watching the bathroom door opening and closing every few minutes. Suddenly, I hear two young women up ahead having a loud and obviously tipsy conversation.

"Did you see her come in?" the first woman says.

"You could hardly miss her," the second woman replies. "She kinda stands out."

"I don't think she's as pretty in person as her photos from *The Nob*."

"Well, it's no mystery what Hari Mistry sees in her. I mean, with that dress, you can see ev-er-y-thing."

"I imagine Mr. and Mrs. Jett will not be pleased about it," the first woman says. "They are practically allergic to scandal. Who even invited her?"

"I heard she's friends with Jett," the second woman says. "I think they know one another from that cancer place he volunteers at."

"That Jett's always been a sucker for charity cases. Do you know the other people she came in with?" the first woman asks.

"Her family, I assume."

"The whole group of them reminds me of our high school trip to Washington when we toured the Hall of First Ladies. The old lady is a bottle-blonde Nancy Reagan, the girl is Jackie O, and Hari's girlfriend is Jackie's daughter-in-law Carolyn Bessette in her Narciso Rodriguez wedding dress. It's like she forgot to wear an actual dress and just wore her slip!"

The two women guffaw like donkeys.

Eleanor's stony face reveals nothing. A middle-aged woman wearing a chenille evening suit and sensible shoes emerges from the bathroom, and the line inches ever so slightly forward.

"What about the last one?" the second woman asks. "Which First Lady is she?"

"There was another one?"

"You saw her—the one who gave a sopping wet anorak to the coat check. I'm pretty sure I heard someone call her Eleanor."

"Well, that's perfect because she dresses just like her namesake—Eleanor Roosevelt!"

The tipsy twins disappear into the bathroom only to emerge a few minutes later, freshly powdered and lipsticked, still gabbing and giggling away. Their faces freeze upon seeing Eleanor and me in line.

"Eponym, not namesake," Eleanor says to the two women as they slink past.

When our turn comes for the bathroom, Eleanor rushes in and closes the door. I have to push hard to force my way inside.

"Eleanor, we need to talk," I say, locking the door behind me.

"Amelia, this is neither the time nor place," Eleanor responds. She grabs a cotton hand towel from the counter, wets it in the sink, and gently pats her overheated face.

"And what, pray tell, is the time and place, Eleanor? If not now, when?"

After a moment's pause, Eleanor turns to me and asks, "How long have you known?"

"Known what?" I ask.

"About Jett and Gisela. Their daughter. The pregnancy. All of it."

"I don't know," I say. "I've known about Gisela's pregnancy since the fall, but I only found out about Laila this week."

"Since the fall," Eleanor says. The words come out like an indictment. "You've known since the fall."

"I promised Gisela I wouldn't tell anyone," I say. "And Hari swore me to secrecy about Laila as well."

"And when did you become Gisela's best friend?" Eleanor asks. "I've known Gisela for years, and suddenly Gisela's sharing secrets with you?"

"Meaning what?" I ask. "Are you jealous that I've made more friends at Arcadia in six months than you have in twelve years? Because that's not about me, Ellie. That's about you. People won't open up to you if you won't open up to them."

"Thank you for that completely unsolicited opinion, Amelia," Eleanor says. "But I'm not jealous—certainly not of you." She pauses to let the words burn.

"Ever since Dad died," she continues, her tone fiery and cold at the same time, "I've been single-handedly holding our family together. For the past six months, I've given you a warm bed and three meals a day, and you have never once bothered to say thank you or offered to get a job. For the past two months, you've been parading around town with a notorious playboy who treats women like baubles to add to his collection, which is not only humiliating for you but also an awful example to be setting for Maggie. But in the immortal words of Edith Piaf, you regret nothing, right?"

I'm stunned. Who knew my sainted sister could hold a grudge?

"I may not be perfect," I say, my fight-or-flight response activated, "but neither are you. I spoke to Chong this week about the lawsuit, and I know you've been lying to Mom and me for months. He didn't want any part of Dad's estate—all he wanted was for us to acknowledge him as our brother. It was only when you refused to meet him face-to-face and hired lawyers to keep him from being recognized as Dad's son that Chong had to bring in his own lawyers. So I don't think you're in a position to be preaching to me about regret. You haven't been single-handedly holding our family together. You're single-handedly ruining us."

"You spoke with that man?" Eleanor cries.

"His name is Chong," I say. "Chong Bae. Just like Dad."

"No," Eleanor says, "not just like Dad. I don't know how he managed to fake the papers and steal Dad's name, but he is not Dad's son. Dad can't defend himself from the grave, and I refuse to believe this imposter's lies."

As Eleanor practically spits out these final words, I realize that my ever-sensible sister has lost her grasp on reality. I think back to my conversation with Hari at Inspiration Point, how he had psychoanalyzed Eleanor's reaction to the lawsuit and tied it back to Edward's death.

"No," I say as soothingly as I can, "Dad can't defend himself from the grave. Neither can Edward. But that doesn't mean we have to deny the truth. Maybe it's time to accept the truth and move forward. Maybe it's time for you to work on your own unresolved feelings about Edward."

Eleanor flashes me a Medusa-worthy glare.

"I found Edward's letters, Eleanor," I say. "It was an honest accident—I was looking for documentation to support Chong Bae's claims—but I found them in your basement." My heart is racing as I admit, "And I read the one he wrote to Tina Gallagher."

"How dare you…" Eleanor splutters.

"I know it was wrong," I say, "but I'm glad I found the letter. It helped me to understand why you're so upset about Chong Bae. Somehow you equate Dad with Edward—no wait, is it that you equate Dad and Chong?—shoot, Hari summed it up so perfectly…"

"You told Hari?" Eleanor explodes.

Once again, my big fat mouth.

"Let me get this straight," Eleanor says, "you have no trouble keeping it secret from me that Jett and Gisela have not one but two children together, but you feel like it's totally okay to go snooping around in my personal papers and share details of my dead husband's private life with a feckless playboy like Hari? Have you no loyalty? Have you no family pride? Do you not care at all about me and my privacy?"

"I'm sorry, Eleanor," is all I can say.

I was furious with Eleanor for putting our family through so much over the past year, but that fury has now vanished. Eleanor's misguided actions came out of loyalty to Dad and the rest of our family, but what was my excuse for my own misguided actions? How could I have spilled Eleanor's most private and painful secrets to Hari? Once again, I let a man take precedence over everything else in my life.

"Get out of here before I do something I will regret," Eleanor says.

I unlock the door and walk out into the hallway. The next woman waiting in line moves forward. For a moment I think Eleanor is going to punch her, but she merely blocks the door.

"My sister's leaving," Eleanor says. "But I'm not through yet."

30

Eleanor's words are still ringing in my ears as I stalk the halls of the Jett mansion looking for a quiet place to think. I see a golden shaft of light from a half-opened door, and I collapse into a mohair love seat in a book-lined study. I click on my Bling Phone again and check the text icon. Still no word from Hari.

I don't know how long I've been sitting there when Leo walks into the room.

"Amelia, darling," Leo says, "we've been looking all over for you. What a night for announcements. I'm simply astonished. How are you doing?"

"I was in the bathroom trying to talk to Eleanor," I say. "She's really upset about it."

"But how about you? It must be a shock for you," Leo says.

"I've actually known for some time," I say. "I felt bad keeping it from everyone, but Gisela and Hari swore me to secrecy."

"You've known for some time?" Leo asks.

"Yeah, Gisela told me about her pregnancy back in October," I say, "and Hari told me about Laila earlier this week."

"Oh dear," Leo says. "So, you don't know then?"

"Know what?" I ask.

"About Preeti? Preeti Singh?"

"Who's Preeti Singh?" I ask.

"My darling, sweet girl," Leo says. "Preeti Singh is the daughter of that Indian real estate mogul. And she's Hari's new fiancée. The Mistrys and Singhs just announced their engagement on Twitter."

Leo hands me his cell phone, and I see the following tweet from TheRaj-Official:

The Mistry Family is honored to announce the engagement of our son Hari to Miss Preeti Singh, youngest daughter of the Singh Family of Mumbai and London and chief curator of Indian Art and Antiquities at the Asian Art Museum in San Francisco.

The accompanying photo collage features the starry-eyed couple, their proudly beaming parents, and a close-up of the breathtaking engagement ring, a canary yellow oval-cut diamond encircled by tiny white diamonds. As if to drive the stake into my heart, the photo collage has a small caption: Jewelry by La Petite Etoile.

WTF???? I text Hari.

I race down the hallway lined with framed Old Master paintings. The ocean of tasteful tweeds and tuxes in the Jett mansion foyer parts like the Red Sea in *The Ten Commandments*, and I'm freaking Charlton Heston as Moses.

As I wait for the coat check attendant to get my salmon-pink stole, I hear not-so-hushed whispers of "Who's that girl?" My mind flashes back to the all-caps article in *The Nob*, and I avoid everyone's curious stares. I glare down at my Bling

Phone, trying by sheer force of will to make the three dots of "someone's texting" appear, but I get nothing.

The attendant offers me my stole, and I reach for it with my left hand. There, I see the faux-diamond ring to go along with my faux-fur stole. Yup, that's me: the faux fiancée. But there's nothing faux about the throbbing in my head.

I need to get the heck out of this faux château.

"May I help you..." the valet asks as I walk out the front door. I ignore him and run down the steps like Cinderella fleeing the ball. Through the pouring rain, I see the glow of a cab on the street corner. I flail my arms around as I race toward the light.

"Where to, miss?" the cabbie asks.

I climb into the back seat and slam the door shut. It's quiet inside the cab. My mind is empty. My brain has flatlined.

"Miss?" the cabbie says.

I can't go to Hari's place. Or Eleanor's flat. Or the house in Atherton. I've lost touch with all my friends from high school, and I don't know another soul in San Francisco.

This really sucks. Things haven't been this bad since I had to sneak out of the Buddhist monastery and hitchhike my way down to California. I thought life had turned around, changed for the better, and now I realize how deluded I was. Absolutely nothing has changed. I'm still as lost and luckless as when I first arrived at Arcadia.

The thought barely has a chance to register when I see the cabbie reach down and take a frothy sip from a green-and-white logo paper cup.

"Arcadia Cancer Retreat Center," I say. "Up past Point Reyes Station. Just keep taking 1 North until you see the signs."

"Motherskippy," the cabbie yells, screeching on the brakes.

My eyes pop open just as the cab swerves and hits something hard on the side of the road—a rock or tree branch, maybe.

"What happened?" I ask.

The cabbie undoes his seat belt, exits, and checks the front of the car. He smashes his fist on the hood.

"What happened?" I ask again when the cabbie gets back in.

"The rabbit survived but my front wheel is effed up," the cabbie says.

"I'm sorry," I say. "I can pay for the damage."

"Yes, you can pay," the cabbie says. "You can pay now."

"Pay now?" I ask.

"Yeah, I don't suppose you have cash?"

The cab's meter glows ominously red. I've never seen a three-digit cab fare before.

"No, I don't have cash," I say, "but you take credit, right?" I point to the Mastercard and Visa logos on his dashboard, click the Apple Pay icon on my Bling Phone, and pass it to him.

"What's this?" he asks.

"Apple Pay," I explain.

"Cash or credit," he says. "No Apple Pay."

"But I don't have cash or credit. I only have my phone. It's linked to an Amex card."

The cabbie smashes his fist on the steering wheel, causing the car to emit a loud beep that triggers me to emit a similarly loud scream.

"Get out," he says.

"You can't be serious," I say, pointing at the rain outside the windows. "I can't get out here."

"Get out," he repeats.

"Here, take my phone," I say. "It's worth hundreds, maybe more than a thousand dollars. You can have it. Just take me a little farther to Arcadia."

"What am I supposed to do with this?" the cabbie scoffs,

turning the phone over in his hands, as if trying to figure out what it is.

"You could sell it," I say. "On eBay or Craigslist."

"And you could tell the police I stole it from you," he counters, returning the phone back to me. "No thank you, I've done my time. Ain't goin' back there again."

"Please," I beg. "I can't go out into this rain."

"There," he says, pointing. "There's a phone booth. Use your Apple Pay to call someone who cares."

The miracle vision appears again. The Portal to the Dead stands there on the hill, its metal-and-glass accordion door open like a faithful wife welcoming her sea captain husband home.

As I tromp up the hill in my stilettos, the rain-soaked earth sucks the shoes into the hillside, leaving me barefoot. Seriously, at this point, I don't care.

"Hello phone booth, my old friend," I say as I walk in. I pat the black metal phone like an owner patting his loyal dog.

The phone booth doesn't say anything back.

"I know you must be mad," I say. "I don't come to visit or anything."

Silence.

I click on my Bling Phone to see if I have service. Barely half a bar. I've never been so grateful to see that tiny white rectangle.

I open the texting icon, and I see two names: Hari and Maggie. I swipe left on Hari and delete all of our messages. Just as I click onto Maggie's name, the half bar sputters out, and NO SERVICE takes its place.

"No!" I scream, desperately jiggling the Bling Phone around. I hold it high, I hold it low, but whatever I do, the Bling Phone refuses to come back to life.

I pick up the phone booth's heavy black receiver. No dial tone, of course. Not that I expected one.

"Happy New Year, Daddy," I say into the receiver. "We've got to stop meeting this way."

Sheets of rain coat the phone booth's glass walls. There's a tiny leak in the far corner of the booth, where the rain enters and dribbles down the interior wall. A small puddle is beginning to form on the shiny metal floor.

"Well, at least there isn't any thunder and lightning tonight," I say. "That's an improvement from last time, right, Daddy?"

My bare feet are freezing standing there on the cold, wet floor. My arms are covered in goose bumps, and my body starts to shiver. How long does it take for hypothermia to set in? Eleanor would know.

I remove my faux-fur stole from my shoulders and place it on the ground. My feet feel warmer already. I sit down on the furry floor and huddle into the smallest ball possible, hoping to conserve my body heat.

I click on my Bling Phone again, taking small comfort in the blue-light glow of the screen. Like a desert island castaway writing a message in a bottle, I type into the message field to Maggie:

HELP! I'm in a phone booth near Arcadia. It's freezing. Please send help.

I click send and hold my breath.

Message not delivered.

I lean my head against the cold glass wall of the phone booth. It's just half a mile farther down the road to the Master's

Cottage. Once there's a break in the rain, I can make a run for it. There's got to be a break in the rain soon, right?

A gale-force wind hits the phone booth, rocking it from side to side, like Mother Nature herself saying "no way!"

While I listen for the rain to relent, I imagine myself running down the hill and along the dirt road toward the Master's Cottage. I left my keys back at Eleanor's flat, but there's got to be some way in. Maybe I could break a window or batter down the front door. I laugh out loud imagining myself as Bruce Willis in *Die Hard*, crashing into the cottage with my feet cut up by the broken glass.

"Oh, Daddy," I say out loud. "What should I do now? How do I get myself out of this mess? I'm officially phoning a friend. Can you give me a clue?"

An icy-cold drop of rain plops from the ceiling onto my face.

I wipe the rain away and realize I no longer feel cold. I think that means hypothermia has set in. I see a light in the distance. Delusions, another sign of hypothermia. Who could it be? God? A visiting angel? Last time, it was Jett, but I can't expect to be so lucky again. This time, it really will be Freddy Krueger.

A dark shadow approaches the phone booth. Someone opens the accordion door and shines a flashlight inside, turning my darkness to light.

"She's here, Eleanor," Brandon shouts into the distance. "She's safe."

Brandon takes off his heavy black raincoat and wraps me in it. The raincoat is still warm from Brandon's body and gives off the scent of his sandalwood cologne and peppermint soap. The torrential rain soaks into Brandon's once-crisp tuxedo shirt, plastering the fine cotton fabric against his surprisingly toned torso. Brandon lifts me out of the phone booth with his steady arms and carries me down the soggy incline.

When we get to the bottom of the hill, Brandon opens the front door of his Land Rover and slips me inside. I look into the back seat and see that it's unoccupied.

"Where's Eleanor?" I ask.

"She left," he says. "In her own car."

"Left?"

"Back to the city," Brandon says. "Everyone else is still at the Arcadia fundraiser. Eleanor predicted you would be headed out here, so we followed as fast as we could."

Brandon gets into the driver's seat, and we remain silent as we make our way slowly up the twisty road. I lean against the window and watch the blue-black landscape passing by. The Master's Cottage appears on the right. We keep going.

"Wait," I say, "where are you taking me?"

"To Leo's," Brandon says. "There's an extra guest room where you can stay."

"But the Master's Cottage. Why don't I just stay at the Master's Cottage?"

Brandon doesn't answer, and something about his demeanor convinces me to be quiet. I draw the collar of Brandon's black raincoat closer to my face and breathe in deeply. I wonder if Dad wore a similar cologne because the scent makes me feel comforted and calm. In just a few minutes, we're in front of Leo's place. Brandon turns off the engine.

"Brandon, are you going to tell me what's going on?" I ask. I turn on the interior car light so I can see him clearly. There's a deep sadness etched on his face that makes me want to reach over and hug him. No one should ever look so sad.

"Eleanor wanted to make sure you were safe," Brandon says.

"Okay," I say. "I'm safe. So why are we at Leo's place?"

Brandon looks pained, as if I've just stabbed him in the heart.

"Eleanor wanted to make sure you were safe," Brandon repeats, "but she says you are not welcome in her home ever again."

Spring

31

There's an Anna's hummingbird flitting in and out of the trumpet vine outside Leo's library. Even with the window closed, I can make out the buzzing sound as the bird zip-zips from flower to flower. After months of wintry rains, spring seems to have finally arrived at Arcadia.

"So, has everyone confirmed?" Leo asks Brandon.

"Yes, Leo," Brandon groans, "for the hundredth time, everyone has confirmed."

I'm lying on the overstuffed couch in Leo's library, pretending to be reading the latest issue of *Nature*, but I'm really soaking in the sunshine while Leo and Brandon bicker like an old married couple.

"One hundred percent?" Leo asks.

"Yes, Leo," Brandon sighs, "one hundred percent."

"Oh, thank goodness," Leo exclaims. He's almost giggling. "Thank goodness."

Brandon stands up from Leo's cluttered desk, plops an inch-thick pile of papers on Leo's lap, and walks out of the room.

I hear him turning the spigot in the kitchen and filling the teapot. I glance at the clock on the library wall. It's four in the afternoon—teatime.

"One hundred percent?" I ask Leo.

Leo looks up from the pile of papers. There's a softness in his eyes—eyes that are already some of the bluest and kindest eyes I've ever seen—that draws me in.

"For the first retreat of the season, I always reserve all ten spots for alumni to attend free of charge. Guests who have been to Arcadia before, who I think might benefit from another week of reflection and relaxation," Leo says.

Arcadia normally charges a couple thousand dollars per person for its weeklong cancer retreats. Even though it's a nonprofit staffed mostly by volunteers, Arcadia needs to pay for its operating costs somehow. Leo must have to curry favor with a lot of rich donors to be able to afford a free retreat for ten people.

"What does one hundred percent mean?" I ask.

"It means all of the guests I've invited have RSVP'd yes," Leo says. "It means they're all going to attend."

"Is that unusual?" I ask.

Leo's eyes turn watery.

"Yes, it's very unusual," Leo says.

My thoughts turn to Eleanor. She mentioned coming to Arcadia for the first time when Edward's cancer had metastasized. He died just six months later. I suspect Edward didn't live long enough to have been invited to come back as an alumnus.

Forget Eleanor, I tell myself. She's apparently forgotten about me, written me off like a bad debt.

Brandon comes into the library with the tea tray. Over the past couple months, I've gotten used to the very English ritual of afternoon tea. In fact, I've gotten used to everything about daily life with Leo and Brandon.

Leo slices a currant scone in half and slathers it with Devon cream.

"By Jove," Leo exclaims. "I think she's got it!" He looks at me with wide-eyed wonder.

"Brandon helped," I demur. "I followed his recipe to the letter."

"You're too modest," Brandon says. He hands me a cup of tea. "The student has become the master."

"Let me guess," I say, rolling my eyes like a teenager. "Lao Tzu? Aristotle?"

"Mr. Miyagi," Brandon says.

"Oh my God, Brandon," I say. "Did you just drop a *Karate Kid* line on me?"

I see Brandon's eyes glowing in pleasure. I take a sip of my tea. Hot, sweet, and creamy. Perfect as usual. Brandon knows just how I like it.

"Are you still willing to take over the kitchen this week?" Leo says to me.

"Do I have a choice?" I ask.

"You have to earn your keep somehow, Miss Amelia," Leo replies.

Even though I know he's joking, Leo's comment contains more than a grain of truth. Ever since the disastrous New Year's Eve party, Leo and Brandon have been beyond generous to me: letting me stay in the guest room, nursing me through my month-long chest cold, carefully avoiding any mention of Eleanor or Hari or Preeti Singh. But Leo made it clear to me that, once I felt ready, I'd need to start contributing to the work at Arcadia. The kitchen seemed like the best fit for my talents—or lack thereof.

"Well, I've been practicing with Jett's menus and recipes," I say, "but I hope you don't expect me to cook to his standards."

"You don't have to cook to Jett's standards, my dear," Leo

says. "You are in a class of your own. Besides, Brandon will be there to serve as your sous-chef, at least until his sabbatical ends."

Leo helps himself to a second scone, pointedly defying Brandon's disapproving glare. "We're taking a hike with Maggie this afternoon!" Leo says by way of excuse.

"We'd better make it an extra-long hike," Brandon says, whisking the basket of scones back into the kitchen. "The doctor warned you about your cholesterol."

"Any further word from Jett?" I ask. I take a bite of my scone and am surprised how well it turned out. The texture is perfect: flaky but tender. The Meyer lemon zest that I added to the recipe gives it just a hint of citrusy perfume.

"He's still being evasive," Leo says. "He's got a lot on his plate right now but doesn't want to leave us in a lurch."

We haven't seen Jett since the fundraiser at his parents' house, but Leo heard through his contacts that Jett has been pulled into the family business. With one teenage daughter headed to college and a new baby on the way, it makes sense that Jett has to start acting like the heir to a global oil conglomerate that he is.

"I'm happy to run the kitchen for this first retreat," I say, "but I don't know if I can do it after that."

"I'd pay you, of course," Leo says. "Jett volunteered his time, but I don't expect that of you. And you are welcome to live here or in one of the employee rooms as long as you want."

"No, it's not that," I say. "I mean, thank you—it would be great to get paid, and of course I appreciate your hospitality."

"Then what is it?" Leo asks.

"It's just," I begin. Out of the corner of my eye, a second hummingbird buzzes into view. The two brilliantly colored birds hover in midair, their wings beating in a blur, until one bird gives chase to the other. I can't tell if they're playing or fighting.

"I don't know if I can do it alone," I say.

Honestly, the only reason I agreed to take on kitchen duties was that Brandon agreed to help me. But come June, Brandon's yearlong sabbatical will reach its end, and he'll have to go back to his position as headmaster of the Muir Academy—a busy job that apparently gets busier once the regular school year ends, summer session begins, and budgeting and staffing decisions need to be made.

Leo looks so placid that I'm not sure he even heard me. He chomps happily on his second scone and washes it down with a gulp of tea. He glances down at his chest and brushes the tiny crumbs onto the floor.

"Teatime's over," Brandon announces as he enters the library.

"Why do you always insist on wearing that silly safari outfit?" I ask, looking up at his familiar figure. "Khaki isn't flattering on anyone. You look so much better in white—preferably rain-soaked."

Ever since Brandon saved me from the Portal to the Dead, I've been teasing him about his "Mr. Darcy moment" with his sopping wet tuxedo shirt plastered suggestively against his body. It's become our private inside joke, something between just us two, although a part of me isn't really joking. He really did look surprisingly hot that night.

"We mustn't keep Maggie waiting," Brandon says, feigning indifference to my comment. He removes Leo's safari hat from the back of the desk chair and places it securely on Leo's head.

While Leo gets up and scrambles to the hallway to put on his jacket and hiking boots, Brandon walks over to the couch and extends his hand to me.

"Ready, Ms. Amelia Bae-Wood?" he asks.

"Ready, Mr. Darcy," I say, letting him lift me up.

Brandon, Leo, Maggie, and I sit on Arcadia's front porch, resting our legs and taking in the scenic sunset view. Our hike was shorter than expected, partly due to a late-afternoon cold front and partly due to my sudden realization that the smoked salmon I planned to serve for the first day's lunch was still lying rock-solid in the walk-in freezer.

Although it was warm all day, a nippy wind rustles the nearby branches. I zip my jacket all the way up to my chin and rub my hands together.

"So much for March coming in like a lion and going out like a lamb," I say.

"Oh, you spoiled California girls," Leo says. "This is positively balmy compared to my days growing up in suburban Boston. Even when it seemed spring had finally arrived, there'd inevitably be one more snowstorm in late April or early May. Ah, good old New England—I don't miss it one bit."

I wish Leo hadn't said those words. Maggie hardly needs another reminder of good old New England. Brandon has been driving Maggie and me to the Muir Academy nearly every day this month to check her email for college admission decisions. Maggie got into all the UCs she applied to except Berkeley, along with a couple private colleges, but she still hasn't heard back from Holyoke. According to their website, Holyoke should send out its admission decisions no later than tomorrow, April 1.

Happy April Fool's Day.

"Mr. Allyn," Maggie asks, "would it be okay if we go on the earlier side tomorrow?"

"Of course," Brandon says, "we can go whenever you want."

"Or maybe we should go on the later side," Maggie says, her

voice unsure. She bends over to untie and retie the laces on her boots. "I wouldn't want to make you go twice in one day, just in case the email hasn't arrived by the morning."

"Brandon, dear boy," Leo interrupts, "you will absolutely kill me for asking, but could we go back to your place right now? I want to check one last time that all our alumni guests will be joining us tomorrow."

Maggie pops her head up and looks over at Leo. Leo holds on to his "nothing to see here, officer" faux-innocent face for a split second before breaking out into a grin. Maggie and I join him in laughter.

"Well, let's be quick about it," Brandon says. "I've got supper still to make."

Although Brandon's tone is as dry and brittle as the few leaves remaining on the winter trees, I see him taking in Maggie's eager face with genuine warmth and affection. I don't know what we did to deserve such a kind man as him in our lives.

Leo and I chatter nonstop all along the drive to the Muir Academy, bantering about the week's cancer center menu, the freshened paint and new furnishings in the guest quarters, Gisela training her partner Sage to substitute teach the yoga classes. Maggie gets the occasional word in edgewise, although I can feel her bristling with anticipation. Brandon, as usual, is silent.

When Brandon pulls his Land Rover into the Muir Academy's curving driveway, a group of students stands aside and watches. They're all young men, dressed in V-neck maroon sweaters and crisp khaki slacks. The whole thing looks straight out of *Dead Poets Society*, except most of the students are Latino or African American.

Brandon parks the car in front of his cottage, and the swarm of boys make their way over to greet us.

"Welcome back, Mr. Allyn," one student says. "We've missed you."

"Thank you, Theo," Brandon says, patting him on the back. "I'm not back for good quite yet, but it's wonderful to see all your faces. I've missed you too."

"I just got into Reed, Mr. Allyn," another student says. "My first choice!"

"I got into Cornell," a third student adds. "Your alma mater."

There's a joyful din as students shout out their admissions and accomplishments. Brandon reaches over and gives each of the young men a high five.

Maggie and I exchange surprised looks. Stuffy old Brandon handing out high fives?

"I am delighted to hear your news," Brandon says, "but I'm not in the least bit surprised. You've all worked hard and deserve every reward. I'll be back here at school to celebrate with you at commencement, but if you'll pardon me, I need to escort my guests inside right now."

With that, Brandon ushers the three of us past the adoring mobs of students and into his ivy-covered cottage.

"Elvis has just left the building," I say as I watch the students disperse. "Or should I call you Mr. Chips?" I look upon Brandon with fresh admiration.

"They're good boys, one and all," Brandon says. "Very good boys indeed." He stamps his leather boots vigorously on the doormat, although I suspect it's more to avoid eye contact with me than to rid his shoes of dirt.

"Miss Maggie," Leo says, settling down on the living room couch, "would you like some privacy as you check your emails?"

Maggie glances nervously over at me.

"You've already been admitted into five great colleges," I say, keeping my voice steady, my eyes glued to hers. "Everything else is gravy."

Maggie nods and makes her way to Brandon's office. Brandon and I stand in the living room, trying not to listen to the clicking of the keyboard.

"Brandon, do you have anything to eat?" Leo asks. "I'm feeling a little peckish, and I'm not sure I can wait until dinner."

Brandon barely has time to shoot Leo an "are you kidding me?" glare before Maggie appears in the archway.

"I got in," she whispers.

"She got in," Brandon and I exhale at the same time.

"She got in!" Leo hollers.

I walk over and wrap my arms around my precious niece, who's now almost as tall as me. We stand there together, rocking side to side, and I can feel her giggling and shaking in equal measure.

"Not to ruin the moment," I say, "but any word about the scholarship?"

"No," Maggie responds. The shaking has now overtaken the giggling. "The email says the financial aid package should come in the mail."

The mail. That's Eleanor's domain. Damn.

"Congratulations, Maggie," Leo says. "What an accomplishment. Now, if you don't mind, I'm going to check my email right quick and then we can head back home in time for Brandon to make us a celebratory supper."

"Maggie, you seem a little shaky," I say, tucking a piece of hair behind her ear.

"Come with me," Brandon says. "I'll get you a glass of water."

I walk into Brandon's study just as Leo checks his email. Over at the bookshelf, I pick up the faded Kodachrome photo of Brandon and Leo and Brandon's now-deceased wife in the silver frame etched with the words *Our Wedding.*

"How long have you known Brandon?" I ask.

Leo takes the framed photo from me and smiles.

"Laura introduced me to Brandon just a month before this photo was taken," Leo says. "They had been friends and colleagues for a long time before they started dating and fell in love. It was Laura's idea for Brandon to create the Muir Academy. She was convinced that his talents would be better spent nurturing young men in need of a strong male role model than lecturing the privileged elite. As you could see from the fine young gentlemen who greeted us just now, Laura was right. She was always right."

"Laura was her name?" I ask. "Brandon's wife?"

"Yes, Laura Lilibeth Lowenstein," Leo says. "My younger sister. Our parents had a thing for *L*s."

"She was your sister?" I say, relieved to hear Leo state what I already suspected.

"Yes, we were sisters," Leo says. "We were so much like you and Eleanor."

The drive from the Muir Academy to Arcadia is the opposite of the ride there. Maggie talks nonstop with Brandon about college, the classes she should take, potential extracurriculars, and so forth, while Leo and I sit in companionable silence.

We drop Maggie off at the Master's Cottage, and I slink down in my seat just in case Eleanor happens to be home. Not that I really need to worry. According to Mom and Maggie, Eleanor's been working double shifts almost every Sunday and staying with her friend Stephanie in Sea Cliff to avoid the long drive to Arcadia at night.

Back in the comfort of Leo's house, Brandon pours two glasses of wine for me and Leo before heading into the kitchen to prepare supper.

"Have I given you a terrible shock?" Leo asks. "Or did you already know that I was Brandon's sister-in-law?"

"Me, shocked? I don't shock easily," I say. "I figured that you transitioned when I first saw that photo in Brandon's office. It's no big deal, really. Caitlyn Jenner was one of my best customers at Amuse."

"You've been awful quiet, though."

"I've been thinking about what you said," I begin. "What did you mean when you said you and Laura were like me and Eleanor? Did you just mean that you two were sisters, or did you mean something else?"

"Oh, that was presumptuous of me to say," Leo says. "An old man remembering himself as a young girl."

"Now, that's not a sentence you hear very often," I say, laughing.

"Too true," Leo says. "Too true."

"Come on, Leo, don't worry about being blunt. Tell me what you meant."

Leo pauses to take a sip of his wine and leans forward on his elbows.

"The instant I met your sister," he begins, "I saw in her so much of my own sister, Laura. Selfless, hardworking, principled, and reserved to the point of…" He hesitates.

"Coldness," I say.

"No, that's too harsh a word," Leo says. "They're not cold, Eleanor and Laura. It's just hard to puncture their armor, to get past that polished veneer of perfection."

"Unlike me," I say. I laugh ruefully. "No veneer of perfection here."

"You're too hard on yourself," Leo says. "Just like me at your age. In fact, the instant I met you, I saw in you the reflection of myself."

"You're too kind," I say.

"No, not really," Leo laughs. "I was seriously messed up at your age."

"Hey," I say, laughing along, "you said I was too hard on myself, and now you're calling me messed up!"

"You can be too hard on yourself and seriously messed up at the same time. The two are not incompatible. In fact, for the young Leona Llewellyn Lowenstein, being too hard on myself—refusing to accept myself for who I was—is what made me so messed up to begin with. Once I embraced my true self, saw my unique qualities as assets rather than liabilities, life got easier."

"So, do you think I should become a man?" I ask.

"Now, that's also not a sentence you hear very often," Leo chuckles.

"No, seriously," I ask in all earnestness, "what do you think I should do?"

"You don't need to become a man," Leo says, "but you do need to man up. Woman up. I don't know what the correct wording should be. Start taking charge of your life instead of letting life—or other people—take charge of you. You don't need Nils or Hari or dear, sweet Brandon to define you. You are Ms. Amelia Bae-Wood, hear you roar."

I lean my head against Leo's shoulder. I know Leo is right. I've thought the same thing for a while, but it helps hearing someone else say it.

"And one more thing," Leo says.

"Yes?" I ask, lifting my head.

"Extend an olive branch to Eleanor," Leo says. "Work to mend the damage that has torn you two apart. I know it may not feel this way, but nothing is ever irreparable. As someone who misses their sister every single day, take it from me—there is nothing more precious than family or more fleeting than life. Don't waste another moment in anger with Eleanor."

With that, I start to sob. Big, messy, full-on ugly crying. Sympathetic soul that he is, Leo starts to sob too. Together, we're a bomb cyclone of tears and snot and blotchy red noses.

Brandon walks into the room.

"Do you two want more wi—" Brandon begins. He's holding a bottle of red. He stops in his tracks once he sees the cryfest taking place before him.

"No," Leo says. We both laugh as we see Brandon's panicked visage, and we wipe away our tears. "I think dear Amelia and I have had quite enough wine for the night."

32

I can't sleep all night. My brain buzzes as tirelessly as the wings of yesterday's two hummingbirds, obsessing about the first cancer retreat of the season, Maggie's college choices, and Leo's advice to me. I toss and turn in bed, glancing at the pale, round face of the clock on the nightstand every few minutes and sighing in frustration. When 4:00 in the morning rolls around, I finally give up and get out of bed.

Leo's house is completely quiet when I walk down the staircase to the main floor. I think about all the wonderful meals I've enjoyed at the large dining table. The hearty laughter, the friendly conversation, and of course the delicious food and wine. In less than nine months, Arcadia has come to feel more like home to me than any place I've lived in since my childhood house in San Jose. More than the cluttered New York City loft that Nils and I used as our home base for so many years, more than the ginormous mansion in Atherton that Mom and Dad bought after his company got successful, and certainly more than the tin-roofed cabin I shivered in for those awful two years in Mendocino County.

I slip on my shoes and open the front door. I hear a rustle in the nearby bushes, and I wonder whether it's a bird or rabbit or other such creature. You'd think I'd have some idea by now, after so many months of listening—or not listening—to Brandon drone on about the flora and fauna of the region, but I'm still as clueless as ever.

Even though the sun won't rise for a few hours yet, the moon casts enough light that I can make my way from Leo's house to Arcadia's labyrinth, which stands in somber silence like an ancient graveyard.

On my first rotation of the labyrinth, I try to emulate Gisela's grace and mindfulness. Gisela told me she walked it every morning to give herself focus, and it's focus that I so badly need. I wonder how Gisela is doing. I haven't seen her all winter, not since the New Year's Eve party, but she's supposed to come to Arcadia today to train her partner, Sage, to be the substitute yoga instructor. She must be ready to give birth any day now. I still have never met Sage. What kind of name is Sage anyway?

Stop thinking about Gisela and just quiet your mind.

On my second rotation, I focus on the dark stones that define the labyrinth's contours. Their smooth, polished surface reminds me of the turtles Dad and I used to watch basking in the sunshine in the lily pond outside the museum at Golden Gate Park. I always associate turtles with Dad, probably because of the jade turtle on my lucky charm bracelet—the one I gave to Hari and never got back. My left hand instinctively reaches for the spot on my right wrist where it used to live, and I feel an aching absence—for the bracelet, for Dad, for Hari.

Focus, focus, focus. Do not think about Hari.

I lose my balance, and one of my feet lands clumsily outside the lines of the labyrinth. There's a hole developing in the right toe of my sneakers. Mom's old sneakers. The Toms slip-ons that I wore on my first bird-watching hike with Maggie and Leo and Brandon. The ones that gave me those painful blisters that Brandon tended to so capably. Good old Brandon. Who would have thought that he would become such a cherished friend over the months since that New Year's Eve party? Who would have thought he could look so hot in a wet tuxedo shirt?

You are not focusing, Amelia!

On my third rotation, my stomach rumbles. I'm looking forward to breakfast, my mouth imagining the buttery layers of Jett's croissants and morning buns, the creamy mascarpone center of his pear-ginger muffins, the subtle sweetness of his apple-walnut bread. But wait, there won't be any Jett today. It's just me in charge of the kitchen. Today and all week.

What the heck have I gotten myself into?

"You're too hard on yourself," I hear Leo saying. "You don't have to cook to Jett's standards, my dear. You're in a class of your own."

Up in the distance, I see a faint beam of light—two beams, in fact. Given the time of day and the general location, there's only one person it could be: Eleanor returning from her Sunday double shift. I wonder how many babies she helped enter the world today.

"Extend an olive branch to Eleanor," Leo said. But how? How do I begin to mend the many mistakes I've made over these past months? How do I earn back Eleanor's trust?

By this point, my focus is blown. I don't even try to finish my third rotation. I step over the rocks that stand in my way and head back to the center to start the day.

★ ★ ★

"Amelia?" Brandon says, walking into the Arcadia kitchen.

"Oh, good morning, Brandon," I say. I open the oven door and feel the blast of heat on my face as I pull out two baking sheets of lime-basil scones.

"I knocked on your door at six," Brandon says. "Leo and I were concerned when we found your bed empty."

"I couldn't sleep last night," I say, "so I took a quick shower and decided to get started on breakfast. Could you get to work on the trifle? The yogurt and berries are in the walk-in."

"Of course," Brandon says, washing his hands in the sink. He leans over to watch as I remove the scones from the baking sheets and transfer them onto the cooling rack.

"I omitted the coconut and added some basil to your recipe," I say. "I hope you don't mind."

"No," he says, barely suppressing a smile. "Not at all."

Moments later, as Brandon is rinsing the berries in the sink and I'm whisking the eggs for the spinach and mushroom frittata, Leo walks into the kitchen wearing his trademark powder blue tracksuit and an amplified look of relief.

"So, she *is* here!" Leo shouts. "Why didn't you come back to tell me, Brandon?"

"Chef Amelia ordered me to work straightaway," Brandon says. "As a mere sous, I could hardly refuse."

"Good morning, Leo," I say, kissing him on the cheek. "I was so eager to do a good job today that I woke up extra-early and rushed down here."

Leo's chest visibly puffs up as he looks around the kitchen and takes in the sights and smells. He reaches over to sneak a scone, and Brandon taps his hand away.

"Just another hour, and the first retreat guests should arrive," Leo says.

"Oh no, Brandon," I say, glancing up at the clock. "I forgot to start the almond milk chai. Could you check the back room for cardamom?"

"I can see I'm neither needed nor wanted here," Leo says. He surreptitiously snags a scone and departs.

Brandon and I work quickly to finish breakfast preparations. We stack the plates, cups, and cutlery on the sideboard, along with the frittata, scones, and yogurt and berry trifle. We wipe the dining tables and straighten the chairs. We ladle the steaming-hot almond milk chai into the stainless-steel urn, and we fill the Mason jars with assorted healthy snacks.

"I picked these yesterday," Brandon says, showing me a bouquet of wildflowers in an antique milk jug. "I thought they might brighten the room."

Before I can say a word, we hear Leo shouting, "They're here, they're here!"

I put the vase of flowers on the sideboard and give Brandon a shaky smile. He gives me a firm nod in response. We stand side by side, waiting to greet our guests.

Over the next hour, the invited guests trickle into the dining room. I slowly come to realize these guests are different from those who normally attend the weekly cancer retreats. They don't arrive with their loved ones but rather on their own. These guests are not cancer patients. They are the partners of cancer patients who have died.

"And you remember Amelia," Leo says, escorting another guest into the dining room. I look up from cleaning crumbs off the sideboard and see Andrew—Chloe's husband. My heart nearly stops.

"Andrew," I gasp.

"Hello, Amelia," he responds.

"I didn't know…" I say.

"She died three months ago," Andrew says.

"Was there a memorial? I'm sorry, I didn't get the notice."

"Just a small one," Andrew says. "Immediate family only."

Chloe had told me she wanted a big memorial service full of friends and family, music and speeches and photographs, flowers and food and wine. It guts me to know that she probably got none of those things, and I feel a burst of anger toward Andrew.

"Thank you for making the time to come," Leo says, gripping Andrew's arm. "I know Chloe's loss is still so fresh. I hope this week will provide you with some small measure of comfort."

I see Andrew's eyes well up as he accepts Leo's compassion, and it makes me feel ashamed. How dare I judge Andrew and the manner of his mourning? What is the purpose of memorials anyway? To fulfill the wishes of the deceased, or to provide some comfort to the living?

"Andrew, I'm so sorry for your loss," Brandon says, joining our small group. "Please accept my deepest condolences. I know the pain of a wife's death. It never ends, but in time, it does soften."

Andrew and Brandon exchange solemn nods. My heart aches thinking about the fathomless well of grief that unites them.

"How wonderful," Leo says. "Our final guest is here."

I close my eyes and gather up my strength for another guest, another human being suffering the absence of a beloved partner from cancer. I think about Leo's and Brandon's generosity and grace in acknowledging the pain of the other guests without judgment, drama, or self-interest, and I steel myself to rise to that same level of empathy.

The final guest appears in the doorway to the dining room, her face pinched with anxiety. I recognize the downward cast of her gaze, the curvature of her weary spine. I'm stunned to see her in person, and yet it makes complete sense that she should be here. She's perhaps the person who deserves to be here the most.

"Eleanor!" Leo says, running across the room to greet her.

Eleanor and I barely have time to say an awkward hello before Michaela and Frank, the two longtime Arcadia therapists, come in and announce that the first day introductory session will be starting shortly. I use the announcement as an excuse to make a quick exit to the kitchen, and Eleanor seems relieved to be able to sit down at Leo's dining table and help herself to some breakfast.

Once the guests have finished eating and leave for the day, Brandon and I sweep into the dining room to clear the breakfast dishes and get ready for lunch.

"You didn't tell me Eleanor was one of the guests this week," I say to Brandon. He's scraping the food scraps from the dishes into the compost bin while I wrap up the leftovers and put them away in the fridge.

"It wasn't my news to tell," Brandon says. "Also, Leo was convinced she would back out at the last minute. It's taken him ten years to get Eleanor to say yes."

"Ten years?" I ask.

"Yes, most of the guests this week lost their loved ones in the past year or two. Like Andrew, for example, although his loss is especially fresh. Leo first invited Eleanor to be a guest the spring after Edward died, but she declined. She chose to become a volunteer instead."

"What about you?" I ask. "Did you ever attend?"

"When Laura first came to Arcadia," Brandon says, "I'm embarrassed to admit I didn't accompany her. I was preoccupied running the Muir Academy and didn't think it was worth taking a full week off. I thought it was a frivolous waste of time, going to group talk therapy, doing yoga, etching lines in sand trays. Leo attended as Laura's companion instead. Afterward, Laura told me it was the most transformative week of her life, and Leo was so taken by the entire experience—including his week as an Arcadia alumnus after Laura died—that he decided to take it over in Laura's memory.

"Over the years, Leo invited me to attend the alumni weeks, even though I did not technically qualify. But I always refused, secure in my belief that a week at a cancer retreat center was nothing but a waste of time. I'm a man of science, after all, not someone who sits in a circle and shares his emotions with strangers. And then, last year, I suffered a mild stroke. My doctor told me it was probably related to stress. He recommended I take a sabbatical, and Leo convinced me to come to Arcadia as his houseguest. I thought I'd stay a week, just to humor him, and then return home to work on my next guidebook revision. My first day at Arcadia was the day of that dinner party at Leo's."

He gives me a wan, almost apologetic, smile.

"The day I met you," he adds.

"Leo's a very special person," I say.

"Yes," Brandon says, "exasperating but special."

I fill the sink with warm soapy water. I remember standing at this spot last October: Eleanor's outburst about both Hari and Brandon being in love with me, and did I really need to add Jett to my doorknob collection.

Now, six months later, Hari's engaged to the beautiful Preeti Singh, their every outing plastered all over the internet. I couldn't help but torture myself by googling Hari's name every time we went to the Muir Academy to check Maggie's college results. Not only is Preeti Singh the daughter of an Indian real estate billionaire, she also worked as a part-time model while getting her MBA from Harvard Business School.

"Your basic nightmare," as Carrie Fisher's character said in *When Harry Met Sally*.

Meanwhile, Jett seems to have disappeared from the public eye, presumably juggling the demands of his high-powered business career and newfound parenthood. Not a word about him, Gisela, or Laila on any of the usual gossip sites. I'm guessing the Jett family paid every media outlet dearly to hush up the scandal.

"Amelia?" Brandon says. He reaches over to turn off the spigot, the water almost filling the sink, the bubbles nearly overflowing the sides.

"Oh, sorry," I say, "I got a little distracted there."

"How about I do those dishes while you get started on lunch?" Brandon says. "As chef, you should focus on the menu and delegate the more menial tasks to your sous."

Before I have a chance to argue, Brandon moves his body closer to mine and gently hip-checks me out of the way. I make my way to the walk-in, thinking about the smoked salmon tea sandwiches, sweet potato and spring onion pancakes with dill crème fraiche, and other delicious things I plan to prepare in the days ahead. If there's one thing I never have trouble focusing on, it's food.

Lunch service begins. Brandon and I stand at a slight distance from the laden sideboard, and the room bustles with guests oohing and aahing over the delectable spread. It fills me with quiet joy and pride of accomplishment.

As the guests slowly settle themselves at the tables, I notice Eleanor's absence.

"Where's Eleanor?" I ask Leo. He grabs a plate, reaches for a sweet potato pancake, and pops it in his mouth. His eyes light up, and he puts three more on his plate. I grab a cloth napkin from the stack and wipe away a smidge of crème fraiche from the corner of his mouth.

"She begged off lunch, saying she had an important matter to discuss with Maggie," Leo says. "I think it's about college."

Yesterday's email from Holyoke had said the financial aid package would be arriving by mail. Eleanor usually stops by the PO box on her way back from the hospital. I can just imagine my sister's confusion when she sees a letter from the Holyoke Admissions Office.

"Brandon, I hate to do this," I begin, but he's already a step ahead of me.

"Your job is done here, chef," he says. "Now go help Maggie."

I'm slightly winded by the time I've jogged uphill to the Master's Cottage. My heart beats hard against my chest as I stand outside the wooden door, wondering if I should knock or just go in.

I knock twice and then, without waiting, open the door.

Eleanor and Maggie are seated together on the love seat, a large white envelope and assorted pieces of paper on their laps. They both look up at me, their eyes filled with tears.

"Aunt Amelia's the one," Maggie says. "She's the one who is responsible."

"You did this?" Eleanor asks.

I glance over at Maggie, not knowing what to say.

Maggie runs over to me and hugs me tightly, squeezing out whatever little breath I have left. I have no idea how to react. I have no idea what's going on.

"I got the scholarship, Aunt Amelia," Maggie says, waving a piece of paper in my face. "Four years, free tuition, room, and board!"

I grab the paper from Maggie's hand and read the letter. It's true: my niece not only got into her dream school but also won the college's prestigious art scholarship.

Eleanor walks over to the two of us. Her face is unreadable.

"You did this," Eleanor repeats.

Just as I'm about to defend myself from my sister's accusations, Eleanor steps forward to hug me. It takes me back to the first time I set foot in the Master's Cottage, that night when I ran away from Jett's truck thinking he was Freddy Krueger and was saved from dismemberment by my sister's urgent embrace.

"Thank you for helping Maggie with her college applications," Eleanor says, finally releasing me. "Thank you for making her so happy."

"You mean, you're letting her go?" I ask.

"She's letting me go!" Maggie shouts, jumping up and down.

"But..." I begin.

"But I said she couldn't go farther than five hours' drive from San Francisco," Eleanor says, finishing my thought. "Yes, I know. I've spent a lot of time talking with my therapist about that very pronouncement. Along with my control issues, my unresolved anger issues, all of the issues you pointed out I need to work on."

"I didn't mean..." I protest.

Eleanor looks at me with a half smile.

"It's okay—you were right. I *am* a control freak," she says. "I'm working on that. And I'm not saying I love the idea of Maggie going to college all the way across the country. I will never forget what happened when you did that. You stayed away for almost twenty years."

"Oh, Mom," Maggie cries. "I'm not going away for twenty years. I'll come back. I promise."

Eleanor looks at Maggie and then at me.

"I will never get over how much you two look alike," she sighs. "How did I give birth to my sister's baby?" She laughs quietly.

"Anyway, it's Maggie we're talking about," Eleanor continues. "Her dreams and her happiness. Not yours, not mine. And with a four-year, full-freight scholarship, there's nothing standing between Maggie and her very bright future. Certainly not her silly old mother."

"You're not silly or old, Mom," Maggie says, still crying.

"Thank you for saying so," Eleanor says, laughing, "but I feel pretty silly and old right now."

"I should probably get back and help Brandon clean up the dishes," I say. "And then we've got to get started on dinner."

"Mr. Allyn!" Maggie shouts, dropping the brochure onto the floor. "I need to go tell Mr. Allyn the good news!"

"Oh my God, look at her," Eleanor says wistfully. As Maggie jumps up and races to put on her sneakers, the sheaf of papers flapping in her hand, Eleanor's face is lit by pure devotion. Then she turns to me with a face that seems to both offer and beg for forgiveness. The months of estrangement suddenly vanish.

"Yes," I say, feeling whole for the first time in months. "Just look at her."

33

The next morning, I'm in the kitchen toasting slices of sourdough bread to just the exact shade of light brown crispness. On the sideboard, I've already placed bowls of honeyed almond butter, sweet creamery butter, and homemade strawberry jam along with a plate of sliced Hass avocados seasoned with olive oil, coarse sea salt, and lemon zest—the perfect accompaniments for the toast.

I hear Brandon open the back door of the kitchen.

"Were there any more lemons on the tree this morning?" I ask absentmindedly.

"Gisela's gone into labor!" Brandon says. "Eleanor's with her now. She says we need to leave right away. Your mother seems to have taken Eleanor's car, so I'll drive everyone to the hospital in mine."

I nearly burn myself pulling the toast slices out of the oven. I place them on the antique sterling silver toast trays that Brandon and I sourced from various local antique purveyors over the past few months.

"Go ahead, Brandon. I can handle the kitchen myself," I say.

Just then, Leo rushes in from the dining room.

"Amelia, your sister asks that you go along to help her with Gisela," Leo says. "I'll stay behind to pass along the news to Sage and take care of breakfast."

"Everything's ready for breakfast," I say. I scan the kitchen to confirm my statement. "We could probably use one more batch of toast. The fruit salad is in the walk-in, and the chai just needs to be ladled into the urn."

"Aye-aye, captain," Leo says, saluting.

"Today's lunch was going to be salade Nicoise," I say, "but if that's too much work for you..."

"Amelia, we need to go," Brandon says. "If worse comes to worst, there's a fridge full of leftovers that I'm sure Leo can lay out, and no one would complain."

Brandon takes me by the hand and pulls me out of the kitchen, through the dining room, and into the foyer. When Brandon and I emerge from the cancer center building into the bright morning sunshine, I'm not prepared for the sight before me: a very pregnant Gisela lying in the back seat of Brandon's Land Rover, screaming at the top of her lungs. What happened to the mindful goddess I knew?

"The contractions are coming fast," Eleanor says when she sees Brandon. "We need to hurry or else she's going to have the baby in the car."

Brandon jumps into the driver's seat, and I strap myself into the shotgun seat. Brandon guns the engine, and we peel out of the Arcadia parking lot as Leo waves goodbye to us from the porch.

"Amelia," Eleanor says, "do you have your phone?"

"No, sorry," I say, "I haven't charged it since New Year's." Not since I ran away from the Jett family mansion after finding out Hari was engaged. I check Gisela's face for a reaction, but she's too busy focusing on her screaming to notice.

"Here," Eleanor says. She passes me her purse from the back seat. "My phone's inside. We should get service around Point Reyes Station. Call Jett and tell him to meet us at Marin General. He's in my list of contacts."

I fumble through the contents of Eleanor's bulky purse. I feel something soft in an inner pocket that piques my curiosity. It's a pure white handkerchief, crisply ironed and with the letters *WBJ* monogrammed in the corner.

Willow Bartholomew Jett.

Eleanor's been holding on to Jett's handkerchief ever since that day they were fixing the roof. I finger the navy blue monogram and notice Brandon glancing over. He shakes his head "no" ever so slightly, and I return the handkerchief to its hidden pocket.

"Found it," I say, holding Eleanor's phone for all to see.

I don't know that anyone has ever traveled from Arcadia to Marin General in the time that Brandon drove us. We must have set a land-speed record for that stretch of Route 1. By the time Brandon screeches into the parking lot, Gisela is pale and damp from sweat.

"Eleanor, I thought you were supposed to be off duty this week," the ER attendant says as he strolls over to Brandon's Land Rover. There's a lilt to his Caribbean-inflected voice that suggests the two of them have worked together a long time.

"My friend is in labor," Eleanor says. "Thirty-nine-year-old female, high-risk pregnancy, 80 percent effaced, 8.5 centimeters dilated."

"First delivery?" the attendant asks, his tone suddenly serious.

Eleanor looks quickly at Gisela.

"No," Eleanor says.

"Baby on board!" the attendant shouts. Another attendant rolls over a gurney, and the two of them whisk Gisela to the elevator bank.

"What do we do now?" I ask my sister.

"Park your car in the lot around the corner," Eleanor says, "and then take the elevators to the fourth floor." She sprints for the elevator and squeezes in just before the doors close.

I look at Brandon, then the glowing ER sign, and then back at Brandon.

"You go up and help your sister," Brandon says, "and I'll park the car."

I instinctively kiss Brandon on the cheek before racing out of the car and pressing the up button for the hospital elevator. When I arrive on the fourth floor, I check in at the reception desk.

"I'm looking for Gisela Mistry," I say. "She just arrived."

The sleepy-eyed receptionist looks up from her magazine and wiggles her mouse to wake up her computer.

"How do you spell the patient's last name?" she asks lazily.

Before I have a chance to answer, I hear a familiar scream from a nearby room.

"Never mind," I say, "I think I know where to go."

When I walk into Gisela's room, there's already a crowd of people gathered around her, babbling about centimeters and milliliters and other metric units I never mastered in elementary school.

"She's lost a lot of fluid," one person says. By her assertive tone and starched white jacket, I assume she's the doctor. "Nurse, please place the IV."

A nurse approaches Gisela's bedside. Another nurse rolls over an IV stand and plastic bag of clear liquid.

"No," Gisela says, her voice more forceful than I'm used to hearing. "No IVs."

Gisela retracts her arms and clutches them tightly around her. She closes her eyes, like a small child trying to ward off the boogeyman. The nurse looks at the doctor, unsure of how to proceed.

I watch as Eleanor washes her hands, rubs on a dollop of hand sanitizer, and pulls on a pair of bright purple latex gloves. She reaches into a cardboard box and takes out a small plastic-wrapped packet and nudges the first nurse aside.

"Gisela," I hear her whisper. "Your baby's coming. We need to make sure you're strong enough to welcome her to the world."

Gisela opens her eyes. She looks at Eleanor, then down at the small packet in Eleanor's hand, and tears trickle down her cheeks.

"I'm a hard stick," Gisela says, her arms still tight to her chest. "My veins don't work."

Eleanor places the plastic-wrapped packet to the side, like a soldier setting down his weapon. She holds Gisela's hands in hers and leans in. She takes a deep breath before talking. She speaks so softly I can barely make out the words.

"I remember when my husband, Edward, finished with chemo after his initial diagnosis," Eleanor says. "Adria was the worst. There's a reason they call it the red devil, right?"

Gisela nods, her eyes fixed on Eleanor's.

I've never heard my sister talk about Edward to anyone outside the family before. She barely talks about him to me, her own sister, and only on the most superficial level. She certainly has never told me about Edward's cancer treatments.

"His veins were ruined after that," Eleanor says. "Whenever we had to go into the doctor's office to run blood tests, the nurses—even the best ones—needed three, four, sometimes five sticks to get a vein that worked. It was pure torture."

Gisela nods again, transfixed.

"I taught myself how to find even the smallest veins that work," Eleanor says. She holds out her own two arms to demonstrate. "The big one on the inside of the wrist is always reliable, although it can be tricky to keep in place. The little ones in the hand are harder to find, but with a little heat and pressure, they're slow and steady. Nurses are often tempted by the big blue ones in the center of the arm, but those are the ones that were used for chemo, right? The ones that don't work anymore. Dry wells."

Gisela doesn't nod or say anything, but she seems to be at ease.

"Trust me, Gisela," Eleanor says, reaching for the plastic-wrapped packet that she set aside earlier. "I know what I'm doing. I will not hurt you."

Eleanor ties a pink rubber tourniquet around Gisela's arm, palpates her skin, and locates a pale blue vein near the wrist. "Now, on my count," Eleanor says, "one...two..."

Before she reaches the count of three, Eleanor has slipped the butterfly needle into Gisela's arm.

"That wasn't so bad, was it?" Eleanor says. She tears off a stretch of clear white tape to secure the syringe to Gisela's skin.

"Thank you, Eleanor," Gisela says. She sounds almost like she's praying.

About ten minutes later, I hear a familiar voice in the hallway. It's Jett, talking with the sleepy-eyed receptionist, with Laila by his side.

"Jett, Laila," I call from the doorway, "she's in here."

As they approach the room, I'm struck by the family resemblance. The same dramatic eyebrows and startling, deep-set eyes. With her small frame, Laila looks like a young Natalie Portman crossed with Norah Jones.

"Are you the father?" the doctor asks when she sees Jett.

Jett hesitates and looks at Gisela for guidance.

"He's the donor," Gisela says to the doctor.

"It's complicated," Jett adds. His comment seems to be directed more at Eleanor and me than at the doctor.

"Well, just tell me who you want to cut the cord," the doctor says to Gisela, "so we can have them scrubbed up and ready to go."

"Sage," Gisela says.

Into the already crowded room walks a Zoe Kravitz lookalike, dressed in tight black yoga pants and matching athletic top with crisscrossed straps that highlight her lean muscles and stunning back tattoo.

"Sorry, babe," Sage says. She glides effortlessly to Gisela's bedside and kisses her on each eyelid. "I guess that'll teach me to run out for a quick latte."

"At least you got here in time," Gisela says. She reaches for Sage's hand, which I notice is adorned with the same stacked silver rings as Gisela's.

"Okay, we have now officially exceeded the max capacity for this room," the doctor says briskly. "Everyone except medical staff and the baby's parents need to exit now."

Jett, Laila, and I leave the room but hover by the door. Brandon soon joins us. We hear Gisela screaming in the next room, and Jett offers a calming smile at Laila. In that moment, I realize Laila and the unborn baby will be full siblings—born of the same genetic material but raised in very different circumstances. I wonder what Jett would think if he knew his monogrammed handkerchief was inside the purse that I'm still holding for my sister.

We hear the ding of the elevator. An elegantly dressed Indian couple gets off and approaches the reception desk. I recognize them from the many gossip and news articles about Hari's engagement.

"Mr. and Mrs. Mistry," Jett yells down the hallway.

"Has the baby come yet?" Mrs. Mistry asks Jett. Her voice is husky and warm, her accent clipped and vaguely British. Mr. Mistry stands silently by his wife's side, dressed impeccably in a navy blazer and plum-colored shirt.

The four of us are about to respond "no" when we hear crying on the other side of the door. The sparkling gold bracelets on Mrs. Mistry's wrist jangle as she pushes open the door.

"It's a girl," the doctor announces.

We watch from the doorway as Eleanor takes the baby from the doctor, wraps her in a soft muslin cloth, and places her in Gisela's arms.

"She's beautiful," Gisela says.

"May we come in now?" Jett asks, although Mrs. Mistry has already burst into the room. She beckons impatiently for her husband to follow.

"Please give us a few more minutes to check the baby and deliver the placenta," the doctor says. "Then they're all yours."

A few minutes later, the door opens, and the doctor smiles as she exits the room.

"You've been very patient," she says. "The baby is perfect. You may now welcome her. Just please wash your hands first."

As each of us takes turns meeting the baby and admiring her ten perfect fingers and ten perfect toes, Eleanor is busy in the corner, throwing bits of paper and gauze into the appropriate bins, double-checking notations in Gisela's medical chart. After everyone has had a chance to welcome the baby, Eleanor approaches the bedside with a clipboard and pen.

"You don't have to do this now," Eleanor says, "but have you decided on a name for the baby?"

Gisela looks down at the puffy little face wearing the pink-and-blue-striped cap, and then up at Eleanor's equally tired but undeniably radiant face.

"I want to name her Eila," Gisela says. She looks at Eleanor, then Jett, and finally Sage for approval. Sage squeezes Gisela's hand and nods.

"That's perfect," Gisela's mother says. "In Hindi, Eila means cardamom tree. Didn't you tell me you drank cardamom tea when you were trying to get pregnant?"

"Yes, Mom," Gisela says, laughing. "I'm naming her after the Arcadia chai."

34

When Brandon and I return to the Arcadia kitchen that afternoon, it's pure chaos. Dirty dishes and utensils piled up in the sink. The compost bin nearly overflowing with food scraps. The back door is wide open, but you can still smell the lingering smoke. There's even a singed pot holder on the counter.

"Thank goodness you're back!" Leo shouts as soon as he sees us.

"What in the world happened here?" Brandon asks. He wipes his finger along the stainless-steel hood of the stove and grimaces when he sees it's covered in black soot.

"I was making another batch of toast," Leo explains, "just as you asked." He points to me. "But you also asked me to ladle the chai into the urns, and somehow, I lost track of the toast and…" His two hands flutter in the air like injured butterflies.

I lean in to give Leo a comforting hug while Brandon puts on an apron and lugs the compost bin out to the garden.

"And then there was the fiasco at lunch," Leo moans.

I take Leo by the hand and walk him over to the dining room.

I take a mug from the sideboard, which still has the remains of both breakfast and lunch on it, get some chai from the urn, and hand it to Leo, who accepts it gratefully.

"All these years, the chefs always made it look so easy," Leo mutters.

"Aren't you going to ask about the baby?" I ask.

"Oh yes!" Leo exclaims. "The baby. Eleanor called the switchboard and told us everything. A girl, right? Baby Eila. How delightful! Do you have any photos? How's Gisela doing?"

"Everyone is great," I say. "Baby Eila is absolutely perfect, but I don't have any photos, sorry. Eleanor does, though, on her phone. She's at the Master's Cottage now."

Brandon comes back into the kitchen from the outside, returns the compost bin to its place, and joins us in the dining room.

"If you intend for your guests not to go hungry tonight, Leo," Brandon says, "I suggest you head back up to your house where you can rest and stay out of harm's way. Amelia and I will have to start right away if we have any chance of getting this place cleaned up and dinner prepared on time."

"Oh, thank you, dear ones," Leo says, kissing us both on the cheeks and shuffling out of the dining room. He seems to have more energy now that he's been relieved of kitchen duty. "Maybe I'll stop by the Master's Cottage and ask to see those photos of the baby."

Within the hour, Eleanor and Maggie join us in the kitchen. Brandon and I have cleaned up the dining room, washed all the dishes, and are getting started on dinner.

"Leo told us about the mess he left you with," Eleanor says. She pulls her hair back with an elastic and washes her hands at the sink. "How can we help?"

"Can you two start on the quinoa salad?" I ask.

"The one with the pistachios?" Eleanor asks.

"Yes, they're roasting in the oven but should be ready soon. Also, instead of the oranges, I thought we'd try adding these kumquats," I say. I show her the bowl of fruit I picked up at the market on the way back from the hospital.

Eleanor reaches into the bowl, pulls out a bright orange fruit, takes a bite, and gives the rest to Maggie to try.

"Are you messing with my recipes again?" Jett says. He's standing in the doorway, with Laila close behind. Jett's got on his Kiss the Cook apron.

"Oranges are so common," I say. "Really, Jett, am I the only one around here with any imagination?"

"The pistachios are ready," Eleanor says. "I can smell them."

"Seems like Amelia isn't the only one in the Bae-Wood family with highly evolved senses," Jett says. He grabs the singed pot holder from the counter and removes the sheet pan of pistachios from the oven.

"Maggie, could you run out to the garden and see if we have any more parsley and mint?" Brandon says. "We need it for the chimichurri sauce."

"Sure, Mr. Allyn," Maggie says.

"Can I come along?" Laila asks. "Jett's told me so much about the garden."

"Sure," Maggie says, "follow me."

All the adults watch as the two young women go out the back door and into the garden. Through the large rear window, we can see Maggie pointing out different plants to Laila. Maggie rubs a leaf between her fingers and offers them to Laila to smell.

"She's a lovely girl," Brandon says. "You should be proud."

"Thank you," Eleanor and Jett say at the same time. Then they turn toward one another, startled.

"They are both lovely," Brandon corrects himself.

"I didn't know about Laila until just a few months ago," Jett says. He takes the roasted pistachios from the sheet pan and places them on the butcher block. The chef's knife makes a satisfying crunching sound as Jett chops the nuts into rough pieces.

"I'm ashamed to admit that when Gisela told me about being pregnant, I assumed she wouldn't want to go through with it," Jett says. "I offered to pay for Gisela to end the pregnancy, and she said she'd think about it. A couple days later, she broke up with me over the phone."

I feel tempted to point out that the pistachios are chopped enough—they shouldn't be too fine—but I don't want to interrupt Jett's story.

"I was heartbroken," Jett continues. "To make matters worse, I heard from friends that Gisela had decided to take a gap year in India. I fled to the East Coast so I could be as far away from her memory as possible. Years later, when I heard she had cancer, I realized my hurt had vanished. All I felt was concern, but I didn't know how to get back in touch with her."

Even though Jett is looking down and seems to be talking to the butcher block, everyone in the room knows he's really talking to Eleanor.

"Then a few years ago, one of my friends emailed me about an article they saw in the Arcadia newsletter," Jett says. "It was an announcement that Gisela had just joined as the new yoga instructor. That same day, I drove all the way out here, not having seen Gisela in decades or even knowing if she would be here, and we started the long process of mending our friendship."

Jett takes the chopped-up pistachios and places them in a medium-sized metal bowl. Then he looks up for something else to do. I hand him a couple lemons to zest.

"When Gisela and Sage decided they wanted to start a

family," Jett says, looking down at the zester, "they asked if I would be the donor. After everything that happened between Gisela and me, it somehow felt like the right thing to do."

"But what about Laila?" I ask. "Didn't Gisela ever tell you about Laila?"

"No, never," Jett says. "I'd always assumed that Gisela had terminated the pregnancy. Gisela never spoke about that terrible chapter in our relationship, and I never asked. Gisela tried to forget about the baby, but she struggled with her decision for years. In her darkest moments, Gisela convinced herself that cancer was punishment for giving up our baby. It was only when Laila turned eighteen and found out about her birth parents that she contacted me, and I finally understood the truth of what happened to Gisela at the end of our senior year."

Jett looks up from the zester and stares directly at Eleanor.

"I'm not proud of some of the things I did as a young man," Jett says, "but I'm lucky that the people I've hurt most have forgiven me and that my parents have accepted, even embraced, Laila. Forgiveness and acceptance are the most precious gifts one can receive—and give. Don't you think so?"

There's a hush in the room as everyone stops their chopping and zesting and stirring, a hush that is broken by the sudden bursting open of the back door.

"You'll never guess what!" Maggie shouts.

"We're going to school together!" Laila says, completing Maggie's sentence.

"What?" I ask. "Laila's going to Holyoke?"

"No, I'm going to Smith," Laila says, "but it's just ten miles away."

"We can be friends," Maggie says.

"Or sisters," Laila adds. "As in the Seven Sisters, get it?"

"You guys can come visit us together!" Laila says to Jett and Eleanor.

"Yeah, Mom," Maggie says, a trace of worry on her face. "Wouldn't that be fun?"

"Wow, this is incredible," Eleanor says. She glances over at Jett. "Don't you think this is incredible?"

"Very," Jett says, holding a completely zestless lemon in his hand.

"I hate to interrupt the excitement," Brandon interrupts, "but we've got less than thirty minutes left to get dinner on the sideboard. Tick-tock."

I watch as Jett brings the bowls of lemon zest and chopped pistachios over to Eleanor, who tucks her hair behind her ear before quietly accepting his offering. I notice that Maggie and Laila are also watching closely. As they exchange sly glances, Maggie and Laila remind me of the separated twins in *The Parent Trap.*

"You heard my sous," I shout, "everyone get to work. Tick-tock."

Dinner is a joyous affair. Everyone is laughing and chatting about recent events—college admissions decisions, Gisela's baby, Leo's kitchen meltdown—and for once, I'm more of an observer than a participant. Eleanor exudes warm affection as Maggie and Laila excitedly talk about their plans for next fall, and more than once, I catch Eleanor and Jett smiling shyly at one another.

I wonder how many more months of therapy it'll take for my sister to finally open herself up to love again. As I instinctively reach for the spot on my wrist where my lucky charm bracelet used to live, I ask that same question about myself.

Everyone helps clean up the dinner dishes. Despite my hearty protests, Maggie insists that Brandon lead us on an evening hike to Lookout Point. The group of us trudge up the hill, Maggie in the lead as usual.

"There's supposed to be a meteor shower tonight," Maggie tells Laila, "and the view of the sky from this place is absolutely amazing!"

"I don't know that I've ever seen a meteor shower before," Laila says.

"Mr. Allyn knows the name of every tree, plant, bird, and animal in this entire area," Maggie tells Laila. "Isn't that right, Mr. Allyn?"

"There might be a few exceptions," Brandon demurs.

"What's the name of that?" Laila asks, pointing to a bush.

"Poison oak," Brandon says, pulling her hand away.

"How about that?" Maggie asks.

"Cushing manzanita," he answers.

And so it goes, on and on. Brandon really is a walking guidebook.

By the time we reach Lookout Point, most of us are panting for breath, but Maggie is right: the view really is amazing. Maggie pulls a water bottle from her backpack and shares it with Laila. Meanwhile, Brandon pulls out a dark glass bottle from his backpack.

"Is that Dom?" I ask, recognizing the matte gold label.

"It was delivered to Leo's tonight," Brandon says, "along with this."

Brandon hands me a plain white envelope. Inside is my lucky charm bracelet along with a handwritten note:

Amelia,

I'm sorry for everything. I'd hoped to propose the night of the gala, but that wasn't part of my parents' ten-point plan.—H

It takes me a moment to remember the ten-point plan he's referring to. The explanation comes to me all at once: perhaps the Jett family didn't pay off the press to hush up the Jett-Mistry love child story. Perhaps the Mistry family timed the announcement of Hari's engagement to Preeti Singh to draw everyone's attention away from Laila. I'll never know for sure. At this point, I don't really care.

I shove the bracelet and the note into the front pocket of my jeans.

"Did you bring wineglasses?" I ask Brandon.

"Who needs glasses?" he says, smiling. He pops open the cork and passes the bottle to me. This is not the Brandon I thought I knew. I take a long draw from the bottle and hand it to Eleanor. We pass the bottle around and feel the tension of the day release from our bodies.

"Mr. Allyn," Laila says, pointing to a hollow in the distance, "what's the name of that pretty tree over there?"

"Salix babylonica," Brandon says. "Commonly known as the weeping willow."

"Your namesake," I say to Jett in a teasing tone before letting out a little burp.

"Eponym," Jett replies. "I'm the namesake. Just like baby Eila is Eleanor's namesake."

"What?" Eleanor and I ask at the same time.

"Eila is a combination of Eleanor and Laila," Jett says. "The two women Gisela and I admire most." He turns to Eleanor with a look of adoration that rivals any British suitor in any Merchant Ivory drama.

My sister appears stunned, her wide eyes fixated on Jett.

"Did I say something wrong?" Jett asks.

"No, Jett," she says, her face suddenly radiant, "you've said everything right."

* * *

I rub the tiredness from my eyes as I walk from the main building to the Master's Cottage. I can barely make out the figure getting out of Eleanor's car.

"What are you doing out so late?" Mom asks when I join her on the porch.

"I could ask the same of you," I say. "Where have you been all day?" Inside the cottage, the small table lamp next to the couch is on, but everything else is dark and quiet.

"Out with a friend," she whispers. Even in the dim light, I can see her face is beaming.

"A friend?" I say, plopping down on the couch. "The same mysterious friend you've been sneaking off to visit the past few months?"

"I'm not telling," she says. Mom slips off her shoes and curls up next to me like a cat. "Not quite yet, at least. Where are you coming from at this hour?"

I'm too tired to go into all the details, but I give Mom the highlights of the day: Gisela's baby, Leo's disastrous kitchen adventure, our hike up to Lookout Point.

"I was just in the center kitchen getting tomorrow's breakfast prepped," I say. "Maggie wanted to have a sleepover with her new bestie, Laila, so I offered them my guest room at Leo's. Now that Eleanor and I are reconciled, I figure we can share a bed again."

"You won't have to share a bed much longer," Mom says.

"What do you mean?"

"Your brother isn't contesting the appeal, and he's even agreed to give back all of your father's estate," she says. "Our bank accounts should be unfrozen soon."

"How do you know?"

"Let's just say a friend told me," Mom says.

"Another friend?" I ask. "Or the same friend?"

"I'm not telling."

I'm tempted to press the issue, but I'm pretty sure I know the answer anyway.

"Will you move back to the Atherton house then?" I ask.

"I don't think so. That house is so large and full of memories. I think I'll probably sell it and buy something smaller. I'll give the difference to you and your sister."

"Speaking of Eleanor," I say, yawning, "I better get to bed. I have to wake up early to make breakfast for her and the other guests tomorrow morning."

"I'm so proud of you, dear," Mom says. "I know what a hard time you must have had after that ugliness with the law up in Mendocino. Dad and I were so worried for you."

"You knew about what happened in Mendocino?" I ask.

"Oh, darling, haven't you figured it out by now?" Mom asks. "I knew about your arrest even before you asked Dad for the money. I have a Google Alert set for any news about you, and there was an item in the *Rockport Record* police blotter about you and Nils. Eleanor even glued your mug shot in that scrapbook we keep of your clippings. I was sure you'd found it in the basement when you found Edward's letters."

"Eleanor knew too?" I ask. "Why didn't either of you say anything?"

"I wanted to talk with you about it, but Eleanor held me back," Mom says. "She said you'd tell us if and when you wanted us to know. It was Eleanor's idea to invite you down here so you could rest and recover from the whole ordeal. Leave it to wise Eleanor—she was right. Look how well you've recovered."

Mom reaches forward to swipe the hair out of my eyes. It's grown so long now that I'll need to get a real haircut soon.

"I don't tell you as often as I should," Mom says, "but I

think you are extraordinary. I've always felt that way, and I always will."

"Oh, Mom," I say, "you only say that because you love me."

"No, I say that because it's true…and I do love you."

We stand up from the couch and hug. Mom slips into the bathroom to get ready for bed, and I walk down the short hall to my bedroom—the one I share with Eleanor.

And there, tied to the doorknob, is an apron.

It says, Kiss the Cook.

Rather than sleeping on the Master's Cottage couch, I decide to give Eleanor and Jett their privacy. I walk up to Leo's house to crash in his library. Before I can even knock on the front door, Brandon appears at the threshold.

"I thought you were spending the night at the Master's Cottage," Brandon says.

"Eleanor seems to have a guest," I reply.

Brandon's eyebrows pop up before the hint of a smile brightens his eyes.

"Well, it's about bloody time," he says. "Took them long enough."

"It was pretty obvious, right?" I say.

"As obvious as the white bar on a tricolored blackbird's wing," Brandon teases.

Last month, after one too many glasses of late-night wine, I finally found the courage to confess to Brandon about Nils' and my misadventures in Mendocino, and the whole incident has become another inside joke between us.

"Oh shut up, you!" I protest, giving him a playful shove.

Brandon clasps both of his hands over my right hand on his chest. I feel the softness of his white cotton shirt, the firmness of his pectoral muscles, the steady rhythm of his beating heart. My breath hitches in my breast.

"From the moment we first met last summer, right here at this very spot," Brandon says, "I was bewitched by you. Not just by your beauty or your charm or even the ridiculous *basso profundo* way you greeted me, but by something I can only describe as your soul. Your wild and precious soul. I've known for some time that you didn't share my feelings, that your affections were directed elsewhere, but the events of today have given me the courage to hope that perhaps that has changed. Perhaps you love me too."

"I do," I say. "I love you too."

I take Brandon's hands in mine, and they are warm—and so is his kiss.

Epilogue

And so, dear friends, it is my great honor to invite Mr. and Mrs. Douglas Park, the most beautiful and besotted couple I've ever seen, to grace us with their first dance.

The gathered guests burst into applause.

Mom exudes the purest joy as Douglas takes her gloved hand and lifts her onto her pale pink satin-clad feet. The newly married couple exchanges a tender kiss under the willow bower embellished with pink tea roses before Douglas twirls Mom like a ballerina onto the dance floor.

I step down from the podium and walk toward the head table. I see Eleanor standing off to the side and watching Mom and Douglas. My sister's wearing an emerald-colored silky wrap dress, which seems a little too body-conscious for a matron of honor dress if you ask me, but I suppose it does match her ginormous emerald engagement ring. Eleanor starts to weep, and Jett reaches into his pocket and offers her a monogrammed handkerchief.

"Ellie's such a hopeless romantic," I say.

"Comes from reading so many books," Brandon replies.

"Not something I'm at risk for," I deadpan.

Brandon gives me that wry, lopsided smile that I've come to know is his awkward way of expressing love—a love that has only grown stronger since our first tender kiss.

"The food, the scenery, everything looks perfect," someone says from behind me.

I turn around and see my brother, Chong Bae. I stand up and give him a hug.

"I'm so glad you could make it back from Korea," I say. "It means so much to Mom and Douglas to have you here."

"But of course," Chong says, "it's not every day that you can watch your bonus mom and lawyer getting married."

"Bonus mom?" I ask. "Where'd you learn that lingo?"

"From Eleanor. I heard her saying it to Laila, and it sounded so nice."

I watch Maggie and Laila rush toward Eleanor and Jett. The girls are home from college on autumn break. Mom and Douglas insisted on scheduling the wedding so Maggie and Laila wouldn't miss a day of school.

"Are you sure you can make it back for Eleanor and Jett's wedding next spring?" I ask my brother. "That's a lot of traveling."

"Would I miss the chance to give my little sister away?" Chong says. "Never."

"It's good to have you here, Opa," I say. I try to smooth out the unruly cowlick at the back of his head. Dad used to fuss with his every morning. If only I had a dab of Brylcreem.

"Douglas is waving me over," Chong says, lifting his chin. "I think he wants me to dance with Mom, and I wouldn't want to disappoint."

As I watch my brother walking over to dance with my mother, I instinctively look up the distant hill. I imagine Dad and Chloe and all the other souls in the Portal to the Dead, watching us gathered together below. My eyes well up with tears, and my chest aches with longing. Stupid pregnancy hormones.

"That was a marvelous speech, by the way," Brandon murmurs. "You've really got talent as a storyteller. Have you thought about writing a book?"

"Seriously?" I say, feigning annoyance. "You know I'm finishing my undergrad degree, getting my credentials as a college counselor, training the new cancer center cooking staff, and helping Eleanor and Jett to figure out the best way for the Jett Family Foundation to ensure Arcadia's long-term future. Not to mention preparing for our little morning bun in the oven. Do you really think I have time to write as well?"

"Seriously," Brandon says, "I think you can do anything you set your mind to."

Good old Brandon. He's the one person who's believed in me without reservation. The one person who makes me feel safe enough to do something completely out of my comfort zone. And I'm doing plenty of those things these days.

"Funny you should say that," I say. "An old friend from Hampshire recently wrote to suggest that we work together on a screenplay about my escapades with Nils."

"You mean the Fugitive Forager of the Fjords?" Brandon asks.

"I didn't think you watched YouTube viral videos," I say, surprised.

"My students can't help but share them with me," he says. "They're a little obsessed by you. As am I."

Eleanor, Jett, Maggie, and Laila stand huddled together and are soon joined by another huddle: Gisela and Sage and Baby Eila. Our super-messy, super-complicated extended family.

"So, what did you say?" Brandon asks. "Are you going to do it? Are you going to work on that screenplay?"

"Nah," I say. I pull Brandon's warm hand onto my round belly and bask in the happy scene before me.

"I think I've got my own story to tell."

★ ★ ★ ★ ★

Acknowledgments

It is a truth universally acknowledged that no writer should tread into Jane Austen territory and expect to emerge unscathed. Janeites are notoriously knowledgeable and protective of their beloved author and rightly so. All the privilege I claim for this modest homage is that of writing from the sincerest place of reverence for Ms. Austen and affection for her first published work, *Sense and Sensibility*. And, in the interest of full disclosure, I must admit I drew equal inspiration from Emma Thompson and Ang Lee's brilliant 1995 film adaptation—particularly the late Alan Rickman's marvelous portrayal of Colonel Brandon—as from Ms. Austen's original. Deepest gratitude to Jane, Emma, Ang, and Alan for sitting by my side and whispering in my ear through the writing of this novel.

To my manuscript group members Lisa Hills, Bill Manheim, Lily Rubin, and Debbie Weissmann: Thank you for reading my work in progress and letting me know how much you loved Amelia and the rest of the Arcadia crew. You gave me courage to keep going.

To Stephanie Wildman and Kirby Kim: Thank you for your kind and insightful comments on my initial drafts. This book is better because of you.

To Danielle Egan-Miller, Mariana Fisher, Eleanor Imbody, and the team at Browne & Miller Literary Associates: Thank you for embracing me as a client and championing my work. Your sage counsel and warm friendship mean the world to me.

To Brittany Lavery, Sara Rodgers, Susan Swinwood, and the team at Graydon House: Thank you for taking a chance on yet another good family—this one a little less dysfunctional than the previous one. I'm grateful for your continued support of my writing.

To my friends in the 2020 Debuts and 2020 Debuts of Color groups, Writers Grotto, and Ann Arbor Writers Network; my morning writing partners, Ehsaneh Sadr and Christi Clancy; and my fellow Fancy Koreans, Lydia Kang and Tosca Lee: Thank you for giving me a community to lean on whenever I need it. Writing is hard, but your humor and good cheer make it easier.

To all the readers, librarians, booksellers, podcasters, and bookstagrammers out there: Thank you for supporting books and authors. We writers would be lost without you.

To my beloved friends from the Bay Area Young Survivors, alive and dead, especially Lynnly Labovitz, Erin Hyman, and Merijane Block, as well as the angels at Commonweal: Thank you for inspiring me to write and to live my best life. You are forever in my heart.

To my family, especially Alice, John, Jonah, Theo, Susan, Kathy, and Anne: This is a book about love, loss, grief, and hope. We've experienced too much loss and grief in recent years, but it's your unwavering love that sustains me and gives me hope.

And finally to Dad, Mom, and Ope: Thank you for the gift of unconditional love. I miss you more than words can say.

RELATIVE STRANGERS

A.H. KIM

Reader's Guide

QUESTIONS FOR DISCUSSION

1. The book opens and closes at a wedding. Did you have any suspicions at the outset about whose wedding it might be? If so, whose wedding did you think it was and why? Did your suspicions change over the course of the book? If so, why? Were you surprised by the ending?

2. The book is told from Amelia's perspective. Do you think she is a reliable narrator? If not, what are some of Amelia's observations or commentary that you think are not wholly accurate? How do you think the story would have been different if told from Eleanor's or Tabitha's perspective?

3. The book is divided into four sections, each covering a week in the life of the Bae-Wood women starting with summer and proceeding through the seasons. How do each of the four sections reflect the season in which they take place?

4. The book is an homage Jane Austen's *Sense and Sensibility*. Have you read the original novel or seen one

of the movie adaptations? How is the book similar to those versions? How is it different?

5. The book's four main male characters—Jett, Brandon, Hari, and Leo—are loosely inspired by the four classical elements: air, earth, fire, and water. What do each of the elements represent to you? Which character do you think aligns with each element?

6. Much of the book describes food and cooking. What is each character's relationship to food and cooking, and how does that relationship reflect the character's personality?

7. The book is set mostly in a cancer retreat center in Northern California. How do you think the setting helps facilitate Amelia's personal growth? Have you ever been to a place that inspired you to grow or change? If so, where was the place, and why do you think it had that effect on you?

8. A central theme of the book is recovering from loss. What are some of the losses that the characters experience in this book, what gets in the way of recovering from those losses, and what finally allows them to move on?

9. Amelia and Eleanor like to quote from movies as a form of inside joke. Do you have inside jokes that you share with your friends or family? What are some examples?

10. If you were to cast the movie version of this book, which actors would you pick for each of the characters?